WITH FATE CONSPIRE

Also by Marie Brennan and available from Titan Books

THE MEMOIRS OF LADY TRENT

A Natural History of Dragons

The Tropic of Serpents

Voyage of the Basilisk

In the Labyrinth of Drakes

Within the Sanctuary of Wings (April 2017)

ONYX COURT

Midnight Never Come

In Ashes Lie

A Star Shall Fall

WITH FATE CONSPIRE

THE ONYX COURT BOOK IV

MARIE BRENNAN

TITAN BOOKS

With Fate Conspire
Print edition ISBN: 9781785650796
E-book edition ISBN: 9781785650802

Published by Titan Books
A division of Titan Publishing Group Ltd
144 Southwark Street, London SE1 0UP

First edition: January 2017
2 4 6 8 10 9 7 5 3 1

Map by Rhys Davies.

A CIP catalogue record for this title is available from the British Library.

Printed and bound in Great Britain by CPI Group Ltd.

WITH FATE CONSPIRE

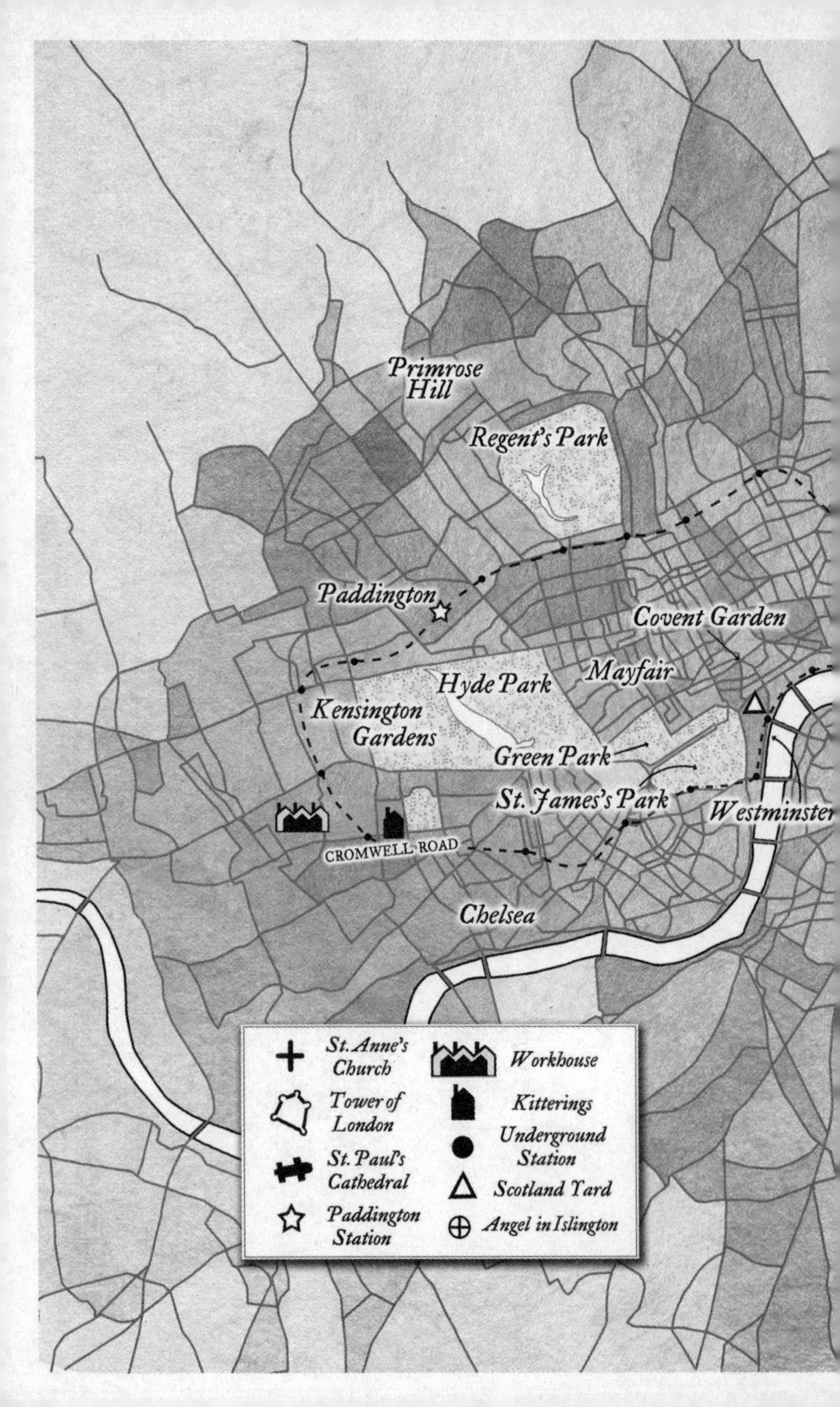
Primrose Hill
Regent's Park
Paddington
Covent Garden
Mayfair
Hyde Park
Kensington Gardens
Green Park
St. James's Park
Westminster
CROMWELL ROAD
Chelsea
St. Anne's Church
Workhouse
Tower of London
Kitterings
Underground Station
St. Paul's Cathedral
Scotland Yard
Paddington Station
Angel in Islington

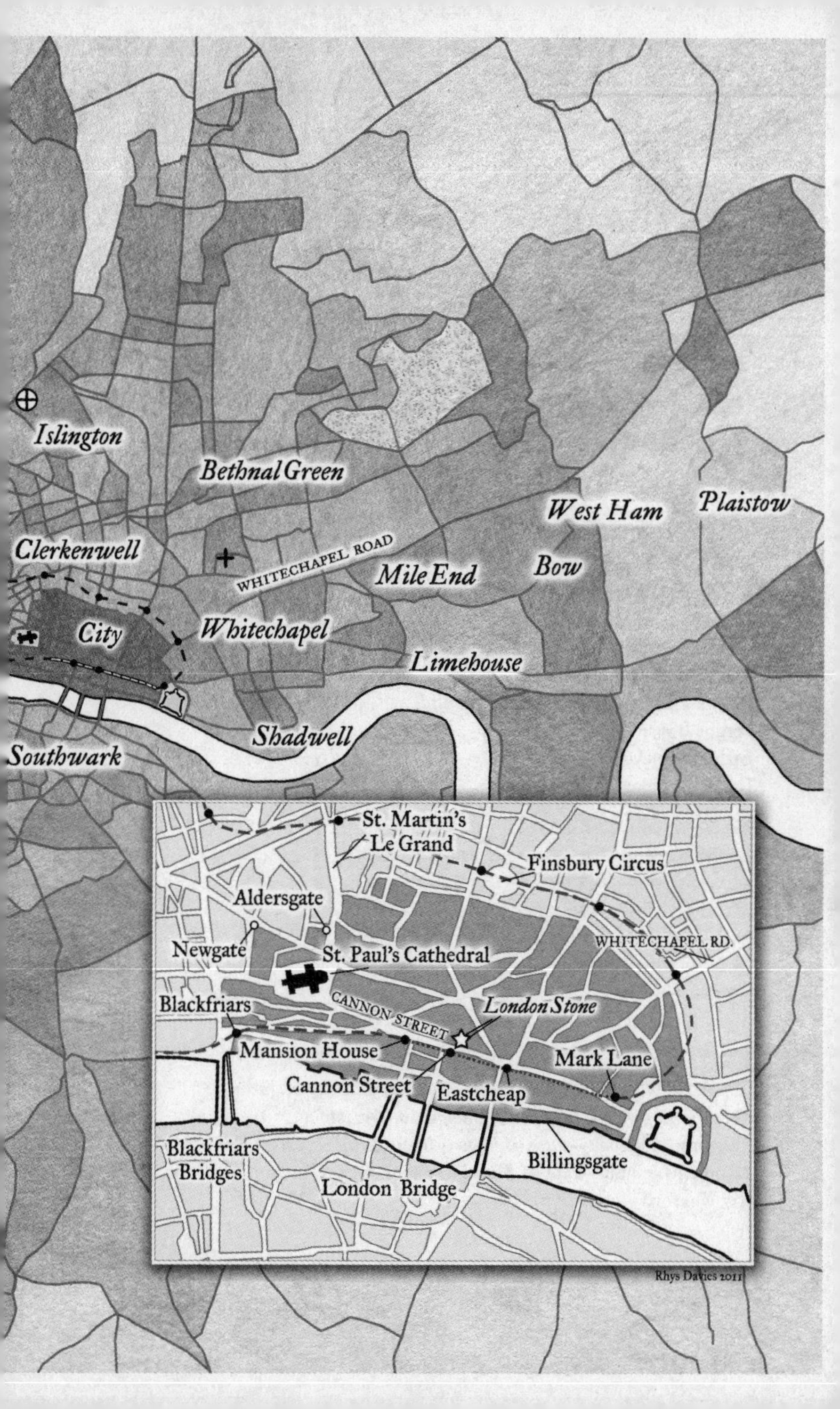
Islington
Bethnal Green
West Ham
Plaistow
Clerkenwell
WHITECHAPEL ROAD
Mile End
Bow
City
Whitechapel
Limehouse
Shadwell
Southwark
St. Martin's
Le Grand
Finsbury Circus
Aldersgate
Newgate
WHITECHAPEL RD.
St. Paul's Cathedral
CANNON STREET
Blackfriars
London Stone
Mansion House
Mark Lane
Cannon Street
Eastcheap
Blackfriars
Bridges
Billingsgate
London Bridge
Rhys Davies 2011

DRAMATIS PERSONAE

Mortals

Those marked with an asterisk are attested in history.

Whitechapel Irish
Elizabeth O'Malley—*a young woman*
James O'Malley—*her father, a prisoner in Newgate*
Owen Darragh—*a boy, missing seven years*
Maggie Darragh—*his sister*
Mrs. Darragh—*his mother, an invalid*
Fergus Boyle—*a troublemaker*
Father Tooley—*a priest*
Dónall Whelan—*a fairy doctor*

No. 35 Cromwell Road
Louisa Kittering—*a rebellious young woman*
Mrs. Kittering—*her mother*
Mrs. Fowler—*housekeeper to the Kitterings*
Ned Sayers—*footman to the Kitterings*
Ann Wick }
Sarah } *maids to the Kitterings*
Mary Banning }

Society for Psychical Research
*Frederic William Henry Myers—*a spiritualist investigator*
*Henry Sidgwick—*his friend, likewise an investigator*
*Eleanor Sidgwick—*wife of Henry, likewise an investigator*
*Annie Marshall—*wife of Myers's cousin, now deceased*
Iris Wexford—*a medium*

Scotland Yard
*Adolphus Williamson—*Chief Inspector of the Special Irish Branch*
*Patrick Quinn—*Police Sergeant of the Special Irish Branch*

*Augusta Ada King—*mathematician and Countess of Lovelace, now deceased*
*Charles Babbage—*an inventor, now deceased*
*Eliza Carter—*a girl from West Ham*
Mrs. Chase—*a widow from Islington*
Eveleen Myers—*wife of Frederic Myers, and a photographer*
Delphia St. Clair—*wife of Galen St. Clair, now deceased*
Francis Merriman—*a mortal seer and founder of the Onyx Hall, now deceased*

Princes of the Stone, in chronological order
Sir Michael Deven
Sir Antony Ware
Dr. John Ellin
Lord Joseph Winslow
Sir Alan Fitzwarren
Dr. Hamilton Birch
Galen St. Clair
Matthew Abingdon
Colonel Robert Shaw
Geoffrey Franklin
Henry Brandon
Alexander Messina
Benjamin Hodge—*the current Prince*

Faeries

The Court of London
Lune—*Queen of the Onyx Court*
Sir Peregrin Thorne—*Captain of the Onyx Guard*
Sir Cerenel—*Lieutenant of the Onyx Guard*
Dame Segraine—*a lady knight of the Onyx Guard*
Dame Irrith—*a sprite, and lady knight of the Vale of the White Horse*
Amadea—*Lady Chamberlain of the Onyx Court*
Tom Toggin—*a hob; valet to the Prince of the Stone*

Bonecruncher—*a follower of the Prince*
Invidiana—*a previous Queen, now deceased*

The Goblin Market
Nadrett—*a criminal boss*
Dead Rick—*his dog; a skriker*
Cyma—*a former lady, in debt to Nadrett*
Gresh }
Nithen } *followers of Nadrett*
Old Gadling }
Chrennois—*a French sprite, and follower of Nadrett*
Valentin Aspell }
Hardface } *Goblin Market bosses*
Lacca }
Orlegg—*a thrumpin in service to Valentin Aspell* Greymalkin—*likewise in service to Valentin Aspell*
Po—*a Chinese faerie, ally of Lacca, and keeper of an opium den*
Hafdean—*keeper of the Crow's Head*
Blacktooth Meg—*hag of the River Fleet*
Charcoal Eddie—*a less-than-bright Puck*

The Galenic Academy
Abd ar-Rashid—*a genie of Istanbul, and Scholarch of the Academy*
Wrain }
Wilhas von das Ticken }
Niklas von das Ticken } *Academy Masters*
Lady Feidelm }
Ch'ien Mu }
Yvoir—*a French faerie, and scholar of photography*
Kutuhal—*a vanara from India*
Fjothar—*a svártalfar from Scandinavia*

Rosamund Goodemeade—*a helpful brownie*
Gertrude Goodemeade—*likewise a helpful brownie, and Rosamund's sister*
Eidhnin } *Irish fae, of a nationalist bent*
Scéineach }
Suspiria—*founder of the Onyx Hall, now deceased*
Father Thames—spirit of the River Thames

Home is a name, a word, it is a strong one; stronger than magician ever spoke, or spirit ever answered to, in the strongest conjuration.

—Charles Dickens, *Martin Chuzzlewit*

PROLOGUE

THE ONYX HALL, LONDON
29 January 1707

The lights hovered in midair, like a cloud of unearthly fireflies. The corners of the room lay in shadow; all illumination had drawn inward, to this spot before the empty hearth, and the woman who stood there in silence.

Her right hand moved with absent surety, coaxing the lights into position. The left hung stiff at her side, a rigid claw insufficiently masked by its glove. Without compass or ruler, guided only by bone-deep instinct, she formed the lights into a map. Here, the Tower of London. To the west, the cathedral of St. Paul's. The long line of the Thames below them, and the Walbrook running down from the north to meet it, passing the London Stone on its way; and around the whole, touching the river on both sides, the bent and uneven arc of the city wall.

For a moment it floated before her, brilliant and perfect.

Then her fingertip reached up to a northeastern point on the wall, and flicked a few of the lights away.

As if that had been a summons, the door opened. Only one person in all this place had the right to interrupt her unannounced, and so she stayed where she was, regarding the newly flawed map. Once the door was closed, she spoke, her voice carrying perfectly in the stillness of the room. "You were unable to stop them."

"I'm sorry, Lune." Joseph Winslow came forward, to the edge of the cool light. It gave his ordinary features a peculiar cast; what would have seemed like youth in the brightness of day—more youth than he should claim—turned into strange agelessness under such illumination. "It is too much in the way. An impediment to carts, riders, carriages, people on foot . . . it serves no purpose anymore. None that I can tell them, at least."

The silver of her eyes reflected blue as she traced the line of the wall. The old Roman and medieval fortification, much patched and altered over the centuries, but still, in its essence, the boundary of old London.

And of her realm, lying hidden below.

She should have seen this coming. Once it became impossible to crowd more people within the confines of London, they began to spill outside the wall. Up the river to Westminster, in great houses along the bank and pestilential tenements behind. Down the river to the shipbuilding yards, where sailors drank away their pay among the warehouses of goods from foreign lands. Across the river in Southwark, and north of the wall in suburbs—but at the heart of it, always, the City of London. And as the years went by, the seven great gates became ever more clogged, until they could not admit the endless rivers of humanity that flowed in and out.

In the hushed tone of a man asking a doctor for what he fears will be bad news, Winslow said, "What will this do to the Onyx Hall?"

Lune closed her eyes. She did not need them to look at her domain, the faerie palace that stretched beneath the square mile enclosed by the walls. Those black stones might have been her own bones, for a faerie queen ruled by virtue of the bond with her realm. "I do not know," she admitted. "Fifty years ago, when Parliament commanded General Monck to tear the gates from their hinges, I feared it might harm the Hall. Nothing came of it. Forty years ago, when the Great Fire burned the entrances to this place, and even St. Paul's Cathedral, I feared we might not recover. Those have been rebuilt. But now . . ."

Now, the mortals of London proposed to tear down part of the wall—tear it down, and not replace it. With the gates disabled, the City could no longer protect itself in war; in reality, it had no need to do so. Which made the wall itself little more than a historical curiosity, and an obstruction to London's growth.

Perhaps the Hall would yet stand, like a table with one of its legs broken away.

Perhaps it would not.

"I'm sorry," Winslow said again, hating the inadequacy of the words. He was her mortal consort, the Prince of the

Stone; it was his privilege and duty to oversee the points at which faerie and mortal London came together. Lune had asked him to prevent the destruction of the wall, and he had failed.

Lune's posture was rarely less than perfect, but somehow she pulled herself even more upright, her shoulders going back to form a line he'd come to recognise. "It was an impossible task. And perhaps an unnecessary one; the Hall has survived difficulties before. But if some trouble comes of this, then we will surmount it, as we always have."

She presented her arm to him, and he took it, guiding her with formal courtesy from the room. Back to their court, a world of faeries both kind and cruel, and the few mortals who knew of their presence beneath London.

Behind them, alone in the empty room, the lights drifted free once more, the map dissolving into meaningless chaos.

PART ONE

February–May 1884

I behold London; a Human awful wonder of God!

WILLIAM BLAKE,
JERUSALEM: THE EMANATION OF THE GIANT ALBION

Oh City! Oh latest Throne! where I was rais'd
To be a mystery of loveliness
Unto all eyes, the time is well nigh come
When I must render up this glorious home
To keen Discovery: soon yon brilliant towers
Shall darken with the waving of her wand;
Darken, and shrink and shiver into huts,
Black specks amid a waste of dreary sand,
Low-built, mud-walled, Barbarian settlement,
How chang'd from this fair City!

ALFRED, LORD TENNYSON,
"TIMBUCTOO"

A great town is like a forest—that is not the whole of it that you see above ground.

MR. LOWE. MP.

ADDRESS AT THE OPENING OF THE METROPOLITAN RAILWAY, REPORTED IN THE *TIMES*, 10 JANUARY 1863

Given enough time, anything can become familiar enough to be ignored.

Even pain.

The searing nails driven through her flesh ache as they always have, but those aches are known, enumerated, incorporated into her world. If her body is stretched upon a rack, muscles and sinews torn and ragged from the strain, at least no one has stretched it further of late. This is familiar. She can disregard it.

But the unfamiliar, the unpredictable, disrupts that disregard. This new pain is irregular and intense, not the steady torment of before. It is a knife driven into her shoulder, a sudden agony stabbing through her again. And again. And again.

Creeping ever closer to her heart.

Each new thrust awakens all the other pains, every bleeding nerve she had learned to accept. Nothing can be ignored, then. All she can do is endure. And this she does because she has no choice; she has bound herself to this agony, with chains that cannot be broken by any force short of death.

Or, perhaps, salvation.

Like a patient cast down by disease, she waits, and in her lucid moments she prays for a cure. No physician exists who can treat this sickness, but perhaps—if she endures long enough—someone will teach himself that science, and save her from this terrible death by degrees.

So she hopes, and has hoped for longer than she can recall. But each thrust brings the knife that much closer to her heart.

One way or another, she will not have to endure much more.

The monster city seethed with life. Its streets, like arteries both great and small, pulsed with the flow of traffic: hackneys and private carriages, omnibuses bursting with riders inside and out, horse trams rattling past on their iron rails. People on foot, on horseback, on the improbable wheels of bicycles. On the river, ships: forests of masts and steam funnels, skiffs hauling cargo to and fro, ferries spilling passengers onto piers that thrust out from the stinking foreshore. Trains thundered in from the suburbs and back out again, the population rising and falling, as if the city breathed.

The air that filled its lungs was humanity, of countless different kinds. The high and the low, glittering with diamonds or the tears of despair, speaking dozens of languages in hundreds of accents, living cheek by jowl, above and below and beside one another, but occupying entirely different worlds. The city encompassed them all: living and dying, they formed part of the great organism, which daily threatened to strangle on its simultaneous growth and rot.

This was London, in all its filth and glory. Nostalgic for the past, while yearning to cast off the chains of bygone ages and step forward into the bright utopia of the future. Proud of its achievements, yet despising its own flaws. A monster in both size and nature, that would consume the unwary and spit them out again, in forms unrecognizable and undreamt.

London, the monster city.

THE CITY OF LONDON

26 February 1884

"Hot buns! A farthing apiece, warm you on a cold morning! Will you buy a bun, sir?"

The cry rose into the air and was lost among others, like one bird in a flock. A burst of steam from the open cut alongside Farringdon Road heralded the arrival of a subterranean train; a minute later, the station above disgorged a mass of men, joining those carried into the City by the power of their own feet. They shuffled along Snow Hill and up onto Holborn Viaduct, yawning and sleepy, their numbers sufficient to stop carriages and omnibuses when they flooded across the street crossings.

A costerwoman's voice had to be strong, to make itself heard above the voices and footsteps and the church bells ringing seven o'clock. Filling her lungs, Eliza bellowed again, "Hot buns! Hot from the oven! Only a farthing apiece!"

One fellow paused, dug in his pocket, handed over a penny. The four buns Eliza gave in exchange had been hot when she collected her load an hour ago; only the close-packed mass of their fellows had preserved any heat since then. But these were the clerks, the ink-stained men who slaved away in the City's halls of business for long hours and little pay; they wouldn't quibble over the truth of her advertising. By the time their wealthier betters came in to work, three hours or so from now, she would have sold her stock and filled her barrow with something else.

If all went well. Good days were the ones where she traced the streets again and again, with new wares every round: laces for boots and stays, lucifers, even larks one time. Bad days saw her peddling cold, stale buns at sundown, with no comfort save the surety that at least she would have something to eat that night. And sometimes a doss-house keeper could be persuaded to take a few as payment, in exchange for a spot on his bench.

Today was beginning well; even a bun of only moderate warmth was a pleasant touch on a cold morning like this one. But chill weather made men sullen in the afternoon and evening, turning up their collars and shoving their hands into pockets, thinking only of the train or omnibus or long walk that would take them home. Eliza knew better than to assume her luck would hold.

By the time she reached Cheapside, following the crowds of men on their way to the countinghouses, the press in the streets was thinning; those still out were hurrying, for fear their pay would be docked for lateness. Eliza counted her coins, stuck an experimental finger among the remaining buns, and decided they were cold enough that she could spare one for herself. And Tom Granger was always willing to let her sit a while with him.

She retraced her steps to the corner of Ivy Lane, where Tom was halfheartedly waving copies of *The Times* at passersby. "You'll never sell them with that lazy hand," Eliza said, stopping her barrow alongside.

His grin was as crooked as his front teeeth. "Wait 'til tomorrow. Bill says we'll 'ave exciting news then."

"Oh?" Eliza offered him a bun, which he accepted. "Scandal, is it?"

"Better. There's been another bombing."

She had just taken a large bite; it caught in her throat, and for a moment she feared she would choke. Then it slid down, and she hoped that if Tom saw her distress, he'd chalk it up to that. "Where?"

Tom had already crammed half the bun in his own mouth. His answer was completely unintelligible; she had to wait while he chewed enough to swallow. "Victoria Station," he said, once he could speak more clearly. "Right early this morning. Blew the booking office and all 'alfway to the moon. Nobody 'urt, though—pity. We sells more papers when there's dead people."

"Who did it?"

He shrugged, then turned away to sell a paper to a man in a carpenter's flannel coat. That done, he said, "Harry thinks it was a gas pipe what blew, but I reckon it's the Fenians again." He spat onto the cobblestones. "Fucking micks. They sells papers, I'll give 'em that, but 'em and their bleeding bombs, eh?"

"Them and their bleeding bombs," Eliza echoed, staring at the remnants of her bun as if it needed her attention. She had lost all appetite, but forced herself to finish anyway. *I missed it. While I slept tied to a bench, he was here, and I missed my chance.*

Tom rattled on about the Irish, allowing as how they were devilish strong buggers and good at hard labour, but one paddy had come up the other day, bold as you please, and tried to get papers to sell. "Me and Bill ran 'im off right quick," Tom said.

Eliza didn't share his satisfaction in the slightest. While Tom spoke, her gaze raked the street, as if frantic effort now could make up for her failure. *Too late, and you know it. What would you have done anyway, if you'd been here last night? Followed him again? Much good that did last time. But you missed your chance to do better.* It took her by surprise when Tom left off his tirade and said, "Three months, it's been, and I still don't get you."

She hoped her stare was not as obviously startled as it felt. "What do you mean?"

Tom gestured at her, seeming to indicate both the ragged clothing and the young woman who wore it. "You. Who you are, and what you're doing 'ere."

She was suddenly far colder than could be explained

by the morning air. "Trying to sell buns. But I think I'm about done in for these; I should go for fried fish soon, or something else."

"Which you'll bring right back 'ere. Maybe you'll go stand around the 'ospital, or the prison, but you'll stick near Newgate as long as you can, so long as you've got a few pennies to buy supper and a place to sleep. Them fine gents like to talk about lazy folks as don't care enough to earn a better wage—but you're the only one I've ever met where it's *true.*" Tom scratched his neck, studying her in a way that made her want to run. "You don't drop your aitches, you ain't from a proper coster family—I know they runs you off sometimes, when you steps on their territory—in short, you's a mystery, and ever since you started coming 'ere I've been trying to work you out. What's around Newgate for you, Elizabeth Marsh, that you'll spend three months waiting for it to show up?"

Her fingers felt like ice. Eliza fumbled with the ends of her shawl, then stopped, because it only drew attention to how her hands were shaking. What was there to fear? No crime in hanging about, not so long as she was engaged in honest work. Tom knew nothing. So far as he was aware, she was simply Elizabeth Marsh, and Elizabeth Marsh was nobody.

But she hadn't thought up a lie for him, because she hadn't expected him to ask. Before her mind could settle down enough to find a good one, his expression softened to sympathy. "Got someone in Newgate, 'ave you?"

He jerked his chin westward as he said it. *Newgate* in

the specific sense, the prison that stood nearby. Which was close enough to a truth—if not the real truth—that Eliza seized upon it with relief. "My father."

"Thought it might be an 'usband," Tom said. "You wouldn't be the first mot walking around without a ring. Waiting for 'im to get out, or 'oping 'e won't?"

Eliza thought about the last time she'd seen her father. Four months ago, and the words between them weren't pretty—they never were—but she'd clean forgotten about that after she walked out of the prison and saw that familiar, hated face.

She shrugged uncomfortably, hoping Tom would let the issue drop. The more questions she answered, the more likely it was that he'd catch a whiff of something odd. Better to leave it at a nameless father with an unnamed crime. Tom didn't press, but he did pick up one of his newspapers and begin searching through a back page. " 'Ere, take a look at this."

The piece above his ragged fingernail was brief, just two short paragraphs under the header MR. CALHOUN'S NEW FACTORY. "Factory work ain't bad," Tom said. "Better than service, anyway—no missus always on you, and some factories pay more—and it would get you out of 'ere. Waiting around won't do you no good, Lizzie, and you keeps this up, sooner or later your luck'll go bad. Workhouse bad."

"Ah, you're just trying to get rid of me," Eliza said. It came out higher than usual, because of the tightness in her throat. Tom was just useful; his corner was the best one to watch from. She never intended more than that—never friendship—and his kindness made her feel all the more guilty about her lies.

But he was right, as far as it went. She'd been in service before, to an Italian family that sold secondhand clothes in Spitalfields. Being a maid-of-all-work, regardless of the family, was little better than being a slave. Lots of girls said factory work was preferable, if you could get it. But abandoning Newgate . . .

She *couldn't.* Her disobedient eyes drifted back to the advertisement anyway. And then she saw what lay below, that Tom's hand had covered before.

> LONDON FAIRY SOCIETY—A new association has formed in Islington, for the understanding of Britain's fast-vanishing fairy inhabitants. Meetings the second Friday of every month at 9 White Lion St., 7 P.M.

Eliza only barely kept from snatching the paper out of Tom's hands, to stare at the words and see if they vanished. "May I?" she asked.

She meant only to read it again, but Tom handed her the paper and flapped his hands in its wake. "Keep it."

The cold had gone; Eliza felt warm from head to toe. She could not look away from the words. Coincidence—or providence? It might be nothing: folk with money babbling on about little "flower fairies," rather than *faeries,* the kind Eliza knew all too well. This new society might not know anything that could help her.

But her alternative was waiting around here, with the fading hope that it would do her any good. Just because there'd been another bombing didn't mean any of the people involved had been *here;* it could have been pure chance last October, spotting him in Newgate. She'd spent nearly every day here since then, and not caught so much as another glimpse. They were tricksy creatures, faeries were, and not easily caught. But perhaps this London Fairy Society could help her.

"Thank you," Eliza told Tom, folding the newspaper and stuffing it into the sagging pocket of her shawl.

He shrugged, looking away in embarrassment. "Ah, it's nothing. You feeds me buns enough; I owes you a newspaper's worth, at least."

She wasn't thanking him for the paper, but saying so would only make him more awkward. "I'd best be moving," Eliza said. "These buns won't sell themselves. But I'll think about the factory, Tom; I will." She meant it, too. It would be glorious to go back to something like normal life. No more of this hand-to-mouth existence, gambling everything on the hope of a second stroke of luck. After these three months, she'd even go back into service with the DiGiuseppes, just to know each night that she'd have a roof over her head.

If a normal life was even possible anymore, after everything she'd been through. But that was a question for the future. First, she had to catch herself a faerie.

Tom wished her well, and she gripped the handles of her barrow again, wheeling it down Newgate toward a fellow in Holborn who would sell her fried fish, if she could dispose of the rest of her current load. Her eyes did their habitual dance over the crowds as she cried her wares, but saw nothing unusual.

Second Friday. That'll be the fourteenth, then. A bit more than a fortnight away. She'd keep on here until then, on the off chance that her luck would turn even better. But Islington, she hoped, held the answers.

THE GOBLIN MARKET, ONYX HALL

2 March 1884

With a clicking of toenails upon cracked black stone, the dog trotted into the room of cages. A half dozen lined the narrow chamber, three on a side, mostly full with sleeping humans. In the nearest, a young girl lay alone on a floor of filthy straw, curled in upon herself. The dog drew nearer, sniffing. His nose brushed her hair, close by the cage's wooden bars, and she jerked awake with a cry of fear.

The dog sat down on his haunches and studied her, tongue lolling just a little. It was as close to an appealing look as a scruffy thing like him could come; his black fur was untidy and matted, and a chunk had been torn from his left ear. But when he made no threatening move—merely sat and watched—the girl moved hesitantly from the corner where she'd retreated. Holding one hand out, she inched closer, until her hand was near enough to the bars for the dog to extend his nose and sniff politely. He even licked her dirty fingers, a brief, warm caress.

At that touch of kindness, the girl burst into tears.

"Oi there!"

The dog rose in a swift turn. A squat, ugly figure stood in the doorway, scratching the wiry hairs of his beard. "Get off it," the goblin said, scowling at him. "'E wants to see you, and not on four feet."

In the cage, the girl had retreated once more. The dog cast a brief glance over his shoulder at her, then sighed, a peculiarly human sound. Bending his head, he concentrated, and his body began to shift.

He heard a faint whimper from behind him as the transformation finished. However little reassurance his dog form had offered, as a man he was worse; Dead Rick knew that all too well. Ragged trousers stopped short of his bare feet, whose toenails curved thick and filthy to the floor. On his body he wore only a torn waistcoat, scavenged off a dead mortal; he hated the confining feel of sleeves on his arms. His hair was as dirty and matted as it had been when it was fur, and as for his face . . . he didn't turn around. He might not be a barguest, with a devil's flaming eyes, but he'd seen himself in a mirror; the hard slash of his mouth wouldn't reassure anyone.

He could have changed elsewhere, out of sight of the

girl. But she was better off learning this now, that even the friendliest creature down here couldn't be trusted.

Gresh's toothy smile would never be mistaken for friendly. "She's a fine bit, ain't she?" he asked as Dead Rick came toward him. "Bit old to be stealing out of a cradle, but 'er mother kept 'er there anyway, as they didn't 'ave nowhere else to put 'er. Living sixteen to a room they was; now it's just fifteen, and she gets this whole cage to 'erself. Better for everyone!"

Dead Rick doubted the girl would agree, or her mother. Then again, what did he know? Perhaps her mother was a gin-soaked whore, and would be glad enough for one less mouth to feed. The girl might be bought by some kind faerie, who wanted a human child to play with like a doll.

Or angels might fly out of your arse, whelp. But she wouldn't age here, and disease would never touch her, which was more than anyone could say for life in the streets above.

"Come on," he said, pushing by Gresh. "You said 'e wants to see me."

"You don't need me to guide you," the goblin said.

Dead Rick paused in the corridor and glanced back. Gresh was standing in the doorway still, shoulders hunched with eagerness. "Don't," Dead Rick warned him. "You spoil 'er, and it'll be your 'ide."

The goblin glared back. "I don't need no dog telling me what to do."

He said *dog* like it was an insult—like Dead Rick should

be ashamed of being a skriker. A habit he picked up from their mutual master. But there were advantages to being a dog; Dead Rick growled low in his throat, holding Gresh's eyes, and sure enough the goblin backed down first. With grumbling complaints, but he came with Dead Rick, and left the girl to what peace she could find.

Laughter echoed off the stone around them as they went along, its source impossible to determine. The warren of the Goblin Market was packed full, fae and the human creatures they kept for entertainment or use; they crowded almost as close as the East End poor that that girl came from. For every faerie that flitted, going in search of a passage beyond the mortal world, another came here to London. To the Onyx Hall, twisted reflection of the City above, the palace that had once been the glory of faerie England—and now was their crumbling refuge against the progress of humankind.

Traces of that glory were still visible, in the sculpted columns and corner posts, the arches spanning high-ceilinged chambers, the occasional mosaic laid into the black stone of a wall. It had all seen hard use these centuries past, though. Much was cracked, or stained, or half-hidden behind the clutter of the refugees. Curtains strung on cord divided larger rooms into smaller, giving the illusion of privacy; fae defended treasured belongings or mortal pets against the greedy hands of their neighbours. But anything could be sold, if the price was good enough: a human child bargained for mortal bread, an enchanted mirror traded for drugs that could make even a faerie forget his troubles.

Gresh was right; Dead Rick didn't need the goblin to tell him where to go. He knew his way through the warren blindfolded. The room he headed for had a broken floor, scuffed stone giving way to bare earth, into which someone had dug a pit; down at the bottom, a red-eared faerie hound, his muzzle stained with blood, seized a rat and shook the rodent until its back broke. The observers—mostly fae, a few mortals—roared him on. Dead Rick shoved through the crowd, making his way toward the short staircase that curved at the far end. By the time he reached it, Gresh had disappeared, into the wagering mass.

The staircase still showed a touch of refinement, though the balustrade's carving had taken some beating over the ages. The room it led to showed a bit more than a touch, largely because the rat-fighting rabble weren't allowed in. If its chairs were mismatched, some were at least carved of exotic wood, and the carpet on the floor was still vibrant with colour. Silks draped along the walls helped cover the cracks behind, the signs of inevitable decay.

And there were only two people inside, one faerie and one mortal. The latter was dressed in a ridiculous parody of a footman's livery, styles that would have been old-fashioned fifty years before, but that hardly mattered; the more important thing was that he was there, uselessly, feeding the self-importance of his master.

Who scowled at Dead Rick. Nadrett waited for the door to close, then said, "I expects you 'ere when I needs you. Not to 'ave to send my goblins searching for you all over the warren."

He made an elegant figure, by Goblin Market standards. Not clad in patches and rags, nor parading around in a gaudy assortment of gypsy silks; his waistcoat might be red as children's blood, but it was restrained in its tailoring. One had to look closely to notice the buttons of bone, the cuff links of knotted hair. He wore no coat, but did affect a gentleman's silk top hat, adorned with a large pin of crystalline starlight.

None of which hid the fact that Nadrett had clawed his way to the top of the Goblin Market heap by a combination of cunning and brutality. Dead Rick was forced to lower his gaze. "Sorry. I was looking in on the cages—"

"You better not 'ave been touching my property."

Dead Rick was no good at lying. His hesitation told enough, and Nadrett spat a curse. "That one ain't 'ere to tithe bread. Got a buyer, wants a girl as stinks of mortality. You go licking 'er, she starts to smell of faerie instead, and then I don't get as good a price."

He should keep his mouth shut, but the words came out anyway. "I ain't 'ere to help your coves in their perversions."

Quick as a striking snake, Nadrett was there, inches from his face. "Yes, you are," the faerie spat. "Because you serve *me*. Those perversions are where I makes my profit, see, and if I don't profit, then I takes the difference out of your mangy hide. So it's in your best interests to make sure my customers ain't unhappy."

Dead Rick opened his mouth to answer—*stupid whelp; you never learn*—and Nadrett's hand closed on his throat. He might weigh a stone less than the skriker, but his grip was iron. "Cross me," Nadrett whispered, "and I will *destroy* you. Everything you used to be. You'll be like this forever, broken, crawling, serving whatever master whips you worst."

Shame and fear twisted in his gut, like a worm, eating away at his pride. He felt a whine build, trapped under Nadrett's hand, and rolled his eyes in desperation. When Nadrett let go, Dead Rick turned his head to the side, casting his gaze down. "I won't cross you."

His master laughed. "'Course not. You'll do exactly what I says. And you're in luck: I've got use for you today. Follow me."

Hating himself for it, Dead Rick obeyed.

Their path was a long one, weaving through the shabby clamour of the Goblin Market. The constant, encroaching decay made it almost impossible to go anywhere directly; too many chambers and connecting passages had vanished. Whole sections were almost completely cut off, their only access being through patches too unsafe to traverse. A faerie who set foot there was liable to come out somewhere else entirely—or not come out at all.

London's foundation is rotting out from underneath it, Dead Rick thought. People still told tales of the glories of the Onyx Hall, but that was all that remained: tales, and these decaying fragments. *And the Goblin Market's the most rotten of all.*

The place Nadrett led him wasn't quite Market territory, and wasn't quite not. The night garden didn't belong to anyone, except the refugees who slept on blankets beneath the overgrown trees. It lay in what had once been the heart of the Onyx Hall, and in past ages had been the favoured haunt of courtiers. But now the Walbrook ran foul through its heart, and the flowers grew among choking weeds.

A trio of goblins lounged on a chipped bench, and rose when Nadrett came through the entrance arch. Scots, and not familiar to Dead Rick; he would have wagered human bread, if he'd had any, that they were newcomers. Temporary residents of the night garden, who'd sold their services to the Goblin Market—to Nadrett—in exchange for a leg up. "We've cleared it," the leader said. "Got two fellows watching each of the other doors."

Nadrett clapped him on the shoulder and turned to Dead Rick. "You knows your job. Get to it."

He stared past his master, into the abandoned wilderness of the garden. "Who is it?"

"What does that matter? Some mortal. She's none of your concern."

Female, then. But not the little girl in the cage. Dead Rick swallowed, tasting bile. Not the little girl; just some other human who likely never did anything to bring this fate on herself.

The mere drawing of Nadrett's breath was enough to prompt him. Grinding his teeth, Dead Rick shifted back to dog form, and ran out into the night garden.

A welter of smells filled his nose. The refugees might be gone for the moment, but their scents remained: hobs and goblins and pucks, courtly elves and nature-loving sprites, some so new they carried echoes of their homes with them. Cool soil, and the thick mat of vegetation that grew over it; once the garden had been planted with aromatic, night-blooming flowers—evening primrose, jasmine—and some of the hardier ones still survived. Up ahead lay the stinking Walbrook. The crumbling enchantments had mixed the buried river's reflection with its polluted reality, poisoning the earth around it.

Dead Rick paused near one of the stream's surviving footbridges, thinking he saw movement ahead. It proved to be just a faerie light, drifting aimlessly through the air. Most of them had abandoned the ceiling, where people said they used to form shifting constellations, but in the distance Dead Rick thought he saw a more solid glow.

He padded toward it, keeping to the underbrush. Yes, there was light ahead, behind that cluster of sickly apple trees. He sank to his belly and crawled forward one paw at a time until he could see.

The mortal was scarcely more than a girl, fifteen years old at most. She sat with her back to a stone plinth, knees pulled tight to her chest. Dead Rick wondered if she knew she was sitting on a grave. Her dress was reasonably fine; she ought to be able to read—but vines had grown over the inscription, making it easy to miss if she didn't look for it. And her attention was elsewhere, scouring the surrounding area for signs of a threat.

Signs of *him*.

Faerie lights floated about the small clearing, as if trying to comfort her. They had just enough awareness to respond to others' wishes; her fear might have drawn them. Or had she called them to her? *Don't ask questions,* Dead Rick growled to himself. *Don't think of 'er as a person—just do your job.*

The growl escaped his muzzle, without him intending it. The mortal gasped, rising to a wary crouch.

She shouldn't 'ave been sitting in the light. She'll be 'alf-blind once she runs.

So much the better for him.

Dead Rick growled again, this time with purpose. There was a gap in the hawthorn bushes; he snaked through it, making no sound, and snarled more sharply. Then circled further: another growl. To a frightened mind, it would sound like she was surrounded.

In every direction except one: the overgrown path that led away from the grave. And sure enough, she bolted.

He was running almost before she moved. She was human, and wearing a dress; he was a dog, and knew his way about the garden. A fallen tree had blocked the left-hand path years ago, so that even if she went that way—and he heard her try—in the end, she had to go right. And Dead Rick was there, waiting to harry her onward.

Nadrett had sent him to do this so often that it was almost routine. But the girl surprised him; she plunged through an overgrown holly bush, hissing as it raked her, to take a less obvious path. Dead Rick cursed inwardly. Two fellows watching each of the other doors—but were they watching *all* of them? Or only the ones that led anywhere anymore? The arch ahead opened on a corridor that went about fifty feet before fading into a bad patch of the Onyx Hall.

It had been fifty feet the last time he looked. It might be less now.

Dead Rick put on a burst of speed. A dry fountain near the wall gave him an advantage; he leapt up the enormous grotesque at the center, toenails scrabbling on the twisted stone, and launched himself through the air toward the arch. He landed with an almighty crash, but that served him well enough: he heard the girl stumble and fall, then claw to her feet and run in the other direction, away from whatever huge monster was lurking by the arch.

Huge, no. Monster, yes. That's what I've become.

Dead Rick shook himself, as if his gloom could be shaken off like water. If he failed at this, Nadrett would see to it he was more than just gloomy.

He trotted rapidly along the girl's trail, following her scent. His pause had given her time to get ahead, and in the absence of his snarls she'd gone quiet. The trail led him over the footbridge; he caught a whiff on the railing, as if she'd paused there, eyeing the filthy water. But for a girl in skirts, who likely couldn't swim, it would just be unpleasant suicide; in the end she'd gone on.

Across an expanse of shaggy grass, almost as tall as he

was. Dead Rick leapt over a fallen urn, hoping to cut her off. The gamble worked: she was coming down the path toward him. Renewed snarling sent her the other way, and now he knew how this would end. Normally he trapped them against the wall, but with a bit of herding . . .

She was nearing the end of her strength. Dead Rick quickened his own pace, baying like a wolf, and burst into the open almost at her heels. The girl flung herself across the torn ground, up the steps of a ruined pavilion, and fell sprawling across the boards of its floor. Dead Rick leapt—

Her scream tore through the air, and then *stopped.*

Dead Rick's paws slammed down on her chest, and his jaws snapped shut just shy of her nose. The girl was rigid with terror beneath him, and her mouth gaped open, heaving again and again as if she were screaming still, but no sound came out.

For a moment, the desire was there. To sink his teeth into that vulnerable throat, to tear the flesh and lap up the hot blood as it fountained out. Death was part of a skriker's nature. It would be easy, so long as he didn't see her as a person—just meat and fear and a voice to be stolen.

But that was Nadrett's way, and the Goblin Market's. Clenching his muzzle until it hurt, Dead Rick backed off, slowly, stepping with care so his rough toenails wouldn't scratch the girl through her dress.

Nadrett was leaning against one of the pavilion's posts, tossing a small jar from hand to hand. "That's a good one," he said with a satisfied leer. "Prime stuff. That'll fetch a good price, it will. Maybe I'll even let you 'ave a bit of the profit, eh?"

If he had any pride left, Dead Rick would refuse it. Since he didn't, he jumped down to the grass, passing Nadrett without so much as a snarl.

His master laughed as he went. "Good dog."

Coming from Nadrett's mouth, the word made Dead Rick ashamed.

WHITECHAPEL, LONDON

4 March 1884

The shift was vivid, as the street's name changed from Fenchurch to Aldgate High Street to Whitechapel Road. In less than a mile, Eliza passed from one London to another, from the grand counting houses and respectable shops of the City to the plain brick buildings and narrow back courts that, until a few months ago, she had called home.

She'd argued with herself all yesterday about coming back. A run of good days had given her money for last night's doss and tonight's, with enough left over to buy new wares to sell, but a day spent not working was one day closer to starvation. Selling as she went would have gotten her run off by the costers who worked this area, though, and besides, she didn't want anything linking her to the woman who sold hot buns and other oddments around the City. So her barrow was in the keeping of a woman in St. Giles who could hopefully be trusted not to sell it the moment Eliza's back was turned, and Eliza herself had taken a day's holiday. A risk, yes—but no more so than returning to Whitechapel in the first place.

"You've got a nerve on you, Eliza O'Malley, showing your face openly around here."

The call came from the doorway of a rag-and-bone shop at the corner of George Yard. Eliza had gone on three more steps before she realised she could stop: it was no longer necessary, or useful, to pretend she was Elizabeth Marsh, good English costerwoman. Those who would give her trouble here already knew who she was.

So she stopped, turning, and saw Fergus Boyle leaning in the doorway, arms crossed over his chest and one foot on the box he'd apparently been carrying. He grinned when she faced him. "Gave you a fright, did I?"

Her skin was still tingling from the sudden jolt of hearing her name, after months of playacting as someone else. The accustomed accents, though, rose to her lips with no difficulty at all. "Get you gone, Fergus Boyle; haven't you anything better to do with yourself than bedevil me?"

"With you vanishing the way you did? I don't." With his foot he shoved the box to the wall, out of harm's way. Eliza stood her ground as he came closer. "You should hear the stories. Some think you've been slung in gaol, like your aul da. The ones who think you're cautious say you went to America, never mind how you'd pay for the journey. *I* put my money on you hiding with the Fenians. Did you and your friends have anything to do with that dynamite at Victoria Station the other day?"

"I'm no Fenian," Eliza said, casting a wary glance across the people on the street. The bobbies hardly cared enough to keep order in Whitechapel, but since last year the new Special Irish Branch kept a lively ear out for any whisper of sedition.

"Sure," Boyle said, grinning in a way she didn't like. "You had nothing to do with Charing Cross last fall. You just happened to see the bomb in time to throw it out the back of the train. Pure chance, that was."

Not chance at all—but what could she tell him? That the Charing Cross and Praed Street bombings hadn't been Fenian jobs, not completely? That they'd had help from faeries? Boyle was descended from good County Roscommon stock, the son of a farmer's daughter and a fellow from the next farm over; they'd brought their stories with them when they came to London during the Great Hunger. He believed in fairies, right enough. But they were creatures you left milk for on the back step, to keep them from witching your cows or tangling your children's hair in the night. Not city-dwelling goblins who bombed railways.

As for telling him *why* she'd followed a faerie onto the Underground . . . she'd tried that before, near on seven years ago. Not Fergus Boyle, but other people. And none of them had listened.

"I can't stay long," she said, knowing he'd take her changing the subject as proof that he was right. "What is it you want? Just to tell me I've got a nerve on me?"

"Not staying long, is it? And what have you to hurry back to?" Boyle stepped even closer, so that he loomed over her. "Or is it that you're afraid the Special Branch boyos will catch you?"

Eliza shoved him, hard, at the point on his shoulder that would spin him back a step. "Sure I have better things to do with my time than spend it talking with the likes of yourself."

Fergus's mocking grin faded a hair. "Ach, you're not going to trouble Mrs. Darragh, are you?"

"I'm not."

She'd always been a good liar, but Boyle still looked at her suspiciously. "Good. Maggie's been glad to see the back of you—says her aul ma got upset when you were around."

Now it was Eliza's turn to look suspicious. "When did you and Maggie Darragh get on such close terms, that you'd be knowing what she's thinking?"

He grinned more broadly, and Eliza sighed. She knew perfectly well that Maggie didn't want her around, and was prepared for that; if she had to dodge Fergus Boyle, though, then this would be even more difficult. But she refused to abandon Mrs. Darragh—not when she was the only hope the woman had left.

Best to distract him with a believable lie. "Unlike some people," Eliza told him, "I have a care for my soul. I'm off to confession—that's a thing we do in church, that is, as I'm sure you've never heard of it." *And lying about that is the least of the things I'm going to Hell for.*

Boyle looked dubious. Fortunately, Eliza saw a stick-thin girl crouching over the crate behind him. "You might want to be watching that, you might," Eliza said mildly, with a nod of her head; then she slipped away while Boyle was busy clouting the girl over the ear.

Her heart beat too fast as she hurried down Whitechapel Road, weaving through the carts and the filthy fog. Four months and more since she'd been here, and it wasn't long enough. Boyle was right: What if some fellow from the Special Irish Branch remembered her face? She hadn't been stupid enough to tell *them* she was the one who threw the bomb from the Charing Cross train; they'd never believe she did it to save the people in the third-class carriage. More than seventy people were hurt that same night, when the other bomb exploded on a train leaving Praed Street. But Eliza was Irish; just being there was almost enough to hang her, and touching the bomb would be more than enough.

That was why she'd done her best to vanish, hiding behind the gift for mimicry and playacting that had always amused Owen so much. With the bloody Irish Republican Brotherhood and their friends in America constantly making trouble, it wasn't safe to be Irish in London right now. And even less safe to be Eliza O'Malley.

Boyle was right: the cautious thing to do would be to scrape together enough money, somehow, to go elsewhere. America, or Ireland, or at least another city. Liverpool, perhaps. But even if she could give up her search, Eliza was London-born; she'd never known another home.

God help her, she even missed the dirty, cramped slums of Whitechapel, so much more familiar than the stuffy businesses of the City.

Not that she had any romantic illusions about the area. It was a sink of vice and crime, filled with the cast-off poor of every race, with tails doing customers in back alleys for tuppence a fuck and gangs taking by threat or violence what little money other folk had managed to earn. But as she passed the narrow alleys and courts Eliza heard familiar accents, and sometimes even the Irish language itself, in raucous and friendly exchange. She pulled her shawl closer about her face and hurried onward, head down, to avoid being seen by anyone else she knew—or seeing them herself. That would just make it all the harder to leave again.

Mrs. Darragh and her daughter lived in a single room in a court off Old Montague Street, with a piece of canvas tacked over the window where the glass had been broken out. At least, they had when Eliza was last here; what if they'd moved on? Boyle wouldn't have told her. If he and Maggie had some kind of understanding, he might have even helped them into better lodgings.

She knocked at the door, leaning close to listen. No footsteps sounded in response, which at least told her Maggie wasn't there. She knocked again. "Mrs. Darragh? 'Tis Eliza O'Malley."

No answer, but the door was unlatched when she tried the handle. "I'm coming in," Eliza said, and opened it enough to peer through.

With fog and the grimy canvas window, the interior was gloomy as a tomb. Slowly Eliza's eyes adjusted, and then she made out the figure sitting in the room's one chair, near the smoldering hearth on the far wall. *Right where I left her, four months ago.* "Mrs. Darragh, 'tis Eliza," she repeated, and came in.

The woman stared dully at the floor, hands loose in her lap as if she could not be troubled to do anything with them. The dim light was kind to her face, smoothing away some of the lines that had carved themselves there, but her hopeless expression made Eliza's heart ache. The loss of Owen had broken his mother, and she'd never mended since.

Eliza left the door open a crack, for the light, and came to crouch at Mrs. Darragh's feet. All the chatter she'd planned faded in the woman's presence: it just wasn't possible to say *Oh, how well you look today,* or anything else so false and cheerful. What good would it do? Nothing would raise her spirits, save one.

"Mrs. Darragh," she murmured, taking the older woman's slack hands in her own, "I've come to tell you good news, I have. I've almost caught him. The faerie."

No reply. Eliza pressed her lips together, then went on. "I told you I saw him, last October? Followed him to Mansion House Station, and saw the others there, getting on the train to Charing Cross. He came from near Newgate, though, and that's where I've been—waiting there, hoping to see him again, or another one. But I'm after finding something better. There's a society in Islington; I'll be going there in a few days to see if they know anything. Once I catch a faerie—any faerie—I'll make it talk. I'll make it tell me how to find Owen. And then I'll go after the bastards who took him, and I'll make them give him up, and I'll bring your son back to you."

The hands trembled in her grasp. Mrs. Darragh's lower lip quivered, too, and she had the despairing expression of a woman who could not even summon the energy to cry.

"I *will,*" Eliza insisted, tightening her grip. Not too hard; the bones felt birdlike in her hands, as if they'd snap. "I haven't abandoned him. Or you. I—"

The brightening of the room was her warning, and the cold air that swept in with it. "Haven't abandoned her?" a sharp voice said from behind. "Odd way you have of showing it, Eliza O'Malley, vanishing without so much as a word."

She didn't rise from her crouch, or let go of Mrs. Darragh's hands, but only turned her head. Maggie Darragh stood in the entrance, a heel of bread gripped in one fist, other palm flat against the door. Her battered bonnet shadowed her face, but Eliza didn't need to see it to imagine her expression.

"You made it clear you didn't want me around," Eliza said.

Maggie made a disgusted sound and shoved the door away, so that it rebounded off the wall and swung a little back. "Not clear enough, I suppose, for here you are again, whispering your poison in her ears."

The hands pulled free of Eliza's, Mrs. Darragh tucking them in beneath her elbows, hugging her body. In the greater light, the pitiful ragged state of her dress was revealed. "Poison?" Eliza said. "It's hope I bring, which is more than anyone else can be troubled to give her."

Maggie's laughter sounded like the cawing of a crow. "Hope, you call it, that makes Ma cry, and never an Owen to show for it. He's *dead,* you stupid fool, dead or run off. Or are you still too much in love with him to admit it?"

Contempt weighted down the word *love*. They'd barely been grown, Eliza and Owen; just fourteen years of age. Too young for Father Tooley to marry them, though everybody knew that was where it would end. But it wasn't love that made Eliza say, "He didn't run off. I know who took him. And I'm going to bring him back."

"You've had seven years," Maggie said cruelly. "What are you waiting for?"

Eliza flinched. In a whisper, she said, "Not quite seven." Not until October. Sometimes she felt like there was a clock ticking where her heart should be, marking off the hours and days and years. Running out of time. When the seven years were up, would Owen come back to them? Or would he be lost for good, beyond any hope of rescue?

Not the latter. She would never let it happen. She'd only let the years slip by because she had no clues, no lead to follow; it had been so easy to wonder if she imagined it all, as Maggie thought. But she didn't wonder anymore. She *knew* they were real, and she had their scent. She would keep hunting until she caught one, and forced it to tell her what she wanted to know.

"Get out," Maggie said, and Eliza could hear the angry tears in her voice. "We've troubles enough without you bringing more around. Leave Ma to mourn her son as she should."

Eliza rose, wincing as her knees protested. "I don't want to bring ye two any trouble, Maggie; you must believe me. Whatever Fergus has been saying about me, I'm no Fenian. I love Ireland as much as the next woman, and God knows it would be grand to get the English boot off our necks—but it isn't my home; London is. I would never do anything to this city, not for a country I've never even seen, and not if it means blowing up innocent people, you may be sure. I didn't leave Whitechapel because I was guilty. I did it because I thought I might be able to find Owen."

Maggie stood silent for a moment, digging her fingers into the heel of bread. When she spoke again, her voice was softer, if not friendly. "Get out, Eliza. We can't live in the past, and there's no future worth speaking of. Stop dancing it in front of us, like it'll do me or Ma any good. Just leave us be."

And that hurt worse than any of it—the hopelessness, the defeated line of Maggie's shoulders. They'd had such bright dreams, when Owen and Eliza were young, and now they'd been reduced to this ash. That, as much as Owen himself, was what the faeries had stolen from them.

Eliza fumbled blindly in her pocket, grabbed everything

there. A little over a shilling in small coins: everything she'd saved, except what she needed to fill her barrow tomorrow, and her doss money for tonight. Those, she always kept in her shoe. She spilled it out onto the bedside table, next to the unlit stub of a candle. "God keep ye safe, Maggie, Mrs. Darragh," Eliza said, and slipped out before pride could overcome need enough for her friend to protest.

RIVERSIDE, LONDON
10 March 1884

Rank moisture made the stone slick under Dead Rick's feet. The area always smelled of damp; in the Onyx Hall's twisted reflection of London above, this was the waterfront, the areas corresponding to the bank of the Thames. Distance from the wall had preserved it against the crumbling caused by the wall's destruction, but the iron gas mains that ran alongside the new sewers brought their own kind of decay.

As the growing foulness underfoot proved. Dead Rick picked his way carefully, but it didn't help him when the walls suddenly trembled around him, and the floor jerked beneath his feet; his heel slipped in something softly disgusting, and only a quick clutch at the wall saved him. He waited there, every muscle tense, until the shaking had stopped.

Train. Mostly they went unfelt, even though iron rails ran through the ground all the way from Blackfriars to Mansion House. The Onyx Hall's enchantments—what remained of them—protected against that disruption; the palace might lie beneath London, but that didn't mean the engines of the underground railway came charging in and out of their chambers. But this, one of the surviving entrances to the Hall, lay near where the line to Blackfriars Station crossed the buried River Fleet, and so the tremors came through more often.

Here, the truth couldn't be ignored. Forget the broken wall; forget the cast-iron pipes laid alongside the sewers. Forget the buildings torn down in the city above. This would be what destroyed the Hall in the end: the mortals' Inner Circle Railway, a ring of iron whose southern reach would spit the palace like a slab of meat over the fire.

Once it was complete. A pair of Cornish knockers in the Market were taking wagers on how long the Hall would survive, after that. So far the numbers ranged from a month to ten minutes. And unless something went disastrously wrong, the railway would be finished before the end of the year.

What would happen then, Dead Rick didn't know. He was certain of one thing, though: when that day came, it would be every dog for himself. Nadrett wouldn't protect him. So Dead Rick needed to be ready, and that meant taking care of his debts now, so he'd have something to hoard against that inevitable end.

The darkness had become absolute—no faerie lights to mark his path—but up ahead he heard the rush of water. Nadrett forbade the skriker to leave the Market without permission, but he'd come this way a few times on orders, and knew what to look for; soon his searching hands found the bronze ring bolted into the floor, and the thick rope knotted through it. He wrapped both hands around it tight, gradually trusting his weight to the line as the floor sloped away beneath him, feeling the black stone of the Onyx Hall end, and the brick of the Fleet conduit begin.

Then the brick ended, and there was nothing to do but screw together his trust and leap.

The wet rope shot through his hands, then burned as he seized it tight once more. For a moment, all that existed was sound and the rope: water below, rough hemp in his hands, and the giddy relief of not having fallen. *Still glad of that, am I? I suppose if I'm going to die, I want it to be somewhere better than 'ere.*

Dead Rick lowered himself into the water, moving carefully at the end. When it rained, the Fleet could rise high enough to drown a man. But the weather outside must have been dry, for when his feet settled flat, the water only came to his knees.

He reached into the pocket of the ulster he'd put on. The coat's sleeves annoyed him, but less than slinging a bag over his shoulder, and sometimes a man needed big pockets. Dark lantern, candle stub, lucifer; he struck the latter against the wall, and a moment later had light.

Not that there was much to see. The tunnel of arched brick stretched in both directions, entombing the River Fleet below the streets of London. But this was one of the few places where strangers could conceivably stumble into the Onyx Hall, and Dead Rick preferred to keep them out. He found the brick tied at the end of the rope, gave the hole above a measuring look, and on his first try sent the brick sailing back through, taking the rope with it. Any faerie who wanted in could go by another door.

Dead Rick began to make his way downstream, lantern held high. Plenty of threats could kill a man down here—pockets of bad air, sudden floods, fellow travelers—but the one that worried him most lurked within the water itself. River hags were cruel creatures to begin with, and the hag of the Fleet had only gotten worse with time. She'd kill anyone, now, mortal or fae. And while the light might draw her attention, if it came to a fight, Dead Rick wanted to see her coming. With his free hand he drew a bronze knife, and then he quickened his pace.

A shudder of relief went through him at the first hint of fresh air. Dead Rick laughed quietly, shaking his head. "Tough bloke you are," he muttered. "Spend your days in the Goblin Market, then run away from Blacktooth Meg like a—"

A splash stopped that comparison short. Dead Rick sank into a crouch, knife at the ready—but it wasn't the hag. Up ahead, a patch of lesser blackness marked the end of the conduit, where the buried river gave onto the Thames; a silhouette had just moved into view there. Dead Rick blew out his light, but it was too late. The figure began to run.

The hunter in him had to pursue. It was why Nadrett

used him in matters like the night garden chase; black dogs were a kind of goblin, terrifying as only a death omen could be, and in the countryside they still hounded men to their ends. The mortality in humans drew them, whether death stood near or far off. Dead Rick would have had to try very hard not to chase the man once he began to run.

But his quarry didn't get very far. Emerging into the sickly brown fog, Dead Rick found the man hip-deep in a sinkhole on the Thames bank, floundering in the waters of a receding tide. The fellow went still when he felt the knife's edge scrape his throat.

A tosher, Dead Rick guessed—one of the men who scavenged through the sewers, hunting out refuse that could be resold. Armed with a knife of his own, but more inclined to run than fight. It was a piece of luck, coming across him right here at the mouth of the Fleet; that might save Dead Rick an unpleasant hunt through London. It was an hour before dawn yet, he judged, and with so few people on the streets, he could have been hunting a long time.

Even coming out this far made his skin crawl like he was covered in spiders. The Blackfriars bridges leapt across the Thames, nearly overhead: long arches of wrought iron. A smaller piece lay inside the man's coat, the knife he used against competitors in his trade. Dead Rick was sensitive enough that his bare feet could even feel a tiny bit of iron in the riverbank nearby, some piece of scrap not yet found and resold by a mudlark. Unprotected, shivering at so much danger so close, he pressed harder than he needed to with the knife, drawing a line of blood.

"I've got sixpence in my pocket," the man gasped, stiffening under his hands. "It's yours, take it—"

"I don't want your tin," Dead Rick said. People always offered money first; after that, their minds went straight to enemies. Before the man could ask who sent him, the skriker growled, "Food. 'Ave you got any?"

A portion of the fear dissolved into confusion. "Food?"

"Bread. A sandwich, or biscuits, anything you might 'ave on you."

Despite the knife at his throat, the man tried to twist around to stare at his attacker. "You chased me because you're *'ungry*?"

Seizing a double handful of the man's torn coat, Dead Rick hauled him free of the sinkhole and slammed him down again, on his back in the shallow water. "Next time I cut your throat and answer the question myself. *'Ave you got food on you?*" Not that it would do him much good to kill the man—but threats did a fine job of helping a man concentrate.

His captive nodded. The motion was spastic; after a moment, Dead Rick realised the tosher was trying to point at his right pocket, without moving anything more than his head. Grunting, the skriker dragged him a little farther up, until they were clear of the water and on what passed for solid ground. Then he shoved a searching hand into the man's pocket and came out with a packet of old newspaper. The whole thing was soaked now with filthy river water, but grease had stained one end, and the aroma of sausage wafted from it.

"Oi, you there! What do you think you're doing?"

The question carried such an air of self-satisfied authority, Dead Rick thought at first it came from a constable. He crouched instinctively. Nadrett's trips above sometimes brought trouble from the peelers, and some of those bastards were too ready with their revolvers. But when he looked up, it was only a man—some sod farther up the shore, in between two of the wharves.

Dead Rick measured the distance between him and the newcomer, wondering if he could change midleap and rip the bastard's throat out. Man form or no, Dead Rick was still obviously fae, and it wasn't safe to walk around London like that.

But the stranger's eyes narrowed, and not like those of a man wondering what he was staring at it. The fellow came forward with three quick strides and said, "You're jumping 'im for bread, ain't you? Fucking goblins. Well, I'm the Prince of the Stone, and I'm telling you, let 'im go."

A disbelieving bark escaped Dead Rick's mouth. "You? The bleeding Prince of the Stone?"

He'd never seen the man himself, only heard stories. Nadrett often complained about the Prince, poking his nose where it didn't belong. Oh, supposedly the man's nose belonged everywhere; he was the mortal ruler of the Onyx Court, after all, consort to London's faerie Queen, with authority over everything having to do with his kind. Only there wasn't an Onyx Court anymore: just a group of self-indulgent courtiers enjoying their last pleasures, and a cockney Prince trying to pretend he had control over anything at all. As for the Queen, she'd been gone for years.

Dead Rick peered through the darkness, sniffing past the reek of the Thames for the man's scent. He could smell the faerie touch that bound the Prince to the Onyx Hall, and see its effect on the fellow's face: he had a strange young-old look, like a man aged long before his time. Well, that was no wonder, with the palace crumbling apart; they said it had drained the Queen down to almost nothing, in the years before she vanished. Dead Rick would be surprised if the Prince had much more in him.

He'd put one foot on the tosher's chest to hold him in place; now he felt the man shift restlessly, confusion winning out over fear. The brief flash of sympathy Dead Rick had felt for the aging, exhausted Prince faded, driven back by more important concerns. "This ain't any business of yours," he said to the Prince.

"The devil it ain't. That bastard you've got there can barely feed 'imself; you can't just go stealing 'is food so you can cause more trouble up 'ere!"

The Prince's sanctimonious reply would have been annoying enough if it were accurate. His complete lack of understanding made Dead Rick furious. Cause trouble? He *wished* he could afford to waste bread on that. Instead he was out here, with the Blackfriars bridges hanging over his head like two axes waiting to fall, because he needed some kind of insurance against the future, and didn't want his ears cut off by any of the half-dozen fae to whom he owed a debt. And every minute this Prince stood there lecturing him was another minute Dead Rick had to put up with a weight of iron that made him want to howl and run for home.

So he didn't bother answering. Instead he just snarled, and threw himself forward.

Trying to change shape out here felt like breaking all of his bones, individually. The iron fought him: it didn't care whether he was man or beast, but it hated letting him shift between the two. When Dead Rick hit the Prince, he was caught halfway in between, a roaring monstrosity, bowling the man down in a tangle of fur and skin and teeth.

Pain stopped him from doing more; his momentum took him into the wooden pillar of a crane, where an iron nail seared against his back like fire and ice. Dead Rick howled, writhing, and abruptly was in human form again. He lay panting on the ground, trying not to vomit, until he had control enough of his muscles to raise his head.

By then he was alone. The tosher had fled, and so, apparently, had the Prince.

So much for 'im and 'is orders. It seemed the man knew just how far his authority went.

Dead Rick forced himself to his feet. Down in the mud, his knife and the packet of newspaper lay untouched; the tosher hadn't bothered to collect his food before fleeing. But it wasn't any use to Dead Rick without the man.

It needed no dog's nose to track him. The footprints

were clear in the mud, heading west, under the bridges and up onto the massive wall of the Embankment. Dead Rick gritted his teeth and began to lope after him. There were iron pipes behind the granite exterior of the river frontage, but that was still better than the bridges, and Dead Rick was light on his feet; he gained rapidly.

The tosher heard him coming, and spun to face him, knife in hand. Dead Rick held out the packet and his own knife alike. Up here, he didn't have much time; the peelers *did* watch the Embankment walk. "I ain't done with you yet. But you do what I tells you, and you'll get out of 'ere without a scratch. Understand?"

Clearly not, but the man nodded warily, willing to listen whatever this apparent lunatic had to say if it meant saving his own skin. "Take this," Dead Rick said, tossing the packet back at him. "Now put that down at your feet and say, 'A gift for the good people.' "

"What?"

Not quite as cowed by fear as Dead Rick thought. "Do it, or lose an ear. Your choice."

Shaking his head, the man dropped the packet onto the stone of the footpath. "A gift for the good people. Now what?"

"Back up." He obeyed. In one swift move, Dead Rick snatched up the packet and retreated. "Now you go. Back home, or into the sewers; I don't care which. Just get out of my sight."

The tosher didn't have to be told twice. He turned and

continued running upriver, toward Westminster, away from Dead Rick.

Who waited to be sure the man wouldn't turn back, then stuffed his knife back into its sheath and tore open the soggy, greasy newspaper. Inside was a sausage roll. Not caring if the thing was soaked with river water, he sank his teeth into the end and ripped a chunk free.

Eating it was like wrapping a warm blanket around himself when he'd been standing all this while in the freezing winter air. The pipes in the Embankment, the gaslight lamps above, the bridges behind him—all became nothing more than human artifacts, bits of metal wrought into useful shapes. A church bell could ring in his ear now, and he would only laugh at it. Mortal food, given in tithe to the fae: the only thing that let them walk the streets of London in safety.

And desperately hard to come by, nowadays. Nadrett's caged mortals served many different purposes, but all of them were forced to tithe bread each day, until they were sold off or ate faerie food or died. It went a long way toward making up for the loss of belief among the people above, who no longer set out food for the faeries, except in scattered pockets far out in the countryside; a long way, but not far enough, not with all the refugees crowding into the Hall. If Dead Rick wanted any hope of surviving once the Market was gone, he had to get some for himself.

He already regretted eating that bite. It meant he had

one bite less with which to pay off his debts, or escape London when the time came. But with all these banes around him . . . he hadn't been above in ages, had forgotten how terrible it felt.

He sighed, staring at the torn roll.

Then he looked around, at the city he almost never saw. London, full of mortals—not caged and broken, but free men and women and children, millions of them, living in blissful ignorance of the decay beneath their feet. And untouched by the faerie stain that would make them unable to tithe. The longer Dead Rick stayed out here, the greater the odds of his master noticing—but the bite he'd eaten protected for a whole day. With that in his stomach, he could find somebody else to jump, get more bread, prepare for the end that was coming.

He would pay a price for it—he always did—but this once, it might be worth it.

Dead Rick stuffed the remainder of the roll into the pocket of his coat and concentrated. Not much; he wasn't one of those fae who took pride in all the faces he could invent, making himself look like a fine gentleman or a little boy or anything else. He was satisfied with looking like himself—just without the faerie touch. For his purposes, it was enough.

Then, whistling "Bedlam Boys" to himself, he set off in search of another poor bastard to rob.

* * *

THE GALENIC ACADEMY, ONYX HALL
10 March 1884

What remained of the faerie palace tended to alternate between rooms overstuffed with refugees and long, empty stretches abandoned even by ghosts. As Benjamin Hodge approached the entrance to the Galenic Academy, the only sound was his own boots scuffing across the floor. But once he passed beneath the silver-and-gold arch, with its motto of SOLVE ET COAGULA curving above his head, noise began to filter down the black corridor. Even before he could make out any details, the sound raised his spirits: this was the one part of the Onyx Hall that felt alive with hope, instead of despair.

Or maybe *madness* was a better word than *hope*. Hodge was too young to have seen the Great Exhibition at the Crystal Palace in '51, but he imagined it must have been a lot like this: a motley assortment of people from all over the world, crowding around displays ranging from the useful to the bizarre, in a crazed display of what human invention could do.

Human invention, and faerie: while there were mortals down here, they were far outnumbered by faerie-kind. The international bit still held, though. For the last century and more, the Galenic Academy had been a place of pilgrimage for anyone from either world who wanted to understand the rules of places like this: not quite Faerie, not quite Earth, but taking on a bit of the nature of both. Some of those who came were philosophers, and they spent their time in the library or various sitting rooms, arguing questions like what ancient curse made iron anathema to European fae, or how it was that a genie could serve the Mohammedan God—but the Presentation Hall which now opened up before him was for the inventors.

As with the Great Exhibition, their work ranged from the practical to the inexplicable. Hodge was very glad of the aetheric engine, which had saved them from the need to find a giant to wind the enormous clock in the Calendar Room every year, but what was the use of an automaton that sang songs like a phonograph? Or a fountain that could be made to pour out any kind of drink? Or the enormous paper wings stretching high overhead?

In truth, the only thing he cared about these days lay at the back end of the long chamber, taking up more space every time he came to visit.

His arrival barely made a ripple in the flow of activity. Passing fae tugged their forelocks briefly—or bowed, in the case of those foreigners for whom it was the customary sign of respect—but otherwise went about their business. Hodge would have done away with even that interruption, if he could; his father had been a bricklayer, and would have laughed himself sick to know his son had become a faerie Prince. *An accident of birth,* he thought wryly, not for the first time. *I was born poor enough to get my start inside the old walls of London—and that's what matters 'ere, more than blood or breeding.*

Not that anybody knew his father had been a bricklayer. Hodge kept that back out of a peculiar kind of shame: he didn't want anyone knowing his father had laid bricks for the very thing now destroying this place. And then been drowned, when the River Fleet burst its sewer and flooded the railway works. Fate had a sharp sense of humour, as far as Hodge could tell.

Two enormous machines lay at the far end, on either side of the door to the Academy library. One was a thing of gears and levers and cranks and dials, those latter marked with a range of alchemical and other symbols. All Hodge understood about that one was that it was some form of calculating machine; the symbols were a language the scholars had developed for describing the elemental makeup and configuration of faerie things, and the engine helped them predict how such things would interact.

Without it, devices like the one across the central aisle would be nearly impossible to build. This one, Hodge understood even less about, except that it resembled nothing so much as a deranged loom—and it had the Academy Masters very excited indeed.

Damn near every last one of them, mortal and faerie alike, was gathered about the machine, arguing in several different languages at once. Lady Feidelm and Wrain; a Chinese faerie named Ch'ien Mu, a Swedish mathematician named Ulrik Segerstam; Niklas von das Ticken had even hauled his brother Wilhas away from sitting over the Calendar Room like an anxious mother hen. The tallest of the fae, a dark-skinned genie, noticed Hodge first and gave him a respectful bow. "Lord Benjamin. Are you all right?"

Hodge had tried to tell Abd ar-Rashid the bows and titles and so on weren't necessary. What few courtiers he had left spent their time idling in one of the palace's remaining gardens and ignoring his commands. The genie, as the Academy's Scholarch or senior Master, had more authority and did more of actual use than Hodge himself. But Abd ar-Rashid seemed to believe the courtesies were all the more important in these degenerate times, and acted accordingly.

The concern in his deep-set eyes made Hodge reach up to touch his own face. His fingers came away spotted with blood. There were two scratches on his cheek: mementos of that black dog leaping on him. Hodge considered saying as much, but remembered fae and mortals all around them; he might not care about courtesies, but admitting that one of his own nominal subjects had knocked him down in Blackfriars was a bit much. "Cut myself shaving," Hodge said blandly, and gestured at the loom. "You lot look excited. Tell me you 'ave good news."

"We do. Or rather, Ch'ien Mu does." Abd ar-Rashid waved the Chinese faerie forward.

When Ch'ien Mu first came to the Onyx Hall, the embroidered silks he wore had been been splendid things, with dragons coiling sinuously about his shoulders and arms; but unless one was a philosopher, constantly in the library, the Galenic Academy was not a good place for clothes. The silks were much mended, and the dragons glared morosely at the barriers of thread that blocked their movement.

They still distracted Hodge terribly, but Ch'ien Mu's mind was clearly on other matters. He shuffled a few steps closer and bowed, but instead of folding his hands inside his sleeves—his customary posture while lecturing—he literally rubbed them together with excitement as he spoke. "The threads no more break! It is, as I suspect, a thing of configuration—though my assumption that the helical is the most stable proves very wrong; we try both solar and lunar configurations, but—"

"Master Ch'ien Mu." Hodge pinched the bridge of his nose, knowing the faerie would go on for half an hour if not stopped. "I knows 'ow to read, and that's about where it ends. Just tell me what you've *got.*"

This seemed to be a more difficult request than he'd thought. The faerie opened and closed his mouth a few times, as if trying and failing to find words for what was in his head. Hodge doubted it was a problem with his English; more likely the fellow was having trouble bringing his thoughts down from the rarefied heights of theory into simple reality. It was a trouble many of the Academy Masters shared. In the end, the Master gave up and gestured at Niklas.

The red-bearded dwarf grinned and spun a small wheel. The small aetheric engine at his feet hummed to life; then he and Ch'ien Mu together made incomprehensible adjustments to a series of pipes and vessels that sat at the base of the loom. Those, Hodge recognised; they were a sort of alchemical retort, used to distill purified forms of the faerie elements, fire and water and earth and air. After a moment, shimmering threads of something that was not quite light began to lace themselves through the loom, forming what Hodge, with his extremely limited knowledge of weaving, knew was the warp: the lengthwise threads that formed the base of fabric.

Except what this loom wove was not precisely fabric. Ch'ien Mu fed one end of a linked chain of crystal plaques into something on the side of the loom, and then Niklas slammed a lever down with a heavy *thunk*. Powered by the aetheric engine, the loom sprang into motion.

Warp threads rose and fell, and the shuttle holding the weft flew back and forth between them. There was a general stampede to the far side of the loom, which Hodge joined, and there he witnessed a miracle.

Growing in the air on the other side of the machine was a glamour. Four isolated bits of gold—golden fur—four paws, it was, and as the legs lengthened above them Hodge suspected it was a lion. He'd seen more impressive illusions before; the fae could do tremendous things when they put their minds to it. But there was no mind involved here: the loom was doing the work. Jacquard had invented something like this years ago, to weave brocaded fabrics more rapidly and accurately than a human weaver could hope to achieve. Ch'ien Mu and the others had found a way to do it with a glamour.

"Bloody 'ell," Hodge whispered, and grabbed hold of

Abd ar-Rashid before he could fall over.

Some of it was just the general infirmity that plagued him nowadays. The Onyx Hall drew on his strength to survive the iron threat driving its breakdown, and it was always worse after he'd gone above—necessary departures, for the sake of his mortal sanity, though he kept them as infrequent as he dared. But the rest of his sudden weakness . . .

It was blinding, delirious hope.

If they could weave the elements of faerie reality into whatever shape they described with those crystal plaques, then they could weave new material for the Onyx Hall.

The genie supported him with one arm under his shoulders, and called for someone to bring a chair. Hodge allowed himself to be lowered into it, too dazed to care about the indignity. Never mind the wings and automata and all the rest; this had been the chiefest project of the Galenic Academy since its founding more than a hundred years ago. *Find some way of mending the Onyx Hall.* Stop, or better yet undo, the decay that had been going on since the beginning of the eighteenth century.

Hodge had known, even before he became Prince, that it wasn't likely to happen. The creation of the palace had been a legendary work, carried out ages before, by a faerie woman and a mortal man. But they were long dead, and so were the powers that had helped them: Gog and Magog, the giants of London, murdered. Father Thames, silenced by iron. Hodge couldn't hope to equal their deeds. He'd devoted his time and energy to slowing the disintegration of the Hall, holding together what remained of London's faerie court, and preparing for the exodus he knew must inevitably come.

An exodus they might—perhaps—be able to avoid after all.

Someone pressed a cup into his hand, and he drank instinctively. Mead, sweet and fortifying, slid down his throat. Then Master Wrain was there, showing a distress Hodge didn't understand at all. "My lord—"

If *he* was being formal, then something really had gone wrong. "What?"

With deep reluctance, the sprite said, "It doesn't last."

Hodge's gaze went past him to the lion, which was now almost completed. The tail lashed, and the paws shifted in place; it was peculiar to see something so apparently real still missing the bulk of its head. No sign of unravelling—but it was in the protected space of the Galenic Academy. The oddly warped relationship between the City and the palace that reflected it meant the Academy lay uncomfortably close to the railway works even now proceeding down Cannon Street—but not so close that it was one of the bad patches of the Hall, where the decay was at its worst.

What the loom produced was pure faerie material. It wouldn't survive for long, if it came into contact with mortal banes.

"How long?" he asked, and downed another gulp of mead.

Niklas answered for Wrain and Ch'ien Mu, in a gruff

voice still coloured by traces of a German accent. "Ve haven't tested it yet. It vould slow the problem—"

"But at a cost," Wrain finished, when Niklas hesitated. "It wouldn't just unravel; the elements that make it up would be destroyed. And we cannot generate those out of nothing. To craft new pieces of the Hall, we would have to distill the raw substance out of existing materials."

In other words, render down the contents of the palace. If that would even be enough. Hodge was out of mead; he stared moodily into the empty cup. Given time, they might be able to find other sources—but even with this machine, time was sorely lacking.

Well, he could set someone to looking, and in the meantime, try to solve the underlying problem. "What would make it last longer?"

Because this was the Academy, he didn't get a wave of helpless shrugs; he got a deluge of speculative answers, everyone talking over each other. "The original anchoring—"; "—given the capacity of the human soul to shelter—"; "—a more suitable weft, perhaps—"; "—perhaps the Oriental elements—"; "—write to Master Ktistes in Greece; he might—"

Hodge put up his hands, and the speculation trailed into silence. "You don't know. All right. Get to work on finding out. Wilhas, is the Calendar Room still usable?"

Niklas's brother, blond haired to his red, chewed on his lips inside the depths of his beard. "Yes. For now. But from the map you showed me, the tracks vill run very close to the

Monument. Ven they put those in, it may destroy the room."

Taking with it anyone inside. But they had to risk it; the Calendar Room, a chamber beneath the Monument to the Great Fire, contained time outside of time. With it, the fae could do months or years of research and planning, at a cost of mere days in the world. "I'll keep my eye on the newspapers and railway magazines," Hodge said, as if he did not read them incessantly already. "We should 'ave some warning before they lay any track."

Nods all around. Wrain began to discuss with the others who would go into the Calendar Room, and who would stay outside. The other machine, their calculating engine, could possibly be used to determine what variable might be added to increase durability; they could look for sources of material. If worse came to worst, they could unravel select parts of the Hall, to weave protection around places like this, that needed to survive.

None of it was anything he could contribute to, not personally. Suppressing a groan, Hodge pushed himself to his feet. "Right, you get to that. Let me know when you've got some answers." For now, the most useful thing he could do for them all was to stay alive.

Memory: 12 April 1840

She both dreaded and longed for the dreams.

Dreaded, because without a doubt they were signs of

the madness her mother warned her about, a shameful inheritance from her shameless and lunatic father. But longed for, because in these dreams she could permit her creativity free rein; her conversational partners not only welcomed but encouraged her wildest flights of fancy, never once murmuring about hereditary insanity.

"Of course he will never get it built," she said to the inhuman creatures that sat on the other side of the tea table. "I hold Mr. Babbage in the greatest esteem, but he lacks the social gifts that would gain him the cooperation of others; and without that, he will never have the funding or assistance he requires."

The taller and more slender of her guests grimaced into his tea. The name of this one was Wrain, and he was a dear friend of her dreams; she had imagined conversations with him many times over the years. "You don't say so," the spritely gentleman muttered, with delicate irony. "We thought to offer him our own assistance, but . . ."

"But he is even ruder than I am," the shorter and stockier fellow said cheerfully, with a distinct German accent. She hesitated to call this one a gentleman, given his dreadful manners. Properly he was Mr. von das Ticken, but Wrain mostly just called him Nick.

Because it was a dream, she could allow herself to laugh. "Oh dear. The two of you, attempting to converse . . . that cannot have ended well."

"It went splendidly," Wrain said, "for all of thirty seconds. But we have begun to pursue the notion on our own, you know; it's too great a challenge to forego."

Of course he was building it; these were her dreams, after all, and she would dearly love to see the Analytical Engine in operation. That Wrain was not presenting it to her right now could only mean that her mind had not yet fully encompassed Babbage's intricate and brilliant design. Such insufficiency, however, did not stop her imagination from leaping ahead. "At this point the challenges are quite mundane, simple matters of obtaining funding and suitable engineers. I have already begun to look beyond."

"I think you underestimate the difficulty of the engineering," Wrain said dryly, but he was half-drowned out by Nick's expression of sudden, sharp interest: "Vat do you mean by 'looking beyond'?"

Happiness lifted her spirit, like a pair of bright wings. These two would not mock her, or warn that she had best confine herself to what was mathematically and scientifically possible. She could tell them whatever she dreamt of, however outrageous. "If we—by which I mean my dear Babbage, of course—can design an Analytical Engine to calculate the answers to equations, can we not design other sorts of engines for other sorts of tasks?"

Frowning, Wrain said, "You mean, other devices that can be instructed by cards?"

"Precisely! Engines which can perform complex tasks, more rapidly and accurately than any human operator could achieve. Composing music, for example: provide the machine with cards that instruct it as to the form of a song—a hymn, perhaps, or a chorale, or even a symphony—and then, by execution of the operations, the engine returns a new composition." Her love for music was an abiding thing, close kin to her love of mathematics, though she suspected her mother—for all the woman's knowledge of the latter subject—never quite understood the similarities between the two. "It wants only some means of presenting notes and their relationships in suitably abstract form. Well, that and the design of the engine itself, which of course is no simple matter; I expect it would require tens of thousands of gears, more even than the Analytical Engine."

Wrain's mouth fell open by progressive stages during this speech; Nick had gone still as a stone. After a dumbfounded pause, the spritely gentleman said, "With sufficiently abstract representation—"

"*Anything,*" Nick breathed, staring off into the distance like he had seen a vision of Heaven itself. "Music. Pictures. It could write books. It could—"

His voice cut off. She felt as if she were flying, lifted above the clay of this earth by the power of her own ingenuity. Only gradually did she realise that while her companions, too, were flying, the path they followed was a very specific one. Wrain and Nick were staring at one another, communicating in half-spoken words and abrupt gestures, too excited to get their thoughts out of their heads before leaping on to the next. "Like a loom," Wrain said; Nick answered him, "But our notation," and the gentleman nodded as if his dwarfish companion had made a very good point.

It produced a strange feeling in the depths of her mind. If these were her dreams, then why did it feel as if they had abruptly become about something she didn't understand? A touch of fear stirred. *Perhaps Mother is right, and this* is *the beginnings of madness.*

Wrain leapt to his feet and seized her hand, shaking it up and down as if she were a man. His grip felt very hard, and very real. "Ada, dearest Ada, *thank you.* Oh, I have no idea how to build this thing—we lack even the notation by which to instruct it; I mean, the system of notation we have is dreadfully inadequate, it would not suffice for a Difference Engine, let alone more—but until you spoke I never even *conceived* of such a device. Not for our own purposes. Will you help us?"

Baffled, increasingly unsure of everything, Ada said, "Help you with *what*?"

Nick laughed, a rolling guffaw that made her certain he, at least, was deranged. "Building an engine of magic calculation. Something of gears and levers and wheels, that can tell us how to create things, faerie enchantments, too complex for us to imagine on our own. And perhaps, in time, to *make* them for us."

No, there was no doubt at all. Ada had taken the first step—or perhaps more than one—down the path of madness her father had followed. Faeries and enchantment, exactly the sorts of things of which her mother disapproved. If she did not turn back now, gambling, poetry, and sexual immorality were sure to follow.

But she did not want to abandon her friends, even if they were phantasms of her diseased mind. Could she not allow herself a *little* madness, and trust to prayer and the rigourous strictures of science to keep the rest at bay?

Augusta Ada King, Countess of Lovelace, daughter of the infamous poet Lord Byron and his mathematical wife Annabella Milbanke, suspected she knew the answer to that—and it wasn't in her favour.

"Please, Ada," Wrain entreated her. "I have seen the disaster that is Babbage's notes; I daresay you understand them better than he does himself. Or at least can explain them to others, which he patently cannot. We will not be able to do this without help."

It would have taken a harder soul than Ada Lovelace's to say no to that desperately hopeful expression. With a feeling of both doom and delight, she said, "Charles Babbage is too rude and too sane to ever help you in this matter. Poor though my own intellect may be, I will bend it to your cause."

ISLINGTON, LONDON
14 March 1884

Eliza had spent the days leading up to the meeting of the London Fairy Society imagining how things might go. The people might prove to be nothing more than a cluster of bored wives, reading collections of stories from the folk of rural England, clucking their tongues and sighing over the loss of a peasant society none of them had ever seen in person. They might be a group of scholars, documenting that loss and forming theories about what defect of education or brain made peasants believe such ridiculous things. They might be the kind of people Eliza had seen at Charing Cross last fall—working hand-in-glove with the faeries to sow chaos among decent folk.

She imagined telling the story of how Owen was stolen away, to the shock and sympathy of her listeners. She imagined haranguing the society's leader until he told her where to find a faerie. She imagined finding a faerie there in person and shaking the truth out of him.

She never got around to imagining how she would get into No. 9 White Lion Street.

Eliza had never been to Islington before. When evening began to draw close on the afternoon of the second Friday, she took her nearly empty barrow and began walking up Aldersgate Street through Clerkenwell. She asked directions as she went, and eventually was directed to a lane behind a coaching inn, in a busy part of town.

The building at No. 9 proved to be a house, and a respectable one at that. Eliza stared at it in dismay. The setting of her various fancies had always been vague—a room; chairs; faceless people—she had presumed it would be some kind of public building, like the ones where workers' combinations sometimes met to plan protests against their masters. Not someone's house, where it would be impossible to fade into the background.

"See here now—what are you doing, standing about like that?"

Biting down on a curse, Eliza turned, and saw a constable eyeing her suspiciously. All at once she became aware of her clothing: two ragged skirts, layered for warmth and because she had nowhere to keep the second but on her body. Men's boots, their leather cracked and filthy. A shawl that hadn't seen a good wash since the last time it rained. Her bonnet had once been some respectable lady's castoff, but that was years ago; the ribbons she used to tie it did not match, and there was a hole in the brim big enough to poke her thumb through.

And she'd been standing there for several minutes, staring at a housefront as if wondering how to break in.

Out of the corner of her eye, Eliza glimpsed a bearded gentleman in a bowler hat knocking at the door of No. 9. "Would you like to buy some oysters, sir?" she asked the constable, her attention on the other side of the street. A maid opened the door, and let the gent in.

"No, I wouldn't," the bobby said, nose wrinkling at their old stench. "Get you gone. The sort of people who live here don't need the likes of you around."

The likes of her would never get into that house, either. Eliza ducked her head and mumbled an apology, pushing her barrow past the fellow, carefully not looking at the house as she went.

He followed her to the nearby High Street; she was able

to lose him in the crowds there. Tongue stuck into the gap where her father had knocked out one of her teeth years ago, Eliza considered her options.

She didn't have many. But she wasn't willing to give up, either. If she couldn't attend the meeting of the London Fairy Society, then at least she could try to see who did.

Making a halfhearted effort to cry her oysters, she turned left on the next street she found, hoping Islington's tangle wouldn't defeat her the way the City's sometimes did. A few narrow courts gave her no luck, before she found an alley that went through, back to White Lion Street. She gave it a careful look before proceeding, but didn't see the peeler anywhere.

Eliza hurried down the pavement, barrow rattling before her. Memory served her well: the house across the street and down one door from No. 9 had shutters drawn and locked across its windows, and the lamp at the door was not lit. Uninhabited, or the residents had gone on a journey. Either way, no one was around to object if she hid in the area at the bottom of their basement steps.

She waited until no one was nearby, then hefted her barrow down, trying not to spill the remaining oysters everywhere, or trip in the darkness. Then she threw the more ragged of her two skirts over them to mute the smell, and peeped through the iron bars to see what happened on the other side of the street.

It seemed almost everyone had arrived already, for she only saw one additional person knock at the door. This was a young lady, she thought; it was hard to tell, for the woman made every attempt at secrecy, even tugging her hood forward and darting glances about the street. Eliza shrank back into the shadows, and when she looked out again, the door was closing behind the mysterious girl.

Then it was seven o'clock, and no one else came. Eliza sat on the cold steps to think some more. Should she go around the back? If there was a garden, she might be able to climb into it, and if the meeting was on the ground or first floor . . . common sense reasserted itself. More than likely she'd be caught, especially with that peeler around.

Better to wait for next month. There were a few people in Whitechapel who owed her favours, or were sympathetic to pleas for help; she might be able to get herself clean and respectable enough to knock on the door.

But that meant a whole month more without Owen. A month closer to possibly losing him forever.

Eliza dug in her pocket and drew out a battered piece of paper, its corners long since torn off by ill handling. She had to stop herself brushing her thumb across the faces, for fear she'd wear them even more indistinct.

Mrs. Darragh, her arms spread wide to embrace the children before her. Little Maggie. Eliza, her black hair unruly even after Mrs. Darragh's efforts to tame it. And Owen, a knock-kneed boy of twelve. It was the only picture of him, taken in celebration of Maggie's first communion.

She had to preserve it. Without the photo, Eliza feared she would forget what he looked like.

Shivering, she crossed her arms on her bent knees and laid her forehead against them. *He's dead, you stupid fool,* Maggie had said. Eliza had proof to the contrary, of a sort, though she didn't dare admit it.

The girl might have guessed, if she ever bothered to think about it. Eliza and Owen had never told Maggie about the faeries, but she knew perfectly well about the ghosts. She'd been there when Eliza saw her mother, a full year after the woman had died. And she knew Eliza had summoned others, or tried to—though not why.

It had been a foolish dream, for the likes of her. Most of the women earning fame, and sometimes money, as mediums or spiritualists were of the middling sort: bored solicitors' wives, ladies too respectable to work for a living, but not rich enough to enjoy their idleness. Not Irish hoydens. And it would hardly have gone over well in Whitechapel, where speaking to ghosts was likely to brand her a witch. But if it had worked . . .

The ghost part worked well enough. But before she could try and make money at it, Owen had disappeared. The only ghost she'd tried to summon since then was his, every All Hallows' Eve.

Five years she'd tried, calling for her lost friend, trying to manifest him in the air before her, or at least feel the comfort of his presence in her mind. Five years of failure, and then she'd given up, because she no longer wanted to know. If he came, she would know he was dead. If she didn't try, she could tell herself he was still alive, and ignore the possibility that perhaps she just wasn't strong enough to raise him.

It didn't make sense, but there it was.

To her surprise, she heard the bell of a nearby church tolling eight. Lifting her head once more, Eliza felt the imprint of folded cloth on her forehead. She'd fallen asleep. *Bloody lucky, you were, not to be caught by the peeler.* Silently calling herself nine kinds of idiot, Eliza stood and looked through the bars again.

Lights still burned in the house across the street, and before long the front door opened. A maidservant emerged, trotting off toward High Street; shortly after she returned, a hansom cab arrived, followed by someone's brougham. People began to depart—Eliza counted seven, ranging from the gentleman she'd seen before to a matronly woman in the gaudiest bonnet she'd ever laid eyes on. The only one missing was the furtive young woman, and just when Eliza was about to give up waiting, she appeared on the steps.

Followed almost immediately by another woman. "Miss Kittering!"

The first one paused, hands on the edge of her hood, ready to pull it up. The light above the steps of No. 9 showed her to be quite a wealthy young woman indeed; she had obviously taken care to choose plain clothing, but her pert little cap had some very expensive feathers in it. The hair beneath was a glossy yellow, twisted into an elegant knot. Eliza caught only the briefest glimpse of her face, though, before the young woman turned to see who had hailed her.

The other woman was remarkable in her very lack of remarkability. Medium-brown hair; medium-age features; medium-quality clothing that could have belonged to the wife of a middling professional man, perhaps a solicitor or a clergyman with a good living. As she hurried down the steps to join Miss Kittering, though, a strange intensity came into her manner, that gave the lie to her drab appearance. "Will you spare me a moment?"

Miss Kittering glanced behind her, to where one last carriage waited. "I must get back—"

"I understand. Would you perhaps let me ride with you? I have a very particular proposition, you see, that I did not want to make before the others—it is for you only, Miss Kittering, because I can see that you are a more . . . *visionary* spirit than the others. I suspect you could accept, even *embrace,* truths the others are not yet ready for."

Miss Kittering's interest sharpened visibly. Eliza curled her hands around the bars, as if they were the only things holding her in place. Otherwise she might fly up the steps and accost this stranger on the spot.

"What truths?" the young lady asked, curiosity clear in her voice.

The other woman hesitated, then stepped closer. Her reply was so quiet that Eliza could only barely make it out. "That the materialistic views which bind so many in this *scientific* age are not the whole of the story. I know more of faeries than I have admitted publicly, Miss Kittering. And I tell you this: You are in a position to do a great favour to one of them, and receive a favour in return."

Miss Kittering's laugh was much louder, and half disbelieving—but only half. "Me? I don't see how—"

"This is not the place," her companion said, a tilt of her head toward No. 9 making her meaning clear. "If I may ride with you, though . . ."

"Yes, of course—I am *quite* intrigued. And I mustn't delay here any longer; Mama expects me home. Come, and we'll talk along the way." Together they went toward the carriage. Desperate, Eliza risked coming up the steps, as if she'd just emerged from the house's cellar; she was rewarded by hearing Miss Kittering tell the coachman, "South Kensington, please." Then they were inside, and the coachman mounted his box once more; with a flap of the reins they were away.

Leaving Eliza standing in the middle of White Lion Street in a daze. *Was she lying?*

It might be like the fraudulent spiritualists who claimed to summon ghosts, only their manifestations were nothing more than a conjuror's tricks. Whitechapel had its share of confidence men—and women, too—swindling the gullible, and Miss Kittering was both young and wealthy enough to be a tempting target.

Or that woman might have been telling the truth.

If only Eliza had gotten her name! But—her feet paused on the pavement—she *did* have Miss Kittering's name. And a district, too: South Kensington. Should the woman's claims prove true, Miss Kittering would have her own connection to the faeries.

Which Eliza could make use of. If she found a way to get close. And for Owen's sake, she would find a way.

She almost forgot her barrow in her haste. Eliza dragged her second skirt back on, hauled the barrow up the steps, not caring if she spilled oysters now. *Miss Kittering. South Kensington. With that, I won't have to wait another month.*

Owen—I'm coming.

THE GOBLIN MARKET, ONYX HALL

19 March 1884

"Dreams, good and bad! Loved ones back from the dead, very cheap right now, or demons chasing you for just a little bit more . . . morning there, my canine friend. I 'ear you're doing well these days."

Dead Rick scowled at Broddy Bobbin, waving for him to lower his voice. "You think I want that shouted all over the Market, man? Just because I've got enough to keep people from breaking my fingers, don't mean I'm ready to go around flashing my bread like some rich toff."

The crate Bobbin stood on only brought him to Dead Rick's height; like most hobs, he was barely child-size. Any child that ugly, though, risked being drowned in a river. He smiled at Dead Rick, but it was a hideous thing, bad enough for a goblin's face. "So you *do* 'ave bread. In that case, let me show you—"

The skriker rolled his eyes. "I told you, I'm paying off my debts. Even if I wanted your grubby little second'and dreams, I wouldn't 'ave anything to spare for 'em. I'm just looking for Cyma."

Bobbin pouted, but his wounded look was even worse than his smile, and he knew it. Giving Dead Rick up as a lost cause, he jerked one knobby thumb farther down the chamber. "She were talking with Charcoal Eddie a little while ago. You tell that bastard 'e'd better steal some worthwhile dreams next time. That last lot was pure rubbish."

They were always rubbish these days. Stealing dreams properly took time and effort; the goblins and pucks who did that sort of thing could no longer afford either. Mostly the Goblin Market made do with what it already had, everyone buying and selling the same trinkets and scraps over and over, like a leech feeding on itself. And the wares got more broken and worn out with every exchange.

That didn't stop them from trying, though. This, the largest of the Market's actual markets, was full of noise and movement. No mortals—those were sold elsewhere, in a flesh market of squalling babies and people in cages—but a thousand kinds of things, from captive dreams to scratched phonograph cylinders. Fae of all kinds and nations came here, to buy or to sell; the majority might be English, but there were Scots and Irish and Welsh, Germans and Spaniards and French, creatures from so far afield they might be a different sort of being entirely. One pen held an enormous three-headed snake, which the alf standing in front proclaimed was a naga from distant India; it watched the passersby with drugged and unfriendly eyes.

Dead Rick found Cyma standing in front of a cracked mirror, holding a dress of printed cotton against her body. It was a strange-looking thing, with a tiny bodice that went no lower than the breasts, and a narrow skirt falling loose from there. "Where in Faerie did that come from?"

Cyma shook her head at him, amused and pitying. "Don't you remember? They used to wear these, years ago—mortal women did. During the Prince Regent's reign. I found them delightful. Very Greek, don't you think?"

It could have been Chinese for all he cared. Dead Rick sidled closer and muttered, "I can pay you back now. Mostly, anyway—I'm still a bit short. But if you let me keep a bite or two, I can probably get the rest."

He'd left Cyma for last because she was kinder than his other creditors. She had been a court lady, rumour said, back when there still was a court beyond the Prince's few followers, but she didn't spend her time dallying in the surviving gardens with the scant handful of lords and ladies that remained. She couldn't: Cyma had her own debts, of a sort that couldn't be repaid in bread, and Nadrett held them. It gave her more sympathy than most; she might forgive him the extra delay.

Dead Rick was startled when she smiled and patted him on the cheek. "You're a sweet one, aren't you? Paying me back, when I know you're all but penniless. You needn't worry. Keep it for yourself; I don't mind."

He stiffened warily. "In exchange for what?"

Cyma's eyebrows rose. "Why, nothing. I don't need it, Dead Rick."

The use of his name was as good as a whole message in code. Nobody else used it; almost nobody in the Market knew it. He was just Nadrett's dog, a nameless slave. Hearing those words on Cyma's lips told him she wasn't playing some game, bargaining forgiveness for some favour from him; she meant it. He didn't owe her.

Why?

Even if she was leading some mortal lovers about on a string, the bread would have been valuable; with it, she could buy practically anything she wanted. That dress, and everything else the bored puck behind her had to sell. Everything but freedom from Nadrett. "What did you do, loot a bakery?"

She laughed. "No, no. Better than that. I'm leaving, Dead Rick. I've had enough of all of this." One hand swept a graceful arc, indicating the tawdry excesses of the Goblin Market around them. "I'm going away."

It produced a strange pang in his gut. "You think you can run away from Nadrett?"

"Not run away, no . . ." Cyma's expression darkened. "I know what Nadrett is like. But I've done what he asked of me, and settled my debt, and now—well, I must look to the future, mustn't I?"

It echoed Dead Rick's own thoughts, and made the cramp in his gut worse. "Where?"

She laid a sly finger alongside her nose. "Wouldn't *you* like to know. But I know better than to say anything; I don't want anyone stealing my place. Keep the bread, Dead Rick, with my compliments. Use it to buy your own way free of that dreadful fellow."

The pain was like a spike through his innards. *If only I could.*

He mumbled thanks to Cyma for the bread and beat a retreat before his bitterness could overwhelm him. Making his way deeper into the warren of the Goblin Market, he sought out the one thing even scarcer than bread: solitude.

The corridor he went to had once branched off to the left, but the buckling of that delicate arch had brought the stone crashing in, closing the way to anything bigger than a mouse. There was a hob approaching from the other direction as Dead Rick neared that collapse, a surly Irish fellow who did the occasional odd job for Lacca, another Goblin Market boss. The skriker leaned against the wall perhaps ten feet from the fallen stones and dug through the pockets of his trousers, as if looking for something in their empty depths, until the hob had turned the corner and gone into the room beyond.

Then Dead Rick leapt for the rockfall.

It *looked* solid, and for the most part it was. But an agile fellow could crawl atop one of the larger blocks, and from there it was apparent that the mass behind had left a small gap, just big enough for someone Dead Rick's size to squirm through. Then he slid on his stomach across a polished bit of marble that had miraculously survived the collapse unmarred, and out into the space beyond.

It was pitchy black, but his hands knew their business. He dropped a dark cloth over the hole he'd come in by, weighted its bottom edge with a thick piece of wood, then found and opened the box. Out floated a trio of faerie lights. Mindless things, they didn't object to a bit of confinement, and that was the only way he could keep them from wandering off in his absence—wandering, and betraying his secret refuge.

By the standards of the Goblin Market, it was comfort. He had blankets and a few cushions, and what odds and ends amused him but weren't worth much in the Market. Everything of real value was beneath a loose stone in the floor, toward the back of this space, where the rest of the collapse had blocked the passage completely.

He inspected it, out of nagging fear. A small engagement ring, taken from a dying spinster, holding her unwavering hope that her fiancé would return from his journey to India. A mermaid's tear, like a lustrous blue-green pearl. A *carte de visite* photograph of a woman. To that he added five pieces of bread: the debt Cyma had told him to keep.

Five pieces. It was enough to see him well clear of London, and Nadrett's influence. Then he could make his way across the countryside, skirting the churches and railways, until he found some other court to take him in.

But it would mean leaving the one thing he truly

desired—the one thing no hidden cache could buy for him, be it ten times this large.

A voice whispered through the air around him, dry as dust. "How badly do you want it back?"

Dead Rick shot to his feet and flattened his shoulders against the wall. His hackles rose, and a growl rumbled instinctively in his throat. But there was no one to direct it at.

"Snarl all you like," the voice said, amused. "And when you feel you've defended your territory enough, then consider my question, and answer it."

Enough? How could he defend his territory at all? Dead Rick's ears were alive to the slightest sound; his nose caught every scent out of the air. No one had crawled over and between and under the stones to his refuge, not even one of the little winged sprites that sometimes flew messages for other fae. No one was hiding anywhere in the small space. He was completely alone—and yet somehow this voice was there with him.

Fae had many strange talents; separating voice from body was hardly the most impressive. But how had the speaker found this place?

"Get out of my fucking 'ome," he spat, hands curling into useless fists. "I ain't answering no questions from no faceless bastard. You want to talk to me, you do it somewhere else."

Unruffled, the voice agreed, "I could do that. But you would still know your sanctuary had been violated—and you would not get what you want. So once again, I put it to you: How badly do you want it back?"

Beneath the anger, the instinct to chase off the intruder, fear stirred. Dead Rick said, "I don't know what you're talking about."

His eyes darted about as he spoke, as if they would be any use. The voice seemed to come from everywhere at once, and there were no scents to help him. But an accent, yes—the refined tone of a gentleman. And the condescending chuckle of one. "You're too honest a hound for that, Dead Rick. But if you will not answer a question, then perhaps you will respond to an offer. Very well: *I can give your memory back to you.*"

"Liar," Dead Rick snarled, coming off the wall as if there were something he could fight.

"Why assume so? Because Nadrett keeps it locked away? This is the Goblin Market; such things change hands all the time, by fair means or foul. Or perhaps you are suspicious of charity. I assure you, I want something in return. And so we come again to the original question, which is how much your memory is worth to you."

Had the speaker been in the room, he would have known the answer to that. Every muscle in Dead Rick's body was rigid with longing. Sweep aside the accumulated dust and rubbish of his time in the Goblin Market, and underneath lay a blank slate—no, that was too pleasant a comparison. Those newer memories were the scab over a wound, concealing the gaping, bloody void beneath. An unhealing wound, robbing him of everything: his past, his *self*—even his name, until Cyma had given it back to him.

How much would he pay, to regain what Nadrett had taken from him?

Wariness helped him regain control of his voice. "You've already got some price in mind, or you wouldn't 'ave made the offer."

"Very observant. Yes, I have my price, and what's more, I think you will find it congenial. I want you to turn on your master."

Nadrett. The hand on the leash, the voice calling him *dog* and making the word hurt. It took a lot to make a hound turn on his master, but Nadrett had passed that bar years ago. But—"If I could kill 'im, I would've done it already," Dead Rick said.

"How fortunate for you, then, that death was not what I had in mind. In fact, at present I would prefer him to remain alive; his demise would not profit me. Not yet, at least. But once I have what I want . . ." The voice laughed. "Then I will slip the chain from around your neck, and watch you tear out his throat."

The mere thought called the taste of blood into his mouth. To hunt Nadrett through the night garden, until the bastard's legs and wind gave out and he fell to the ground, and then to leap upon him with teeth bared . . .

Or just to shoot him, or knife him in the back. Dead Rick honestly didn't care how Nadrett died. Just so long as he got his memories back.

But, as the speaker had said, this was the Goblin Market. And nobody here could be trusted. "You expect me to risk my neck for you—when I don't even know who you are?"

Whatever face was on the other end of that voice, Dead Rick could imagine it smiling. "Not at present, no. We will enter into this alliance one careful step at a time, each watching the other for signs of betrayal. For now, what I ask is no particular risk. Merely information, that I want you to find for me."

Dead Rick spat onto the stone, wondering if the stranger could hear it. "No. I ain't doing nothing for a cove I can't see. 'Ow do I even know you can do what you say?"

A sigh answered him. "Very well. As proof of my goodwill, let me give you something: a fragment of your past."

The skriker stopped breathing, hackles rising again—but not in anger or fear.

"The first task Nadrett demanded of you," the voice said, "was to steal a mortal from the world above. A young man—little more than a boy, really. Irish, and poor. He had a friend, a girl of the same age; from what I hear, she attempted to kill you when she realised what you were doing."

A pause. Dead Rick worked spit back into his dry mouth and said, "From what you *hear*. So you got the story; so what?"

"The story doesn't end there. Or rather, it doesn't *begin* there. The boy you stole, and the girl who was his friend—they were both friends of yours."

Her screams were one of the first things he remembered, echoing in the empty void of his memory. Only half-coherent—only half-*English*—he'd never understood what she was saying, but the intent of the words was easy to make out. As was the betrayal on her face.

The voice said, "Nadrett was testing his control over you, making certain you remembered nothing. You would never have harmed either of them if you knew. And it amused him to make you turn on those who trusted you."

The fury rising inside Dead Rick was a strange thing, with a hollow void at its core. He couldn't be properly angry for the friends he'd betrayed; he didn't remember who they were. *No, it's worse than that,* he thought, with grim despair. *I don't remember what* friends *are.* Who could he give that name to? Cyma? But the instinct was there, the impulse to loyalty, whatever beating it had taken in the last seven years, and it left him shaking with rage that had nowhere to go. Dead Rick almost howled, just to let something out.

At the moment he reached that breaking point, the stranger spoke again, as if he had measured Dead Rick's endurance to the last inch. "Nadrett has isolated you from everyone who knew you before, forbidding you to leave the Goblin Market without his orders, cowing those who might be able to say more. I am not bound by his restrictions. For every piece of information you bring to me, every task you undertake on my behalf, I will tell you a piece of your own past."

The unvoiced howl had lodged like a knot in his throat,

painful to swallow down. Thickly, Dead Rick said, "You could make things up."

"I could. But I won't; in fact, I may give you ways to verify what I say. But that is beside the point; in the end, the point is to do harm to Nadrett. Will you assist me?"

The thick nails on Dead Rick's feet scraped against the stone, his toes curling down as if he were about to leap. But which way?

It's stupid. It's fucking *stupid. Agreeing to work with somebody you can't even see—you know nobody in this place can be trusted—*

But yearning, and the desire for revenge, were stronger than common sense. And the stranger had called him by name.

"What do you want me to do?"

"Excellent." Pleasure radiated from the word, but quickly gave way to cool instruction. "Tell me: What do you know about passages to Faerie?"

Dead Rick snorted. "Ain't you the one who came in 'ere pointing out I don't 'ave no memories?"

"You've had seven years to gain more. Do you know nothing?"

The skriker slid down the wall until he was tucked into a comfortable crouch, scratching his torn ear. "Just the usual bosh. Everybody says 'e knows something, and pretty much everybody's lying."

"Because most of the passages we knew are gone. The railways are not only a threat to the Onyx Hall; they've wrought a great deal of destruction in the countryside.

You've seen the refugees here, of course. Their homes are the least of what's been lost. These lines of iron mortals have laid across the land act like dikes and canals, shaping how the water flows. Making the usual roads impassable."

"You want me to find you some way to get to Faerie?" The first step was easy: *leave England.* Go someplace that hadn't been so thoroughly carved up by iron, not yet. And then hope you could find a passage somewhere in the American frontier, or convince the rakshasas or whoever in India to let you through, and take your chances with whatever *their* part of Faerie looked like.

"No," the voice said. "I want you to find out what way Nadrett has."

The skriker's heart thumped hard against his ribs. "The 'ell with you. 'E don't 'ave nothing of the sort. Don't you think we'd know, if 'e did?"

"It depends. The longer Nadrett waits, the greater the desperation; the more fae will pay for the escape he offers. But I suspect he does not have it *yet.* A new passage to Faerie cannot be a simple thing, or cleverer minds than his would have worked it out by now; they have certainly tried. No, I believe Nadrett is working toward this end, and is close to succeeding."

No need to ask why the stranger wanted the information; it would be more valuable than bread, more powerful than the empty throne of the Onyx Court. But— "And 'ow exactly am I supposed to find this out for you?"

"In stages. Have you ever heard of a fellow named

Rewdan?" Dead Rick shook his head, then realised the voice must not have any way of seeing him, and repeated the denial out loud. "I want you to find him for me. Rumour has it that he went to Faerie—from some foreign land—and returned, on Nadrett's orders. I'd like to know why."

Dead Rick licked his lips. He'd be better off keeping his mouth shut, but he had to ask. "Why send me? If you knows the Market, you knows there's a bloke named Valentin Aspell. 'E buys and sells this kind of information every day."

"Which means he might very well turn around and sell the news of my asking to someone else. You, on the other hand, are desperate enough to help me, and stand to gain very little by betraying me."

That was true enough. Still— "Nadrett might find out, though. I ain't that subtle."

"Then try harder."

The annoyed reply was a little victory, and Dead Rick wondered if the speaker noticed it; for the first time, he'd prodded the stranger into an answer that hadn't been rehearsed. *Those three words told me more about 'is real nature than everything 'e said before them.* Whoever this cove was, he was accustomed to giving orders, and had little patience for fools. "I'll do what I can," Dead Rick promised. "When I 'as something, how will I tell you?"

What followed after was almost as telling as the three words; the stranger regained his composure with speed. "Nadrett permits you the night garden; it won't attract suspicion if you go there. Bury a bone near the old pavilion, and I will speak to you again back here soon after."

"No," Dead Rick said instantly. In part because the choice of a signal felt like mockery, but mostly because of how the conversation began. "I told you to get out, and I meant it."

The impatience was back, and stronger. "Will you argue with everything I say? There is nowhere else in the Goblin Market that might be considered remotely safe; anyone in this warren would cheerfully sell news of your dealings for a scrap of mortal bread. If you leave the Market too regularly, it will draw Nadrett's attention, and that would be equally detrimental to my plans. If you insist on defending your territory, then I will promise not to return until your signal—but I will *not* undertake pointless risks just because of your canine instincts."

Dead Rick gritted his teeth. The bastard had a point. However little the skriker liked it. "Not until my signal."

Venemously, the stranger said, "Just don't take too long."

Then silence. Dead Rick waited, utterly still, every sense alive; but there was nothing.

He let out his breath slowly, and realised his heart was beating at twice its normal pace. "Bloody shit-sack," he muttered, and shifted to dog form before circling the whole space, sniffing every last corner. Nothing but cold stone and his own scent, so finally he sank into a wary posture on his pile of blankets, from which he could watch the entrance.

He couldn't trust a bit of it. But Dead Rick was just

desperate enough to agree anyway. And whoever this stranger was, he knew it.

Well, no point wasting time. Turning himself into a man once more, Dead Rick began the hunt for Rewdan.

CROMWELL ROAD, SOUTH KENSINGTON
24 March 1884

The mere sight of No. 35 Cromwell Road was almost enough to make Eliza give up.

She felt uncomfortable simply walking around South Kensington. This was the area where the Great Exhibitions of '51 and '62 had been held, before Eliza was born; afterward, some rich gents had decided to build grand museums in the area, and the people who lived around them were grand enough to match.

But even by the standards of the area, the houses along that stretch of Cromwell Road were intimidating. Their fronts stretched five windows wide—twice as much as an ordinary house—and rose a full four stories, plus attics, all of it brilliantly white, even in London's dirty fogs. The columned entrances looked like a row of maws, all waiting to devour her.

If she'd had to go in one of those doors, her nerve might have broken entirely. But those were never for servants. Instead she went to the western end of the row, where No. 35 stood in detached glory, and found the staircase leading down to the area. Before she could question the wisdom of her plan, Eliza hurried down the steps and rapped on the basement door.

It opened almost immediately, revealing a skinny girl of perhaps twelve. Her hands, red with hot water and harsh soap, marked her as the scullery maid. "If you please," Eliza said, "I'm here to apply for a job."

The girl waved her in silently. Eliza stepped through into a narrow entryway, then followed the girl through a dimly lit basement larger than some people's entire houses. All around her, Eliza could hear people working. How many staff must a house like this employ?

Entering a room dominated by a heavy trestle table, the girl curtsied and spoke for the first time. "Mrs. Fowler, there's someone here to speak to you."

A woman sat at one end of the table, counting through a stack of fine linen napkins. Like the table, she was heavily built, with a face like soft dough and eyes like bits of granite. Hoping her nervousness did not show, Eliza echoed the scullery maid's curtsy and said, "Good afternoon, ma'am. My name is Elizabeth White, and I heard you had a position open for a housemaid."

Getting that information hadn't been difficult, not once she found where the Kittering family lived. Servants gossiped here as much as they did in Whitechapel; more, even, because there were so many of them. Eliza had thought it a stroke of unimaginable luck—at first. She soon discovered that open positions were a common thing in the Kittering household.

Mrs. Fowler, the Kitterings' housekeeper, said nothing at first, but kept counting napkins. Only when she had finished did she stand and say, "Follow me, Miss White."

The housekeeper led her elsewhere in the basement, to the room that apparently served her as bedroom and office both. It had its own little coal grate, and gas lamps Mrs. Fowler cranked up to a brighter state—luxury that made Eliza's eyes pop. The room itself was comfortably furnished, with a modern brass bed stand and pictures on the walls. The chair she was gestured into, however, was hard and straight backed: no comfort there.

Mrs. Fowler held out one hand, and after a blank moment Eliza realised what the woman wanted. Trying to appear confident, she gave the housekeeper a paper from her pocket.

She carefully did not hold her breath as the woman read it over with a frown. Getting that paper, and the tidy dress she wore, had taken everything she had: every spare penny, and every favour she could call due from friends back in Whitechapel. Applying for a maid's position in Mrs. DiGiuseppe's household had been a simple enough matter; nobody who relied on a single maid-of-all-work could afford to be deeply fussy about the quality of servant she attracted.

But that was the East End of London, well supplied with Italians and lascars and Jews, much less so with respectability. This was the West End, and it might as well have been another city entirely.

A city of privilege, rank, and above all, wealth.

From what she had learned, gossiping with other servants, the previous Mr. Kittering had made a small fortune in a railway speculation, and his son had, through clever investments, transformed it into a very large one. He then married the daughter of a man who imported exotic goods from Japan, and that had made their wealth secure. They were exactly the sort of upstarts that attracted gossip—both of the envious sort, from those who craved money, and of the disdainful sort, from those who insisted that no amount of it could replace good breeding.

It wasn't hard to guess why Miss Kittering—youngest of six children, and the only one still unmarried—had to go in secret to meetings of the London Fairy Society. Wealth, her mother had; good breeding, she could not buy; that left respectability as the final component of an ideal life, and Mrs. Kittering pursued respectability with everything in her power.

Which posed certain difficulties for Eliza. The easiest way to keep watch over Miss Kittering would be to join the household as a maid. To do that, however, she needed a character from her previous employer. Mrs. DiGiuseppe had been a decent enough sort, but her recommendation would not help Eliza here; the word of an East End Italian would more likely see her kicked out on the spot.

Fortunately for her, the Kittering household could not keep maids for love or money. Mrs. Kittering, it seemed, was the problem; she was a dreadful mistress, eternally sacking maids for trivial shortcomings, and those she didn't sack soon quit to seek a position elsewhere. Had Eliza been looking for employment on ordinary terms, she would never have applied here. But she only needed to spend a little while in the Kittering household, and the rapid change of staff made the housekeeper more desperate in her hiring choices than she might otherwise be.

Or so Eliza hoped. The character in Mrs. Fowler's hands was falsified; if she was the sort of sensible housekeeper who visited the previous employer to inquire in person, she would soon discover the lie. *But surely she cannot spare such time, not when she's so often hiring.*

Mrs. Fowler sniffed and turned the paper over, as if expecting there should be more to say about a good maid's morals, honesty, cleanliness, capability, temper, and health. "Elizabeth White," she said. When Eliza nodded, she shook her head. "Not here, you won't be. The missus is still mourning Hannah—the only good maid she ever had—and doesn't see why she should learn a new maid's name. If you work here, you'll be Hannah. How often do you go to church?"

Eliza hadn't attended Mass since last October, but she suspected "never" would be a more welcome word out of her mouth than "Mass." Mrs. Fowler, according to rumour, was a stout evangelical. "Whenever I can," she said, "work permitting. I study my Bible at nights, if I cannot go to church." *Why did I just say that? I'll never be able to afford a Bible.*

But it made Mrs. Fowler look pleased. "How would you wash a silk handkerchief?"

Mrs. DiGiuseppe had never owned such a thing. "Gently," Eliza said, trying to think what would make sense. "I would, ah—soak it for a time, and see if that lifts the dirt free, and if not—ah, perhaps scrub at any stains with my fingers—"

The pleased look faded; clearly there were secrets to the washing of silk handkerchiefs that Eliza did not know. "And the recipe for starch?"

There, she was on firmer ground. "Half a pint of cold water, and one quart boiling, for every two tablespoonfuls of starch; but the hot water must be properly boiling when it's added. And I stir it with a wax candle to prevent the iron from sticking."

"Which also gives a smooth appearance to the linen." Mrs. Fowler seemed satisfied with that answer, at least. "Show me your teeth— Well, I suppose they will suffice. What illnesses have you had?"

"Measles and scarlet fever. And my mum took me to be vaccinated against smallpox." Actually it had been Mrs. Darragh, behind the back of Eliza's mother. They had to go to an English doctor for it, and many of Whitechapel's residents were suspicious of that, even though the vaccination was free. Or perhaps especially because it was.

Mrs. Fowler pursed her lips at Eliza's character again, as if something about it was bothering her. But after a moment, she folded it briskly and said, "I can take you on as an under-housemaid. You don't have the skills for more, but if you last here you might learn enough for a better position. Your pay will be twelve pounds yearly plus an allowance for tea, sugar, and beer, and you will have one evening off each week, one day off each month. On Sundays you will accompany me to church."

She said nothing about an annual holiday; Eliza doubted maids stayed long enough to claim such a thing. "Thank you, Mrs. Fowler. That sounds very good." And it did, strangely enough. Twelve pounds yearly! Without her having to pay for lodgings every night, or walk miles through London's streets shouting herself hoarse. It was more than she earned as a struggling costerwoman, and for that matter, more than she'd earned as Mrs. DiGiuseppe's slavey. *So this is what working for wealth looks like.*

But it came with a price: working for Mrs. Kittering, and lying about who she was. And an under-housemaid would have less opportunity to spy upon Miss Kittering than one who worked above stairs. Eliza's enthusiasm was therefore tempered by the time Mrs. Fowler asked, "How soon can you begin?"

"Oh, as soon as may be," she hastened to assure the housekeeper. "Today, if you like."

"I will show you the house, then, and tonight you may go fetch your things—" She broke off at Eliza's muted reaction. "What is it?"

Eliza ducked her head, embarrassed. "There—there isn't anything to fetch, ma'am. Just this." She touched one shoe to her bundle on the floor, then jerked her foot back before Mrs. Fowler could notice the shoe was a man's boot, with cracked leather and worn heel. Every last penny had gone into the dress and the character, with tuppence left over for a bath; shoes could run as much as a shilling, even secondhand. No one in Whitechapel could, or would, spare her that kind of money.

The housekeeper's expression turned forbidding. "You have nothing else to your name?"

If she didn't come up with a good explanation, Mrs. Fowler might follow up on that character, and then the entire thing would fall apart. Eliza tried to hide her worry—then thought the better of it, and let her distress show through. "I'm sorry, ma'am—I know it's disgraceful—it's my brother, you see, he fell sick. Measles, it was, and I nursed him, because I'd had it before; but then it got into his lungs, and we paid all we had to the doctor, but it wasn't enough. He's dead now. This is the last good dress I have, and I sold my good shoes, and—please, ma'am, I *need* this job. I promise I'll save every penny, and make myself respectable again as fast as I may."

Mrs. Fowler sniffed, but her expression softened by a hair. "Very well. Ann Wick is the upper-housemaid; she will lend you a dress until you receive your first week's pay. I'll expect you to look better by this day week."

"Yes, ma'am." Eliza had risen from her chair during that inspired bit of lying; now she bobbed a curtsy. *In one week's time, I could be gone entirely. But I'll have four shillings and more to show for it, and that's never a bad thing.*

"Follow me, then," Mrs. Fowler said, opening the door and leading her toward the stairs. "I'll show you the room you'll share with Ann, and then you can begin cleaning the carpets in the morning room."

THE GOBLIN MARKET, ONYX HALL

26 March 1884

"Get 'im! Come on, rip 'is fucking throat out!"

Dead Rick's lips peeled back in a snarl. Half at the dog across from him, half at the voices egging them on. *Stupid whelp,* he cursed himself. *Should 'ave knowed better than to do your sniffing in dog form. Gives the bastards ideas.*

He had plenty of reason to curse himself out. On the one hand, he'd found Rewdan: good for him. On the other hand, Rewdan was the stringy padfoot cur snarling back at him, and the mob was howling for one of them to die.

What the other faerie had done to land himself here, Dead Rick didn't know. Maybe he'd just wandered by in dog form, as Dead Rick had, and run afoul of some drunk goblin, again as Dead Rick had. Or maybe he'd gotten on the wrong side of Nadrett. They were in the pit outside the master's chamber, and that was the place for two things: entertainment and punishment.

The crowd was out for blood, sure enough; the pit floor was strewn with the broken bodies of three dead dogs, mortal beasts thrown down here to challenge the padfoot, and if Dead Rick wasn't careful he'd be the fourth. Rewdan was tired, though, and waiting for his opportunity. Dead

Rick circled, crouching low, trying to think of a way out that didn't involve one or the other of them bleeding his last into the filthy sand of the pit. He couldn't ask the padfoot any questions if either of them was dead.

The mob didn't like the delay. A chicken bone clipped Dead Rick's ear, hurled into the pit by some impatient spectator, and he flinched; in a flash, Rewdan attacked.

Dead Rick twisted under the padfoot's rush, barely managing to keep his feet. He reared up, trying to get an advantage of height, but the other faerie did the same; their chests slammed together, paws scrabbling for purchase, breath hot in each other's ears. Dead Rick managed to get a bite of something soft, and Rewdan yelped, but then toenails raked his ribs and he echoed the sound. They broke away from each other, snapping, feinting lunges, and the watchers cheered them on.

Now he had to keep a bit of his awareness on everything else, not just the other dog, for fear he'd be caught by surprise again. But the padfoot was panting hard; he probably couldn't manage so quick a rush again. *Tire him out a bit more, then go for his throat—*

They wouldn't let him stop short of tearing it out, though. Unless . . .

A shift in the air made him tense, expecting another hurled bone. What it brought instead was a new scent, barely discernible over the blood-stink of the pit, and the oddly sour smell of the other dog. And it gave Dead Rick a very dangerous idea.

Probably won't work. But I ain't got nothing better.

He feinted another lunge, then pulled up short as if it pained the bleeding scratches where the other dog had raked him. Rewdan took the bait, and leapt for him again.

This time Dead Rick let himself go under. He kept his paws between their bodies as best he could, fending off the padfoot's weight, hoping he was right and Rewdan was too tired to resist if Dead Rick tried to throw him off. But he let himself be wrestled onto his back, matted fur grinding into the filthy sand, and the padfoot's jaws dove for his throat—

A thunderclap obliterated the cheers. Rewdan jerked sideways, and all the strength went abruptly out of his body; he collapsed onto Dead Rick, no longer fighting, his snarls twisting off into an agonised whine. The reek of blood flooded Dead Rick's nose, obliterating the sour smell: blood, and acrid gunpowder. He squirmed out from under the padfoot's twitching, dying body, and looked up.

Nadrett stood at the top of the stairs, a smoking pistol in his hand. Raggedly, the arena fell into silence; even those cursing their losses over the padfoot stopped when they saw the cause.

Dead Rick's master waited until he had quiet, except for the padfoot's last, gasping breaths. Then he said, "Who put my dog in the pit?"

No one answered. Nadrett lifted his gun again. It was a Galenic Academy design, adapted from the American Colt so as to fire elfshot; the cylinder clicked smoothly around as the master cocked it a second time. "*I* decide 'ow long my dogs live, and 'ow they die. And I ain't given no orders for this other one to die. Who put 'im in there?"

Confession would win nothing for the guilty party, except possibly a bullet between the eyes. Betrayal, however, was more profitable. A dozen hands moved to point, at seven different targets. Nadrett aimed his revolver at the one who had collected the most fingers: a puck in a knee-length leather coat. "Nithen, put 'im in the cages. I'll deal with 'im later."

The fetch shoved his way through the crowd to obey. Dead Rick, crouching in the pit, didn't look at the dead padfoot. He'd hoped Nadrett would end the fight; he'd known Nadrett might end it with murder. It told him what he needed to know, which was that the master had, in fact, given the order for Rewdan to die. Which meant there never would have been any chance to question him, regardless of how the fight ended. Dead Rick hadn't found him fast enough.

The master left the room, trailed by his lieutenants. Only when he was gone did the voices feel safe to rise, grumbling to one another and settling their bets. Dead Rick gathered his back feet under himself, waiting for a small gap to open up in the crowd; with a tired leap he made it to the pit's edge. Then he wormed his way between the legs until he reached the wall, where he could safely change back to man form.

"Bloody clever of you." Gresh leaned against the wall nearby, digging in his pockets for pipe and tobacco.

"Getting Nadrett to settle it like that. Cost me a mint, you bastard; I'd bet Rewdan wouldn't drop 'til the fifth fight."

Maybe there was still some hope of finding out what the padfoot had been doing. "Who was 'e, anyway, and did 'e bite Nadrett in the knackers, or what? 'Ow'd 'e get 'imself stuck down there?"

Gresh shrugged. "Ain't seen 'im before myself. I 'eard 'e's some kind of courier, and tried to sell some of 'is shipment to the Academy. You know, make a little bread on the side."

"Shipment?" Dead Rick straightened, despite the complaints of his weary back. "What was 'e carrying?"

The goblin hawked and spat, then began sucking on the pipe. "The sort of thing the Academy likes. I look like a bleeding scholar to you?" Dead Rick held his breath, not wanting to betray his curiosity by prompting. Gresh got his pipe properly lit, then said, "Compounds of some kind. Lunar caustic, satyr's bile—valuable, from what I 'ear, but not if it gets you on Nadrett's bad side."

Dead Rick knew enough to recognise those as faerie compounds, rather than mortal. Brought in from Faerie itself? Perhaps. One of them must have been what he smelled on the padfoot, that oddly sour scent. Dead Rick opened his mouth to ask what Nadrett wanted them for, but closed it before he could be that stupid. Gresh wouldn't know—but he'd take note of the fact that Dead Rick had asked. And maybe sell that information to others.

Someone in the Academy might know what they were

useful for, at least. Whoever Rewdan had tried to sell to, if that rumour was true. Some of the scholars weren't above getting their materials from the unclean hands of the Goblin Market.

To distract Gresh from the real point, he said, "Am I going to 'ave 'is friends coming after me?"

"Friends, hah. Think anybody's 'is friend, after 'e got dropped in there?" Gresh jerked his patchy beard at the pit.

Well, that was one less worry. *Now all I've got to worry about is Nadrett.* "Sorry you bet on Rewdan. I'll buy you a beer in the Crow's Head, to make up for it." One good thing from the breakdown of the palace: it had forced the pub to move from its old location to a spot inside the Goblin Market, where Dead Rick could go freely.

"That don't 'alf make up my losses," Gresh complained, but he was never one to turn down beer. And it would give him reason to forget anything Dead Rick had said. Clapping one hand on the goblin's shoulder with a friendliness he didn't feel, Dead Rick headed for the pub.

CROMWELL ROAD, SOUTH KENSINGTON
27 March 1884

To the uncritical eye, Miss Louisa Kittering's bedroom appeared a model of respectable young femininity. It was agreeably papered in a floral pattern, with sunny landscapes and paintings of birds upon the walls, and a soft rose carpet upon the floor. The lace-trimmed curtains at the windows were neatly tied back; the one minor sign of disarray was an embroidery frame balanced upon the arm of a chair, as if the needlewoman had set it down just a moment ago, and would return at any second. But the frame had lain there since Eliza began working in the Kitterings' house three days ago, and not a stitch had been added to its contents in that time: one of many little marks of Miss Kittering's rebellion.

Eliza studied the room, running the tip of her tongue absently through the gap in her teeth. She kept being distracted by the Kitterings' unfathomable wealth; the lace on the curtains alone was worth more than she would earn in a year. Every time she touched something, she felt guilty, as if the basic grubbiness of her own birth would somehow stain the finery. If the Kitterings weren't so desperate for servants, she never would have had a place here; everything around her, even the servants' quarters in the garret, shouted that she didn't belong.

I'm only here for one thing, Eliza reminded herself. Once that was done, she could go back to where she *did* belong. But first: Where would a young lady hide her secrets?

Not under the mattress. In a house like this, mattresses were turned every day, and the linens aired; Eliza would have seen it her first morning. Nor behind the headboard of the bed, which had been her second guess. She'd had regrettably little time for prying, though; if she fell behind on her tasks, Mrs. Fowler would come looking. And if Eliza were found with her nose in the young miss's belongings, a sacking would be the *least* of her concerns.

But she had to keep trying. As quietly as she could, Eliza dragged a chair to the wardrobe, then tossed a rag over the seat to protect it from her shoes. The top of the wardrobe, unfortunately, held nothing more than a shameful quantity of dust, undisturbed by any human touch. Underneath was cleaner, but likewise empty.

She put the chair back, wondering if she dared search the writing desk. There was little reason for any honest maid to be going through those drawers, and if someone were to find her . . . Eliza told herself it was not merely caution that kept her away, but common sense. Mrs. Kittering was very obviously the sort of mother who had no compunctions about going through her daughter's letters. If Louisa was keeping secrets—and her behaviour in Islington made it clear she was—then she had to be keeping them elsewhere.

Such as *inside* the wardrobe. Eliza threw the doors open, preparing a variety of suitable lies in case someone were to come upon her, and began to rummage through.

If there were any false panels built in, she'd have to find them another day; she couldn't spare that kind of time now. But Eliza dug swiftly through the clothes and shoes, making sure there was nothing tucked away in a back corner—and then her eyes fell upon the hatboxes at the top.

Instinct overcame caution. Eliza dragged the chair back over, pulled the front boxes out of the way, and reached for one at the back. It proved to be inappropriately heavy, and when she lifted the lid, a smile spread across her face. "Caught you."

Whatever hat had once occupied this box was long gone. In its place were books, magazines, and pamphlets. Eliza paged through them, hardly breathing. A pair of gothic novels, showing signs of repeated reading. A book of poems by someone named Oscar Wilde. An advertisement for a mesmerist. Scattered numbers of a few spiritualist magazines, and some pamphlets by Frederic Myers, whose name Eliza recognised. He and some other fellows had done a great deal of research into mediums and ghosts, even forming their own Society for Psychical Research.

Was Miss Kittering interested in contacting a departed spirit, or did she fancy herself a medium? Eliza supposed it didn't matter. Either way, this collection held a great many things Mrs. Kittering would not approve of in the slightest, not with her insistence upon perfect respectability. Nothing on faeries, not that Eliza could see without a more detailed search—but plenty that spoke of disreputable things.

At the creak of the stairs, her heart leapt into her mouth. Eliza hastily crammed everything back into the hatbox, shoved it into place, threw the doors shut—catching them at the last instant so they would not slam—and put the chair back more or less where it belonged, before flinging herself at the fireplace, where she ought to be hard at work.

When the door opened, she knew that only vanity had saved her from discovery. Not hers, but that of the footman Ned Sayers, who invariably paused to admire himself in the looking glass mounted at the top of the family staircase. Mrs. Kittering did not sack footmen as often as she did maids, because of the necessity of keeping a pair who were reasonably well matched in height and looks; as near as Eliza could tell, Ned Sayers's face was the only thing keeping him in his position.

She offered him a smile, hoping he wouldn't notice that she had only just begun to rub black lead into the iron bars of the fireplace grate, when she should have been nearly done. Sayers smiled back, and held up a pair of delicate ankle boots. "Just returning these," he said.

"I hope they weren't too much trouble to clean," Eliza said. Servants' gossip was her other great hope of learning anything; they knew far more about their masters and mistresses than those employers liked to consider. But Mrs. Fowler, who watched over their meals, had little tolerance for idle chatter; and when Eliza went to bed at night, she was far too exhausted to question Ann Wick, the upper-housemaid whose room she shared. Hoping to get something from Sayers, she added, "From what I hear, Miss Kittering can be dreadful hard on her belongings. A real hoyden, that one."

The footman shrugged, going past her. "I suppose." Eliza watched surreptitiously as he opened the wardrobe doors and tossed the boots casually onto the bottom shelf; she prayed he would not notice anything out of place. Then she saw her rag still lying on the chair, and jerked her eyes back to the grate, cursing silently. But Sayers only said, "If you'd like, I could shine your shoes up for you. Such a pretty ankle you have."

A hand settled on Eliza's calf, exposed where she knelt to do her work, and she jumped in surprise. Her sleeve caught on the knob of the ash pan; for a moment she was off balance, almost falling. Sayers caught her. Eliza dropped the brush in her haste to be free of him. "Mr. Sayers—"

"Ned, please." He smiled at her.

Eliza did not like that smile at all. Maids could be turned off for dallying with men; perhaps Mrs. Kittering was not solely to blame for all the departures. But if she made him angry with her, that could be trouble, too. "I'm already behind in my work," she said, dodging the question of what name to use. Picking up the brush, she frowned; it had rolled off the canvas she'd put down and left a smear of oily black lead on the floor. Then she bit back a curse in Irish, seeing that she'd gotten some of it on her hands, too. Even if Sayers left, there would be no returning to those hidden pamphlets; she'd leave dirty finger marks everywhere.

"You'll always be behind. Sunup to sundown, and Mrs. Kittering will be displeased at *something* you've failed to do; what's a bit more, in exchange for some fun?"

It cut too close to the bone. Sayers was right about the work; this house was so big, and the staff perpetually shorthanded, that Eliza found herself busy every waking minute. A stray thought had her wondering how deeply Miss Kittering slept, and that frightened her into sensibility: if she was considering sneaking into the young woman's room at night, then she had lost every last shred of sense.

All of which made Eliza's tone harder than was perhaps

wise when she said, "I need this job, Mr. Sayers. Mrs. Kittering may be displeased whatever I do, but that's no reason for me to add to it a-purpose."

Sayers frowned. She could hardly bring herself to care; surely any trouble he posed would take time to really vex her, and she had no intention of being here long enough to give him the chance. What mattered was Miss Kittering, and her secrets.

"I thought you a more friendly girl than this," he said.

Eliza almost laughed in his face. Fergus Boyle had said much the same to her once, and she knew well what kind of "friendliness" they were trying to coax out of her. *But no; if I laugh he* will *be angry, and I should avoid that if I can.* "I'm sorry, Mr. Sa— Ned. It's just that life has been miserable hard for me lately, and this position is the best bit of luck I've had in ages. I don't dare risk it. Please, forgive me."

His given name stuck in her craw, as did the apology, but it had the desired effect; the footman's hard mouth softened into a more accepting line. And he didn't even offer to make life easier for her—not yet, anyway. Eliza had little doubt such false promises would come. "How could I not forgive a pretty face like that?" he asked—stretching the truth close to the breaking point, for Eliza knew herself no beauty. Her life had been much too hard for that.

When the door opened a second time, she wasn't sure whether to be relieved or dismayed, for she was sure it would be Mrs. Fowler, come to thrash Eliza for being a sluggard. But the figure in the doorway was half a foot shorter and half the housekeeper's size, and dressed ten times more finely: Miss Louisa Kittering herself.

Eliza shot to her feet and curtsied. Sayers rose more lazily, and though he stood behind Eliza, out of her sight, she was sure he tried one of his smiles on Miss Kittering, for the young woman's mouth twisted in disdain. "Don't you have work to do?" she asked him.

"Of course, miss." He had the gall to pinch Eliza's rump as he left. She went rigid, then remembered herself and curtsied again. "I was just polishing the grate, miss. I'll come back later—"

"No, help me change clothes." Miss Kittering shut the door again and tossed her bonnet carelessly toward the bed. It fell short, and rolled across the carpet.

With that black lead on her fingers, Eliza knew she ought to call for Lucy, the lady's maid. But this was too splendid an opportunity to pass up; Mrs. Kittering was firm on the subject that servants should be seen only when they were needed, and ideally never heard at all, which meant she might never have another chance to speak with the young woman.

So she retrieved her rag from the chair while Miss Kittering's back was turned and gave her fingers a hard scrub, until the black lead no longer came off at a touch. "A walking dress," the young woman said, pulling off her elegant little shoes with a sigh; Eliza went to the wardrobe and fetched one out, hoping she remembered the subtleties of ladies' clothing well enough to have chosen the right outfit.

"It's a lovely day for walking," she said to Miss

Kittering. Not that she'd put her nose out of the house past taking deliveries at the cellar door, but the last two days had seemed much warmer, and there was even some sun.

Miss Kittering made an unenthusiastic sound in reply. Determined to get more than that, Eliza asked, "Are you going up to Hyde Park, then?"

"Kensington Gardens," the young woman said. She bent to see herself in the mirror, smoothing her polished golden hair, then straightened so Eliza could unbutton the back of her morning dress. "Mama's idea, of course. She would send me out in a thunderstorm, if Mr. Twisleton-Wykeham-Fiennes asked."

"Who?" Eliza bit her lip an instant after the question slipped out. She couldn't help herself; the name was so absurdly long.

Miss Kittering didn't comment on her rudeness. "Eldest son of Baron Saye and Sele. *Only* a baron, as Mama put it—'but at least it's not a *new* barony.'" She spoke those last words in perfect mimicry of her mother's voice, then sniffed in disgust.

"You don't care for him, then?" Eliza laid the morning dress aside for later folding.

"There's nothing wrong with *him,*" Miss Kittering said, holding her arms up for Eliza to slip the walking dress over her head. "But it's 'Louisa, go here,' and 'Louisa, go there,' and 'Louisa, don't waste your time dancing with anyone who doesn't have a title,' and it's enough to make me *scream*. All because she still thinks she could have married that viscount, if only her figure had been of higher quality, and so she's determined to—"

Miss Kittering stopped there; apparently she had just noticed herself gossiping with a servant. Eliza devoted her attention to the row of little buttons, as if she'd heard nothing at all. So Miss Kittering had a rebellious nature, did she? It didn't surprise Eliza in the slightest. But what, aside from the general impulse to kick against her mother, did that have to do with faeries?

Experimentally, she said, "I imagine you'd rather just curl up with a book."

The back beneath her hands stiffened. Eliza cursed her tongue; what if Miss Kittering realised she'd been snooping in the wardrobe? The young woman said, again in mimicry of her mother, " 'Too much reading rots a girl's brains.' " Then Eliza finished with the buttons and Miss Kittering pulled away. "My ankle boots, and the yellow shawl; it is not so warm out there as all that."

Eliza curtised and fetched the requested articles. And then Miss Kittering was gone, leaving her with a half-polished grate, and only a few tantalizing hints of an answer.

THE GOBLIN MARKET, ONYX HALL

30 March 1884

Even in the Goblin Market, few people paid attention to a dog.

They were too common to mind. The Onyx Hall held some actual strays—mostly pets, abandoned by faerie owners who tired of them. Cats sometimes slipped through the hidden entrances by means no one could explain, but it was a rare dog who stumbled upon one of the holes in the palace's fabric. There were also faerie hounds, creatures of some intelligence, but no shapeshifting ability. And then there were fae like Dead Rick, who walked equally well as men or dogs: skrikers, padfoots, galley-trots, and more. It was possible to tell the various kinds apart, but only if the watcher paid attention.

So Dead Rick could and did crisscross the warren that housed the Goblin Market without attracting much notice at all. Far less notice than he would have attracted if he'd gone asking for Cyma, when he had such a particular question for her. He finally picked up a trail that smelled more or less recent, and followed it into a quieter part of the warren, until it was drowned out by the overpowering scent of opium.

Dead Rick briefly considered waiting. He hated the opium den; it was full of delirious mortals in varying states of mental decay, easy prey for the fae who had lured them below. And if Cyma had been smoking it herself, she might be in no state to help him.

But he didn't want to waste any time. And if he stayed low to the ground, out of the worst of the smoke, he could get in and out before it had too much effect on him. Peeling his lips back in annoyance, Dead Rick slipped through the brocaded silk curtains that had taken the place of the den's missing door.

The light inside was murky, partially from the smoke, partially from the various covers placed over the faerie lights: oiled cloth, coloured glass, anything to soften and warm that cold brilliance. He couldn't smell anything through the opium reek, though, and was glad the abundant shadows gave him useful concealment until his eyes adjusted enough to make his way around the room.

Most of the people he saw were mortal. With the introduction of faerie opium from China, this had become the most common means of harvesting dreams: men and the occasional woman lay in loose-limbed stupor on narrow pallets, and from time to time figures would take shape in the smoky air above their heads. Once bottled, those were worth a bit on the market, though not as much as the clean product. And besides, the only sorts of people fae could usually lure down here were the dregs of London, beggars and cripples and madmen, poor folk who would sell their souls to forget their troubles for a little while. Not much variety to be had from such stock.

The fae who slipped among them weren't Nadrett's people. The opium den was under the control of a Chinese faerie with a long, elaborate name that had soon been shortened to Po, and he did business only with Lacca, another Goblin Market boss. Together they defended the opium-dream trade against Nadrett's attempts to take it over. But they allowed individuals to pay for use of the dens and, as Dead Rick suspected, Cyma was among them.

She was in a back corner, leaning up against a low couch, helping a golden-haired young mortal woman in a nightgown steady an opium pipe carved of ivory. The pupils of Cyma's eyes were slightly contracted, but he guessed that to be the mere result of sitting too long in the room; the young woman, on the other hand, was thoroughly lost to the drug. After a long drag on the pipe, she opened her eyes, saw Dead Rick, and fell to helpless giggling. He felt disgruntled at her reaction: he was a death omen, after all, not some lady's idiot lapdog. But perhaps that was the opium at work.

Cyma turned to see what her mortal was laughing at, and frowned at Dead Rick. "What are you doing here?" she whispered.

It was possible to speak in dog form, but not easy. Dead Rick shifted back, then said, "I was going to ask you that." He, too, kept his voice low, but not out of consideration for the opium smokers. If any of them were alert enough to pay attention, he didn't want them overhearing more than necessary. "Wasn't you supposed to be going somewhere? Away from 'ere?"

"Soon enough." An unfocused smile spread across her face; the drug was affecting her, after all. "Soon I'll be safe. I'm done chasing mortals for Nadrett . . . London will be mine, and I won't need him anymore."

Dead Rick had no idea what she meant by most of that, but one thing was clear enough to prick his curiosity. "Who did 'e send you after?" His attention went to the girl on the couch. " 'Er?"

"No!" Cyma said. It was abrupt enough that he believed it, especially with the way she shifted as if to protect the girl; for a moment, he thought she might say more. But Cyma wasn't so far gone that she would spill her secrets that easily. "Nadrett's business," she muttered, subsiding. Was he imagining the guilt on her face? "It was a man he wanted, and nothing to do with you."

Could this have something to do with the plan the voice had spoken of? Dead Rick doubted it. Nadrett sent his minions after people all the time; Gresh harvested them regularly from the East End, for bread and less pleasant things. Rewdan's business was something less usual. "Cyma . . . do you still talk to that fellow over in the Academy?"

"Yvoir?" Cyma's gaze sharpened, and she said in something more like her regular voice, "What do you want, Dead Rick?"

He'd practiced the lie until he could tell it convincingly. "I might know 'ow to get my 'ands on some compounds from Faerie. But I ain't no scientist; I don't know what they're good for. And that means I don't know what they're worth. I was 'oping you might be able to find out for me."

"What compounds?"

"Satyr's bile. Lunar caustic. Maybe some others, but those two for sure."

The mortal's hand groped absently through the air, from where she had sagged back along the couch. Cyma caught it, then hung on as if she could read the answer to Dead Rick's question in the young woman's palm. He held his breath, waiting. Cyma was the only person he halfway trusted; if she couldn't help him—or wouldn't—he'd have to buy the answer from someone else. Valentin Aspell sold information, but it came at a high price.

Cyma frowned. "Won't your master be angry? If you go making deals behind his back."

Not 'alf so angry as 'e'll be if 'e finds out what I'm really *doing*. "I can't afford to be safe, Cyma." He gestured around: at the opium den, the Goblin Market, the Onyx Hall. Maybe at London itself. "It's all falling apart, ain't it? Nadrett's got me chained to 'im now, sure, but I ain't stupid enough to believe that'll 'elp me much when the end comes. 'E'll leave me to drown, I know it. I got to be ready to run on my own."

Cyma's gaze softened. One hand reached out to stroke his cheek; he flinched away. To his surprise, he saw the bright glint of tears in her eyes. "We shouldn't have to run," she whispered.

The opium was starting to make him light-headed. He fought it back with bitter anger. "Unless you've got a new palace stuffed down the front of your dress, we ain't got much choice. Bloody 'umans are going to crush us underfoot, and never know we was 'ere." He glared at the oblivious young woman on the couch.

"Some of them know," Cyma said, and stroked the girl's hand. "Maybe if they all did—"

"What?" Dead Rick's skin jumped all over, as if he'd turned around to find Nadrett pointing a gun at him. "Are you bleeding mad? They'd kill us."

Cyma gestured languorously at the slumped figures all around the opium den. "These don't. The ones in the Academy don't. The idea isn't mine, Dead Rick; you'd be surprised who else agrees. We're a part of London, damn it—have been for centuries. Why shouldn't we admit it?"

"Because we'd 'ave priests waving crosses in our faces, blokes shoving us into cages for raree-shows, little girls wanting us to dance in the bloody flowers for 'em. We're a part of London? So's the rats. Even the Irish and the Jews would be lining up to kick us."

Cyma had started giggling at his complaint about the flowers, and was having trouble stopping; she said something half-intelligible about nobody going to church any longer, but Dead Rick didn't listen. The trouble was, he *wanted* to agree with her. Wanted to charge up into the streets and shred anybody who threatened his territory, the Onyx Hall. Bare his teeth and say, *This place is mine,* until the mortals backed down, showed throat, left him in peace.

Stupid whelp. It ain't your territory. It belongs to the ones strong enough to 'old it—and they don't care a toss about defending it, not against the bastards upstairs. Curs like you get kicked to the gutters, by both sides.

His thoughts must have shown on his face, for Cyma reached out and took him unexpectedly by the shoulders, too tight for him to easily twist away. "Dead Rick—I'll help you if I can. When the time comes."

"'Ow?" he growled, hearing his own rough voice as if it came from a great distance. Nobody touched him, except to hurt him; he wasn't at all sure that Cyma wasn't doing the same, to something other than flesh. "You ain't going to be 'ere, are you?"

"I—I'll find a way. If what I'm doing works . . . I'll come back and tell you. Maybe see if I can help you do the same thing. I promise, I'll explain everything then. And I'll ask Yvoir about the compounds; you don't have to pay me. Is that enough that you'll forgive me for leaving? Just a little bit?"

He had to get free of her hands, and free of this room, with its gentle smoke beckoning him to let down his guard, relax, slip into oblivion. "Sure. A bit. Just keep it quiet. You've got your secrets, and I've got mine."

She seemed about to say more, and would not let him go. His heart beating too hard against his ribs, Dead Rick resorted to changing his shape; Cyma exclaimed and flinched back from the shifting of his skin and bones beneath her hands. A dog once more, he fled into the shadows, stumbling around lost before a breath of cleaner air from the curtains guided him to his escape.

Memory: 13 August 1878

She entered the room in perfect silence, well cloaked by charms. The man in the bed, one Frederic William Henry

Myers, did not stir; this had been a bad night, one of several in a row, and he'd helped himself to sleep with brandy.

She'd been waiting for such a night to come. The dreams of mortals were more easily influenced when their hearts were troubled; a man at peace offered her little chance to work this art. Fortunately, the closest Myers came to peace was at the bottom of a bottle, and that created its own kind of opening.

Cyma drew back the curtain, letting the light of the full moon fall upon her target's face. He stirred slightly, and she waited, allowing him to settle; only when he was quiet did she move again, across the carpeted floor to the side of his bed, where she laid a feather-light touch upon his temple.

For weeks she'd sampled his dreams, sifting from them the face and voice and manner she needed. They were more valuable than photographs, for her purposes; Cyma's interest was not in what the woman had actually looked like, but rather how Myers had seen her. She'd gathered more information than strictly necessary, perhaps; his mind would fill in any gaps or errors she might make, so long as they weren't *too* jarring. But it had been ages since she had this kind of freedom to walk among mortals, protected by their bread, and she could not resist stretching it out for as long as possible.

Which brought her to this night. Closing her eyes, Cyma lifted one foot from the floor, then the other, until she floated above Myers in his bed.

She was not the best at this. But she was good enough, and she owed Nadrett a debt.

Beneath her, Myers dreamt of Annie Marshall. His

cousin's wife, who drowned herself two years ago. Not nearly enough time for the grief to fade. In his dreams, Myers could do as he had never done in life: profess his love for Annie, kiss her lips, touch the flesh he'd only ever imagined. The hard part was not making him dream of Annie; it was making him dream of something other than their unconsummated love.

But Cyma was nothing if not determined. Fear had that effect, even on a faerie. Nadrett had sent her to do this; Nadrett held her debt. Why Nadrett wanted a pet spiritualist, Cyma didn't know, and didn't ask. All that mattered was creating the vulnerability in Myers, the belief that his dead inamorata had a message she wanted him to hear. Mediums had not been able to contact Annie on his behalf, though not for lack of trying; but the woman might come to him in dreams.

So she gave herself the face, the voice, the manner of Annie Marshall, and she told Myers what Nadrett wanted the man to hear. That there were people who could help him; that he must seek them out, and they would give him the proof he so ardently desired, proof that the spirit could persist after death. That her suicide meant neither that she was gone from him forever, nor that she had been damned to some tormenting hell. He would have all the reassurances he could want, so long as he found the strangers and shared with them what he knew.

Tears streamed down Myers's sleeping face, as the moon's light carried Cyma into the defenseless realms of his mind.

He wasn't the first man Nadrett had sent her to pursue. But with this one, she was sure, she would find success. He was the perfect target: a scholar of spiritualism, keeping company with similarly learned friends, but wounded at heart as the others were not. Once Nadrett had him, surely the master would be satisfied, and Cyma's debt would be repaid.

She might even be free as soon as next month.

She believed it, as Myers believed in the ghost of Annie Marshall, and for the same reason. Because the hope kept her going, however impossible it might be.

ADELAIDE ROAD, PRIMROSE HILL
6 April 1884

The lowering of the gas lights had given the room a chill, tomblike aspect. Outside, the night was shrouded in fog, the moon playing hide-and-seek among the clouds. Wind rattled the shutters from time to time, and created a faint moaning in the chimney. It was, in short, a poet's notion of what a night for a séance should be like.

Cyma hoped it would inspire the medium to her best efforts. Mrs. Iris Wexford was typical of the breed: the wife of a vicar in Aylesbury, past her childbearing years, and bored senseless by her respectable life. She held fast to the conviction that spiritualism was the cure for Christianity's ills, that it vindicated instead of disproving the Bible, as some claimed.

Like most of her kind, she was probably a charlatan. But Frederic Myers had great hopes for her, and so Cyma was here.

She fancied it was fate, encountering him again. Once Myers had been thoroughly ensnared by his dreams, Nadrett had taken over all dealings with the man, closing Cyma out. Without bread to protect her, she had no way to visit him, and so in time Myers had faded from her thoughts: one more mortal caught up in faerie matters, not likely to emerge intact.

Or for that matter, to emerge at all. That Frederic Myers was still a free man, not someone's mad slave in the Goblin Market—or dead—told her Nadrett had not yet let go of him, not entirely. In which case it would have been far safer for Cyma to keep her distance. She was almost free of Nadrett at last, and had no desire to trap herself again. But Myers had intrigued her, with his melancholy grief and undying hope of seeing his lost love again, and she could not pass up the chance to see what path he followed now.

Much the same as when she first knew him, it seemed. Testing mediums, hoping to find one who could communicate with the late Annie on his behalf. He sat now around the table with his friends Henry and Eleanor Sidgwick, and various others Cyma didn't know; unlike those first two, they were not members of the new Society for Psychical Research. She had joined them as one "Miss Harris," and now sat with her attention more on Myers than Mrs. Wexford. He had not changed: still the same tremulous eagerness in his wide eyes, his slightly parted lips, as Mrs. Wexford's head sagged to touch the back of her chair.

In a husky voice, the medium said, "I feel the other world draw near!"

Miss Harris, of course, was not cynical in the slightest about these things; Miss Harris had her own ghosts she desperately wanted to see. A dead fiancé, most particularly, for whom she still pined. It gave her and Mr. Myers something in common. But Cyma, beneath her human mask, was impatient. In her time haunting Myers, she'd seen more than enough bored housewives go through similar acts—even exposed a few frauds, when they annoyed her too much—and her initial excitement had long since worn away. She endured this tedium only for the renewed connection to Myers, which she might make use of once she was free of Nadrett.

Then tedium fled, without warning, and every hair on the back of Cyma's neck stood to attention. "A child," Mrs. Wexford whispered. "A boy child—oh, he's like a little angel."

On the other side of the table, one of the sitters, an elderly woman whose name Cyma had forgotten, pulled her hands free of the circle and clasped them over her mouth, tears springing to her eyes. Sidgwick, who sat to the woman's right; immediately turned a suspicious gaze upon her; he was far less credulous than Myers, and knew such movements were often used as cover for tricks. His wife Eleanor kept her attention on Mrs. Wexford, in case the upset woman was a diversion for the medium instead.

But if those two had any tricks planned, they could save themselves the effort. Cyma knew when she was in the presence of a genuine ghost.

Mrs. Wexford shuddered, then began to speak in a high-pitched voice. From the conversation that ensued between the medium and the crying old woman, Cyma gathered that this was the lady's firstborn son, lost years ago, when infection from a rotted tooth spread to his brain. Next to her, she felt Myers heave a silent sigh. Once again, his lost love had failed to appear.

Cyma wondered how the mediums did it—how they called up particular spirits, long since gone. Regular apparitions were one matter, and the recently dead another; both were decidedly less common than they had been in centuries past, but contacting them had never been difficult for those with skill. The little boy's spirit, however, must have moved on. How had Mrs. Wexford summoned him back? One of countless mysteries about the human soul, whose answers she could not fathom. Cyma was no Academy philosopher, but sometimes she understood what intrigued them so.

Her interest sharpened as something formed in the air behind Mrs. Wexford. Its shape was vague, but it was the right size to be a little boy. Cyma held her breath, teeth sunk deep into her lip. True visitations were rare; true physical manifestations might as well have been unicorns. Real, but almost never seen in this day and age. Myers had found himself a true medium after all.

Upon that thought, his hand slipped from her grasp. He and Sidgwick had promised this first sitting would not be any kind of formal test—too many mediums grew nervous and failed to produce anything at all when they knew scientists would be examining their every move—but it seemed Myers's curiosity had overcome him, for he crossed the intervening distance in two quick strides and reached his hand out for the manifestation taking shape in the air.

It vanished with a startled jerk, and Mrs. Wexford's eyes flew open. "I—what—"

She seemed genuinely disoriented, which happened sometimes. The old woman who'd lost her son burst into tears; Eleanor Sidgwick comforted her, while her husband bent over Mrs. Wexford, explaining what had occurred.

Cyma rose and went to Myers's side, curious. "Was it truly physical?"

"For a moment," he said distantly, still looking where the ghost had been. "I felt it, so briefly . . ."

Mrs. Wexford might be able to summon dear Annie for him. Cyma frowned at the notion, and spoke again, to keep Myers's thoughts on matters scientific. "What are such things made of? Is it some coagulation of the air, a curdling that results from the ghost's presence?"

Myers came back to himself with a sigh that said his thoughts had gone exactly where she guessed. "No one knows for certain. It felt gauzy against my fingers—"

"Usually it *is* gauze." Sidgwick had joined them. He gave his friend a sympathetic, pitying look. "You know such things are so often faked."

"Often, yes—but always?" Myers shook his head, rubbing his fingertips together as if he could still feel the substance. "I see no wires, Henry, nor mirrors. I believe this one was real."

Cyma laid a supportive hand on his arm and smiled up into his sad eyes. "As do I. In fact, I'm sure of it."

"You had a theory about the stuff, didn't you, Frederic?"

"Did I?" Myers shrugged at his friend. "I don't recall."

Sidgwick tapped one finger against the bridge of his nose, eyes closed in thought. "*Ectoplasm,* you suggested we should call it. Some kind of emanation from the ghost itself—you never told me the details. Spirit made physical, or some such; a thumb in the eye of the materialists, you said. But you never wrote the article you promised."

They began wrangling amiably about the *Proceedings* of their society. Cyma didn't attend to any of it. *Spirit made physical.* It was one of the basic discoveries of the Galenic Academy last century, that in faerie realms, spirit and matter were the same thing; faerie bodies were a particular configuration of the four classical elements that made up their spirits, intermixed with the aether that permeated their world. Was it somehow possible for human spirits to achieve a similar unity?

She could ask in the Academy—but that might be a very dangerous thing, if it touched on Nadrett's business.

Cyma knew she should keep silent. *You're almost free of him; knowing will only put you in danger.* But encountering Myers last month, after not seeing him for so long—she couldn't let this go.

Sidgwick went to crank up the gas lights, thoroughly breaking the mood; there would be no more raising of ghosts for now. Experimentally, Cyma said, "I recall reading an interesting theory once, from someone in the Theosophical Society. You're familiar with their notion of the astral plane?" Myers nodded. "I do not agree with them on the matter of spirits, of course; clearly the souls of the departed *do* sometimes stay near to comfort those they leave behind. It is not all trickery on the part of the medium. But what if some of it is indeed trickery, as they suggest—on the part of something else?"

His fingers had begun to pull at his beard in a gesture she recognised very well. "Madame Blavatsky's 'spooks, elementaries, and elementals,' you mean. Lower principles cast off by human spirits on their way to a higher existence."

"Not precisely," Cyma said, hoping she could invent well enough to keep Myers from dismissing her entirely. What she was about to say was pure balderdash; the point was to see what *he* said in response. "There is, after all, a long-standing association in folklore between faeries and the spirits of the dead. Is it possible that the spiritual realm—the astral plane, as the theosophists would have it—is in fact shared by those two classes of being? And when a medium is deceived, it is by a creature we might in other contexts term a 'faerie'?"

She was watching very closely as she said it, recording every movement of eye and brow and mouth. Goblins *did* sometimes deceive mediums, it was true, but only as an occasional lark. Myers pursed his lips, then shook his head. "I confess, I've never given the possibility much thought. It is an interesting theory, at least."

Not a single twitch, not the slightest spark of recognition.

He doesn't remember.

Myers *had* given the possibility some thought, in the days before Cyma handed him over to Nadrett. It was why her master had wanted the man, though what purpose such an erroneous idea could serve, she didn't know. Did Nadrett think this "spiritual realm" or "astral plane" was Faerie itself? Or did he think to extend his control over such a place?

That question was far too dangerous for Cyma to allow it to remain in her mind. Myers had considered such things, and now did not remember; that meant Nadrett had taken the memory from his mind. Just like he'd done to Dead Rick, though in this case, the removal appeared more precise. Myers was not broken like the skriker.

Perhaps because Nadrett still had use for Myers's knowledge. After all, he'd let the man walk free, back to his friends in the Society for Psychical Research.

I should get away from him. Cyma was suddenly cold in a way that had nothing to do with the séance. She murmured something inane when Myers took his leave, going to coax Mrs. Wexford into trying again; after a paralyzed moment of standing where the manifestation had been, she slipped out the door and asked the footman to fetch her a cab.

She was almost free of Nadrett. Not even for Frederic William Henry Myers would she trap herself again.

WHITE LION STREET, ISLINGTON
11 April 1884

Eliza smoothed the bodice of her borrowed dress with nervous hands. "Borrowed" might be the wrong word; Ann Wick didn't know she'd taken it. But the wages she'd saved so far weren't enough to buy a respectable dress—something that wouldn't instantly advertise her as somebody's maid—so she'd sneaked this one from a hook in the room they shared, and changed into it once she was away from Cromwell Road. It wasn't stealing, not when she intended to put it back.

Thus disguised, she was going to attend a meeting of the London Fairy Society.

It was the best she could think of to do. A fortnight of working for the Kitterings had gotten her no further than those few stolen minutes of nosing through Miss Kittering's things; she'd uncovered nothing about faeries, and had no further opportunities to speak to the daughter. So, a month later, she was back where she had been before—but this time, with more preparation.

She would never have dared show her face at the

meeting, except that she knew Louisa Kittering wouldn't be present. Mrs. Kittering had decided to host a dinner party tonight, with the Honourable Mr. Twisleton-Wykeham-Fiennes in attendance. The row between mother and daughter had been audible two floors in either direction, and when Miss Kittering lost, Eliza had gone promptly to Mrs. Fowler with news that her mother was gravely ill. That had sparked a second row, nearly as fierce as the first, for with the missus planning this dinner party, the housekeeper needed every servant on hand. But Eliza was a good deal more stubborn than Miss Kittering, and had generally been a good enough worker that Mrs. Fowler was not eager to sack her; and Eliza had sworn she would quit if she were not permitted to go.

A threat that worked because she came quite close to meaning it. Louisa Kittering did not matter very much at all, except as a connection to her friend, the one she'd met at the previous society meeting. Eliza's time in the Kittering household had failed to show her that woman again, though, or to turn up her name. It was worth risking her position at Cromwell Road to come to Islington, where she had a better chance of seeing the woman again.

Eliza's optimism had been sufficient that she paid for an omnibus fare out to Islington, rather than walking the whole distance. She even looked respectable enough that a gentleman gave up his seat inside the 'bus so she wouldn't have to climb the ladder to the knife-board bench on top. Crammed in between a mother with three squalling children and a clerk who somehow managed to sleep through all the disturbances, she'd felt very pleased with herself . . . until she got to Islington High Street.

Where she had stood for the last five minutes, staring down White Lion Street at the innocent facade of No. 9, trying and failing to convince herself to knock on the door.

The problem was that she still didn't know what to expect inside. How many people would there be, and of what sort? Her skill at lying went as far as pretending to be English, but she'd never masqueraded as anything other than the lower-class woman she was. She did not know how to be a housewife, or a bookish bluestocking—would there even be women in there? Yes, there must; last time there had been Miss Kittering and her unknown friend. But she didn't have the first notion what would go on at such a meeting, whether they would discuss books, or poetry . . .

Or personal encounters with faerie-kind.

She heard a church bell ring the hour. Seven o'clock. The time had come either to go in, or to admit that she was a coward.

For Owen's sake, she could not be a coward. Eliza squared her shoulders, marched down White Lion Street, and rapped the knocker on the door.

It opened almost immediately. No footmen here, and Eliza recognised the signs about the maid's appearance that said she'd hurriedly cleaned herself up for door-opening duties, and would go back to dirtier work as soon as the meeting was underway. Which put Eliza slightly more at ease. Any family that could possibly afford a manservant to answer the door had one; that meant the people here were not so high above her as she'd feared.

The maid prompted her, "Yes?"

She'd been so busy thinking that she hadn't said anything. "Oh! I'm, ah—Elizabeth Baker. I'm here for the meeting?"

"Yes, of course. They're just getting started. If you'll follow me?"

Eliza stood aside in the narrow front hall so the maid could close the door, then followed her up the stairs. *I'm late. I should have known it; nobody went in while I was standing there, like an indecisive fool.*

The house was old and a little shabby, the linoleum scratched in places, the stair railing well worn by countless hands. Voices came muffled through a door on the first floor, which stopped when the maid tapped on it. She waited until she heard a reply, then opened the door. Warm gaslight flooded out, and Eliza had her first proper sight of the members of the London Fairy Society.

There were only seven, but that was enough to crowd the small drawing room, taking up most of the seating. The gentlemen—three of them—stood as she came in, and Eliza dropped into a curtsy before realizing it made her look like a servant. "I'm sorry, I know I've come late—is this the Fairy Society?"

She straightened, and found herself staring at Louisa Kittering.

The young woman was seated on a chair by the

windows, looking like the very picture of horrified surprise. Eliza feared she mirrored that expression, but her months of lying had been good practice; when she wrenched her gaze away, she saw only mild curiosity in the others' faces, and nobody was looking between the two of them as if waiting for an explanation.

The remainder were a trio of gentlemen; a pair of middle-aged women who were very obviously sisters; and an elderly woman by the hearth, who answered Eliza. "Yes, do come in—it's no trouble; we haven't yet stopped ourselves chattering long enough to do anything like business. What is your name, child?"

Doubt paralyzed her tongue for an instant. Miss Kittering would expect her to say White; the maid had already heard Baker. *You'll already have to do something about Miss Kittering. Don't connect yourself to Cromwell Road.* "Elizabeth Baker," she said, and made herself lift her eyes to the woman's face. It was a friendly countenance, wrinkled by many smiles—entirely unlike Mrs. Kittering or Mrs. Fowler, whose forbidding expressions had trained her very thoroughly to keep her gaze cast down.

"Welcome, Mrs. Baker—or is it Miss? Miss Baker. I am Mrs. Chase, and as this is my house, so far I have been the de facto president of our little society, though we have not yet gone so far as to establish rules or any kind of official leadership. We are quite informal here, you see."

Eliza was profoundly grateful for that informality; she'd already had enough of a fright. Mrs. Chase introduced her to the three gentlemen—Mr. Myers, Mr. Graff, and a Scostman named Macgregor—and to Miss Kittering and the sisters, a pair of spinsters named Goodemeade. "Please, have a seat," the woman said, after all the greetings were done.

The furniture was mismatched in a way no elegant woman would ever have permitted, a mix of heavy new chairs with thick padding and older, sticklike pieces. Mr. Myers surrendered one of the former to Eliza, startling her; she was more accustomed to gentlemen ignoring or making crude suggestions to her. She settled into it, trying not to fidget with the skirt of Ann Wick's dress. Mrs. Chase said, "You have an interest in fairies?"

"Oh, yes," Eliza answered. She glanced around as she said it, partly to see if the others read her heartfelt tone as enthusiasm, but mostly to see what Louisa Kittering was doing. The young woman's face had settled like stone. It didn't look like anger, though, or the self-righteous indignation of a girl who had caught her maid in a lie; it looked more like confusion and dread.

Then understanding came, and Eliza fought not to laugh. *I'm not the one who's been caught out*—she *is!*

Mrs. Kittering had forbidden her daughter to go out tonight, because of the dinner party. She was utterly inflexible upon that point. It therefore followed that Miss Kittering must have sneaked out of the house. Her supposed plan for the evening had been to attend a theatrical performance with a friend . . . but Eliza's presence made it seem as if the truth had been discovered. In which case she had to be wondering where her mother was, and why Eliza had not seized her by the ear to drag her home.

Let her chew upon that for a while. A plan was taking shape in Eliza's mind, but it could not be put in motion until the meeting ended.

Which left her with her original purpose in coming. She was disappointed not to see the other woman, Miss Kittering's friend, who had claimed to know more of faeries than the others here. Still, there might be something of value to learn.

Mrs. Chase had gone on talking, words Eliza only half heard; something about there being a great diversity of interests present. "Mr. Graff, you had indicated that you wished to speak upon—anthropology, was it?"

He rose at her words, tucking his thumbs into the pockets of his waistcoat. "Yes, anthropology. Ladies, gentlemen—I recently returned from missionary work in Africa, and as a result have taken quite an interest in the superstitions of primitive peoples. As some of you may be aware, this often takes the form of animism, totemism, and similar beliefs. Well, the chaps I was dealing with were full of such things, always talking about lion-men or what have you, and it occurred to me that what they were describing were not so different from our own English fairies. More primitive, of course—a reflection of their own lesser development—but the kinship can be seen.

"Visiting places of that sort . . . it's like looking back into our own, less civilised past. And so I have begun to wonder whether the fairy beliefs we have here might not be a relic of similar practices back in pagan days."

Eliza did not like him in the slightest. He did not look at anyone as he spoke, but rather directed his gaze above their heads, which had the effect of lifting his nose to an arrogant angle. She liked him even less when he chose an example to illustrate his point. "Take the legends—very common in the north of England, but found elsewhere as well—of supernatural black dogs. We know that the dog was an object of veneration for ancient Celtic peoples; think of Cú Chulainn, the Hound of Culann. Might there not have been a dog cult in northern England? Perhaps a funerary cult, given the association of such phantasms with death; or perhaps they were warriors, garbing themselves as dogs before going into battle. Then we might very easily explain the legends as folk memory, preserving a faint, distorted echo of past truths."

Her one comfort, upon hearing those words, was that nobody else in the room looked terribly impressed, either. One of the Goodemeade sisters made a faintly outraged noise at the word *distorted;* the other laid a quelling hand on her knee.

There was no one to quell Eliza. "What of people who have *seen* those black dogs?" she asked.

His mustaches did not hide his condescending smile. "What have they seen? Supernatural creatures? Or merely some neighbour's black-furred mongrel, that startled them along a lonely road at night?"

"If I may," Macgregor said. The habits of deference made Eliza hesitate, forgetting that she had a right to speak here, and by the time she found her tongue again, the Scotsman had already begun to air his own theory. "I agree that we must look to the past for explanations—but not to superstition. As an educated man, Mr. Graff, you must of course be familiar with Darwin's theory of evolution . . ."

As he began outlining a place for fairies in that scheme, Eliza sank back in disgust. If these people believed in evolution, there was no point in wasting her time listening to them. *No wonder that other woman took Miss Kittering aside.* The young woman was observing all this with condescending amusement, while Mrs. Chase exchanged a look with the Goodemeade sisters, who shook their heads. Eliza wished she could leave the meeting, without drawing unwanted attention.

Mr. Myers finally broke in, interrupting the increasingly heated argument between Graff and Macgregor. "Gentlemen, you are debating theory, without evidence. Would it not be more productive to ask ourselves what *proof* we have of fairies?"

Graff's exhalation of annoyance ruffled his mustaches. "What proof do you think exists?"

"People who have seen them," Eliza said again. Then she hesitated. Now was the moment to tell her own story—

But what would it gain? Graff wouldn't listen to her; she could tell that just by looking at him. Her suspicion was confirmed when Myers said, "Scholars of folklore have been collecting such stories for some time. Indeed, some claim to have seen fairies themselves, particularly in Ireland—"

"Ireland! Bah!" Graff dismissed that with a contemptuous wave of his hand. "Superstitious peasants, the lot of them, and probably drunk to boot."

Myers stiffened, giving him a very cold look. "As a scholar, sir, I should look first to the evidence they present, rather than the nationality of those who present it."

He, at least, might listen if Eliza spoke. But it was clear from what Myers said, continuing his argument with Graff and Macgregor, that he had no personal experience of faeries himself. He could not help her. Glancing across to the silent Miss Kittering, Eliza saw her own frustration mirrored. *Of course; she probably came here hoping to meet her friend. Now she's gone and disobeyed her mother—and been caught out—and all she has to show for it is a stupid argument among men who love the sound of their own voices.*

Mrs. Chase finally managed to calm them into something like a truce, once it became obvious that neither of the men was going to sway the others. Unfortunately, she then turned her attention to Eliza. "So, Miss Baker. We have already heard from Mr. Graff, who is the other newcomer among us, but you have been rather quiet. Tell us, what is your interest in fairies?"

I want to know how to catch one and wring his neck. Eliza pasted a vague smile onto her face, covering the anger beneath. "Oh," she said, "I've always found the stories very interesting—the Irish ones particularly," she added, as a jab at Graff. He snorted.

Mrs. Chase, however, brightened. "Indeed? Then surely you've read the works of Lady Wilde?" Eliza was forced to shake her head. "Oh, but you *must*—she's quite a famous poet, really, under the name of 'Speranza,' and she has been publishing articles based on her late husband's research. Here, I should have one on hand—"

One of the Goodemeade sisters rose on the old woman's behalf and found it, and they passed the remainder of the time in listening to Mrs. Chase read. Only Mr. Myers seemed to pay much attention, though, and so the meeting straggled to an unhappy close.

Eliza rose promptly from her chair, intending to go straight over to Miss Kittering. She no longer cared whether anyone guessed they already knew each other. Before she could take a step, though, the Miss Goodemeades appeared in front of her. "We didn't have a chance to welcome you properly before the meeting, but we wanted to say we're very happy you came. Did you see the advertisement we placed in the newspaper? Or did a friend tell you about our society?"

"The newspaper," Eliza said, distracted. Miss Kittering was speaking to Mr. Myers, but she couldn't hear what the young woman was saying.

"You see?" Miss Goodemeade said to her sister. "I *told* you that would catch the right kind of eyes! Well, some of the right kind; I fear we've pulled in a few we might have done without." This last was said in a lower tone, easily hidden under the argument Graff and Macgregor had resumed.

"But we're very glad to have you," the sister said. The two women were almost impossible to tell apart: both short, both honey haired and honey eyed, in dresses of brightly printed cotton. Only the roses on one and the daisies on the other kept them from being identical; unfortunately, Eliza had forgotten their given names. "In fact, we should like to invite you to join us at another meeting—more a private circle of friends, really, that—"

Eliza risked a glance over at Miss Kittering and Mr. Myers, only to find Mrs. Chase had taken the fellow aside into private conversation, and the drawing room door was swinging shut behind Miss Kittering.

Her heart leapt into her mouth. If she were to salvage anything from the wreck of this evening—and keep it from getting any worse—she could not let the young woman go off without her!

"I'm sorry," she said, cutting Miss Goodemeade off. "I'm afraid I have to go."

"Oh, you mustn't," the daisy Goodemeade said, trying to catch her hand.

Eliza pulled away, making some half-coherent excuse, not caring anymore that she was catching people's attention. "At least come back next month—" the rose Goodemeade said.

"Yes, certainly," Eliza lied; anything to get away without being inexcusably rude. *Why do I even care? I've no reason to see these people again.* But she was reluctant to hurt the sisters' feelings, when they obviously meant well. "I'm very sorry—I've stayed too long already—goodbye." She flung herself out to the staircase.

Even with her haste, those words proved prophetic. When she got downstairs, Miss Kittering was gone, and the maid nowhere in sight. Eliza hurried out into the street, but it was no use; the gaslight showed her a variety of people and vehicles, but not her quarry. "Stupid girl," Eliza muttered. "You should have tried to talk to me, bribe me to lie—" Instead, she'd run. To her home? If not there, then Eliza didn't have the first guess where she'd gone; so Cromwell Road it was.

If she hurried, she might even be able to stop Miss Kittering from doing anything else stupid. The Angel Inn was just on the corner, a few doors down, with cabs standing outside. Cursing the expense, and the optimism that had made her waste money on an omnibus earlier, Eliza went to hire a driver, and try to race Miss Kittering home.

CROMWELL ROAD, SOUTH KENSINGTON

11 April 1884

She saw no one outside when she arrived, and hesitated for just an instant, wondering. Had Miss Kittering gone elsewhere? If she'd come here, and already gone inside, there was nothing Eliza could do for her; by now she'd certainly been caught.

Then she saw a furtive shape dodging from shadow to gaslight shadow, toward the servants' entrance on Queensberry Place.

Eliza couldn't be both fast and quiet. She ran, and the furtive shape did, too, throwing herself down the steps to the area. Eliza caught her halfway down, with a grip hard enough to bruise.

Miss Kittering drew breath to scream, until Eliza clapped her other hand over the young lady's mouth. "Hush, you stupid girl," she hissed, half her attention on the servants' door. "Unless you want them out here, before you've had a chance to save yourself from what's waiting inside."

The struggling stilled. When Eliza was sure Miss Kittering had calmed, she lifted her hand, and the young lady turned to face her.

Standing on a higher step put her at eye level with Miss Kittering, who licked her lips and tried to regain a measure of dignity. "What do you think you're doing, grabbing me like that? You have no right to treat me this way; I'll—"

Her voice was far too loud; the basement would be full of servants, swarming like ants in a kicked hill, and if Eliza didn't stop her Miss Kittering would bring them all out to investigate. But she held an advantage: whatever secrets Miss Kittering might keep, she was a sheltered soul. Eliza, on the other hand, was a daughter of London's Irish slums. Brendan Hennessy, a petty criminal she'd known in Whitechapel, had once told her people weren't much different from dogs: the one who came out on top wasn't necessarily the bigger or the stronger, but the one who growled louder, bit harder, and scared the other into submission.

Brendan Hennessy ended up hanged in Newgate for his growling and biting, and maybe Eliza would end the same way. But it was worth the risk, for Owen's sake.

She seized hold of Miss Kittering's shoulders, ignoring the young lady's indignant squeak. "You'll close your mouth and listen, you will. You've gone and sneaked out, without your mother's permission, and her with no idea why . . . sure I could spin her such a tale, it would turn her hair white. A spiritualist meeting, it could be—even a secret lover—"

Miss Kittering went even more rigid. She might not want to marry that baron's son, but if she lost her reputation, she'd be lucky to get any marriage at all.

"Or," Eliza went on, before the girl could find her tongue, "I could be telling her something more respectable. It won't save you the thrashing, and that's the truth of it—but 'tis better than you'd have otherwise."

The girl licked her lips again. She had no ability to hide her nerves; how had she evaded her mother's control for this long? "Why . . . why would you do that?"

Thank Heaven for sheltered idiots, who don't see a chance for power when it's in their hands. But Miss Kittering didn't know Eliza had told her own lies tonight; she was entirely vulnerable.

Eliza showed her teeth in a smile, and not a friendly one. "Because you'll be helping me in return, you will. I—"

She didn't get a chance to say anything more. The

servants' door opened to reveal Ann Wick, bracing a bin of refuse against her hip. The housemaid gaped at them, and Eliza seized Miss Kittering's arm once more, stepping behind the young woman to hide Ann's borrowed dress. With an effort, she summoned something more like her usual false demeanour. "She followed me," Eliza said in a brisk tone, dragging the girl down the stairs. "Heard my mum was sick, and wanted to help; but as soon as she came, I turned around and marched her right home again. We shouldn't bother Mrs. Kittering, I think, Mrs. Fowler can tell me what to do with the silly chit."

Miss Kittering, blessedly, had the sense to keep her mouth shut.

THE GOBLIN MARKET, ONYX HALL
11 April 1884

Under the cool glow of a faerie light, the *carte de visite* in front of Dead Rick assumed an otherworldly aura. Who the stern-faced woman depicted in it was, he had no idea; it didn't much matter. Her image fascinated him. The photograph was shoddy work, nothing to the sharp detail of a daguerreotype, but that very vagueness allowed him to spin a hundred stories about her. She was an upper-class wife, devoting all her time to the pressing question of what pattern her china should bear. She was a suffragist, campaigning to extend the vote to women. She was a frustrated bluestocking, more interested in books than a lady's pursuits.

All he knew of her was that she was real: that she had lived, and sat for a photographer's portrait, and given the resulting cards to her friends.

Proof of her existence. *I should be lucky to leave so much behind.*

The stone of his hidden refuge trembled faintly beneath him. A train, perhaps, or just one of the periodic tremors that shook the Onyx Hall. Dead Rick held his breath, waiting to see if it would grow stronger, but after a few seconds it subsided. As if the tremor had been a bell at the door, the voice spoke.

"What have you learned?"

Dead Rick stuffed the *carte de visite* into his waistcoat pocket and pushed his back against the wall. Even though he'd summoned the stranger, burying the bone near the pavilion in the old garden, it still made him uneasy to have anyone else sharing this space. Even if that someone else was just words in the air.

He said, "I knows a few things. But afore I go telling you anything, I need some proof."

"Proof of what?"

"That you can get my memories back."

The silence that followed sounded a great deal like a suppressed sigh. He could hear the stranger's irritation echoing in his next words. "Haven't we been through this before?"

"You told me something I didn't know, and I think it's true. But there's lots of ways you might 'ave learned it. That don't mean you can get my memories back. Do you know where Nadrett keeps them?" Dead Rick's crossed arms were pressing in hard enough to make his ribs hurt. "Do you even know what they *look* like?"

It would be so easy for someone to play him. Dead Rick almost wished the stranger had never come to offer him hope; it made it that much harder to endure his life under Nadrett's heel. Hope kept him from sinking into the blinding embrace of despair. It meant he had to keep fighting. But he couldn't make himself give it up, and anybody who knew that could use it to lure him into damn near anything.

The voice was silent for long enough that Dead Rick wondered if it had been a bluff after all, and so easily called. Then came the answer: "Pieces of glass."

He squeezed his eyes shut, before any tears could escape. It didn't stop his ears, though, and the memory of sharp, shattering sound. When Nadrett wanted to punish Dead Rick, or just to remind him of the chain around his neck, he broke one of the stolen memories. The wisp of light that escaped was too vague for any detail to be made out, but it carried something—not quite a scent—that told Dead Rick it was his own.

Lost forever.

Through his teeth, he asked the question that really mattered. "Do you know 'ow to put them back?"

This time, the hesitation was much briefer. "No."

Dead Rick slammed his hand against the floor, hard enough to bruise. "Then what fucking use are you to me?"

"I can get them away from Nadrett; surely that is some use. And it may be I can help you discover how to return them to their rightful place. Once they are in your possession, many things become possible. Now, do you have anything for *me*?"

The skriker drew a series of breaths, each one deeper than the one before, shoving his knotted emotions out of the way. "You ain't given me nothing yet. I already knowed about the glass, so you tell me something else. Something I've forgotten."

The annoyance was much more distinct now, but Dead Rick didn't care. "Are you going to haggle every time we speak? Never mind; I'm sure I know the answer to that. Very well . . . something you've forgotten." The stranger paused, then said, "You were once a faithful Queen's man."

It wasn't at all what he'd expected. Lune, the Queen of the Onyx Court: he didn't remember her, but he'd heard stories, even in the seven short years since his mind was wiped clean. How she'd won her throne from the cruel Queen Invidiana, centuries past. How she'd battled a Dragon to save London, twice. How she'd struggled to hold the Hall together, in the face of human destruction.

Noble stories, that all ended the same way: *But that was a long time ago*. However great a Queen she'd been in past ages, she was gone now. "Me, a courtier?"

"I never said that. Merely that you served her on several occasions—her, and the Prince of the time. And not because they held your leash, either."

It was like their first meeting, when the stranger had spoken of those mortals as Dead Rick's friends, the boy he'd stolen, and the girl who damned him for it. *A Queen's man.* Against his will, the concept wormed its way under his skin and lodged there, irritating and impossible to ignore. A master—or rather a mistress, and a changing series of masters, the Princes who ruled at her side—more worthy than Nadrett. The stories spoke as much of Lune's flaws as her virtues, but at least she *had* some of the latter. More than he could say of his current master.

"Is that why you're doing this?" Dead Rick asked, the sudden thought dragging him up from the depths of his own mind. "Not the bit where you find a passage to Faerie—the bit where you tear down Nadrett along the way. Is it for 'er sake?"

The voice answered with cold disgust. "No. I do not serve the Queen."

Which ruled out him being the Prince, even if Dead Rick believed that cockney sod could speak like such a gentleman. "So all you're after is profit."

"Is that a problem?" the voice asked, calmly.

His immediate reaction was suspicion—but that was just reflex, born of living in the Goblin Market. *Once I've got my memories, I can do whatever I like. If I stay, this bastard* might *demand somebody's firstborn child in payment for going to Faerie . . . but I* know *Nadrett would. And so long as there's two of them selling, there's a way to pit them against each other.*

Many things became possible, once he had his memories back.

"Not a problem," Dead Rick said, "*if* you can give me

some proof you ain't just spinning lies."

The reply had the unmistakable sound of being delivered through clenched teeth. "More damned haggling. What proof do you want? The Queen, on a platter?"

"If you know where she went, sure—but I was thinking of somebody who knowed me. Before."

"That will be dangerous," the voice pointed out. "Nadrett has gone to some effort to cut you off from the life you had before. If he discovers you talking to an old friend, I will not be blamed for the consequences."

"I don't care."

A note of amusement. "So the dog has begun to recover the pride he once had. If you believe I will be patient until you have had your confirmation, you are wrong; tell me what you know, and I will make arrangements."

He was unlikely to get anything better. Dead Rick slid one hand into his waistcoat pocket, and pulled out the *carte de visite*. The stranger couldn't see him, but he held it up anyway, studying the woman's face once more. "Rewdan was bringing compounds in for Nadrett. Faerie chemicals, not the mortal kind. I asked around, and found out they're used for photography."

"Photography?"

He'd been hoping the stranger might see meaning in that, but judging by the surprise in the voice, the hidden speaker was as confused as Dead Rick. "So they say. I guess there's faerie cameras?"

"In the Galenic Academy, yes . . . mortal techniques

cannot capture our images properly. Issues of light." Dead Rick wished, not for the first time, that he could see his ally's face; he would have dearly loved to see the stranger's expression as he paused for thought. "Are you certain this has something to do with a passage to Faerie?"

Not in the slightest—but he wasn't stupid enough to admit it. "I ain't 'eard about nothing else."

As if musing to himself, the voice said, "Some sort of optical trick, perhaps? . . . I will look into it. Can you get anything else from Rewdan?"

"Not since Nadrett shot 'im."

"Ah. Then we will have to proceed on our own. What were the compounds?" Dead Rick named them, and the voice made a thoughtful noise. Then he said, "I can't keep sending you to the pavilion; someone will notice. Next time, leave a bone near the monument to past Princes, at the other end of the garden. And if I need to contact you, I will put my own sign there, by the flame that burns in its base. A spill of ashes. Keep watch for it."

Dead Rick nodded, then remembered. "And you get me somebody who knowed me."

"Yes, yes, I haven't forgotten."

Again, no farewell. The voice simply fell silent, and did not speak again. Dead Rick leaned his head back against the stone and thought, *Good. Because while you look into this photography business, I'll be looking into* you.

* * *

CROMWELL ROAD, SOUTH KENSINGTON
12 April 1884

Tongue stuck firmly in the gap in her teeth, Eliza bent over the brush in her hands, giving the floor of the water closet the hastiest scrub she could without risking Mrs. Fowler thrashing her for it later. The housekeeper was out this morning, which meant everyone was being decidedly slower about their work—everyone but Eliza, who was determined to finish quickly so she could sneak off and talk to Louisa Kittering.

Miss Kittering had been confined to her room, with only the barest contact permitted. Ann handed trays of bread and tea through the door, and Eliza went in long enough to clear away cinders from the grate, fill the lamps with paraffin, and gather up dirty laundry, but all of this happened under Mrs. Fowler's disapproving eye. She'd had no chance to finish the conversation they'd begun outside the house, after the London Fairy Society meeting.

That was good enough. Eliza sloshed a bit of clean water from the sink to rinse the floor, mopped it up, wiped the tiles dry, and hurried to the servants' stair. If she was quick about returning her supplies to the basement, she could be out again before anyone thought to question what she was doing next.

A lovely and plausible hope that was dashed when she reached the bottom of the stairs. Almost every single maid and footman in the house was gathered there, gawping and whispering amongst themselves.

Apprehension gripped Eliza's heart. Had Miss Kittering done something else foolish? *If she's gotten herself banished to the countryside . . .*

It might not be Miss Kittering at all. But a heavy dread had settled upon Eliza, making her go forward, to where Ann Wick peered up at the ceiling as if she could see or hear anything from the floors above. "What is it, Ann?"

Sarah, the little scullery maid, answered before anyone else could, her face bright with curiosity. "A police constable! Come to talk to Mr. Kittering. I wonder if—"

"You shut your mouth," Ann said, interrupting her. "It isn't our place to be speculating about the master's affairs." But there was no conviction behind it, and she kept looking up.

The word *police* had made Eliza's skin jump, as if she'd been splashed with cold water. "Scotland Yard sent a man *here*?"

"Nothing to fear," Ned Sayers told her, sidling close. "If it's burglars they're worried about, we'll deal with that right quick. But should you need comforting—"

Eliza tried to sidle away without being obvious, and was helped by Mr. Warren, the butler, who cuffed him sharply. " 'Comforting' is not what Mr. Kittering pays you for, Sayers. Move along, everyone; Ann is right. This is none of our affair. What would people say, if they saw us hovering about here, like prying little mice? Back to work, the lot of you."

Grumbling and speculating, the clump of people began

to break up. Eliza moved away from the stairs without paying the slightest scrap of attention to where she was going. Her heart was beating double-quick. *Scotland Yard, here at Cromwell Road.* It might be nothing—burglars, or some difficulty with Mr. Kittering's business, or a thousand other things that weren't her concern.

Or it might be a Special Branch man, asking after an Irishwoman with black hair and hazel eyes, answering to Elizabeth O'Malley. Or even a young woman matching that description, without the name and the accent.

I must find out. Her mind began to work properly once more, like a cart getting traction in deep mud. She followed Cook and Sarah back to the kitchen, then stepped into the scullery, where she changed out her mop and bucket for a bottle of ox gall, a soft brush, and a rag. Then she hurried upstairs, to the billiards room.

It was, of course, empty. Eliza had already cleaned the grate that morning, and Ann had dusted the pictures and animal trophies; with the Kitterings' three sons already married, and Mr. Kittering more often socializing at his club, the room saw only occasional use. Mrs. Kittering would never set foot in such a masculine domain—and besides, at present she was busy answering letters in her boudoir, enjoying her last few minutes of ignorance before someone came to tell her of the damage her family's respectability was taking from the constable in the house. Louisa was still shut up in her room, and Eliza should have taken advantage of that . . . but first she had to know what the constable was doing here. Talking to Louisa would do her no good at all if she went to prison ten minutes later.

She dug a small fragment out of the coal scuttle, then went on silent feet to the room's other door—the one adjoining Mr. Kittering's library.

There Eliza dropped the coal onto the carpet and ground it in with a merciless heel. It left a gratifyingly black smear. She pocketed what remained of the fragment, then knelt and virtuously began to clean the stain away, every scrap of her attention bent upon the voices coming through the door.

"I fail to see what concern this is of mine," Mr. Kittering said.

Muffled though it was by the door, the peeler's reply made her spill too much ox gall over the stain. "'Tis a matter of general safety, sir. Sure ye all will rest better once we catch these fellows and get them locked away."

Spoken in the clear accents of western Ireland, undiluted by a childhood in London. A great many constables came from Irish stock—and almost every last member of the Special Irish Branch.

She wanted to believe this man was the ordinary sort of constable, but couldn't lie to herself that convincingly. Eliza bit her lip and forced herself to continue working. Mr. Kittering said, "We certainly would be pleased to see Scotland Yard do its job. But what I do not understand is why you're sniffing around South Kensington. This is a respectable neighbourhood; we have no Irish here."

"Not even servants, sir?"

The vulgarity of Mr. Kittering's reply would have given his wife the vapours. "Shiftless, filthy lot—kept an Irish bootboy, once, and he repaid us by stealing. Men like you, Sergeant Quinn, are a credit to your race, but regrettably rare. The rest are good enough for simple labour, nothing more."

"I understand, sir."

Eliza tasted blood, and realised her teeth were clenched hard on both her lips, as if nailing them shut to prevent any sound escaping. *Aye, we're good enough for my father to lose an arm digging your damned railways—good enough to make your clothes for pennies a day and pick through your sewers for lost rubbish to sell—but no more than that. And if we starve, or our children die of disease, then surely that's God's hand at work, keeping the vermin in check. Sometimes I wish the Fenians* would *blow the bloody lot of ye straight to Hell.*

With thoughts like that possessing her mind, she heard little of what Quinn said next—until she was broken out of her distraction by the word "Whitechapel."

"Most of the men involved are American Irish," Quinn went on, while Eliza cursed herself and wondered what she'd missed. " 'Tis fair certain we are they're getting their dynamite from the United States—possibly routing it through France. But they have allies here in London, and we think one of them has come to South Kensington."

"Well, you won't find any such criminals in *our* household, I assure you."

With the same neutral politeness he'd been using all

conversation, the constable said, "I've been asked to check all the households, sir; it's no reflection on you. If you do learn anything, though, don't hesitate to say. You can write to me at the Special Branch offices in Scotland Yard, or to Chief Inspector Williamson, who's overseeing these investigations. You may be sure we'll be discreet."

"I doubt I shall," Mr. Kittering said, with monumental disdain, "but very well. Carry on with the good work, Sergeant Quinn."

"Thank you, sir."

The stain was only half dealt with. Eliza stared at it, trying to will herself to clean the rest away. Mr. Kittering's words had left a bitter taste in her mouth. What did she care if these rich toffs had a smear on their expensive Turkish carpet? The entire room disgusted her: all this space, dedicated to *billiards,* when it was more than Mrs. Darragh and her daughter had for living in. And how many Whitechapel beggars could have been fed on the money that instead went for Chinese silk curtains and Moorish lamps?

Filled with that fury, Eliza snatched up her rag and left the stain where it was, soaked in gall. She almost stormed out the billiards room door, but caught herself at the last instant; although the constable was gone, she could hear Mr. Kittering on the landing, speaking quietly with the butler, Mr. Warren. She waited until the master went upstairs, and Mr. Warren down to the ground floor. Then she slipped through to the servants' staircase. There would be no going up to talk to Louisa, not right now. Not with Mr. and Mrs.

Kittering above, discussing the untrustworthy Irish.

She wondered if she should run. If Special Branch had followed her this far . . . they must have caught wind of her in Whitechapel, when she called in her favours there. But no, she couldn't leave, not when she had such a perfect chance to make Louisa Kittering talk!

Eliza slipped her hand into her pocket, feeling the tattered old photograph there. For Owen's sake, she had to be brave. As soon as she learned what Miss Kittering knew, she could run again. Hide under a different name, hunt the faeries, get Owen back; once that was done, she could do anything. Even leave London, if she had to—though that would be like carving out her own heart, to abandon the only home she'd ever known.

She just had to wait a little longer. *You're not Eliza O'Malley,* she told herself, straightening her apron and heading for the servants' stair. *You're not even Elizabeth White. You're Hannah, a sorry replacement for the only good maid Mrs. Kittering ever had. Eliza O'Malley would run, and that sergeant would notice. You'll stay, and be patient, and God willing, get what you want.*

THE GOBLIN MARKET, ONYX HALL

12 April 1884

Given enough time, Dead Rick could track just about anyone through the Goblin Market. But that was if he knew who he was hunting. His current question was one his nose couldn't answer for him: who he was working for.

The obvious suspects were the other powers in the Goblin Market, the fae who challenged Nadrett for control. There were three of any importance: Lacca, Valentin Aspell, and a Welsh gwyllion whose name nobody could pronounce, so they just called him Hardface. Any of the three would leap at the chance to steal Nadrett's idea out from under him.

None of them, however, sounded like the voice that spoke from the air. That didn't necessarily mean much; he could tell the stranger was making an some effort to disguise his speech. Lacca could lower her voice, Hardface could hide his Welsh accent, Aspell could discard the oily contempt that dripped from his every word. There were other reasons to set them aside, though. Aspell wouldn't need Dead Rick's help for something like this; he had plenty of his own spies. Lacca didn't have the subtlety for it; she would just shoot Nadrett and be done with it. Hardface *did* have the subtlety, but he'd rather cut off his right arm than ask Dead Rick for help, ever since the skriker had chased him into the sewers six years ago.

It didn't have to be someone at the top. If there *was* some way to make a passage to Faerie, control of it would be enough to make anybody a king.

Which might be enough to tempt Charcoal Eddie. The shape-changing puck worked for Nadrett, but believed he could rule the Goblin Market better than anyone if he only got the chance. Creeping about once more in dog form, Dead Rick found Eddie near a busy crossroads of the Market, drinking and boasting to his mates about his exploits this All Hallows' Eve past. "Scared three men straight to death," the bird-man said, lowering his voice to what he clearly thought was an impressive growl. "And that's how it should be, you know? *All* the time, not just one night a year! Time was, men were afraid to stick their noses out of doors after dark, for fear we'd snap them off; now they've got lanterns and gaslight and all, and they're more afraid of bashers with truncheons than they are of us. Did you hear about the electrical lights they tried on the Embankment?" Charcoal Eddie spat in disgust. "Ought to smash them, I say. Smash it all."

He got noises of agreement from his listeners, huddled around the old door that served them as a table. But they were only a small knot of goblins and pucks, thoroughly drunk, and none of them with bread enough to do anything about Eddie's ideas. And it seemed awfully complicated, Eddie trying to get Nadrett's secret so he'd be rich enough to cause better trouble in London. The puck wasn't smart enough for that.

Hafdean, on the other hand, was. The hob had managed the Crow's Head since before fae who weren't Dead Rick could remember, and he dealt in information, too—sometimes, but not always, on Aspell's behalf. Spitting out the rank-tasting bone he'd been chewing on for cover, Dead Rick licked an itchy part of his foot instead, considering.

He didn't get far in his thoughts. Through the constant din of the Market, Dead Rick's sharp ears caught a swelling uproar, one passage over.

The skriker leapt to his paws and ran to see, weaving through legs that paused as their owners realised there was trouble nearby. Through a broken doorway, around a corner, down a short hall—and then he stopped, because he'd gotten more than close enough.

The half-dozen fae edging their way toward the fork in the passage were not part of the Market; a glance made that obvious. Three were elf-knights, two men and a woman, in ordinary clothing, but with a fineness that stood out in this ragged place. The others were a mixed trio, a puck, a sprite, and a goblin Dead Rick recognised as the barguest Bonecruncher. Every last one was armed to the teeth—in Bonecruncher's case, quite literally. He snarled at everyone in front of him, eyes flaming red, and pointed his pistols at anything that moved.

The six of them formed a protective ring, weapons facing outward, and in the center of it was a cluster of mortal children. That, in combination with the elf-knights, told Dead Rick everything he needed to know: the Prince had decided to assert his authority over the Onyx Hall, and sent his underlings to carry out a raid.

It happened every once in a while, on no particular schedule. Maybe the Prince heard about some atrocity too big to ignore; maybe he just woke up one day with the burning need to prove he wasn't completely impotent.

Dead Rick always avoided these raids when they happened. Sighing, he turned to go.

And found a gleefully drunk Charcoal Eddie charging straight for the intruders, brandishing his pint glass like a weapon.

The tense stalemate broke instantly. A sound went off like a gun firing underwater, and an enormous web spread itself over Eddie and his friends. One strand at the edge caught Dead Rick's tail; when he pulled away, all the stuck fur ripped free, leaving him with a bald patch. He howled in pain. Then a second time, when a fleeing hob stepped on his paw.

The rushing crowd parted enough for him to see most of the raiding party fleeing down the right-hand passage. Covering their retreat was the sprite, a slender, almost boyish thing, far too skinny for the absurd-looking gun she held. She whirled to shoot someone else, and Dead Rick saw another web cough out of the barrel, expanding as it went.

Then she ran. But her delay had separated her from the group, and when she reached the fork in the passage, she went left.

Dead Rick wasn't even sure why he ran after her. To steal that gun, in the hopes of selling it for bread? To point her back toward her friends, in some misbegotten echo of his former self? Or just for the pleasure of the hunt?

None of those three, he realised when he finally caught up to her, and his brain caught up to him. He'd followed because of the brief flicker in her brow when she saw him, before she turned to shoot the others. A flicker that returned when she whirled to shoot *him,* and saw he was alone. They'd lost the rest of the pursuit.

"Dead Rick?"

He skidded to a halt on the stone, paws splaying wide. *Is this who 'e sent?*

Sounds behind him. They hadn't lost everybody, not yet. Dead Rick twisted upward into man shape, grabbed her by the arm. *I'm a bleeding idiot.* The voice was right; this was dangerous. But he didn't care.

She swallowed her protest as he dragged her toward a broken slab of stone, leaning against a pillar. Gun shoved into the band of her trousers, the sprite scampered up it with more agility than he could manage in following, but they both made it to safety before the hunt came streaming through.

Perched in the crook where the stone vaulted outward to arch across the small chamber, they waited until the place was as close to silent as it would get. This was too near a bad patch of the palace for anyone to live in the room, though there were fae nearby.

The sprite let out the breath she'd been holding, turning it into a quiet laugh. "Blood and Bone—am I glad to see you. I went the wrong way, didn't I?" Dead Rick nodded mutely, trying not to stare at her. "I never did learn my way around this warren. Doesn't help when bits of it keep falling off, either."

The sight of her mesmerised him. *She knows me. I should know 'er.* But there was only blankness in his mind.

When he found his tongue, he whispered, "Who sent you?"

Another quiet laugh. "Who else? Hodge, of course. Heard Aspell had a flock of children he was going to trick into swapping places with changelings, so Hodge sent us to get them out. Well, he sent Peregrin and the rest; I begged to come along. Can't pass up a chance to tweak Aspell's nose."

Hodge. It took a moment for him to recognise the name, so few people used it. *The Prince.* "Nobody else? Nobody told you to come find me?"

She gave him a peculiar look. "Why should they? I thought you'd gone in search of Faerie years ago."

About seven years, he guessed. Or maybe longer; for all he knew, those lost memories included a hundred years away from the Onyx Hall. But he doubted it. "Peregrin. Or the others. Are they trying to do anything about Nadrett?"

The sprite had begun lowering herself down; there really wasn't room for two of them in the crook of the pillar. She paused long enough to make a disgusted face at him. "If only they could. We're fool enough to make the occasional raid, Dead Rick; we're not suicidal."

Those two elf-knights would sound like gentlemen, surely; the puck might be able to pretend. And they served the Prince now, not the missing Queen. Dead Rick pursued the sprite back down to the floor. " 'Eard any rumours about 'im? Maybe that 'e's got some secret plan, some way to get to Faerie?"

She'd been brushing her palms off against her trousers; at his words, her hands froze in midair. Dead Rick cursed his tongue, so ready to wag at the first sign of a friend. "A passage, you mean? One people don't know about?"

Better not to say anything more than he already had. "Something like that."

Her green eyes went very wide. "If something like that existed . . . Ash and Thorn, Dead Rick. Half the Onyx Hall would sell their souls to the devil for a path to Faerie. The half that have to worry about iron. What do you know?"

This wasn't how it was supposed to go. He'd demanded the voice send someone as proof partly because he wanted to learn more about himself, but mostly because it would give him a chance to identify his mysterious ally. So far, he hadn't made much progress with either. And this was a terrible place to be having any kind of conversation, but his refuge lay too far away to take her there, even if he was willing to show that kind of trust.

Dead Rick compromised by jerking his chin toward the far corner of the room. The sprite watched in interest as he pried up a hinged stone in the floor, revealing a tight passage beneath. "It runs right past a bad patch," Dead Rick warned her.

She flashed him a grin before dropping into the hole. "I'm not afraid."

I am. If the bad patch had grown since he last went this way, at best they ended up in another part of the Onyx Hall. At worst, they would find out where the fae who vanished had gone. Dead Rick doubted it was Faerie.

But at least the tunnel was private, even if he nearly

planted his knee in his teeth with every crouched step. "I don't know a lot," he said, edging his way along. How much to tell her? *You were once a faithful Queen's man.* "There's . . . rumours that 'e's got something secret, or 'e's working on it, anyway. Something really big, and I figures it's about selling passage to Faerie. But the only secret thing I've found 'im doing is photography."

"Photography? That sounds more like Academy business, not Market."

"If it 'as anything to do with this, then it's power. And that's Goblin Market business."

"True." For the first time, a grim note entered her voice. But a howling mob hadn't been able to depress her spirits for long; neither did this. More cheerfully, she said, "I still have a lot of friends in the Academy. I can ask."

Dead Rick's heart thumped harder. "Be careful. This gets traced back to me, I'm dead."

Then they were at the other end of the hidden passage, and he directed her in how to open the panel. No way to check if there was anyone on the other side, but not much need; the sprite gagged at the smell of sewage that rushed in. Even hardened goblins avoided this spot. Dead Rick climbed out after her, leaving the panel open behind him, and cocked a thumb to the right. "Go through there, turn left, and you'll see a hole in the stone. It's where the sewers broke through into the palace. Sorry to put you into the mortal world, but I couldn't get you to the other doors, not without you 'aving to shoot 'alf the Market."

"I wouldn't have minded." She pulled the web gun from her trousers, cocked it, then looked at him with a sharpness that took him by surprise. "Are you a prisoner?"

His skin jumped as if she'd pointed the gun at him. In the wake of that shock came shame. *She knowed me before. I don't want 'er to know what I am now.* But he had to say something, and he didn't have time to think of a good lie, even if he could tell it convincingly. "No. Not exactly. It's complicated."

"Come with me. You can explain as we go."

Shattering glass echoed in his memory. *'E'd destroy 'em all.* "I can't. Look, you've got to get out of 'ere, and I've got to get back. Just—if you 'ear anything about Nadrett, can you send word? Without anybody knowing."

Her mouth quirked at the added requirement, but she said, "If it will help you, I'll try."

"It will."

She turned to go, and the question burst out of him. "Who are you?"

It gave away too much. He saw a degree of understanding come into her green eyes, and prayed she wouldn't ask. He couldn't bear having to explain.

She didn't ask. She merely said, "Irrith," and then she was gone.

Irrith. He knew that name; she'd once put Valentin Aspell in prison for a hundred years. *Can't pass up a chance to tweak his nose.*

Had she, too, once been a friend?

Whispering the name to himself, Dead Rick crawled back into the tunnel and closed the door behind him.

THE PRINCE'S COURT, ONYX HALL
12 April 1884

The door swung open dramatically, and Irrith announced, "I'm not dead."

None of those gathered in the Prince's chambers tried to hide their relief. Ever since Sir Peregrin's raiding party had come back without Irrith, Hodge had been pacing, using up energy he could ill afford. It had been a risk, sending them in the first place. In the early years of Hodge's reign, Sir Peregrin and the rest of the Onyx Guard had been eager for any chance to strike at the festering sore known as the Goblin Market. Some of them died there, and others fled when the decay brought on by the opening of Blackfriars and Mansion House stations ate great chunks out of the Hall. The rest soon learned pragmatism: if they stood foot to foot with those thugs, they would lose. Especially if the thugs belonged to Nadrett.

His elf-knights were down to three, Sir Peregrin, Sir Cerenel, and Dame Segraine. To that meager strength he added Bonecruncher, Cuddy, and Irrith. That was all he had, to occasionally peck at the evils of the Goblin Market. Losing even one would be too much.

Without fear to keep his knees strong, Hodge sank into a chair. The furniture was ludicrously elegant for him; the whole room was. The chambers traditionally assigned to the Prince had crumbled a few years before, but Amadea—Lady Chamberlain to a court that had long since vanished—made sure he got the best of what was left. The black stone of the walls was carved at regular intervals with decorative columns, fluted into delicate spirals. The tapestries in between showed grand scenes, their colours unfaded by passing centuries, and the wood of the furnishings was rare, exotic stuff, taken equally from Faerie and the Orient. A little island of quality, in the midst of decay.

Wiping his brow, Hodge said, "Where the 'ell did you go? Bonecruncher 'ere said you was there one minute, gone the next."

"Ran into an old friend," Irrith said, with her usual breezy unconcern. "And I heard a very interesting rumour. If somebody had a passage to Faerie—here, I mean, or somewhere nearby; not off in a foreign country—how much would people pay to use it?"

"It don't exist."

"Pretend for a moment that it did."

The rest of the raiding party looked just like Hodge felt. Skeptical, baffled, hopeful, confused. "Depends on who's buying," Hodge said, after a moment's thought. "The ones as think they can manage 'ere wouldn't go if the price was dear—but the desperate ones, they'd pay anything."

Dame Segraine said, "Oaths, even. All those refugees in the night garden, the Goblin Market—they'd swear fealty to anyone who could promise them safety."

Irrith dropped heavily into a chair. “That’s what I was afraid of. According to my little bird, Nadrett might have something of the sort up his sleeve.”

Cries of dismay burst from the others, rising above their exhaustion. Having any Goblin Market boss in control of a passage to Faerie would be bad enough, but Hodge would choose Hardface or Lacca—maybe even Valentin Aspell—over Nadrett. “How *could* he?” Sir Cerenel asked, in a tone that suggested the answer he wanted to hear was, *He can’t.* “There’s nothing near London, not anymore; we would know if there were. They were destroyed years ago, and it’s not as if we can *make*—”

He cut off abruptly, a sudden expression of hope fading into horror. Peregrin swore, then asked, “Is that even possible?”

“I’ll ask the Academy,” Hodge said, grim and cold. The means to *make* a passage to Faerie . . . that could save any number of lives.

In the right hands.

“I say we avoid the whole problem,” Bonecruncher said, fingering the guns he was never without. His eyes flamed brighter. “Kill that bastard now, like we’ve always wanted to.”

“But if he has something useful—”

“Bonecruncher, if we go after Nadrett we’ll be dead before we get ten steps—”

Hodge thumped the arm of his chair, and got silence. “We ain’t going to kill Nadrett. If ’e does ’ave some way to make a passage, we need to know about it, and get it away from 'im."

"Small chance of that," Peregrin said. "For the same reason we can't kill him. Nadrett's too powerful in the Market."

"And anybody who knows anything is surely sworn not to tell," Segraine added.

A thoughtful smile began to grow through Hodge's weariness. "Maybe not. Remember La Madura?" Their grins said they certainly did; the Spanish nymph had spent no little time in Hodge's bed, before he lost the strength for such exercise, and Sir Adenant escorted her to a safer land than London. "She told me something interesting. So far as she knowed, nobody in 'is gang swears any oaths."

It got him an array of disbelieving looks. Then Irrith's eyes widened, and she said, "Ash and Thorn. He's an oathbreaker?"

They were rare, so far as Hodge knew. Faerie oaths were more than just words; they bound their speakers to obey. Breaking one was all but impossible. Any faerie who managed it found he could no longer swear oaths—*or* receive them. One's word, given to a fellow who didn't keep his own, was meaningless.

Someone else could accept oaths on his behalf—a trusted lieutenant, perhaps—but that would require Nadrett to trust his ally. And he wouldn't want to draw attention to his oathbroken status by such measures, anyway.

Bonecruncher growled low in his throat. "No wonder he's such a ruthless bastard. He's got nothing but fear to keep them in line with."

"Lucky for us, frightened people ain't the same thing

as loyal," Hodge said. "Irrith, who's your little bird with the rumour?"

The sprite frowned, fingers twisting about each other. "I'd . . . rather not say. I think there's something odd going on there."

If it was someone in the Market, "odd" probably meant "bad." But he'd let it pass for now. "Well, can you try to find out more? Maybe nose out somebody in Nadrett's gang that might turn on 'im, since they ain't bound by oaths?"

She nodded, and the bands around the Prince's heart relaxed a notch. Locked carefully away in another room was a stockpile of bread, in preparation for the final collapse. When that day came, he would do his best to ensure that every faerie here had enough to see them clear of London. But if he could give them a path to true safety instead, in Faerie itself . . .

It was a Goblin Market rumour, one of the most untrustworthy things in the world. The hope was too great to ignore, though.

Sighing, Hodge levered himself to his feet. "Get to that, then. The rest of you, let's 'elp Amadea with the kids you brought back."

ST. ANNE'S CHURCH, WHITECHAPEL
13 April 1884

Mrs. Fowler might be a stout evangelical, but no one in the Kittering family itself felt any deep religious sentiment.

The family attended church regularly because it was the respectable thing to do; some of the servants didn't even bother with that much. Eliza herself had never been reliable about going to Mass—mostly because she was either working, or too exhausted from work to bother.

But six months and more away from the familiar ground of her parish created a weight of longing that finally broke her common sense. Special Irish Branch was looking for Fenians in South Kensington; going from there to a Catholic church for Easter Mass was very nearly the stupidest thing Eliza could do, short of walking into Scotland Yard and cursing the peelers out in Irish. She knew that, and she didn't care. She wanted the comforts of the familiar. So she asked for, and received, permission to visit her supposed mother for Easter Sunday, and went back to Whitechapel.

With precautions, of course. She left Cromwell Road before dawn, when the streets of South Kensington were almost completely deserted, and walked along the edge of Hyde Park, up Piccadilly, before plunging into the tangled quarters of Soho. Skirting Seven Dials—as bad a district as Whitechapel, and more dangerous for being unfamiliar to her—she paused in a back alley of Holborn to change into the clothing she'd bought from a secondhand shop, an old-fashioned full-skirted dress with an equally old-fashioned bonnet. It made her look like an old woman, and that suited her very well.

Thus disguised, she took the long way around the City, bending north through Clerkenwell and Shoreditch. Nearly seven miles in total, and the sun was well up when the familar rose window of St. Anne's came into view.

By then she was hardly alone on the street. Nowadays it was lawful to worship in a Catholic church, even if the English wished no one would; and Easter drew out many people who found more frivolous uses for all the other Sundays in the year. It was easy for Eliza to lose herself in the crowd. If there were any Special Branch men doing the same, out of uniform, they shouldn't recognise her in these old clothes. And if they'd managed to follow her from South Kensington, without her noticing, they were better than anyone gave them credit for.

Eliza's throat tightened at the first notes of the choir's entrance chant. The priests began their procession down the aisle, robed in their Easter vestments, followed by the deacons and the altar boys. *That's Biddy McManus's youngest boy,* Eliza thought, seeing that one of them was much shorter than the others—and that was her undoing.

Tears sprang to her eyes, and would not die down again. She fought not to sob such that others would hear, but every time she looked about, another familiar face met her eyes. Thomas O'Rourke, and Sarah Flaherty, and all the Kinsellas; their eldest daughter was carrying a babe in her arms, and Eliza wondered if it was the girl's own—had she finally married Will Cleary?—or if it belonged to some relation of hers.

She had no family to miss; her mother was dead, her father in prison, and of her three siblings who survived childhood, Mary and Bridget had gone to America, and Robert had gone to sea. Coming back now, though, she realised she missed something else very profoundly indeed. Whitechapel was *her* London, from the buildings to the people who lived there, whether they were kin or not. Even the ones she didn't much like seemed dear to her now, because they were like her. They were not the Kitterings, frantically courting respectability, terrified that someone might discover their human flaws, trying to convince even themselves that they had none; the people here drank and laughed and had fights the whole neighbourhood could hear. *I don't remember the last time I screamed my lungs out at anyone,* she thought—and then a hysterical giggle rose in her throat, that she could miss something like *that*.

She choked it down. Father Tooley was among the priests; of them all, he would recognise her if she drew his eye. Instead Eliza lost herself in the comforting patterns of the Mass, kneeling and rising with the rest of the faithful, her voice in the responses only part of a much greater whole. Mrs. Darragh had always made sure she went to Sunday Mass, after Eliza's mother died in the last cholera. The other woman had stopped going, though, after Owen was taken.

I will pray for him, Eliza thought, while Father Kearney read the offertory verse, beginning the liturgy of the Eucharist. *And for myself—strayed lamb that I am.*

Upon her knees as he recited the intercession, Eliza bent her thoughts to Owen, lost somewhere among the faeries.

The Latin phrases washed over her, their sense known even if their specific meaning was not; she knew when the commemoration for the dead came, and her gut clenched. *He isn't dead. I'm sure of it. I couldn't call his ghost.* But she hadn't tried in two years.

It was blasphemous to think of such things, especially on Easter morning. Eliza forced the thought from her head. Hands clasped before her like a pious old woman's, she joined the river of people flowing slowly toward the altar, where the priests had ranged themselves for the Eucharist. Within the depths of her bonnet, no one could see her face as long as she kept her head bowed. But it also meant she could see little of where she was going, and so by the time she realised which direction the eddying movements of the crowd had taken her, it was too late to shift without attracting attention.

She came to the front of her line, and lifted her head to receive the wafer from Father Tooley.

He recognised her immediately, of course. She saw it in the lift of his eyebrows—a brief crack in his well-practiced solemnity. But he would never disrupt Mass just because one errant parishioner had shown up without warning. He murmured "*Corpus Christi*" and placed the wafer on her tongue; Eliza moved on to receive the wine; and no one who was not watching his face at precisely that moment would have noticed anything out of the ordinary. But now Father Tooley knew she was there.

Eliza returned to her pew and knelt, trying to put such

worldly concerns out of her mind. *Lord, protect and watch over Your son Owen Darragh, who was betrayed by one he trusted. Guard him against those unholy spirits that envy us our immortal souls. May he return to the family that loves him and the Church that shelters him—and may he do it* soon. *Help me to save him; 'tis only with Your aid that I have any hope. Amen.*

It brought a measure of peace—but only a measure. After the *De profundis*, her thoughts turned quickly to leaving before anyone else could recognise her. She would have liked to confess her sins, but this was neither the first nor the last Mass the priests would conduct today; Easter brought Catholics popping up like snowdrops after winter, and St. Anne's could not hold them all at once. Confession could wait until later.

But when she turned to go, a hand caught her sleeve. It was Brian McManus, the altar boy she'd spotted before. "If you please, ma'am," he said, "Father Tooley wants to see you."

Brian obviously didn't recognise her. To a boy like him, anyone over the age of twenty was old, and her disguise was as good as gray hair for making her into a crone. But if she refused, he'd remember that, and oh, she should never have come here in the first place.

She had little choice now. Eliza nodded, and let Brian lead her to the sacristy.

Father Tooley waited there alone. Once the door had closed behind her, Eliza lifted her head; there was little point in hiding now. "Eliza O'Malley," the priest said, and she could not tell what he meant by it: Disapproval? Concern? Resignation?

"I'm sorry, Father," she said in a rush, hands bunching up the wool of her old skirt. "I should have confessed before taking communion—not that I've committed any mortal sins, I don't think, but it's been months, and—"

He stopped her confused apology by coming forward and taking her shoulders in his hands. They were big hands, with big knuckles; those and his broken, florid nose attested to a turbulent past before he joined the priesthood. It made him ideal for this parish, where tending to his flock occasionally meant wading into a drunken brawl and separating his parishioners by force. The warmth of his palms was as much a comfort as communion had been—a reminder that, while her father might be in prison, she still had a Father watching over her.

Which he had been doing, even in her absence. "I wanted to warn you," he said. Quietly, as if he didn't want his words carrying beyond the sacristy door. "Fergus Boyle's been spreading trouble."

Bloody Fergus. She stopped herself from saying it out loud. "What do you mean?"

"I mean there's been lads from Special Irish Branch up and down Whitechapel, asking questions. Some of them about you. They think someone here is helping the Fenians, and maybe 'tis you. Maggie Darragh's kept her mouth shut, but I'm not sure Boyle's done the same. I've heard some rumours you'd gone to the West End, looking for some kind of work there. If he knew anything about that, then 'tis a good bet Scotland Yard knows it now, too."

This time the curse did escape her. Father Tooley didn't blink; he'd heard worse before. *I should have known it was Boyle that sent the bobbies after me.* "He doesn't know much," Eliza said, trying to remember what she'd let slip while gathering what she needed to apply for the position in Cromwell Road. Not much, surely, or Sergeant Quinn wouldn't have been going from house to house through all of South Kensington. "Just that I—"

The priest stopped her with a finger on her lips. "We aren't in the confessional," he reminded her. "Don't tell me anything you wouldn't want known, if the police asked. But Eliza . . . if you *have* anything to confess, come back late tonight. I'll wait up for you."

She shook her head, and when he took his hand away, said, "Not like that. I'm no Fenian, Father, and that's the truth of it. I was at Charing Cross, yes, but not because I went there to blow anything up."

"The peelers think there's more trouble planned for the Underground; I got that much from the fellow they sent to question me. If you know anything about it—"

He broke off as her expression changed. Eliza shook her head again, meaning to say that no, she didn't know anything about it—but it was a lie, because she *did* know something. She knew that faeries had helped the men who bombed Charing Cross, and maybe the ones at Praed Street, too; and they must have had a reason for it.

Iron, she thought. She'd always assumed it was just goblin mischief, or maybe sympathy for the Fenian cause; maybe Irish faeries immigrated during the Great Hunger, just as mortal folk did, and wanted to see their homeland free of British rule. If they were striking at the Underground in particular, though . . . but why hadn't they bombed railways before?

It was all speculation. Just as likely the Fenians were the ones planning more Underground trouble, because it was a good place to make people afraid. With their dark tunnels and clouds of choking steam, they were already a little like Hell on earth.

"Eliza," Father Tooley said gently.

She gripped his hands in her own and said, "'Tis all right, Father. If I find out anything, you may be sure I'll not just sit on it. I don't want to see anyone hurt, any more than yourself—or the peelers, for that matter." Hesitantly, her mind ventured past that hazy day when she would have Owen back, and thought about what she could do once he was safe. *Could be I can do more than just help him, and myself. And that might get the Special Branch boys off my back at last.*

He kissed her on the forehead, then blessed her. "But you still need confession," he said, with kind sternness. "If you've spent the last six months as a lily-white saint, then I'm a Methodist."

Lying, spying, threatening Louisa Kittering. No, not a lily-white saint. But it wasn't worth the danger of coming back to a place where the constables knew to look for her. "I will when I can, Father," Eliza promised.

If God granted her prayer, "when" might even be soon.

CROMWELL ROAD, SOUTH KENSINGTON
14 April 1884

When Eliza went up to air out Louisa Kittering's bedding the next morning, Mrs. Fowler was not on guard at the door, and the bedroom itself was empty.

"Mrs. Kittering reckons church yesterday did her some good," Ann Wick said, when Eliza questioned her. "Won't let her out of the house yet, but she's at least free of her room." The other housemaid frowned at Eliza and added, "I don't know what nonsense went on the other night, but you'd best not repeat it, if you know what's good for you. Mrs. Kittering won't just have you beaten; she'll find a way to toss you into prison, she's that vindictive."

It hardly mattered. Louisa Kittering was free—free enough that Eliza could contrive a way to speak with her privately—and that meant her time at Cromwell Road might be drawing to an end at last.

Any further doubts that God had heard her prayer were banished when she carried the ashes out to the bin behind the house. The gardener, Mr. Phillips, caught her before she could go back inside. "Miss Kittering says she wants to see you, girl. In the conservatory."

Eliza thanked him, and added a second, silent thanks to God as she hurried to the conservatory, wiping her hands clean on her apron.

Inside, the glass roof of the structure magnified spring's faint warmth; that and the blooming flowers made the place a miniature Eden. It formed a pretty background for Miss Kittering, who stood in an ivory morning dress in the far corner, fingering the half-opened buds of an Oriental poppy.

They were alone, and as long as no one shouted, the gardener would not hear them outside. Eliza still dipped into a curtsy out of habit, thinking as she did so that this was not the best way to begin following up on a threat. Before she could say anything, though, Miss Kittering spoke.

"You addressed me in a very unacceptable fashion the other night." Her fingers brushed the brilliant tips of the poppy petals, then curled around the stem. "In fact, I would go so far as to say you attempted to blackmail me."

Eliza's breath drew short. *I should have done this sooner. Before she had time to think about it.* But if Miss Kittering thought strength of will alone would be enough to protect her, she was wrong. "Call it whatever you like, miss; it doesn't change anything. I can still tell your mother things that will make life very hard for you, whether they're true or not."

"You can—but you won't." Miss Kittering turned to face her. The young woman's face looked pale and bruised, as if she'd not slept well during her captivity, but above the dark circles her eyes glittered like two brown agates. "Because I heard two interesting things lately. One was gossip about a constable who came to question my father the other day. And the other was your voice that night—sounding very distinctly Irish."

At those words, a lump of lead took the place of Eliza's heart. It felt like her blood had truly stopped flowing, and metal coldness spread throughout her body.

"I may have secrets," Miss Kittering said, a small, triumphant smile curving her lips, "but so do you. And it seems we're each in a position to ruin the other. So *this* is our agreement: that you will say nothing, and neither will I. Out of gratitude for your assistance the other night, I will tell no one of how you threatened me; but that is all the help you will receive. Whatever further price you intended to extort from me, you can give up on it now—for if you attempt to force me, then you will end in prison. However little I inherited from my mother, I can promise you, that is one thing we share."

All Eliza's hope of a moment before had crumbled into ash. Darkness at the edge of her vision made her realise she wasn't breathing; when she gasped air in once more, Miss Kittering's smile deepened. How could she *rejoice*? A boy's life was at stake, maybe his very *soul*—

But Eliza had never told her that. And now it was too late. Miss Kittering might have believed, had she heard the tale sooner . . . but not now, not after Eliza's terrible misstep. Or rather, if she *did* believe, she still would have no reason to help. What did a rich, sheltered young miss from South Kensington care what happened to a poor Irish lad from Whitechapel? She wouldn't give tuppence for Owen, any more than the peelers had when he disappeared.

Eliza refused to give up. Not when she was this close. "Then let me help you," she said, coming forward with her hands raised in supplication. "If you sneak away again, your mother will thrash you within an inch of your life; but what if I helped you hide it? Say you'd gone to call on a friend, or—or close the windows behind you, if it must be at night."

Miss Kittering laughed. She'd pulled the bud off its stem, and was now shredding the delicate, half-formed petals, letting them fall to the ground like drops of bright blood. "I have better allies than *you,* and shan't have to worry about my mother much longer. Now get out of here; I've said what I must, and have no desire to hear anything else you might say."

Eliza went. There was nothing to be gained by staying; she had missed her chance. But like a drunken man in a brawl, the hits she'd taken only made her angrier, and more determined. Louisa Kittering could go to the devil; Eliza O'Malley would rescue her friend.

She went about her duties like the clockwork doll she'd once seen exhibited in Covent Garden, while her mind wrestled her problems toward a solution. The next meeting of the London Fairy Society was in a bit more than a fortnight. Eliza would be there if she had to quit her position to go—but in the meantime, she might as well stay here. Her long vigil in Newgate had produced nothing, and her earnings as a costerwoman were barely enough to keep her fed. Better to stay where there was actual money, and look for another opportunity to get the upper hand over Miss Kittering. Given the young woman's behaviour, surely she'd have one before long.

Failing that, she could at least get a bit of revenge in parting.

Lips peeled back in an expression that might have been mistaken for a grin, Eliza went about her work.

SEWERSIDE

1 May 1884

"Remember Moor Fields?" Gresh asked, spitting tobacco juice onto the floor.

He'd been kind enough to spit in the other direction from Dead Rick, and so the skriker didn't bite his head off for bringing up the painful subject of memory. "What are you talking about?"

"It's May Day, old chap! We ought to be outside, with bonfires and feasts and such. Dancing. Music. Nymphs from nearby villages, willing to spread their legs for anyone. Mortals we'd lured in, that we'd be nice to for once." Gresh spat again, then fingered something out of his mouth that didn't look like tobacco leaf. "But they've gone and built all over it. So we sits 'ere and gets drunk, and it's no different than any other day."

Dead Rick bent his attention to the dirt under his fingernails, as if that could be his excuse for not answering. Fields, and celebrations in them: two more things he didn't remember. He felt like punching Gresh.

But an approaching scent brought him into a wary crouch, not sure whether he was about to growl or show throat. Nadrett swept into the room, trailing a trio of other fae: the fetch Nithen, a thrumpin named Old Gadling, and a sprite Dead Rick didn't recognise, who was lugging an unwieldy leather case. *Showing throat it is.*

"On your feet," Nadrett said. Dead Rick stood, warily, not liking the sense of purpose in his master's posture. "Take these." His hand flicked outward, twice; Gresh and Dead Rick both caught what he threw. "Now come with me."

Dead Rick uncurled his fingers, his nose telling him what he held before his eyes did. *Bread.* Nadrett was taking them outside.

Gresh cackled and threw his piece up into the air, catching it in his mouth as it came down. "Moor Fields!" he said to Dead Rick, chewing. "Think 'e's laid on any nymphs for us?"

Nadrett was far enough ahead by then that he either didn't hear or, more likely, didn't think Gresh worth answering. Nithen did it for him. "Moor Fields has been paved over as Finsbury Circus, idiot, and the only way you're going to see a nymph there is if you get a head full of

Po's opium first. Now shut up."

They were still in the Goblin Market; Nadrett would have ripped the guts out of anyone stupid enough to say anything of their purpose where others could hear. It didn't take Dead Rick long to figure out where his master was leading them, though. There were only four ways out of the Market: two passages to the rest of the Hall, one concealed entrance to Billingsgate above, and the sewers.

His hackles rose as he remembered bringing Irrith here. Had Nadrett learned about that? *Stupid whelp; 'e wouldn't give you bread if 'e 'ad.* But they *did* have bread, which meant they could have gone through the door into Billingsgate without worry. The sewers were mostly used by unprotected fae, willing to brave the filth and the danger of drowning in order to avoid the worst of the iron.

Could be what Nadrett sought was *in* the sewers.

The black stone of the Hall gave way to a brickwork wall, with a hole knocked in it big enough for a faerie to slip through, so long as he wasn't a giant. This wasn't one of the proper entrances, built into the Hall's fabric; it was a break, a spot worn thin and finally through by the cast-iron gas main running alongside the great intercepting sewer. They couldn't keep a glamour over the hole for more than a short while, and mostly only bothered when men came through to inspect the tunnel. Any tosher who spotted the gap and climbed through was fair game for the Market inhabitants on the other side: a small compensation for when the sewer flooded through to their chambers.

Dead Rick helped the unnamed sprite maneuver his case through the hole. "Careful, that's delicate—" the sprite said in a distinct French accent, but swallowed his words when Nadrett spat a warning curse. Dead Rick sniffed, but couldn't smell anything beyond a hint of leather over the sewer.

He dropped through the gap last, into water that came up past his knees. Nadrett produced a hawthorn box from one pocket, and slid aside a disk on one end until a will-o'-the-wisp floated out of the small hole there. It was considerably safer than a lantern, which could ignite the bad air and kill them all, but Dead Rick didn't put good odds on the wisp's survival. Those things couldn't eat bread. Nadrett covered the hole again and put the box away. "Follow me."

It was hard going, in water that deep; the brickwork was slick below his feet, and Nadrett had them walking upstream. Dead Rick hoped it wasn't raining outside, and watched the water in the dim faerie light, ready to flee if he saw it rise. It remained steady, and when they'd gotten some distance away from the Market, Nadrett stopped.

"Tell them," he said to Nithen.

The fetch grinned. In the scant light, he looked even more cadaverous than usual. His voice echoed weirdly over the sound of the water, making his words hard to understand. "So there's stories of a ghost in these sewers. Every year on this night, for a couple of years now. We're going to hunt it down."

Gresh looked confused. "But it ain't All 'Allows' Eve."

Old Gadling smacked him on the back of his head.

Nithen said, "Ghosts can appear at any time. The night they died, for example. This isn't an All Hallows' Eve ride, us sweeping away ghosts with the dawn; we don't want this ghost going anywhere."

"We're going to capture it," Nadrett said.

Dead Rick's eyes went back to the sprite's heavy case, which Gadling had taken control of. The water came nearly to the thrumpin's waist, but he didn't seem to care; the stocky faerie balanced the case on his head and waded through without apparent trouble. There were ways of capturing ghosts, but none of them—so far as Dead Rick knew—required anything so bulky.

He'd see what it was soon enough. "Where's the ghost?"

"That's what you're 'ere to find out," Nadrett said. He let out three more will-o'-the-wisps, then gestured ahead, and Dead Rick saw dark shadows along the walls ahead, openings into the smaller sewers that connected to this main trunk. "Start looking."

That seemed to be directed at him, Gresh, and Nithen. Old Gadling braced his feet and served as a stand while the sprite unlatched the case. And Nadrett, of course, could not be bothered to help. Dead Rick went without complaint. He wanted to be the one to find the ghost—and maybe warn it to flee.

Iron shivered against his senses as he went, not hurting him, but palpably there. They were close to the Underground works, where navvies laboured day and night to build the railway's final extension; no tracks had been laid yet, let alone trains run along them, but there were spades, mattocks, nails for the bracing beams, carts to bring cement and drag the spoil out. The doom of the Onyx Hall, less than a hundred feet away.

Right, left, or straight. Dead Rick went left, climbing the slick bricks to enter the smaller tunnel. The flow here was neither so deep nor so fast, but that was at best a mixed blessing; without the force of the water to scour material away, the passage was much fouler. Dead Rick held his breath as best he could and peered ahead, searching for the telltale flicker of a ghost.

A dead tosher, most like, he thought. People didn't seem to be leaving ghosts as often as they once did. Or maybe ghosts, like fae, were being worn away by the changes in the world. All he knew was that Gresh complained every year about the loss of the old All Hallows' Eve ride—an event he missed far more than May Day in Moor Fields—but the inability of the fae to sweep away weak ghosts each year, as they used to do, hadn't left London neck-deep in phantoms. Maybe some Academy scholar was trying to answer that very question, and Nadrett intended to sell this ghost to him.

Another fork. The side passages were narrower still, barely large enough for Dead Rick to fit through. He didn't want to go down them. But he was a skriker, a death omen, and instinct led him left.

He didn't have to go far. Mist floated in the air ahead, where no mist should be; then it eddied as if turning to face him, and took more solid form.

Dead Rick found himself staring. This was no tosher. Nor was it a recent ghost. He didn't need memories to know that knee breeches had gone out of style generations ago for anybody who wasn't some rich swell's footman. And footmen didn't carry themselves the way this figure did.

It was a young man, slender of build, with the habitual dignity of a gentleman. He seemed relieved to see Dead Rick. "Oh! Thank goodness you found me. I seem to have gotten lost."

Dead Rick was too startled to prevent his will-o'-the-wisp from streaking away. He hadn't put on a glamour; despite his human form, he was clearly a faerie. And yet this ghost seemed completely unsurprised. Was it because he was dead, and therefore accustomed to strange things? Or had he seen fae before?

The ghost glowed faintly, just enough for Dead Rick to make him out. The skriker said, "What do you mean, lost?"

A laugh almost as faint as the light answered him. "I mean that unless I am *very* much mistaken—addled by death, perhaps—I ought to be in the Onyx Hall. But I haven't seen so much as a bit of black stone in four years, now. Am I in a cesspit?"

The quality of the echoes changed. Dead Rick cursed. The wisp hadn't bolted; it had gone to fetch Nadrett. They could take simple commands well enough.

Whoever this ghost was, Dead Rick wasn't inclined to help Nadrett capture him. "Look, you've got to get out of 'ere. Go back to wherever you came from."

"I'm sorry?" The phantom drifted closer, cocking his head to one side as if that would help. "I couldn't quite understand you."

Because Dead Rick had spoken quietly, not wanting the untrustworthy echoes to carry his words to Nadrett. He grimaced and flapped his hands, trying to shoo the ghost back, but the young man peered as if he could not quite see, either. *Of course not, because I ain't glowing.*

Then it was too late. "Out of the way, dog."

When he didn't move, a hand seized the back of his waistcoat and yanked, dropping him onto his arse in the built-up muck. Nadrett shoved him against the sewer wall, then stopped, staring at the ghost. In the light of the gathered wisps, Dead Rick saw a wondering and unpleasant smile twist Nadrett's lips. "Well, well. Ain't *this* an interesting surprise. Evening, milord—out for a walk, are we?"

The ghost frowned. "Do I know you?"

More hands, grabbing Dead Rick under the arms; with slime and shit greasing the passage, Gadling was able to pull him out with only the most casual effort. "If you remember much, you might," Nadrett said. "Though after this long—a century? No, more—I'll be surprised if you do. Don't much matter either way. Chrennois, get to it."

Nadrett moved out of the way. Dead Rick, climbing to his feet, saw the sprite go to the mouth of the ghost's tunnel with something in his hands. A box, about the size of a man's head but wider, with flexible canvas sides that allowed him to extend the front forward. Two silver-rimmed lenses were set into that front board, winking clean brilliance in the dim light.

Wary, but not yet afraid, the ghost said, "What is that?"

Dead Rick answered him silently, held frozen by sudden, half-formed understanding. *It's a camera.*

Lunar caustic, satyr's bile. Nadrett *was* doing something with photography—or rather, this French faerie was, on his behalf. Were they about to open a passage to Faerie? In the filthy sewers of London? Dead Rick tensed, unsure what he was going to do, but ready to do something.

Chrennois peered through an opening in the top of the box, then pulled a lever set into the side. With a most peculiar noise—halfway between a moan and a *huh* of surprise—the ghost vanished.

It didn't even fade; it simply blinked out of existence. The figure of the young man disappeared, leaving behind only faint wisps of phantasmal substance, which dissipated before they could fall to the sludge below. Those weren't even gone yet when Nadrett demanded, "Did it work?"

The sprite shrugged, collapsing the front of his camera back into the rest of the body. "I'll have to develop the plate to be certain. But he went *somewhere;* it seems likely."

"Good."

There was no mistaking the malicious pleasure in Nadrett's voice. For the camera's work, or the capture of that ghost in particular? Maybe both. He'd clearly recognised the young man, and just as clearly didn't like him. That alone was enough to make Dead Rick feel sorry for the unknown phantom. But he couldn't regret the fellow's imprisonment too much, because it had just handed Dead Rick another piece of the puzzle.

Now if only he could figure out what it *meant*.

There was certainly no sign of a passage to Faerie. Were Nadrett and Chrennois planning on using the ghost in some fashion, later on? Or was this a test of the photography concept, a stepping-stone on the way to something greater? Dead Rick had no idea; what little he knew about science came by way of the mortal and faerie inventions that occasionally appeared in the Goblin Market. But the voice, he was willing to bet, would know more.

For one unpleasant moment he thought he'd given his intentions away, when Nadrett turned without warning on him and Gadling. In a voice colder than ice, the master said, "You don't tell nobody about this. Understand? First one to open 'is mouth gets an iron knife through the eye."

"Nobody," Gadling said, and Dead Rick echoed him. Nadrett hadn't guessed his thoughts; it was just the master's usual vicious caution. Probably he had some hold over Gadling, as he did over Dead Rick, more fearsome than even an iron knife. Nadrett wouldn't have brought anyone out here he didn't think he could threaten into silence.

Which meant Gresh and Nithen, too. Half-considering a test of his theory, Dead Rick said, "You want me to go find the other two?"

Nadrett shook his head. "I've got no more use for them tonight. They can find their own way back."

PRAED STREET, PADDINGTON

7 May 1884

The nearness of freedom made Cyma brave.

By tomorrow morning, she would be free of Nadrett's control. No longer dependent upon him for bread or a place within the Onyx Hall; gone where he was unlikely to track her. Free of the Goblin Market, with its grasping, hateful ways. She wasn't like the rest of them, happy to kidnap humans and tear away their voices and dreams, seeing people as little more than things to either be used or feared. Cyma had been a lady once, in a far-off court, and had come to London because she wanted to live closer to the mortal world, to bask in their bright warmth. She adored the city, in ways fae like Nadrett could never understand.

Soon, it would be hers.

Before that happened, though, she was determined to face the demon.

The building to which her steps led her was entirely innocuous. Twenty years of London smoke had darkened its low walls to the same drab, black-streaked shade as everything around it, but Cyma knew it was only her imagination that gave the stone a sinister cast.

The threat came not from the building, but from what lay below.

She hesitated on the corner of the street opposite, nervous hands twirling her parasol. A dozen times she'd thought of doing this, and a dozen times her fear had gotten the better of her. Philosophers might extol the virtue of confronting one's fears, but Cyma was generally happy to live without that particular virtue. Yet morbid curiosity compelled her, every time she passed near one of these innocuous low buildings, so that she wasted precious minutes of her protected time standing on corners like this one, arguing with herself.

This is your last chance to see. Starting tomorrow, you need never fear it again; but you should face it once before that happens. So you will know.

Gripping her parasol like a weapon, Cyma crossed the busy street and went inside.

The morning rush had ended; only two people stood in the queue ahead of her, and they made their purchases quickly. Far too soon, she reached the counter, and stood blinking at a posted sign full of names and numbers.

"Where are you going?" the fellow behind the counter asked, not bothering to hide his bored annoyance with her delay.

She must look like a country lady come to the city for the first time. Cyma sat on the impulse to tell the rude young man that she'd lived in London longer than his grandfather had been alive, and scanned the list of destinations. "Ah—Mansion House, please."

"Single or return?"

Flustered, she asked, "What's the difference?"

He looked as if she'd asked what the difference was between night and day. "Are you coming back to Paddington later today?"

"Oh—no, I only want to go to the City."

"Single, then. First class? That'll be a shilling." He accepted the half-crown she gave him—a real coin for once, not faerie gold—and gave her a shilling and sixpence and a paper ticket in return. "Across the bridge to the opposite platform. First-class carriages are marked by a sign. Thank you."

She was too unnerved by this entire experience to give him the set-down his rudeness deserved. Clutching her coins and ticket, parasol tucked under her arm, Cyma ventured deeper into the Praed Street station.

No amount of telling herself there was absolutely no danger would erase her fear. Iron, iron, everywhere she looked; iron fixtures for the gaslights, iron railings on the stairs, an iron bridge crossing over the iron tracks below. With tithed bread in her stomach, none of it could harm her directly, not unless she flung herself from the bridge as a train approached. But these were not the ordinary trains that had been around for ages; these ran underground.

These were the trains destroying the Onyx Hall.

She crossed the bridge with her breath held, and descended the stairs on the opposite side without touching the rail. People ranged themselves along the platform, with third-class undesirables at the far end; many read newspapers, hardly attending to their surroundings, as if this were nothing out of the ordinary. Cyma took a deep breath, grimacing at the damp, foul air, and tried to mimic their behaviour.

An attempt that failed the moment she heard the rumble of an approaching train. *I will hold my ground,* Cyma thought, even as the platform began to tremble beneath her feet—but her nerve broke the moment the engine came thundering into the station.

It might have been some terrible black beast out of legend, belching steam and smoke, its wheels screeching along the rails like the cry of a great raptor stooping for the kill. An enormous weight of iron, moving as if it were alive, radiating the heat of Hell itself—Cyma's hands ached, and she realised she was pressing them flat against the wall, in the arched brick alcove where she'd instinctively retreated. The only thing preventing her from bolting for the stairs was the irrational, inarguable conviction that if she moved, the creature would *see* her.

"Are you all right, ma'am?"

For an instant, she thought it was Frederic Myers, come to save her from the beast. But no, it was some stranger, a different bearded gentleman from the one she knew; he stood a polite distance away with one hand outstretched in concern. Cyma opened her mouth to answer him, but nothing came out. Frowning, he stepped closer. "Shall I fetch you a doctor?"

"No! No, I—I—"

People were exiting the carriages, and those on the platform taking their places. It all happened in a rush—down at the third-class end some of the men were even shoving each other aside—as if there were no time to lose. The gentleman cast a brief glance over his shoulder, then clearly abandoned his intention to get on the train. "Come, have a seat on this bench, and I will fetch you a drink."

"That won't be necessary," Cyma said, in something like better spirits, though she allowed him to guide her to the bench. "I'm afraid I just came over faint." She clamped her jaw shut on anything else she might have said when another gust of steam burst from the train. With a ponderous clanking, its wheels began to turn once more, and the carriages rolled with increasing speed into the waiting tunnel.

The noise precluded conversation; the gentleman waited until it was gone, then said, "It is a common affliction, I fear. The Metropolitan Railway Company insists the air here is very healthful, especially for asthmatics, but I cannot imagine it is so. I take it you have not ridden the Underground before?"

Would you ride something that was trying to destroy you? But that was untrue; *trying* implied will. The terrifying thing about the trains was that they were *not* beasts. A creature out of legend could be fought, bargained with, controlled; this was mindless. A machine, doing that for which its maker had built it, without thought or desire. The true problem was people: the men of the railway companies, who had designed such a thing, and the millions that thronged London, making the thing itself necessary—none of them with any notion as to the damage wrought by their iron demon. And she had come here to face it of her own free will. For reasons she could not, at this instant, recall.

She hadn't answered the gentleman. "I have not," Cyma said. "In truth, I have a—a phobia of such things, which I thought to conquer by coming here."

"Alone? I cannot think that wise. If you will permit me, I would be more than happy to accompany you to your destination. You may grip my hand if you become frightened, and if at any point you feel you cannot continue, I will guide you out at the next station."

A wash of gratitude swept over her. Her glamour was of a woman more than old enough to be married, and therefore to venture out without a companion, but it had indeed been foolish to come here alone. She had enough bread to spare a piece for some other faerie—if she could have found one willing to set foot in this place.

It wasn't long before the next train came. This time Cyma was prepared, and she had her companion to steady her; he guided her into a first-class carriage, and they found a pair of leather-upholstered seats next to one another. Cyma couldn't help but exclaim in relief when she saw there were gaslights hanging from the polished wooden ceiling, bright enough that a man might read by them. "Yes, they are a necessity," the gentleman said. He'd introduced himself as

Mr. Harding, and she'd given her name as Mrs. Campbell. "No one would travel underground if they were forced to do so in darkness."

Even in the Onyx Hall, where goblins and other creatures of shadow made their home, that was often true. Cyma held her breath again as the train lurched into motion.

Natural light vanished almost immediately, as they passed from the glass-paneled roof arching over the station into a proper tunnel. The air was indeed foul, though now and again the train ran through an open cutting, houses rising high to either side, to ventilate the track. Cyma found the noise and motion deeply unpleasant, but so long as she did not dwell upon the terrible mass of iron that was dragging her along at such speed, her fear faded; she did not need Mr. Harding's hand very much after all.

She wished, though, that he would not persist in extolling the virtues of the underground railway. The movement of cargo into and across the city did not interest her in the slightest, and every time he spoke approvingly of slums razed by the construction, she could not help but think of the Onyx Hall. What would Mr. Harding say, if he knew about that?

It doesn't matter, she told herself, staring fixedly at an advertisement for bicycles posted on the far side of the carriage. *Soon enough, you won't have to worry about any of this any longer.* And that was why she'd come: to face the thing she feared, and to know its power over her would not last.

The train carried them through Kensington, through Westminster, into the Embankment that now chained the great Thames. That, at least, was one improvement she could applaud; the construction of sewers to prevent human waste from flowing into the river was beneficial even to fae. But as they departed Temple Station, she found her hands tightening upon her parasol once more.

Was the shudder that went down her spine her imagination at work? Or did it strike at the exact moment when the carriage passed the buried River Fleet, crossing the line of the old City wall and entering the precincts of the Onyx Hall?

Cyma found herself peering out the window as if she would be able to see the faerie palace in the shadows. An absurd thought; the picks and shovels of mortals would never breach the enchantments, even crumbling as they were. But the rails that now carried her were the ones breaking those selfsame enchantments: them, and the iron pipes for gas, and the loss of the wall itself. But the railway most of all.

Mr. Harding led her out again at Mansion House Station, having explained the situation to a conductor and paid the difference on his own ticket for Charing Cross. They emerged into the heart of the City, a stone's throw from the Bank of England, as if all the intervening miles of London had vanished. "Will you be all right?" Mr. Harding asked her.

"Oh, yes," Cyma said, smiling at him with so much

cheer he must think her deranged. "Thank you so much for accompanying me. I don't want to keep you from your business any longer—"

When he was safely on his way back to Charing Cross, Cyma let out a tremendous exhalation of relief and sagged against the blackened wall of the station, not caring if she made her dress filthy. *I did it. Faced the demon—rode it—and here I am, alive still.*

Perhaps tomorrow she would do it again, and laugh at the thing she had so recently feared.

Made bold by that thought, she stepped toward the road, hand outstretched to wave down a hansom cab. The sun was setting; it was time to go claim her freedom.

CROMWELL ROAD, SOUTH KENSINGTON

8 May 1884

Eliza counted the days like a clock counting down to midnight: twelve days until the next meeting of the London Fairy Society. Ten days. Seven. Four. Three days until she would leave the Kitterings behind forever, and go seek Owen's salvation elsewhere. She would give her notice the day before the meeting, and shake the nonexistent dust of Cromwell Road from her shoes.

The morning she was to give notice, Eliza went upstairs, as usual, to clean the cinders from the various grates.

Miss Kittering was already awake.

The drapes were thrown wide, and the young woman had what looked like all her garments out of the wardrobe and draped across every piece of available furniture: the unmade bed, the chair, even the writing desk. It might have suggested she was about to run away for good, except that when Eliza entered, she was smiling delightedly into the mirror, holding her least favourite walking dress against her body. More than anything, she seemed like a young girl who had gotten into her mother's jewels, and was trying them all on with abandon.

Some of her delight faded when she saw Eliza in the mirror. Clutching the dress with a faint air of guilt, Miss Kittering peered across the room as if trying to study her face, then said, "Oh. It's you. What do you want?"

"Ah . . ." Eliza was startled enough that she almost answered in her natural voice. Even now, she couldn't risk others hearing it. When she was certain of her accent, she said, "I'm here to clean the grate, and lay a fire, and open the drapes, miss. Is—is there something you need?"

"Oh, no, I'm quite well—you can go about your work." Miss Kittering waved her hand vaguely in Eliza's direction, then hesitated, as if she were not sure of the answer she'd just given.

Was she drunk? Eliza supposed she might have sneaked some of the brandy from the library. Miss Kittering was *humming* as she sorted through the dresses. She never hummed.

Unsure of what to think, Eliza knelt and began her

work on the grate, casting glances over her shoulder when she thought Miss Kittering wouldn't notice. The third time, Eliza spotted something shoved underneath the bed—something that looked a great deal like a rope made from knotted sheets.

So not the brandy from the library, then. Gin, perhaps, from some gambling hell, that she'd sneaked off to in the middle of the night?

"What *are* you doing?"

Eliza jerked, thinking Miss Kittering had noticed her staring under the bed. But no; the young woman was looking in perplexity at the grate, where Eliza had begun the task of rubbing in black lead. "I'm polishing the grate, miss," she said, even more baffled.

"Do you do that every day?"

The clever course of action would have been to answer her questions, and hopefully draw out her reasons for asking them. But Eliza was so unsettled by the oddity of the entire encounter that she said what actually came into her head. "Why in the name of the Blessed Virgin do you *care*?"

Miss Kittering flinched back. Then she went very still, eyes wide; then she laughed, and in that sound was an unmistakable note of nervous relief. "Oh, I—I suppose I don't. Carry on."

It was inexplicable—or so Eliza thought, until an explanation came into her head. An explanation so outlandish, it should have been utterly impossible; and so it would have been, to any young woman not convinced her love had been stolen away by the faeries.

She watched Miss Kittering move about the room, playing with the strands of her golden hair, and saw the way the girl peered at things; and Eliza knew that *none* of it, from the curiosity to the way she walked, was anything Miss Kittering would ever have done.

Hand gripping the brush so tight it hurt, Eliza thought, *That is not Miss Kittering.*

She had been stolen away—and replaced by a changeling.

THE GOBLIN MARKET, ONYX HALL

9 May 1884

Fae did not dream. It was one of many things for which they envied mortals: the ability to experience strange fantasies as they slept, whether born of fears or their dearest wishes come true. Fae could imagine; under certain conditions they could hallucinate; on rare occasions, they could receive visions, whether of the past, the future, or something happening in a distant land. But when they slept, their minds filled with nothing more than a black absence of thought.

So when the world began to tremble around Dead Rick as he lay in his secret refuge, he knew at once that it was real.

Real, but unimportant. The days when the Onyx Hall did *not* shake periodically were long enough ago that he couldn't remember them. Even away from the Fleet entrance, these tremors were reasonably common. Some claimed they were caused by the trains, but Dead Rick doubted it; the trains ran many times each day, through Blackfriars Station to Mansion House and back, and the quakes were not that frequent.

Frequent enough, though, that he'd learned to ignore them. Dead Rick, jarred from his sleep, growled and lowered his head to his paws once more, waiting for the disturbance to end.

It didn't.

A whine rose in his throat as the trembling went on. No, not trembling; this wasn't the usual effect. The trains, or whatever caused the quakes, made everything rattle, as if something heavy were being dragged across a wooden floor. This—

Suddenly afraid, he rose to his feet. Then left them again, staggering and collapsing to the stone, as the palace *twisted*.

For one horrific moment, he had an impression of the Onyx Hall as a beast: an enormous creature, writhing in pain, trying to throw off its tormentor and failing. Nadrett sometimes flogged the people who angered him, making the rest of his followers watch. This was like being inside the faerie chained to the post, feeling the body around him flinch and cringe, recoiling at each fresh blow, trying and failing to avoid the next.

Only a moment; then the impression faded. But Dead Rick, tasting blood where he'd bitten his tongue, knew that nothing had improved. He'd just lost that moment of sympathy, the connection between his mind and whatever spirit might personify the palace.

What in Mab's name is going on?

His three faerie lights were whirling in agitation—no, only two; the third had somehow escaped. Or been snuffed out? Dead Rick changed to man form, rushing it as much as he could, swallowing a yelp as his body protested the speed. Then he yanked aside the cloth covering the entrance and squirmed through the broken rock to the passage beyond.

He almost didn't make it; the stones had shifted, narrowing the gap. The collar of his waistcoat caught on something and tore. Terror at the thought of being crushed by a further collapse propelled him forward, until he tumbled into the corridor. For once Dead Rick didn't care if anyone saw him come from a supposedly closed passage; he was just grateful for the free air. When he looked up, though, he found himself alone.

Another shift, back to dog form; he'd needed his hands to climb, but now four feet would be more stable than two. The tremors hadn't stopped: occasionally there would be a brief pause, an instant of calm, as if the Hall were fighting against whatever was hurting it, but always another wrench followed, all the worse for that fleeting respite.

Sounds echoed off the black stone from both directions. Shouts, screams, someone weeping; also noises that told him some of his fellow shape-changers had made the same calculation he had. Dead Rick picked a direction and ran.

In the first chamber he came to, all was chaos. A human child sat on the floor, naked and bawling, surrounded by panicking fae. Dead Rick saw a sprite he knew, and slipped through the press until he was close enough to shift back again and speak. "Pollikin—what the bleeding 'ell is going on?"

The sprite opened his mouth to answer. As he did so, however, one of those pauses came; and by now they'd happened enough times that everyone knew what it meant. The noise in the room dropped sharply, half the fae holding their breath—and the pause stretched on, and *on,* just long enough for the hopeful to think that maybe the trouble was over.

Then the palace bucked around them as if it were a tatterfoal trying to throw off its rider. Pollikin fell into Dead Rick, and they both went down, the skriker cracking his head against the stone.

But it didn't hurt as much as it should have. As if the stone were not quite there.

"Blood and Bone," Dead Rick whispered. His eyes met Pollikin's, and he saw his terror echoed in the sprite's eyes.

One shove got Pollikin off him; another brought Dead Rick to his feet. For one crazed moment, he wished Nadrett were there—simply because the master would know what to do, and would give Dead Rick some kind of direction, if only by running. But there was no one to lead him, and everyone else in the room looked even more panicked and lost than he was. Seizing on his one good thought—Nadrett running for his life—Dead Rick drew in a lungful of air and bellowed as loudly as he could, *"Get out of 'ere, damn it!"*

A few fae started moving before he'd even said the words, probably from sheer unfocused panic. Others stared at Dead Rick. He fought the urge to hit them. "The palace is breaking," he said. By now he had something like silence, aside from the screaming mortal boy, but his voice was still loud, as if his heart were pounding each word out of his mouth. "Never mind if you don't 'ave bread; right now, London's safer than this place is. Get out of 'ere." They were still staring at him, the stupid sods. The stone writhed around him again, and he could almost hear it howl in pain. *"Go!"*

As if the command had unlocked a door, the room sprang into motion. And sound; screams immediately drowned out the child's. Dead Rick fought his way through to where he'd last seen the boy, and found him curled into a tight ball on the floor, bleeding where the stampeding feet had kicked him in passing. The skriker grabbed the boy around the middle and tucked him under one arm, using the other to shove people out of the way.

By now the motion had become a river, a torrent of bodies sweeping through the far door and into the warren beyond. Here and there a faerie battled the flow, and soon Dead Rick realised why; they were rushing to save what they owned, whether that was Goblin Market wealth or the few scraps they'd brought when they fled their homelands.

And then he remembered his own scraps, hidden behind the rockfall.

Instinct told him stop; he had to go back! But the moment his feet slowed, a satyr slammed into him from behind, making Dead Rick stagger and nearly drop the child. The boy wailed and clung to the skriker's hip. *Ash and Thorn, I can't just abandon 'im.*

He pressed his back to the wall, on the edge of the flood, and looked back desperately. The bread, he *had* to get the bread at least; if this wasn't just a break, if this was the death convulsion of the entire Onyx Hall, then he would need bread to have any hope of making it out of London alive.

But the boy he carried was scarcely more than an infant. Even if he could walk on his own, he'd never survive this chaos, let alone find an exit. And Dead Rick wouldn't care to wager on the likelihood that being mortal would save this child from whatever was about to happen to the faerie palace.

Nobody would help him. There were fae who believed in the value of mortal life—but none of them lived in the Goblin Market.

Well, maybe one does. And 'e's a fucking idiot.

Dead Rick shifted the boy higher, cradling him against his chest, and rejoined the river's flow.

There weren't many directions it could go. The warren had many passages, but few exits. Two corridors led toward the rest of the Onyx Hall, which might or might not be safe. One chamber contained a hole where the fabric of the palace had frayed thin enough that the two worlds touched; it led into the great intercepting sewer, where he'd sent Irrith. And the last led up: a proper entrance, from the days when the Hall was built, giving into the cellar of a pub near Billingsgate Market.

Dead Rick and the boy were going up, whether they liked it or not.

Along with dozens of other fae. The pace slowed to a crawl as they drew near the entrance, bodies packing in tighter and tighter until Dead Rick was afraid the boy would be crushed. *Forget the boy;* I *might be crushed.* This wasn't any orderly procession; fae were elbowing and shoving, using claws if they had them, and then Dead Rick heard a gunshot, deafening in the tight space. But if it was supposed to scare anyone into getting out of the way, it failed. Everyone was already as scared as they could get. And if the shot was aimed at a body . . . Dead Rick stepped on something soft and bony a little while later, and smelled blood, but didn't look down to see its source.

A gust of air made him shiver, despite the frantic heat of so many fleeing bodies. Then Dead Rick realised it wasn't physical cold. Up ahead, the passage ended in a chamber scarcely large enough for two or three desperate fae, and above lay the mortal world.

Flapping wings shot overhead, some bird-shaped faerie bolting for safety. She didn't quite make it. The bird flew into the chamber and up; then she fell again, screeching as the atmosphere outside forced her body into a woman's form. Dead Rick, holding the boy almost on his shoulder to protect him, shuddered in sympathetic pain.

Then he was in the chamber at last, with dubious salvation above. He could feel the chill of nearby iron—tools, barrel hoops, all the metal humans could not seem to do without—but right now, it felt safer than the Hall behind him. The ladder that should lead into the cellar, though, was splintered and broken, only one cracked rung still holding the legs together.

Here, at least, something like help was to be had; the fae behind him, eager to take his place, were more than willing to shove him upward if that would speed his progress. With his free hand Dead Rick clawed for the hard-packed dirt of the cellar floor, bare feet twisting in someone's grasp, trying not to crush the child he'd brought all this way. He ended up heaving the boy up and onto the floor, then dragging himself after, curving his back over the mortal to protect him when somebody else staggered and fell over them both.

Gasping, he crawled clear, flinching away from the iron all around them. *It's no worse than Blackfriars. You survived that, remember?* But he didn't know how long he would have lasted, if he hadn't caught that tosher with food.

All at once his will gave out. Dead Rick collapsed against a wall, the rough brickwork scratching him where his waistcoat had torn, and watched fae escape the Onyx Hall. Already they packed the cellar; some must have gone upstairs, into the pub on the ground floor. What would the mortals think, with faeries flooding into their midst like that?

It might not even matter. For all Dead Rick knew, this

was the end; whatever indomitable will held the Onyx Hall together had finally given out, just as his own had, and now that shadowy reflection would at last fray into nothingness. And the fae who called it home would scatter to the four winds: some going to Faerie, some finding refuge in what other courts remained, some dying under the oppressive weight of the mortal world's hostility.

Dead Rick didn't know which of those fates would be his. And lying against the wall, with a mortal child crying into his bruised ribs, he couldn't much bring himself to care.

PART TWO

May–August 1884

A Lord of Steam and Iron am I
A monster in the land;
While puny men of bone and blood
Are slaves at my command.

"MONSTER SCIENCE,"
NINETEENTH-CENTURY SONG

Thy form is clothed with wings of iron gloom;
But round about thee, like a chain, is rolled,
Cramping the sway of every mighty plume,
A stark constringent serpent fold on fold:
Of its two heads, one sting is in thy brain,
The other in thy heart; their venom-pain
Like fire distilling through thee uncontrolled.

JAMES THOMSON,
"TO OUR LADIES OF DEATH"

Wandering between two worlds, one dead,
The other powerless to be born . . .

MATTHEW ARNOLD,
"STANZAS FROM THE GRANDÊ CHARTREUSE"

If she had breath, she would be gasping for air. Exquisite agony still lances through her body, new knives to join the old. When they pierced her, all control vanished; there was no thought, no endurance, nothing but an endless, voiceless scream.

She claws it down, forces herself to think past the pain. Forces her body to stillness, accepting the fresh mutilation. Fighting it will only hurt her more, and so she bends *herself around it, drawing back the bleeding edges of her flesh. The further she retreats, the less it hurts, but she knows this has consequences she cannot accept. What those consequences are, she cannot recall, but that much stays with her: that she* must not *retreat too far.*

Pain has the power to startle her, to weaken her control, but it is not the real threat. Her own response is. Like a woman above a great drop, clinging to the edge of a blade, she must not loosen her grip—whatever it costs her in blood.

She remembers this, though she cannot remember why.

And so she will cling on, until memory fades, and oblivion claims her at last.

WHITE LION STREET, ISLINGTON:
16 May 1884

The maid escorted Frederic Myers into the ground floor parlour, where Mrs. Chase sat with her mending. The old woman rose as he entered, despite his exhortations for her to remain seated; she moved remarkably well for a woman of her age. *Or perhaps it is not so remarkable,* he thought, remembering what he knew of her. There was more in Heaven and Earth than even the Society for Psychical Research dreamt of in their philosophy.

"They're downstairs," Mrs. Chase said, "but not yet started, I think. I must wait for a few more guests; you may go on down."

She went to a patch of wall left oddly bare of any pictures or furniture, and brushed her hand over the roses that sprawled across the wallpaper. At her touch, they came to life. The blossoms acquired depth and scent; the vines twined themselves into a flowery arch; and then the wall within that arch was not there anymore, and a set of worn wooden steps led downward.

Myers's breath quickened at the sight. He'd seen it only once before, and could no more catch the manner of its happening this time than he could the first. They would not let him study it, not yet; for now, he was only a guest in this home. *Both* of these homes: the one above, and the one below.

Hat in hand, and ducking his head to avoid scraping it against the low ceiling, Myers descended into the hidden realm of Rose House.

Voices trailed up the staircase toward him, one of the Goodemeades speaking. He could not yet tell them apart, not without seeing the embroidery on their aprons. ". . . loom-thing, whatever Wrain and Ch'ien Mu are calling it, *ought* to help—but the best it can do is to slow the problem."

"It may cushion folk against more incidents like last week," her sister said, and then Myers emerged into the sitting room below.

The second speaker proved to be Rosamund Goodemeade, who popped to her feet the moment she saw him. "Mr. Myers! Oh, I'm so glad you could join us again. Please, do be seated—"

She scarcely came to his belt, but somehow managed a presence much larger than her actual size. Aside from the height, she was almost precisely as she had been when he came to his first meeting of the London Fairy Society back in March: the same honey-coloured curls, the same friendly demeanour. Just a foot shorter, and with an odd cast to her features that marked her not as human, but faerie.

Mrs. Chase had said nothing of that when she

approached him at the April meeting about joining a second, more select group. Explanations had waited until he came to tea a week later—explanations, and a test; his reactions then, he suspected, had determined whether they would open the rose arch in the wall and admit him to the Goodemeades' home below. He had passed, and thereby joined the *real* London Fairy Society.

It was not a topic he'd ever known much about. Myers's notion of "fairies" owed a great deal to the sort of sentimental picture books published for children nowadays, with delicate winged creatures floating about flower gardens. Instead he found himself in an underground house furnished like an idyllic, rustic cottage, taking tea with a mixture of mortals and fae, none of whom were tiny and possessed of wings. The Goodemeades, while small, were plump, homespun creatures; Lady Amadea was the height of an ordinary woman and statuesque in her beauty. Another short fellow, by the name of Tom Toggin, had a face that could have belonged to some lady's Chinese pug—though he assured Myers that goblins were often *far* uglier than he.

And then there were the mortals: men and women carefully selected by the Goodemeades, judged trustworthy enough to know the secret of the faeries' presence in London. Myers made his greetings to them, then settled himself in a comfortable chair, waiting for the meeting to begin.

He caught Tom's murmured question to Gertrude Goodemeade. "How many refugees do you think you could pack in here, if you had to?"

"It depends on how well they like each other," she said—but her levity was a thin mask over real concern.

"I think Hodge is about ready to start—"

Footsteps on the stairs interrupted him. A slender faerie flamboyantly dressed like a carnival barker leapt into the room, struck a grand pose, and announced in a thick Irish accent, "Mistresses and masters, my lady Wilde!"

Startled, Myers rose with the others. The woman who entered was not the grand lady that introduction led him to expect; her shabby-genteel clothing, in widow's black, spoke clearly of having fallen on hard times. She had the drooping look of a lush-bodied woman reduced by age and circumstance; though Myers judged her to be younger than Mrs. Chase, she moved like the older of the two. Tom hurried forward to help escort her to a chair.

"Lady Wilde?" Myers repeated, when they were introduced. She had not been here the previous month; he would have remembered. "The poetess? I did not know you were in London."

"I have lived here for some years now," she said, as he bent over her hand. "With my two sons." Her own accent was a musical lilt next to her faerie companion's thick brogue.

Myers bowed again. "I heard your name mentioned at one of the public Society meetings; I might have guessed you would be involved with its more private face. It is an honour to meet you, Lady Wilde."

People settled into their seats once more. "Who else are we waiting for?" Lady Amadea asked. "You said there was another young woman you were considering—"

Rosamund shook her head. "Miss Baker, but unfortunately she didn't come to last week's public meeting. Next month, perhaps. We haven't seen Miss Kittering again, either, so no decision yet as to whether we should invite her."

"What about Cyma?" the Irish faerie fellow asked.

The Goodemeade sisters exchanged worried looks. "We haven't seen her," Gertrude said quietly. "Not since the earthquake."

Earthquake? Myers saw his own confusion mirrored among several of the mortals in the room. Not Lady Wilde, though. Or any of the fae. Rosamund took a deep breath and spoke. "It's time we shared a few things with the rest of you. It—well, it sounds terribly dramatic to say this is the 'true purpose' of our Society, particularly since nothing says we must have only *one* purpose, and all the others must be false. But there is something else Gertie and I had in mind, when we decided to begin these meetings, and given events elsewhere, the time for it has come."

"The time to *talk* about it," her sister corrected her.

Rosamund nodded. "Yes, of course. We don't want to rush into anything.

"All of you—our human friends—know the difficulties we faeries face here in London. Religion isn't so bad anymore; people aren't as pious as they used to be, and it doesn't hurt too badly if a man uses the name of divinity as a curse, without much believing in what it stands for. It's still a problem, of course, but not nearly as much as iron is."

Mrs. Chase had come quietly downstairs while they spoke, having presumably closed the parlour arch behind her. When Rosamund paused, Myers said guiltily, "I neglected to bring bread. But I will fetch some when we are done here, and tithe it upstairs before I leave." Others echoed him.

"Thank you," Rosamund said, and it sounded heartfelt. "But unfortunately, while bread helps, it can't solve our problems."

Gertrude gestured at the rustic comfort of their home. "Rose House isn't the only place of this sort in London. There's another one, much bigger than this, but it's falling apart; all the changes in the City are destroying it. Soon enough, all the fae who live there now will have to go somewhere else. Out of London. Maybe out of this world entirely."

"Flitting," Lady Wilde said. "Collectors of folklore have been gathering the stories for years."

Rosamund nodded. "But some folk are determined to stay. The two of us certainly are, and we'll take in whoever we can. We know that someday, though, our house may face the same problem. Likely it *will*. So we have to think about what we can do to prevent that."

She drew in a deep breath, then held it, as if unwilling to release the words it bore. Gertrude did it for her. "Rose and I have wondered for a long time now if maybe it wasn't a mistake, keeping our presence here secret. What might have happened if we showed our faces, right from the start, and been a part of the city as it grew. An open part. We can't go back and change that, of course—but there's always the future, isn't there? And we're thinking of telling the world that we're here."

Again, none of the fae were surprised. It was, as Rosamund had said, a notion they had in mind when they formed this society. But among Myers's fellow mortals . . .

"It has been done a bit in Ireland," Lady Wilde said, while everyone else gaped. "When my late husband withdrew to Moytura and began collecting the local folklore, two Connemara faeries came to him and told him their stories. He never published them, and I myself have not yet decided what to do with the tales. But in Ireland, 'tis still common for people to know about the faeries nearby—if not as common as it once was."

Myers found his tongue at last. "Are you not afraid that this might be even more dangerous to you?"

"Of course we are," Gertrude said, with a touch of sharpness. "That's why we're being careful. The public meetings to see who's interested, and then these private meetings for the ones we decide we can trust; and now we're going to discuss it until we're blue in the face."

"And no matter what we decide, we aren't doing anything yet," Rosamund added. "Admitting our presence in London won't save the Onyx Hall—that's the other place we mentioned—and not everyone there thinks we should do this." By the faint embarrassment in her tone, the opposition was in a clear majority. "But we intend to talk to the ones who do end up staying in London—

especially the ones staying with us—and we'd like to be able to present them with a plan. Some notion of how this might be done, as safely as possible, with the best chance of success."

Excitement of an unfamiliar sort was building beneath Myers's ribs. Nothing had fired his imagination like this in years, not even his work with mediums. *Annie would have been delighted,* he thought. It brought with it a familiar lance of pain—but not as sharp as he would have expected. For the first time since she died, he found himself eager to pursue something that was *not* about communicating with her spirit. Eager, and guilty, as if he were somehow betraying her by thinking of other things.

Mrs. Chase rescued him from these thoughts by addressing him. "What do you think your friends in the Society for Psychical Research would make of this, Mr. Myers?"

Henry Sidgwick meeting faeries. The very notion made his head hurt. But— "It falls outside the purview of our usual work," Myers admitted. "Then again, most of our members view fairy tales as a literary matter rather than a scientific one. If I were to write an article, or speak at one of our meetings—"

"Not yet," Lady Amadea cautioned him.

"No, of course not. What I mean is, once aware of the situation, I imagine they would be eager to investigate." He laughed ruefully. "They would probably make a new committee, and force me to be in charge of it. But if faeries are willing to meet with them, and show proof of their—

your—natures and capabilities, then my colleagues will establish this field of study so quickly, it will make your head spin."

"Will they be *friendly*?" the Irish faerie asked bluntly.

Myers blinked. "Why would they not be?"

"What I mean is, sure I don't fancy being tossed in a cage like some kind of ape for folk to gawp at—"

"Eidhnin," Rosamund said. Mild though her voice was, it hushed him. "Nobody will do *anything* until we're sure. And if we can't be sure, we won't do it. But don't gallop to meet future difficulties before you must. Mr. Myers, please continue. You mentioned committees; what exactly would this one do?"

By fits and starts, with contributions from fae and mortals alike, the London Fairy Society laid plans for a future beyond the death of the Onyx Hall.

CROMWELL ROAD, SOUTH KENSINGTON
19 May 1884

For days the storm built, an unsubtle tension that put all the Kitterings' servants on their toes, jumping at shadows. Mrs. Fowler struck anyone, maid or footman, who fell short in their duties; even the usually pleasant butler, Mr. Warren, began to employ the sharp side of his tongue. Little Sarah, the scullery maid, ceased to speak to anyone, and more than once Eliza caught Ann Wick looking through the "help wanted" advertisements in newspapers.

The source of the storm, of course, was Mrs. Kittering. Not her daughter; no, the creature pretending to be Louisa seemed the only one unaffected. She flitted through the house like a butterfly, delighting in the smallest things—when she was there at all. Her absences were frequent, despite her mother's attempts to curb them, and that was the source of Mrs. Kittering's fury; never tractable at the best of times, Louisa had become a wild thing indeed, and threatened to overturn every plan her mother had for her future.

When at last the thunder came, it was almost a relief. Almost—but not quite, for instead of breaking upon Louisa, the cause of all this trouble, it broke upon the servants.

Eliza's fears took on sharper form the moment the bell rang on the downstairs wall, as if she could hear doom in that brassy, imperious sound. It signaled the drawing room, a place usually unoccupied at this hour of the morning, and Mrs. Fowler went to answer it. Within two minutes the housekeeper was downstairs again, her brows drawn together like those of an unpitying magistrate, and she ordered every last one of them up to the first floor.

Everyone: not just the maids, but Cook, the footmen, even the gardener and the grooms from the stables. Mrs. Fowler and Mr. Warren lined them all up against the north wall, facing the windows; the curtains had been drawn back, and despite that brilliant light, the gas lamps had also been lit. The effect reminded Eliza of a theater she'd gone to once, when she and Owen had a little money to spare;

the searing limelights there had illuminated the actors for all to see. She did not think the staff had been assembled to entertain anyone, though.

Mrs. Kittering was an ominous shadow against the left-most window, looking out over the back terrace into the garden. The missus's hands were locked above her bustle, and her spine was even more rigidly straight than her stays demanded. Unlike many women who had borne a large number of children, her aging body had not run to fat, and in her dark dress she looked like a skeletal, ravenous crow.

An impression that did not change when Mrs. Fowler murmured that all the servants were present, and Mrs. Kittering turned to face them at last. Eliza could see nothing of the missus's expression—which was, she was sure, exactly as Mrs. Kittering wanted it. With slow, deliberate strides, the woman paced the length of the room, studying them all; then she pivoted by the grate and came back along their lines. Only when that was done did she speak.

"I want to know," she said, carving each word into the air as if with a knife, "what has possessed my daughter."

At the word *possessed,* Eliza tried not to jump. Fortunately, Mrs. Kittering's attention was on Ned Sayers at that moment, so she did not notice her under-housemaid going rigid.

"It is not possible to keep secrets in this house," Mrs. Kittering went on. This time, Eliza was better able to hide her reaction. *You like to think that—or maybe you think that by saying it, you can make it be true.* "I *will* discover what Louisa is hiding. Whatever you know, speak up now. I will be very grateful to the one who assists me in this matter."

Keeping her mouth shut was no difficulty at all. Mrs. Kittering wanted an answer, but she didn't want the truth; if Eliza spoke, the best she could hope for was a beating and immediate dismissal. Though part of her wanted to do it, just to see the incredulous look on Mrs. Kittering's face. *Your daughter's gone, and I'm the only hope you've got for ever bringing her back.*

Her own thought startled her. Bring Louisa Kittering back? Eliza scarcely cared two pins for the girl; had this been some other kind of trouble, she would have abandoned the silly chit to it, and good riddance. But she couldn't save Owen and leave Louisa behind. Not if she had a chance to rescue both.

She might not. Among the few things Eliza was certain of, one was that the faerie who'd taken Louisa's place was not the one who had stolen Owen, seven years ago. To begin with, this one was undoubtedly female. But there could not be many faeries in London; it beggared belief to think the changeling and the thief were not connected in some fashion. Find Louisa, find Owen—and then find a way to bring them back. If she could. Should it come to one or the other, Eliza would choose Owen in a heartbeat, and anyway there might not be a choice: in some of the tales it took true love to win a prisoner free, in which case Louisa was out of luck. But Eliza would cheat the faeries of both if she could.

Fortunately, cheating was another thing that happened in the tales.

With a start, she realised Mrs. Kittering was standing in front of her. In a cold voice, the woman said, "Anyone caught keeping secrets on Louisa's behalf will regret it most acutely."

Eliza disciplined her face, trying not to look as though her thoughts had been wandering. After a moment, Mrs. Kittering moved on, to stop in front of the coachman and his grooms. "Where has Louisa asked you to drive her, these last few months? I want to know every destination."

Hearn began to stammer out a list, naming off dressmakers and dancing masters, museums and friends' houses. He gave dates when he could, and Eliza wondered if Mrs. Kittering heard what she did, that the pattern had changed in recent days. The faerie had different interests than Louisa—strange ones, a fascination with matters that a human considered mundane or distasteful. What well-bred young lady wanted to tour the halls of a hospital, other than as part of some charitable visit?

In almost all these cases Louisa was chaperoned: by a friend, or one of her married sisters, or Lucy, the lady's maid. Mrs. Kittering descended next upon the maid, interrogating her mercilessly about every last detail of Louisa's activities. And here arose some oddities, for there were moments for which Lucy could not entirely account; she had become distracted, or occupied in some unnecessary task, and could not swear with a clear conscience that she knew what Louisa had done during that time. Mrs. Kittering soon reduced her to tears, provoking some sympathy from Eliza—but sympathy was soon pushed aside by the realization that Lucy's distractions had begun before the changeling took Louisa's place. *Faerie trickery,* she thought. It wasn't random; the changeling had been following her target for some time before stealing her away.

It ended as it must, with Mrs. Kittering sacking Lucy, without any of the pay she was owed. "Count yourself fortunate I do not bring you to the attention of the police," she said, viciously and without much cause; Lucy had committed no crime. But it was a favourite threat in the household, and the Kitterings wealthy enough that they could possibly follow through, condemning their erstwhile maid to the prison, the workhouse, or the lunatic asylum.

Eliza's relief to have escaped the ax faltered when Mrs. Kittering turned her attention to the remaining servants. "I want to know everything she does. What she reads, from whom she receives letters. She will see no callers without me present; if I am not at home, then you will say that she is not, either. And above all, she is not to go out. Am I understood?"

They all answered promptly and with vigor, eager to avoid Lucy's fate. It thwarted Eliza's hope that she might contrive to be the changeling's companion on a trip out of the house, and thereby corner her away from watchful eyes and ears; she would have to find another way.

She tried to pretend the prospect didn't call up a note of fear, and failed. It was one thing to force information out of Louisa, a sheltered young woman whose notion of cruelty was to ignore someone at a garden party, but a faerie . . . Eliza's breath shallowed at the thought, and her palms grew sweaty-cold. She knew firsthand how cruel they could be.

Think of Owen. Think of Mrs. Darragh, and Maggie. You're willing to dare the Special Irish Branch for him; surely a faerie can be no worse.

Mrs. Kittering's eyes were upon her once more. Eliza curtsied, her face a perfect mask of obedience, and left before the missus could guess at the plan forming behind her eyes.

NIGHT GARDEN, ONYX HALL
22 May 1884

At first glance, nothing in the night garden had changed. The Walbrook's foul waters still flowed sluggishly through the rank plants; faerie lights still drifted aimlessly about; the blankets and miserable possessions of the refugees still littered the ground.

But the population of those refugees had changed. In the aftermath of the terrible earthquake, a great many of them had fled, if not in search of Faerie, then to somewhere else less dangerous than London. Into the gaps they left came the dregs of the Goblin Market.

When the first brave souls ventured back into the warren beneath Billingsgate, they found half of that warren had disappeared. Of the two passages connecting it to the rest of the palace, one had fallen in; some of the Cornish knockers tried to dig it out, but new dirt fell to replace what they carried away. That part of the Hall now let into the ground beneath London. Even if they could dig through, there would be no palace on the other side.

Part of Dead Rick's reason for coming to the night garden was to get out of the Market. The part that vanished had included Lacca's entire lair, from doss-houses to Po's opium den; now the goblin woman was fighting tooth and claw—literally—to keep from being forced out by Nadrett and Hardface. And so it went, down to the lowest sprite, everyone kicking and shoving to find new space or keep what they had, and the losers coming here, to the garden.

He didn't have to claw for a new place—because Nadrett had decided to shorten his leash, keeping Dead Rick in his own chambers more often than not. But if it weren't for that, he would be homeless. The stone of his refuge had finished its collapse, burying his few treasures under broken marble and onyx. With no bread to shield him, fleeing through London now would be suicide.

The rest of his reason for coming lay near the chamber's eastern end. Two obelisks rose there, one a gravestone, the other a memorial. The dirty surface of the latter held a list of names and dates, marking the reigns of past Princes of the Stone. In its base, a small flame burned: one of the few things in the garden that wasn't broken or fallen or stained.

No doubt the names would have meant something to Dead Rick, once. He knew the first one, Michael Deven, belonged to the man buried under the other obelisk, where he'd found and chased that girl. The rest were mysteries to him. Hodge, the only Prince he remembered, hadn't yet joined his predecessors in the stone; the twelfth and final name carved into the obelisk was Alexander Messina, dead in 1870, long before Dead Rick's memories began.

The skriker paused, looking at the dates. Doing the precise sums would have taken too long, but a glance was enough to show the pattern: each Prince's reign had been shorter than the last, for quite some time now. There were two in the middle of the last century who only made it a handful of years each, Hamilton Birch and Galen St. Clair; the next, Matthew Abingdon, had done a good deal better, but after him it went steadily down.

"Probably the palace killing them," he muttered. "Which one will go first: Hodge or the Hall?"

At the rate of progress on the Inner Circle Railway, it would be the Hall. The navvies were laying a short stretch of rail already, from Mark Lane partway toward Eastcheap Station at the Monument; that had been the cause of the earthquake. From there it was just a short gap to Mansion House, along Cannon Street and past the London Stone. The newspapers said it would be open for service by the autumn.

He scowled and jerked away from the obelisk, with its forlorn list of mortal men who'd served the Onyx Court. The finger bone he'd laid on the ground alongside it was still there, he saw, with no ashes anywhere nearby to signal that his ally the voice had seen it. Dead Rick dug in his pocket and pulled out a beef bone, cracked open for its marrow, dropping it onto the dead grass. Perhaps the finger, placed there after the incident with the ghost in the sewers, was too small, and his ally had overlooked it.

Unlikely. Much more probable that he'd given up. Or been discovered and cut down by Nadrett.

Or been in the Goblin Market when part of it vanished.

Dead Rick nudged the bone into better position with his toes and retreated, not wanting to be seen there. Intending to take a different path out of the garden, he headed toward the center and the Walbrook—only to stop short at the sight of a familiar figure, sitting on the edge of a dry and leaf-choked fountain.

Irrith spotted him at the same time and let out a dry huff of a laugh. "Seven years I don't see one hair of your tail, and now I can't turn around without tripping over you."

"Are you following me?"

It came out hard and suspicious, and her eyebrows went up. "No. I came here because—"

She looked away suddenly, but that did little good against a skriker who sensed the world as much through his ears and nose as his eyes. He heard the catch in her voice, the choked noise after she stopped speaking. He smelled a hint of salt, over the dirt and half-rotted leaves, even if her face hadn't shown any sign of tears.

Nobody in the Goblin Market cried. Nobody who let herself be that weak lasted long there.

Dead Rick didn't know what to do or say. He just stood there, wondering if he should go away, until Irrith spoke again. "I used to love this place," she said quietly, still looking anywhere but at him, across the overgrown tangles of the night garden. "It reminded me of the Vale. I love London, understand—I wouldn't stay here if I didn't. But I needed a bit of green, some grass and trees and flowers, to keep from going mad."

He didn't know what the Vale was—her original home?—but he heard the ache in her voice, and answered with the only words he had, pathetic and useless as they were. "I'm sorry."

"So am I." Irrith hung her head, hands braced against the fountain's edge so her shoulders hunched up like a hawk's. Then he heard another laugh, short and hard. "And I keep thinking about Lune."

The vanished Queen. "What about 'er?"

The sprite gestured with one hand; he couldn't tell what she meant by it, and maybe she couldn't, either. "Those speeches she used to make. She would have stood up in front of the court—not just the lords and ladies, but common fae like you or me—and said something about how London is our home, all of us who came here from somewhere else, and we weren't going to give up on it. People would stay, instead of flitting. And we'd find a way around this problem."

This problem. As if it were a simple thing, an overturned cart in the road, and all they had to do was figure out which narrow side lane would lead them past it. Harshly, Dead Rick said, "Too bad she's gone and pushed off with the rest of 'em, and left us behind."

Irrith's head came up so fast, he twitched back. "What? Lune isn't gone!"

"Oh, is that so? Then where is she, eh? You tell me that."

"I don't know."

He snorted in disgust. "Of course you don't."

Irrith glared at him, expression darkening. "She's still here, though. Somewhere in the Hall. Hodge talks to her sometimes; he says—"

"Oh, the *Prince,* the fucking *Prince.* Of course 'e'd say; without the Queen, 'e's nothing but a jumped-up cockney bastard, playing at being King of the Faeries. She's *gone,* Irrith."

"No, she isn't!" Irrith shot to her feet. "Dead Rick—just who do you think is holding this place *together*?"

He frowned, not following her. "It *ain't* 'olding together. That's the problem."

The energy possessing the sprite seemed far larger than her slender body. "You must have felt it. When the tremors hit. Like a body in pain, but trying so hard to hold still, until it gets too bad; then the whole thing thrashes, like it's screaming—like *she's* screaming. I think Hodge hears that, too, though he'll never say so. She keeps as much of it from us as she can, but even Lune has limits. And she's being pushed past them more and more often."

Dead Rick's skin crawled, thinking of the moment when he woke inside his refuge. That sense of the Onyx Hall as a prisoner chained to a post, writhing beneath the whip.

It's the Queen.

Irrith nodded. Her cheeks hollowed briefly, as if she were biting the insides of them to keep from crying. "When they laid the rails . . . sometimes I think it would be better to just pull her away. Let us all move on to something else, rather than hanging on here like the desperate things we are; let the Hall have a clean death, instead of this horrible torture. If I knew where she was, I might try to do it. But I don't."

With the railway so fresh in his mind, the answer was obvious. "The London Stone. Ain't it the 'eart of this place?"

"Yes," Irrith said grimly. "But where's the Stone? The part below, I mean; not the part above. Hodge is the only one who knows, and he swore an oath not to tell."

Human oaths meant nothing. But fae had ways of binding men to keep their word; Hodge's promise would certainly be of that sort. A secret like that, they couldn't risk getting out. Even now, control of the London Stone might be a valuable thing.

"Speaking of the Prince . . ." Irrith sidled closer. "I've been thinking about what you told me before. About Nadrett? I was wondering if you knew anything more, or had any proof—"

With a jolt like his brain popping back into place, Dead Rick realised what he was doing: carrying on a friendly conversation with the sprite who recently helped the Prince's minions carry out a raid on the Goblin Market. In the middle of the night garden. In easy view of any number of Goblin Market refugees, who would be only too happy to sell news of this event in exchange for a place in the warren.

He drew a slow, deep breath through his nose, and spat the last of it back out as a near-silent curse. *We're being watched, all right.* By at least one person, and maybe more, if his nose was any judge.

Irrith raised her eyebrows, waiting for his answer. Dead Rick had to end this, before she said anything else that could get him killed. Hoping the sprite's hearing was good, he whispered, "What I'm about to do—sorry."

Then he backhanded her across the face.

His knuckles only clipped her cheek; the sprite was fast, and his vague warning had at least put her on alert. She stumbled back out of his reach, staring, halfway to angry. He had to stop her before she could say anything loudly enough to be overheard. "Is that why you came 'ere? Looking for me, thinking you could get me to talk? Went after Aspell, now you're going after my master—well, you'd better know, you set foot in 'is part of the Market, you won't get that foot back. And you tell your cockney Prince: Nadrett could kill 'im any time 'e wanted to. And what do you think that would do?"

Every bit of colour drained out of Irrith's face, freezing her anger into sudden horror. Dead Rick cursed his choice of threat. Killing the Prince—if it wouldn't destroy the Hall outright, it certainly wouldn't help the Queen any. There were some crazy fae around; he prayed he hadn't put that idea into anybody's head. *They may not know where she is, but they can sure as 'ell find* 'im.

Her jaw clenched hard, and then she drew herself up with contempt worthy of the elf-knights she'd joined for that raid. "Iron rot your soul, Dead Rick," she spat, and strode off in rigid fury.

He shut his eyes and went through every profane oath he knew. *Stupid fucking whelp. Should never 'ave said nothing to 'er. That's what you get for trusting somebody you don't even remember.*

This was why he'd spent seven years under Nadrett's thumb. Because he wasn't clever enough to scheme and lie and trick his way out. The moment he tried, he nearly got himself killed.

But he couldn't give up. The voice had cracked the shell of despair that had hardened around him, these past seven years; there might be something like hope, if Nadrett's scheme was real. And Dead Rick could barter that hope for aid in getting his memories back.

If you can get your paws on it.

He couldn't wait forever for his ally to come back. Stupid whelp though he was, Dead Rick would have to keep going on his own.

Memory: 7 July 1798

Lune's messenger—a pigeon from the world above, given very precise instructions—fluttered into the chamber and settled upon a small table by the wall. Placing her right hand upon the London Stone and extending her left to Robert Shaw, the Queen said, "It is time."

The Prince mirrored her without hesitation or outward sign of fear. He was a brave man, a colonel in the Horse Guards, and had distinguished himself in battle before taking up his position as Lune's consort; if the knowledge that he might not survive the next moments unsettled him, he did not show it. He merely braced his feet, set his own hand upon the Stone, and sank alongside the Queen into the deepest of trances.

Once the Stone had stood alongside the Walbrook, at the heart of the City of London. An ancient relic, placed there long before the creation of the Onyx Hall, it seemed eternal, immutable, the perfect foundation for that edifice of enchantments.

But given enough time, even the eternal changed. The mortals of London had already moved the Stone once, from the south side of Cannon Street to the north, where it would be less of an obstruction to traffic. Now, finding it a nuisance still, they were moving it a second time.

With it, they moved the entirety of the Onyx Hall.

Lune and Shaw prepared themselves for the upheaval. Joining their spirits in concentration, they reached out through their realm, binding it together, from their hidden place within the Queen's chambers to the farthest reaches of the palace. The frayed edges flared with pain, where the loss of much of London's wall had damaged the integrity of the whole. There had been some fraying the previous time, too, but it had grown worse in the last fifty years; deep within the quiet of her mind, Lune worried what the effect now would be.

She did not have long to fret. In Cannon Street above, workmen jammed long crowbars beneath the Stone's exposed base, and began to lift.

A bone-jarring tremor ran through the Stone they touched. This one, suspended from the chamber's ceiling, was a reflection of the Stone above, the linchpin that held London and its shadow together. The shattering jolts that ensued as its original began to move could destroy the Hall in an instant—if Queen and Prince did not stand together, cushioning the blow.

Whether the ache Lune felt was in her body, or in the Hall itself, she could not say. At that moment, there seemed no difference between the two. Painful as it was, she knew it was only the first stage of the process, and she steeled herself against the next.

The shifting of the Stone to its new home.

Direction lost all meaning as the linchpin, the immovable point around which all else was fixed, began to move. Nausea rose up in Lune's gorge; distantly, she heard Shaw retch. With her attention spread throughout the entire Onyx Hall, she had little sense of her own vertigo, but she fought to keep that disorientation from the palace itself, fought to hold all the chambers and galleries and entrances to the world above in place. All except the reflection of the Stone itself: not even one of the great powers of Faerie could have held that in position. Once it had resided in a secret alcove at the heart of the Onyx Hall's power. The first shifting had moved it to Lune's chambers. Where it would be when this process was done, she could only guess; she had no power to control it.

Still the world shuddered and whirled, until Lune wanted to let go, allow the maelstrom to fling her away. She had no teeth to grit, but she strained every particle of her soul, desperate to hold on. If she released her grip now, it might destroy the Hall; the final moments of this change surely would.

Shaw held on with her, and she felt the Prince prepare himself, sheltering her soul with his own.

In the world above, the workmen grunted and swore, and finally pushed the London Stone into the setting that awaited it.

The exterior wall of St. Swithin's Church.

Sacred power washed through the connection between the two worlds. Shaw took it into himself, contained it, kept it from flooding on into the Onyx Hall itself. Then Lune, working with him in the shadow of his protecting spirit, reached deep into the Stone. It, too, was an entrance to the Onyx Hall, though it answered only to the Queen and the Prince; but if the palace were to survive having its central point embedded in the wall of a church, that doorway must be closed.

With a sound like grinding rock, the portal sealed, and Lune and Shaw returned to their bodies.

The Queen blinked, dizzy with effort, and looked about to see where they were. The chamber was a larger one than before, perhaps ten paces across, and Lune recognised it as lying in a part of the Hall few fae ever came to; it was very nearly beneath St. Paul's Cathedral. A consequence, no doubt, of the new placement at the church. She felt peculiar, as if she were looking out over familiar ground from an unaccustomed vantage point.

Shaw wiped sweat from his brow and said, "We'll need to hide this."

Yes, they would. Even if few fae ever came here, some did, and the London Stone was a vulnerable point. Extending her hand once more, Lune said, "If you have the strength?"

Robert Shaw's strength was an endless thing. He wrapped callused fingers around hers, and together they went through the archway into another room, this one larger, just by the stairs that led to the cathedral above. Turning to face that arch, they concentrated, and the black stone grew shut, until it seemed there had never been an opening there at all.

The Onyx Hall would be safe a while longer.

SHADWELL, LONDON

24 May 1884

With much shouting and cursing, the packed body of men surged forward across the dockyard, past the fallen chain that until a moment ago had held them back. Not far ahead, a group of foremen waited on a platform of boards laid across barrels, raised just high enough to allow them to survey the charging mass. As the first runners reached them, the foremen began to bellow with powerful voices, naming off the work they needed done, and calling out the men they would hire to do it.

This was only the Shadwell Basin, not the West India Docks, nor any of the other great pools that had been built in the East End of London to accept the commerce of the world. Even in those places, the foremen could not hire more than a fraction of the fellows who came each morning to beg for work. Here, only a fraction of a fraction met with luck; the rest were turned away, grumbling or silent with despair, to find what employment they could.

Or to drink away what coin they still had. Eliza had watched the scrimmage from the safety of an empty cart along a warehouse wall; she stayed where she was, letting the energetic men depart again, waiting for those who had nothing to hurry on to. As she expected, Dónall Whelan was among the last of these, and one look at him was enough to tell that he'd be lucky to afford a dram of gin, in his current state.

So much the better for her. Eliza hiked up her skirts and jumped over the cart's rail to land on the filthy cobbles in front of Whelan, startling him from his weary shuffle. She smiled broadly into his surprised eyes. "I knew I'd find you here, for all that you're too old; sure you know the calling-men will never choose yourself. But I've a threepenny bit in my pocket, and that's enough to get you blind drunk—after you help me."

Whelan's face had seen hard wear since she last saw him. He was old for a dockworker, old for any job in the East End; nearly forty, she thought, for he'd been a boy when his father came over during the Hunger. Whelan followed after his mother perished in Galway, waiting for money that never came. His shoulders, though still broad, had taken on a hunch, one riding higher than the other, and most of his hair was long since gone. One of these days he would drown himself in the Thames, or find work and then be killed by it. Or drink himself to death, if he could get enough money to do it in one go.

His rheumy eyes took on what he probably thought was a cunning look, and Eliza wondered if he was thinking of robbing her. Let him try; she had a knife under her shawl, and in his state she was probably the stronger of the two.

"You're looking wondrous fine, Miss O'Malley," he said, with a mockery of a bow. "Fine enough to be buying a dinner of whitebait, even. And a man can help much better on a full stomach, he can."

How bad had things been for him lately, that he wanted food more than drink? Against Eliza's better instincts, a touch of pity stirred her heart. Grudgingly, she said, "Not whitebait, or do you think silver sprouts up wherever I walk? But you'll have oysters now, and a hot baked potato afterward, if you can keep your hands to yourself. Grab my paps like you did last time, and you'll have a knee in the bollocks instead, understand?"

Whelan had fewer teeth, too, since the last time she saw them, and what remained were badly tobacco stained. But his smile looked sincere enough. "You always were a spirited lass. Oysters first, and then we'll talk."

It was true, she could have afforded more. For all the many things Eliza hated about working on Cromwell Road, her wages were not one of them; between the pace of her work and her own instinct to keep her head low, she'd scarcely spent a penny more than she had to. It might have been nice to go into one of the riverside taverns, get a table in a bay window, have a proper meal of fish and beer—like a normal woman.

But not in Dónall Whelan's company. They ended up perched on two piles of rope on one of the sufferance wharves, licking oyster juice off their fingers while gulls circled in predatory hope. Eliza kept one eye on the birds and one on Whelan, not trusting him more than an inch. At the moment, though, he was fully involved with his food, bolting it as if he hadn't eaten in days—and perhaps he hadn't.

When he paused for breath, she said, "I need to know what to do about a changeling."

She was glad she'd waited; her statement set Whelan to coughing, and she wouldn't have wanted him to choke on an oyster. The coughing turned to laughter soon enough. "A changeling? And you with your harsh words before, swearing it would be a cold day in hell before you asked

Dónall Whelan's advice again, on fairies or any other thing."

Eliza remembered those words very well. She'd gone to Whelan after Owen vanished, because Mary Kinsella said his father had been a fairy doctor in Ireland, with knowledge of how to treat the ailments they brought on mankind. Supposedly the father had passed that knowledge on to his son. If that was true, Whelan had forgotten half of it, and scrambled the other half. He wouldn't even believe her about what she'd seen, swearing blind these English had no fairies, that they'd run them all out with their soulless Anglican church. But all Eliza knew of changelings was some half-remembered tales; she needed advice, and Whelan's—bad as it might be—was the only advice she knew how to get.

"It won't be your missing lad," Whelan said, picking bits of oyster from between his teeth with one ragged fingernail. "You'd have more panic in you if it were, and more hope. So who's been stolen this time?"

" 'Tis none of your concern, who it might be."

"I could say it was." Whelan shifted to find a more comfortable perch on his rope. "Could tell you it matters, for disposing of a fairy. But the truth is I want to know, and I'm thinking you owe it to me—call it an apology. You hurt my feelings something dreadful, last time."

Eliza scowled. "The devil with you and your hurt feelings. Answer me, or I'll be off, and you'll get nothing more than the oysters you've already had."

But Whelan's gap-toothed grin told her the bluff had

failed, even before he spoke. "And you'll be asking the next fairy doctor instead? If you knew one, you'd be asking him already. You're desperate, Eliza O'Malley; it may not be your lad who's gone changeling, but either you care about whoever it was, or you still think you can get him back. So tell me what I want to know, and we'll go on from there."

A fellow passed by them, pushing an empty wheelbarrow. Eliza's skin drew tight, muscles tensing to readiness. She'd taken one of the workmen's trains that morning, leaving Cromwell Road before five o'clock to pay her fare and join the throngs of labourers on their way to work. She'd reckoned the Underground a safe enough way to go; few people boarded the third-class carriages from South Kensington Station, especially at that hour, and none rode so far around the incomplete Inner Circle, a horseshoe journey north and east and south to the Tower of London. If anyone had followed her, she would have seen. But the peelers kept watch over the docks, and especially over the Irish there, to stop dynamite being brought in. She waited until the workman was gone, then said, "Not that it means anything to you, but Miss Georgiana Barlow."

It was the first name that came to hand, a friend of Louisa Kittering's, likewise making her debut in London. "*Miss,*" Whelan said, as if tasting the courtesy. "Some young nob, is it? And why do you care?"

"I don't. But as you said, it might help Owen. Now you've got what you want; give me what I'm paying for."

Whelan eyed her, sucking in his hollow cheeks, as if

gauging whether he could squeeze anything more from her first. Eliza glared at him, not having to pretend a mounting fury, and he gave in. "Sure 'tis simple enough; I've done it a dozen times. Sometimes, with infants, you can give them back: put the changeling on the seashore, or where two rivers come together, or on the edge of a lake, and the fairies will reclaim their own, knowing 'tisn't wanted. But more often, you have to make it go away on its own."

She didn't even know why it had come in the first place, except to disguise the theft of the real Miss Kittering. "How?"

"There's medicines, but I don't know how they're made. Better to be straightforward: beat the changeling, or kick it, or starve it; forcing it underwater can work, or holding it over a fire—"

"I can't do that!" Eliza exclaimed in horror, cutting off his rambling suggestions. For one fractured instant, her mind tried to imagine dragging the false Louisa down to the kitchen, flinging the pots and saucepans off the top of the range, forcing the screaming young woman into their place. *I wouldn't live long enough to be arrested.*

Whelan shrugged. "If the fairy leaves, they have to give the stolen one back. But it isn't easy to make them leave."

"How do you know they have to give the human back? They took Owen, and didn't leave anyone in his place."

"True." Was it her imagination, or did Whelan look troubled? He bent his attention to his fingernails, picking at the ragged edge of one until it broke off. "If you're clever, then sometimes it works to use trickery instead."

It said something very unpleasant about Whelan that he suggested drowning and roasting before trickery. "Tell me about that," Eliza said, trying not to let her relief get the better of her. What followed next might not be any better.

But it was better—if not terribly convincing. "Some say if you can trick the changeling into admitting that 'tisn't human, then it will be bound to leave."

"How—by asking it questions that the person should know the answers to?"

He shook his head. "No, they often seem to know quite a lot." And indeed, Eliza knew, that was true of the false Louisa. Whelan said, "I've only heard the one story of this, and I don't remember it well. But there was a woman with a little child that had been stolen away, and she did something unnatural to confuse it. The thing said it had never seen that in all the centuries of its life, and so showed it was a changeling; and after that, it had to go away."

A much safer path than attacking Louisa Kittering. But still, a thin thread upon which to hang her hopes. Staring out over the filthy brown waters of the Thames, Eliza said, "And that's the best you can say?"

"Don't you be insulting me again, Eliza O'Malley—not when I've been as helpful as I can."

She rather thought he had, and forced herself to murmur an apology. Her heart was still heavy, though, and she couldn't immediately bring herself to move; instead she sat and watched a ship floating gently into the tight quarters of the Shadwell Basin, where dockworkers more fortunate than Dónall Whelan waited to unload its cargo of rice or tobacco or wine. And when the ship's stern had passed from view behind the high walls of the closed dock, Whelan spoke again.

"I suppose I'm owing you an apology of my own."

Startled, Eliza turned back to him. Whelan had hunched down upon his coil of rope, fingers jabbing at its tarred strands. A sharp breeze off the water made them both shiver. "For grabbing my paps?"

His unrepentant laugh said she'd missed the mark. Then Whelan sobered. "No. For doubting what you said, near seven years ago. About fairies in London."

Eliza was off the rope in an instant, tired feet slamming onto the boards of the wharf. "You've seen them?"

"No." The word struck like the grim blow of an ax. "But I've had others come asking for help. From West Ham, out past Mile End. Girls have gone missing, and they say the fairies took them."

The energy of a heartbeat before drained out of her, its place taken by slow horror. "How many?"

Whelan spread his gnarled hands. "Three? That I know about. There might be more. A girl named Eliza Carter, ten or fifteen years old . . . I don't remember the other two. The police looked, I think. But of course they found nothing." He spat onto the planks, still damp from that morning's rain. "The police never find anything in the East End, unless it went missing from the West. You could murder a dozen women here and never be caught."

They certainly hadn't been able to find Owen. One patronizing fellow had told Mrs. Darragh her son probably ran off to America. Eliza never understood it, how one minute these English could talk about the irrational closeness of the Irish family, and the next assume a young man would abandon the mother and sister who needed him. And was that where they thought Eliza Carter had gone?

West Ham. That was on the very edge of the city, a good five miles from Newgate. But the horse-tram was cheap, and Eliza had the whole day off. It might be worth going out there, to see what she could learn.

But first she had a debt to pay. "On your feet," Eliza told Whelan. "We're going to find someone selling potatoes, and some butter to put on them, too; and while we do, you'll be telling me everything you know about this girl and the others. Starting with where their families live."

THE GOBLIN MARKET, ONYX HALL:
26 May 1884

There were fae in the Goblin Market who were very good at stealing secrets.

Dead Rick was not one of them.

But he gave it his best try anyway, knowing it wouldn't be good enough. *Counting* on it not being good enough. Because when Nadrett asked questions later, the master needed to be satisfied that the story Dead Rick told was true.

So he slipped through the chambers and passages of the Market, making his way toward the one corridor that still led to the rest of the Hall. A lot of fae had to pass through that area, making it the perfect territory for the Market's biggest buyer and seller of secrets.

When Nadrett asked later, Dead Rick would say, with perfect truth, that he was looking for proof of an alliance between Lacca and Valentin Aspell. The goblin woman no longer had any territory in the Market; if she wanted to survive, she needed help, and about the only thing she had left to sell was the information in her head. So it was reasonable to think she would offer it to Aspell, who traded in such things, in exchange for something that would help her avoid being crushed by Nadrett and Hardface. It was also reasonable to think that Nadrett would be pleased with any faerie who brought him proof of that offer.

Not that Dead Rick was going to succeed. But Nadrett wouldn't have to question why he tried. For a skriker who was absolute rubbish at lying, it was important to have these things in place beforehand.

A fidgeting sprite stood watch at the edge of Aspell's territory, no one Dead Rick recognised. Slipping past him was easy; all it took was a charm of concealment, persuading eye and ear there was nothing worth noticing. That was only a doorman, though, not an actual defense. The first layer of that waited in the chamber Dead Rick soon came to, where Aspell's underlings lounged at their ease on stolen silks, playing cards or talking idly. No dogfighting here, no pit stained with blood; Aspell's crew was more disciplined than that, if no less ruthless.

Some of these were fae Dead Rick knew. Orlegg, for example, whose thick muscles made him an intimidating enemy. The thrumpin, though, wasn't half the threat Greymalkin was; her feline nose might not be as sharp as a dog's, but it was enough to catch his scent on the air. And scent was a good deal harder to charm away than sight or sound.

Dead Rick had optimistically thought he might get past this room, to where the actual guards kept watch. No such luck: Greymalkin's head came up in swift alert, and then before Dead Rick could decide whether to try and run, they had him.

Orlegg growled impressive threats about breaking his arms, but it was just talk—Dead Rick hoped. Aspell's minions were disciplined, more so than most in the Goblin Market. They wouldn't really lay into him until their master gave the order.

And that meant seeing the master.

This was the part that most worried Dead Rick. He didn't dare ask to see Aspell; people would take notice of that, and while the discipline here also extended to information, he couldn't trust it wouldn't get out somehow—maybe on Aspell's orders. So when Greymalkin asked him what he was doing there, what he had seen, Dead Rick gave the most threatening laugh he could manage, and said, "More than you want to know."

She swiped his face with her claws, but he smiled through the blood, because one of her companions had gone away with a worried look on his face. When the other faerie came back, he jerked his thumb at the door and said, "Bring him."

Dead Rick let them drag him; it wouldn't do to look eager. And for once luck smiled on him, because they shoved him into a chair, bound him in place, and went out again, leaving the skriker alone with Valentin Aspell.

Who studied him with an expression forbidding enough to make Dead Rick hope this wouldn't turn out to be a fatally bad idea. Aspell's thin mouth was pinched close, his brows drawn in over sharp green eyes. The wingback chair in which he sat shrouded him partially in shadow, as if it were the hood of a cobra. In a straight-up-and-down fight, Dead Rick would win—he didn't even think the other faerie was armed—but Aspell knew that, and would never let it come to such a fight. Tied to a chair, with plenty of people just beyond the door, Dead Rick was potentially in a great deal of danger.

So he spoke before Aspell could. "I didn't see nothing, and I didn't expect to. I only broke in so I'd 'ave a way to talk to you, private."

The sharp eyebrows rose. "Oh? There are accepted means of doing so. Violating my territory is not one of them."

Aspell should have looked ridiculous, dressed as he was. The former Lord Keeper had been imprisoned for a hundred years of sleep, ever since the middle of the last century, and when he awoke he'd been unimpressed with the dreary simplicity and dull colour men's clothing had taken on. He still wore the long, decorated coats of that previous era, usually in a serpentine green, though he'd given up the absurd wigs Dead Rick had seen in old engravings. Seated at the heart of his power, however, Aspell could have worn a pantomime costume and still been terrifying. The skriker had to swallow before answering.

"You're good, guvner, but you ain't perfect. I go anywhere near you, I got to assume Nadrett will find out. And if I don't 'ave a good answer for it, I'm a dead dog. So I'll tells 'im I wanted to know whether you and Lacca are plotting something, and in the meantime, I tells *you* I'm 'ere to buy information."

"Of what sort?"

Dead Rick thought he'd managed to intrigue the other faerie, at least a little bit. Intrigue was good; it gave Aspell a reason to keep listening. "Information that gets close to Nadrett. You see why I can't 'ave 'im finding out about this."

Aspell settled deeper into the embrace of his chair, one slender hand stroking its arm with an idle motion. "Indeed. Very well; what do you wish to know?"

After leaving the night garden, Dead Rick had decided he had a choice: give up on his absent ally's mission, or continue pursuing it himself. The former choice would just sink him back down into the pit of helplessness that had trapped him before. The latter might get him killed—but if it didn't, he might have something valuable enough to buy the help he needed. "I 'ear tell Nadrett's got a fellow named Chrennois working for 'im. I wants to know more about Chrennois." Dead Rick paused, licked his dry lips. "What's the price for answering that?"

His options for payment were limited. Dead Rick didn't have anything resembling wealth, not since his little store of valuables had been crushed beneath falling stone. That left information—but selling any of Nadrett's secrets could get him killed. The skriker curled his bound hands into fists and prepared to bargain hard.

Aspell sat in thought long enough to make him squirm. Then an unreadable smile curled one corner of his mouth, and he said, "You intend to betray your master."

Dead Rick shook his head. "No, I ain't that ambitious. I just need to know what 'e's planning, so I can—"

The former lord put up one hand, silencing him immediately. "You needn't bother denying it. I know you have been in contact with someone, who has asked to you investigate . . . let us say, certain of Nadrett's activities."

It felt like someone had thrown a bucket of icy water over him. Dead Rick's skin jumped, and his hands clenched tight. " 'Ow in Mab's name do you know that?"

This time the smile curved Aspell's entire mouth, but not pleasantly. "You approach me to buy information, and ask how it is I know things? I will not tell you. All that matters, at least for this conversation, is that I *do* know. But be at ease; I shan't ask you anything about your master. Instead I want to know about your ally."

That was safer—maybe. Aspell smelled *intent,* in a way Dead Rick didn't like. "I ain't seen 'im in a while," he said, hedging.

"Do you meet regularly?"

"No, I—" Dead Rick stopped. On the one hand, this was a betrayal of the voice; on the other hand, for all he knew the owner of that voice was dead or gone. On the third hand—he switched to paws—his scant knowledge might not be enough to satisfy Aspell; on the fourth paw, that made it not much of a betrayal.

Making up his mind, he said, "If you already know 'e exists, that's the dangerous bit, I suppose. I think the cove's somebody in the Goblin Market—or was."

"Was?"

"Like I said, I ain't seen 'im in a while. Think 'e might 'ave died when everything fell. We've got a way of signaling when I wants to talk to 'im, but I did that days ago and ain't 'eard so much as a whisper."

Aspell frowned. "Where does he speak to you?"

"In—" Dead Rick stopped again. "In my old 'ole," he said slowly, thinking. *Which is gone. Maybe that's why I ain't 'eard back. Could be 'is trick only worked there, or 'e don't know where to find me now that my 'ole's gone.*

None of which he shared with Aspell. The other faerie asked, "What else do you know about him?"

'E ain't you, and that's about all I know for sure. "'E talks like a gentleman," Dead Rick said. "But 'e ain't nobody in the court, I don't think—I asked 'im what 'e

thought of the Queen, anyway, and 'e don't seem to like 'er much. Knows a bit about the Goblin Market, but I think 'e also knows people in the Academy."

"What else?"

Dead Rick racked his brain, trying to find anything else to say. Otherwise Aspell would declare that wasn't payment enough, and then he'd end up betraying Nadrett as well as the voice, which was a quick way to end up dead. "'E's got some ventriloquist trick, making 'is voice sound where 'e ain't." Aspell still didn't look satisfied. Then Dead Rick thought of one more thing. Reluctantly, he added, "And 'e knows some things about me."

That got Aspell's interest. "What kind of things?"

"Things I . . . I don't remember."

He wasn't sure whether to be relieved or not that Aspell didn't ask what he meant by that. *Relieved, I guess. If Aspell's knowed all this time that I don't 'ave my memories, 'e 'asn't used it against me, not that I've seen. And that means I ain't told 'im nothing about myself 'e didn't already know.*

Either way, he'd rather be talking about anything but himself. "Is that good enough?"

"It is," Aspell said, surprising him. The former lord sounded obscurely pleased. "So—Chrennois. French, as you may have guessed, though not from the Cour du Lys; he originally hailed from some provincial court. He came to the Onyx Hall more than twenty years ago, with the intent of studying at the Academy. If memory serves, he wanted to develop some new kind of faerie photography.

But he and Yvoir, another French fellow working on the same topic, had a serious falling out—not surprising, as Chrennois was a cold-blooded sort, far more willing than Yvoir to try . . . let us say, *unorthodox* methods."

The frog worked for Nadrett; by *unorthodox,* Aspell likely meant *horrible*. But Dead Rick needed better specifics than that. "Like what? And what kind of photography?"

Aspell spread his delicate hands. "I'm afraid that sort of technical matter falls beyond my expertise. If you truly wish to know, however, I can make inquiries in the Academy."

No need; the methods didn't really matter, and as for the kind, Dead Rick could guess easily enough that it had to do with ghosts. As if the voice of his ally were in his head, he thought, *But what 'as that got to do with going to Faerie?*

He didn't know, and his ally wasn't around to ask. On impulse, Dead Rick said, "How much to find out who it is I been talking to?"

Aspell controlled his expression, but Dead Rick heard the hitch in his breath that indicated a suppressed laugh. "When I have only just now gathered the first scraps of information? Once I know the answer to your question, I can quote you a price; until then, I do not know how much it is worth."

Dead Rick hunched his shoulders and glared, putting as much threat behind it as he could while tied to a chair. "You'd better be quiet about it."

"Yes, yes; you do not want Nadrett to find out. Your

lack of faith in my discretion is really quite offensive. Well, I believe our business here is done . . ." Aspell smiled in a way that raised Dead Rick's hackles. "Except for one simple matter."

The other faerie paused, clearly wanting to make Dead Rick nervous, and to force him to ask. On another day the skriker might have refused to cooperate, but right now, he just wanted out of that chair. "What?"

"You broke into my chambers, Dead Rick. Quite aside from my feelings on that matter, Nadrett will expect to hear you were punished for it." Aspell ran the tip of his tongue over his lips, considering. "You did not make it very far, I suppose. A simple beating should suffice."

It could have been worse. Dead Rick nodded, and at some unseen cue the door opened, revealing Greymalkin on the far side. She was a slender thing, but wiry, and her claws were wickedly sharp. *Could 'ave been worse—could 'ave been Orlegg—but this won't be good.*

"Take him outside first," Aspell instructed the waiting faerie. "I don't want blood on my carpet."

CROMWELL ROAD, SOUTH KENSINGTON:
27 May 1884

In the aftermath of Lucy's sacking, Ann Wick quit, and Eliza was promoted to the position of upper-housemaid, with her pay increased to a full five shillings a week. She spent most of the additional money on coffee: Mrs. Kittering could not find a lady's maid who satisfied her, relying instead on Eliza's clumsy hands, while the new under-housemaid, Mary Banning, was lazy and slow and drank Cook's sherry when she thought no one would notice. Which meant that Eliza was worked so hard, she could scarcely drag herself out of bed in the mornings. Exhaustion rendered her nerves uncertain; one harsh word from Mrs. Fowler could make her angry enough to murder the housekeeper, or put her on the brink of tears.

The thought of confronting the faerie—even with trickery—terrified her nearly into paralysis. Once taken, such a step could not be called back; the faerie would know that she knew, and what little safety Eliza had would be gone. Then there would be only two paths before her: get Louisa Kittering back, or flee. And it might be that neither one would save her from the faerie's revenge.

Failure wasn't the most frightening thought, though. The prospect of success was far, far worse.

Say it tells you what you want to know, Eliza thought, while changing the linens on Mrs. Kittering's bed one afternoon. *Say it confesses,* Yes, we steal humans away, *and tells you where to find them. Miss Kittering, and Owen, and even Eliza Carter of West Ham, whose sister told you she was so afraid of "them" before she vanished. Then what?*

For seven years she'd dreamt of rescuing Owen. With the moment possibly at hand, though, Eliza was learning how little of a hero she was.

It had been easy to pretend, before. When it was a matter of spying on people, and skulking about, and lying. Now the time had come to act directly, though, and the fear gripping her heart made her wonder: Was it really true that she couldn't act before? All these months since Charing Cross, when she'd had the courage to throw a bomb out the back of a train, but not to catch the creatures who put it there. The six long years before that, when she gave up on searching, telling herself she didn't know what to do. Keeping herself safe, at every turn.

And all the while, Owen paid the price of her cowardice.

In the middle of opening the curtains in Louisa Kittering's bedroom the next morning, Eliza's nerve broke. She looked out onto Queensberry Place, and for an instant she could feel the cobblestones beneath her feet, pounding against her heels as she fled back to Whitechapel. Not to safety, but the relief of failure, of giving up and trying no more.

Under her breath, she snarled, *"No."*

Eliza spun, putting the street at her back, and looked toward the bed. The changeling slept there, innocent and false, one hand dangling over the mattress's edge. Vulnerable—but one cry would bring the other servants running. Instead Eliza took a deep breath, squared her shoulders, and picked up a chair.

She didn't attempt to be quiet. Mary Banning would be dawdling over the grates in the morning room still, and Mrs. Fowler discussing the plans for dinner with Cook; Louisa's bedroom was three floors up from where any other servants were likely to be. The only person Eliza was likely to wake was the changeling, and that was exactly what she wanted.

It took less than a minute for the creature to stir and sit up in bed. Where a human might have yawned or rubbed blearily at her eyes, the faerie looked perfectly alert—and then perfectly confused. "What are you doing?"

"Dancing your furniture," Eliza said. Her breath came in short pants, and her arms were already tiring; Louisa's chairs, like everything else in the house, were the pinnacle of conventional fashion, which meant heavy and well upholstered. "I'm sorry for waking you—please don't tell Mrs. Fowler—should have done this yesterday. Has to be done every month, you see."

The changeling stared as she completed one last, lurching turn and set the chair down. Casting about for something lighter, Eliza decided on a small table, and shifted a potted plant off it into the washbasin.

"Dancing . . . my furniture," the faerie repeated, watching her maid begin a second bad waltz about the room.

"Yes!" Whelan's half-remembered story had involved the mother cooking something strange, but the changeling would never have reason to come down to the kitchen. Eliza had thought of several possibilities; this had been the most immediate to hand.

Out of the corner of her eye, she saw the faerie's mouth open and close, and her head wag slightly in denial. *Say it,* Eliza thought, barely keeping the growl behind her teeth.

Tell me how old you are, what strange things you've seen, but this the strangest of all. Admit what you are. Say it!

"Are you drunk?"

Eliza stumbled, lost her balance, nearly fell into the wall. "What?"

The young woman's mouth pressed tight. The way she drew her shoulders back was a perfect echo of Mrs. Kittering in a ferment of disdain. "Put that table down this instant, back where it belongs—and then get out. We do not tolerate drunken servants in this house."

"But—"

She didn't even know what would have followed that protest. It hardly mattered, though, for the girl smacked one hand against the bedclothes, cutting her off. "Did you not hear me? I said get out!"

Hands cold and shaking, Eliza did as she was told. Table replaced, and the potted plant atop it; then she curtsied like some streetside entertainer's clockwork automaton and slipped from the room, closing the door behind her. After one frozen instant of staring into the hallway mirror, she fled to the refuge of the servants' staircase.

She made it halfway up the narrow steps before sinking into a trembling heap. *Saints preserve me . . .*

I failed.

Because her effort hadn't been good enough? Or because she was wrong—and there was no faerie?

The plain, white-painted boards of the wall swam in Eliza's vision. What evidence had she, that the young woman in that bed was *not* Louisa Kittering?

Changes in her behaviour. An interest in unladylike things. And that brief flinch, weeks ago, when Eliza spoke of the Blessed Virgin.

A flinch only. Shouldn't there have been more, if the creature truly was a faerie? And the other things could be explained away; after all, Miss Kittering had always had unladylike interests. She might simply be kicking harder than ever against her mother's control.

The rest could be explained by Eliza's own fears.

And what of Owen . . . ?

Eliza slammed her fist down onto the step, hard enough to bruise. *No.* That was no trick of her imagination. Whatever Maggie Darragh thought, *that* faerie was real; Eliza had seen him often enough to know.

But that was all. The girl in the bed might very well just be Louisa Kittering.

She heard sounds a couple of floors below: a door opening, and footsteps upon the stairs. Eliza shoved herself up and hastily wiped her face with her apron, scrubbing away sweat and tears alike. Bolting upward would only trap her in the servants' quarters, so she headed down instead, and almost ran into Mrs. Fowler on the landing.

The housekeeper looked at her suspiciously. "I heard a noise. What are you doing up here?"

Eliza dropped a curtsy, hoping it would hide the effects of crying. "I'm sorry, Mrs. Fowler. My foot slipped on the stairs, and my heel came down dreadful hard. I didn't mean to disturb anyone. I just finished in Miss Kittering's room."

But Mrs. Fowler was too practiced at seeing through the lies of maids. "And that sent you up to the attics? You certainly weren't coming from Miss Kittering's room just now. You look a fright, girl; what has happened to your hair?"

An exploring hand found sweaty tendrils escaping from beneath her cap, no doubt from her exertions with the furniture. "I—I'm sorry," Eliza stammered, grasping for any plausible excuse. "I'm afraid I'm not feeling well—"

The housekeeper took her roughly by the shoulder, pressing the back of her other hand to Eliza's forehead. "You're very clammy. Perhaps you're falling ill. Well, we can't have you coughing and sneezing around the family, can we? You'll take over that new maid's duties below stairs; she can do your work above." Mrs. Fowler released her, and when Eliza did not immediately move, said, "What are you waiting for? There's stains that need cleaning, and you've wasted enough time already. Get on with you!"

A shove sent her stumbling toward the stairs. Eliza caught herself on the railing, and thought, *Now is your chance.* She could quit—blame Mrs. Fowler's insistence upon her working while ill, as if she had any right to expect otherwise—and go. Run away before Louisa had a chance to tell anyone what she'd done.

And do what? Without the changeling, she had nothing. No hope except to march up to Scotland Yard and ask the Special Irish Branch whether they arrested any faeries along with their Fenians.

She had nowhere to go, not even Whitechapel. But she had a position here, unpleasant as it was; and if Louisa didn't have her sacked, then at least Eliza could save a bit more money while she tried to think of a plan.

"Yes, ma'am," she mumbled to Mrs. Fowler, and made her way downstairs.

Whole minutes passed—whole hours, it felt like—before Louisa Kittering was able to move.

She spent those minutes staring at the bedroom door, as if the maid would come leaping back through, reciting prayers and waving a solid iron cross to banish her. Not that it would do much good; that might overcome the protection of bread, if the human was devout enough, but not the armour that shielded her now. Still, no amount of safety was enough to erase the inevitable flinch, the instinctive fear.

Especially if the maid knew what she was.

An absurd thought. This was not some rural village, where people still believed in faeries; this was South Kensington, literally across the road from the Museum of Natural History, where humans kept the preserved corpses of exotic animals from around the world, and specimens to illustrate their own supposed descent from apes. And while the maid might be from a less scientifically minded part of England, it would be quite a leap for her to think of faeries—especially when the girl who once lived in this room swore she said nothing of it to anyone.

Yet the maid—Hannah, that was what the girl had called her—must have had some reason for waltzing about the room with furniture. And Louisa had heard cautionary tales of fae, innocents less familiar with the mortal world than she, caught by such tricks, forced out of their changeling roles and back to whence they'd come.

She was not surprised to find, as she swung her legs out from beneath the bedclothes, that her feet were trembling. So were her hands. That had been one of the oddities of her new life, discovering that cold bothered her as it never had before; but this was nerves more than chill. For all that her changeling state protected Louisa more than mere bread, she felt naked, exposed, *vulnerable*. This was no brief masquerade, a glamour thrown over her faerie face and discarded when it was no longer needed. She had taken over the life and name of the girl who was once Louisa Kittering, and until she managed to break free of that young woman's ties, it meant subjecting herself to the constant scrutiny of those around her.

She was only safe so long as they didn't know what she was. The Goodemeades and their mad plan to come out of the shadows looked a good deal less appealing, now that she stood to lose very directly by it. Then *everyone* would know how to recognise the signs of faerie things. As long as they remained ignorant, though, she remained safe—and *free*.

Gloriously free! Louisa could not help but grin at

everything around her, from the pictures on the walls to the brass knobs of her bed, as if she'd never seen any of it before. The touch of her bare toes against the floor steadied her after that fright, and she bounded over to the window to peer out at the street below.

A carriage rolled by, bearing on its doors some peer's coat of arms; she could not make it out from up here, and likely wouldn't have recognised it anyway. She'd thought to go along with Mrs. Kittering's plans and marry that baron's son, the one with the absurd name—or perhaps someone even more highly placed. Taking on a human life didn't mean giving up all of her faerie charms, after all, and the glittering beauty of the *haut ton* did have its appeal. But wedding a peer would limit her freedom too much, unless she kept her husband continually enchanted; and besides, Louisa had never desired to be a faerie bride. She'd known such a creature once, a nymph who left her husband after he struck her three times, and didn't see the point.

No, she would not marry. There was no need for it anyway. Once she was settled into her new role, she would cut her ties with this family, and go wherever she liked. After Frederic Myers, perhaps. He had a wife in Cambridge, but surely it wouldn't take much to change that, especially if Louisa Kittering suddenly discovered a mediumistic talent and began channeling the spirit of Annie Marshall. She even looked a bit like the dead woman, if she turned her head to the right angle; Myers had sneaked glances at the girl all through that London Fairy Society meeting, back in March.

Now that the face was *hers,* she could make use of that.

Silly fool, she chided herself. This was her escape from Nadrett, so that she no longer depended on his shelter and bread. She'd known from the moment she saw Myers at the meeting that spending time around him would be . . . unwise.

But just because Nadrett thinks he might *have another use for the man later on, doesn't mean he will,* whispered the part of her that had grown tired of caution and control. *With your help, Myers could even take steps to protect himself. Wouldn't that be better than leaving him in danger?* She stood with one foot in each world now; why not make use of that? She could do anything Louisa Kittering could, and more.

But a glance back at the door sobered her. That freedom was hers only so long as she *was* Louisa Kittering. One direct admission of her true nature, and the bond would be broken. Which was hardly a concern in the ordinary way of things—but what of the maid?

There were other ways to force a changeling out. It all depended on how strong the maid's nerve was.

Louisa tried to recall what the girl whose place she'd taken had said about the maid. A prying sort—and Irish; yes, now she remembered. Irish, though hiding it, which might explain why her mind went to fae. Louisa shuddered. They had harsh ways of dealing with changelings in Ireland.

Biting her lip in thought, she went to sit in front of the grate, staring at the coals glowing softly in their harmless iron nest. *The Goblin Market answer would be to dispose of her.* It wouldn't even be hard; servants vanished all the time, with little or no explanation. Fetch a will-o'-the-wisp from the Onyx Hall and lure Hannah Whoever over the rail of a bridge, or into the path of an omnibus. Easy and sure.

But she'd taken on this life precisely to get away from the Goblin Market—that, and to stay in London, when the Onyx Hall finished its collapse. It would be a poor escape if she brought all those habits of thought and behaviour with her.

So what, then?

The door opened. But the woman who came in wasn't Hannah; it was some other maid, and she stared wide-eyed at Louisa—who realised she was on her feet with her hands raised in defensive claws. She lowered them hastily, and assumed an expression that implied they'd never been raised at all, that she *certainly* hadn't been on the verge of attacking the maid. *It will take more than a new name to banish my Goblin Market habits, I suppose.* "Yes? What is it?"

The maid, a slump-shouldered woman with a nose made florid by drinking, gave an awkward curtsy. "I'm here to help you dress, miss."

"Oh." Now Louisa felt even more foolish. She couldn't get used to all these people about, waiting to help her. In the old days, before the Onyx Hall reached its present degenerate state, she'd been a minor member of the court, and then of course she'd had servants. But the menial work—the lacing of her stays, the cleaning of her shoes, all the little tasks—had been handled by creatures so small and mindless they ranked one bare step above furniture in her notice. Humans relied on people for these things, and Louisa kept being surprised by their presence. "Pick out something—no, never mind; I will do it myself."

She rummaged through the wardrobe, half her mind on which of her myriad of outfits to wear—*It's morning; I should choose a morning dress; now, which ones are those? It's been ages since I was able to mind proper fashion*—the other half on the problem of Hannah the maid.

I'll see to it she keeps quiet, Louisa decided at last, fingering the sleeve of a dress. *Scare her, if I must. But no sense drawing more attention than necessary, as long as she doesn't go wagging her tongue where she oughtn't.*

She turned around, garment in hand, and saw the maid's eyebrows shoot up. Looking down, Louisa found she'd picked up what even she could tell was a ball gown, in eggplant-coloured silk. Scowling, she shoved it back into the wardrobe and plucked out something else. *But if she threatens more trouble . . .*

If that happened, then Louisa would have to take steps to remove her. Not deadly ones; having her sacked might do. Or reported as Irish, at which point she'd likely be sacked anyway, and no one would listen to a word she said besides. If that wasn't enough, there were fae in the Onyx Hall who would help out for a price, making sure Hannah went somewhere very far away, and didn't return.

There were possibilities. But this much was certain: under no circumstances could the maid be allowed to threaten Louisa's safety. There was still enough Goblin Market left in her to guarantee *that*.

RIVERSIDE, ONYX HALL:
28 May 1884

Coming out of the Crow's Head, where Nadrett had sent him to question the owner Hafdean, Dead Rick caught an odd scent.

Sour. Sharp. I've smelled this before, I know I 'ave—

On Rewdan, the padfoot who'd been Nadrett's courier from Faerie. Satyr's bile, Dead Rick guessed; it was a kind of acid. But what in Mab's name was it doing here?

He stepped warily, following the trail. It led away from people, toward a broken bit of the palace, close enough that nobody wanted to spend much time there. Which made it a perfect place to do secret work—but also to ambush anyone who came looking. *Nadrett wouldn't do that; if 'e wants you dead, all 'e 'as to do is snap 'is fingers.* Chrennois might be a different story, though.

The light faded fast, but he could feel that the stone around him was mazed with cracks. This part of the Hall, like the Market, lay close to the riverside; that meant both cast-iron pipes and the forward progress of the Inner Circle were eating away at its structure. Dead Rick's hackles rose. But there was light up ahead—a faerie light—surely that meant he could trust the fabric to hold together a little while longer.

He paused to sniff the air. Nothing. Just dust, cold stone, and the sour smell of bile. No scent of anyone, faerie or mortal. It didn't reassure him: How had the acid gotten there, if no one had brought it?

Ears and nose could not answer that question for him. Dead Rick crept forward on silent feet and peered around the edge, into the light.

He saw just one faerie light, drifting slowly through the air. Its weak glow illuminated a round chamber, rings of stone benches surrounding a low depression in the center. Dead Rick didn't know what the place had been originally—some kind of theater? There were no other exits, just the passage by which he'd come. He strained his senses, afraid someone had followed to trap him in this dead end. Again, nothing.

Except the smell of acid.

He glanced back into the chamber. A lighter smear marked the black stone in the center. Bait, he was sure—but damn it, it worked; he couldn't leave without investigating.

Gritting his teeth, Dead Rick went down the steps between benches, to the floor of the chamber.

"My apologies for the absence."

He actually leapt into the air, and only just stopped himself from shifting to dog form as he came down. A strangled noise came from his throat, a growl and several different curses all fighting to get out at once. Dead Rick sucked in a huge breath of air, held it, then spat out, "You fucking *bastard*."

The voice didn't dispute it. "I'm glad you found—and followed—the hint I left for you."

Dead Rick swiped at the mark on the stone. It burned his fingers faintly: bile, of course. He wondered where the voice had gotten it. "Where in Mab's name 'ave you been?"

"Had you not taken to sleeping at your master's feet, you might have heard from me sooner. But arranging a new location in which to speak required some amount of effort, and time. I take it you have news for me?"

More than a little. Dead Rick wrestled with himself. Honesty could get a dog killed—but in this case, so could deception, if Aspell decided to sell what he knew. "Secret's out. I don't know 'ow, but Valentin Aspell knows we've been dealing."

A long pause. His muscles all tensed. Just because his ally had never presented himself as anything more than a disembodied voice didn't mean he wasn't in danger. There might be an ambush here, after all.

"What did you tell him?"

The question was presented far more mildly than he had any right to expect. Still, Dead Rick was careful to say, "I thought you was gone, understand? Tried to signal you for days, got no answer, but I didn't want to just give up, and this was 'is price for what I needed to know."

"Spare me the excuses; just tell me what you said."

So Dead Rick did. Mostly. He left out any hint that he'd been investigating the voice, trying to find out who he was; but as he'd thought before, the information itself didn't amount to much. "You was right to be careful," he added at the end, still wary. "Keeping separate like this—I don't know nothing to betray."

"How fortunate," the voice said dryly. "So, you sold me to Aspell in exchange for something about Nadrett. I think it only right I should have a share in that information, don't you?"

This time Dead Rick answered with enthusiasm, spurred by relief that his ally had not abandoned him. *Maybe 'e's one of the Prince's fellows after all. They're the only ones as play so kind.* "I saw the camera. And the cove using it, too." Quickly, the words stumbling over one another, he related what Aspell had told him about Chrennois.

His ally seemed far more interested in the camera than the sprite behind it. "Where did you see this? And did they use it in front of you?"

"They did. Out in the sewers—west of where it breaks into the Market, and a bit south of the intercepting line. Nadrett 'ad us out there 'unting a ghost, me and a few others, and Chrennois. 'E used it to capture the ghost." Dead Rick settled himself on the cracked stone of the lowest branch and described the device, and the way the ghost had vanished. "I don't think 'e'd tried it before. Ain't many ghosts around anymore, are there? But I guess this one appears every year—proper 'aunting, not just something that ain't been cleared away yet—and so 'e decided to test the camera on it."

The voice hummed in thought. "Appears every year . . . when was this?"

"May Day. It were an old ghost, too; knee breeches, the whole bit."

Silence. Then Dead Rick heard something he'd never expected from his ally: a bark of laughter. "Knee breeches! Do you mean to say that Nadrett captured the ghost of Galen St. Clair?"

Dead Rick opened his mouth to say he had no idea who that was, then stopped. Because he *did* know the name; he'd seen it before he talked to Irrith.

On the memorial listing past Princes of the Stone.

"Why would 'e be 'aunting the sewers?" the skriker asked, disbelievingly.

"No direct reason. It must be a consequence of the palace's disintegration. He's buried in front of that memorial, you know—well, no; I suppose you wouldn't. One of two Princes laid to rest in the Onyx Hall. And his ghost appears here every May Day, or used to. But the chamber where that occurred vanished several years ago, and he wasn't seen again. The general presumption was that his connection here had been broken. It seems he went instead to the place the chamber had been, beneath London." Another thoughtful noise. "Near the Monument, it sounds like; almost beneath it."

Dead Rick wasn't sure what any of it meant. "So Nadrett's scheme needs a dead Prince?" Then he shook his head, dismissing his own words. "No, 'e was surprised; 'e recognised the cove, but didn't expect 'im. So 'e just wanted a ghost. Why?"

"That is a very good question."

In the following silence, Dead Rick tried to think of what a ghost might be useful for. Tithing bread? He doubted ghosts could—and in any case, the Princes all carried a touch of faerie in them, which meant St. Clair, dead or alive, could hand over bread until he was blue in the face and it wouldn't do any good.

The voice, it seemed, had been thinking about something else. "You didn't try to demand any price of me, before telling me what you knew."

Dead Rick shifted uncomfortably on the stone bench. He muttered, "After that bit with Aspell, I figured I'd used up my luck."

A dry chuckle, much more restrained than the laughter of a moment before. "Wise of you. I think I shall set you a new task—a dangerous one. Consider it penance, if you like."

"What task?"

"I doubt we'll be able to determine what Nadrett is doing by force of reason alone. Therefore, we must pursue his photographer."

The skriker leapt to his feet, shaking his head as if the voice could somehow see him doing it. "No chance. Nadrett would kill me."

"Only if he discovers you at it. I have faith in your ability to be subtle."

He might, but Dead Rick didn't. "I won't do it."

The answer carried a note of malevolence he hadn't heard before. "Yes, you will. What other choice do you have? Who else will help you regain your past? You are running out of time, Dead Rick; your home is crumbling around you. How long before a falling piece of stone crushes your memories to dust?"

Fear rose like nausea in his gut. It might have happened already, in the earthquake of a few weeks before. Dead Rick trusted that it hadn't only because the alternative was unthinkable.

More quietly, the voice said, "We have a deal. Keep your word, and I will keep mine."

What's the worst Nadrett can do to you, anyway? Smash your memories? This bloody sod is right; that'll 'appen anyway. Kill you? I almost wish 'e would.

Through clenched teeth, Dead Rick said, "All right. I'll find your fucking photographer."

THE PRINCE'S COURT, ONYX HALL: *29 May 1884*

Twisting pain in his gut brought Hodge awake. He sucked in air through his teeth, pressing one hand below his ribs as if that would do any good. This back-and-forth was a familiar pattern: he hurt too much to sleep, until exhaustion beat the pain down and he collapsed in the middle of whatever he'd been doing. When he had energy enough to wake, the pain roused him again, and so the cycle went.

He wiped drool from his cheek and looked ruefully at

the wet newspaper that had been his cushion. *Some Prince I make.* He probably had ink on his face.

These days, he was lucky to get any sleep. Hodge had thought his life difficult before; the laying of the new track had showed him how much worse it could get. And yet, no cloud without a silver lining, and all that rot: the Academy was making progress as rapidly as it could on Ch'ien Mu's loom. Wrain already had plans to use it as a shield against the next extension of the track, in the hopes that the unsupported material would take the brunt of the effect, cushioning those in the real Hall. Hodge didn't know if it would work, but he was willing to let them try.

Of course, it meant he had to know when the extension would come. Hence all the newspapers, and railway magazines, and everything else that might contain a shred of information on the progress of the Inner Circle. They made for dreary reading: more tunnel dug, more bricks mortared, more signals set into place. Scowling, Hodge shoved them all aside.

Something fluttered off the edge of the table that did him for a desk. He frowned after it. A piece of paper, folded and sealed. He was almost sure it hadn't been there when he fell asleep.

Sighing, he reached for it. His valet—and wasn't *that* a funny idea, a cove like him having his own valet—knew better than to wake him, on those rare occasions that he got rest; this wasn't the first time he'd woken to find a letter waiting nearby. Perhaps Amadea had brought more bread from the mortals in that Society the Goodemeades had set up. Or it might be another report from the Academy, telling him of improvements to the loom, that still fell short of it saving them all.

But it wasn't either of those. The paper was unexpectedly fine, and the seal a sinuous pattern, like a knot. Hodge broke it and began to read.

We are not friends. You are aware of my past deeds, and revile me accordingly; I understand this very well. But I trade in information, and I have some of sufficient value that I believe you would bargain even with me to gain it.

Nadrett of the Goblin Market has taken prisoner the ghost of Galen St. Clair. Should you wish to rescue him, I can supply details that would assist you in your task. My price is this: that you grant me access to Lune.

You have never made use of my services before now, but some of your followers have. When you decide to accept my offer, notify Bonecruncher; he knows how to contact me discreetly. During my conference with Lune, I will tell her how to rescue the Prince's ghost. As I am sure you will have me guarded during this conference, if I fail to uphold my end of the bargain, you will have no difficulty in retaliating as you see fit.

Do not delay. I am sure you, of all men, know how little time you have.

Valentin Aspell

Hodge stared. The words, crisply inked in an old-fashioned hand, didn't go away.

A few seconds later, with no memory of having moved, he flung open the door and stormed into the outer room. Three fae shot to their feet in alarm, and Hodge held up the letter in one fist. "When did this get 'ere?"

Irrith and Segraine both looked to Tom Toggin, the hob who served as his valet. Tom peered up at the paper. "What is it?"

"It's the bleeding letter you left for me to find. 'Ow long was it sitting there?"

His valet shook his head, wide-eyed. "I didn't leave any letters for you."

Hodge went very still. It was that or drop the letter—as if the paper held any threat. The threat was long gone, along with whatever faerie had sneaked past these three to leave a sealed note by his head. He knew better than to think they'd left him alone; everybody was far too afraid for his safety to let that happen.

"Who's it from?" Irrith asked.

Of course she'd be the one to ask. Hodge made sure to pull the letter close before he answered, so she couldn't snatch it out of his hand. "Valentin Aspell."

Sure enough, her face immediately went pale with anger. Segraine tensed—possibly to grab Irrith, in case she did something stupid—and Tom, who never seemed to get angry at anything, looked curious. "What does he want?"

"To sell us information." Hodge's knees shook; the burst

of energy that had carried him through the door was fading fast. *Bloody 'ell. You'd think I was an old man.* He didn't like to do the math on how old he actually was. Or rather, how young. *I've already survived longer than I expected to.*

It was mention of his predecessor's ghost that made him think that way—that, and the pain that had woken him. In blunt terms, Hodge told the others what Aspell wanted, and what he demanded in return.

"You can't let him near Lune," Segraine said immediately. "He's a traitor, and can't be trusted."

Hodge watched Irrith. Her delicate face was going through an amazing series of expressions, one piling atop the other: suspicion, worry, anger, hope, disgust. When she noticed the Prince looking at her, she grimaced. "He wouldn't try to kill her—I think. He knows the Hall would melt right out from around us if he did, and if he wanted to die he'd find some more elegant way to do it. Segraine's right, though; I don't trust him. On the other hand, it's Galen. If Aspell's telling the truth, and that bastard Nadrett has him . . ." She shuddered. "We can't leave him there."

No, they couldn't. Hodge had only ever known two other Princes of the Stone: his predecessor, Alexander Messina, and Galen St. Clair. The latter haunted the Onyx Hall—or had, until recently—so as to help those who remained. He'd been a scholar in life, and over the years since his death had contributed far more to the repair efforts than Hodge ever would. *They'd be better off with 'im than with me.*

But Hodge was who they had, and he needed to know whether Aspell was telling the truth. His offer didn't give any proof of that; he'd set up a good method for trading for his information, but the information itself could still be a swindle. "*Does* Nadrett 'ave 'im?"

Tom said uncomfortably, "We just assumed he was gone, after the Prince's chambers vanished, because that's where he'd always appeared. And if he'd returned to some other part of the Hall, wouldn't he have come looking for us?"

"Maybe he couldn't," Segraine said. "The Hall has . . . changed a lot, since his time."

Hodge snorted at her delicacy. But it wouldn't do morale any good to suggest the phrase she wanted was, *The Hall is falling down about our ears*. Irrith said, "Aspell . . . wouldn't lie. Not like this. He's a manipulative bastard—I'm sure whatever he wants Lune for, we won't like it—but if he says Nadrett has Galen, then he does." Her mouth pinched, as if that idea caused her pain. Then she drew in a deep breath and went on. "I'd say offer him something else, but I doubt he would take it. So it's your choice, Hodge: Are you going to let him see her?"

He felt the anticipation in all three of them. *Nobody* got in to see the Queen; that was common knowledge. Nobody except the Prince.

Hodge stood, crumpling Aspell's letter in one hand. "It ain't my choice," he said, hearing the roughness in his own voice. "It's Lune's. I'll talk to 'er."

No one said anything, and he couldn't meet anyone's

eyes. For privacy's sake, he turned and went back into the inner room, which held only his table, his bed, and a few faerie lights for company.

With the door shut behind him, he laid one hand on the black stone of the wall.

Reaching out hurt. It meant sinking his mind into the torn fabric of the Onyx Hall, feeling every spike of iron, every gap where the wall had been. It always made him think of the old tortures, thumbscrews and pincers and the rack: no wonder men said whatever their questioners wanted, after being put through such pain. But here he was, putting himself through it, and the only reason he could was because he reminded himself that Lune felt the same thing. Constantly. For years on end.

If she could survive that, he could share it for a little while.

Lune?

Her mind stirred, like a sleeper caught deep in a nightmare. Hodge reached out for her, tried to lend her what strength he had. *Lune. I . . .'ave to ask you something.*

He phrased it as briefly as he could: Aspell's offer, the price, their guesses as to his honesty. By the end of it, she was alert; he could feel her consideration. *Do you have any hint as to why he wants to see me?*

Hodge never knew if his body actually moved during these conversations, or if the shaking of his head was entirely a mental thing. *None. I can try to find out.*

If you succeed, I'll be much surprised; Aspell was

always good at keeping secrets, and I doubt he has lost the skill. Lune paused, and Hodge gritted his teeth—or at least thought the action of gritting them—as a train rumbled along the buried track, from Blackfriars to Mansion House. When they could both spare thought for something else again, she said, *I will not see him, of course. But I will speak to him, through you; he must be content with that.*

He wondered if he should tell her the rest of what they knew about Nadrett, the possibility that he might be creating a passage to Faerie. Would she go, if she could? If it meant bowing to Nadrett, not a chance . . . but what if it didn't?

She loved this city. Had loved it for more ages than Hodge could really conceive. Lune had poured so much of herself into preserving the palace, and the court that inhabited it; he wasn't sure she could abandon it, even if palace and court were gone.

No point in mentioning it, not until they knew if it was more than a dream born from some opium pipe. She would see it as hope, for her subjects if not for herself, and he didn't want to take that away from her if it proved false. Hodge merely said, *I'll tell 'im. Thank you, Lune.*

Surfacing was like pulling a knife from his own flesh: both pain, and the relief from it. Hodge sucked in a great gasp of air as he opened his eyes, and then laid his forehead against the cool stone.

Aspell would not see the Queen. Nobody did.

Not even the Prince.

There was no point. Lune sat in a trance, dedicating every

shred of her concentration and strength to maintaining the Onyx Hall. The only way he could talk to her was through the palace. All going to visit her would do was tell other people where her defenseless body rested.

She'd made him Prince—and then left him to it. He hadn't laid eyes on her in fourteen years.

Valentin Aspell would have to be content with talking. If he didn't like it, then he and his deal could go to hell. They would handle the problem of Nadrett themselves.

NEWGATE, CITY OF LONDON:
31 May 1884

"Come out, ye bastards! I know ye're here!"

Eliza's shout echoed from the brick and stone facades of the buildings around her. For once it was audible, not drowned out by a hundred others; she didn't know what time it was, but midnight had come and gone long since, and the streets around Newgate Prison were deserted. She cackled, remembering the clerks she'd scraped after for pennies during her months here, and shouted again. "Buns! Hot buns, only a farthing apiece!"

It made her miss Tom Granger, and his newspapers at the corner of Ivy Lane. He probably thought she'd gone to work in the new factory and never bothered to tell him. "Sorry, Tom," Eliza mumbled, and took a swig from the bottle of gin she carried, letting it burn down her throat and set her eyes to watering. The gin was responsible for the latter, surely. "Should've said goodbye. Or never left. They're here somewhere, I know it."

She paused, casting around, and finally pointed toward Warwick Lane. "Over there. That's where I saw him. Should've jumped him then—but I'm a bloody coward, I am, and then I lost them. Missed my chance. But they're here, I'm sure of it. Ye're here!" That last was a shout again. She put her mouth to the gin bottle, found it empty, threw it at the entrance to Warwick Lane. It came up short, but shattered satisfyingly against the cobblestones.

Why Newgate? She snorted. Might as well ask, why Whitechapel, where she'd first seen the dog? Why London at all. None of the stories said anything about that, faeries in the city, but they were here—and once you accepted *that,* Newgate was no stranger than anywhere else. Maybe the faeries were drawn by the money, all the wealth of the City's bankers. The traitor had told enchanting stories, about a beautiful and tragic Queen with a string of mortal consorts, but no doubt they had all been lies. Like everything else he said.

Eliza's feet brought her stumbling to the corner of Warwick Lane, where she began to run her hands over the walls, as if she would find something. A hidden door, maybe, that would lead her through into a realm of sunlight where nobody ever got old. But she didn't get far in her search before a voice stopped her. "You there! What do you think you're doing?"

She rested her head briefly against the bricks, then rolled it sideways until her shoulders followed, flattening themselves against the wall. That held her up while she focused her eyes on the source of the voice.

A bobby, of course, in his dark coat and hard, round-topped hat. His left hand held a lantern, adding to the dim gaslight in the street; his right gripped a truncheon. Eliza put her hands up in innocence. "Don't mind me," she said, offering him a grin. "Only looking for something I lost."

He frowned and scraped his shoe along the ground, hitting fragments of her gin bottle. "I ought to run you in for public drunkenness."

"No need, no need." Eliza straightened up, to prove she didn't need the wall, and only swayed a little this time. "I'm, uh—I'm on my way home."

"Is that so?" He came closer, lifting the lantern toward her face. "Where's home? What's your name?"

"Eliza," she said, then cursed herself for telling the truth. And for speaking in her natural voice, she realised belatedly; now he knew she was Irish. *Have to give an Irish name.* "Eliza . . . Darragh." It was the first thing that came into her head, and a stupid answer. Grief rose up in her throat, bringing nausea with it. *Owen. We should have been wed by now.*

"And where's your home, Eliza Darragh?" he repeated, showing no sympathy for her distress.

This time, at least, she managed to think before she spoke. "St. Giles."

His lip curled. The rookeries of St. Giles were even worse than Whitechapel, full of the poorest Irish crammed in ten to a room. But it lay in the right direction from here, if he sent her along—which he did. "Get back where you belong, then. And quietly, mind. I'll be putting your name on the books, and if you're caught disorderly again, we'll see if a night in gaol doesn't settle you down."

"Ye lot couldn't catch a fish if someone gave ye one with a hook through its lip," Eliza mumbled, moving to obey.

"What was that?"

She laughed at him—then stopped, because it wasn't really funny; they'd failed to catch the one who took Owen, too. Shuffling off down Newgate, she said to the night air, "Nothing. Nothing at all. Don't mind me; I'm just a poor Irishwoman. Nobody cares about us."

CROMWELL ROAD, SOUTH KENSINGTON: *31 May 1884*

She woke the next morning in confusion, with no idea of where she was. Damp cold had settled into her bones, making every bit of her body ache, but under her cheek was clean dirt, and she smelled flowers nearby. Head swimming, Eliza lifted her head and looked about.

Jesus, Mary, and Joseph, I'm in the garden. The back face of the Kitterings' Cromwell Road house rose nearby, full of respectability in the morning light; she was lying on the ground behind a bush, with little idea of how she'd gotten there.

The aftertaste of gin in her mouth, and the unsteadiness of the world as she pushed herself upright made her remember drinking—which make her remember Newgate—and the policeman. She'd staggered far enough toward St. Giles to satisfy him if he'd followed her, then turned south, feet carrying her onward while her mind tore again and again at the problem of Owen and the faeries. She hadn't even meant to come back here, not consciously; yesterday she'd taken the evening off, and left with all her money in the pocket sewn to the inside of her skirt, thinking it might be best just to quit. What was there for her in South Kensington, except a family of rich swells with a rebellious daughter?

But habit brought her here, where she'd climbed the wall into the garden, before being defeated by the locks and shutters on the house. Eliza vaguely recalled sitting with her back against the bricks, meaning only to rest a moment while she considered what to do. And that was the last of it.

Sounds from the mews told her the coachman and grooms were up and doing; well, of course they were, it must be at least nine o'clock. Eliza should long since have been inside the house, and hard at the day's work. The very thought of walking through those doors made her ill—and then she remembered what her heart had known, what she'd forgotten last night, with the gin fogging her brain. She'd brought her money, but left behind the photo of Owen.

For that, she would go back inside. And then leave, and do . . . something.

Eliza climbed to her feet and spent a moment ineffectively brushing the dirt and leaves from her dress. Then she went out through the now-opened gate, and around to the western side of the house and the basement door.

Sarah clearly expected some kind of delivery when she opened the door; her eyes widened at the sight of Eliza, who mumbled an apology and pushed past the scullery maid without attempting an explanation. Cook was more difficult to avoid; she sniffed ostentatiously at the reek of gin and said, "You'll be lucky to avoid a sacking."

"I don't care if I'm sacked," Eliza said, splashing a little water from the tap over her face. "I'm done. I've only come to get my things."

Cook's exhalation was just shy of being a snort. "Lucky to do that, too. Mrs. Fowler isn't above confiscating a thing or two, in 'compensation' for you quitting."

"I'll hit her if she tries." Maybe it was the gin—or just the boiling frustration of all the time she'd wasted here. Anger built with every step Eliza took up the servants' staircase, all the more bitter for having no suitable target. She wanted to hit *something*, and the worst part was, one of the people she wanted to hit was herself.

She heard the voices before she made it past the ground floor. In the Kitterings' household, where respectability was more precious than gold, someone was shouting.

And it sounded like Mrs. Kittering.

Eliza didn't care. She didn't want to know. But the stairs took her right past the concealed servants' door into the drawing room; it was impossible not to hear.

"—not tolerate it any longer. Do you hear me, Louisa? I will not have it! If you persist in this manner—"

Louisa's response was too quiet to make out. Every shred of common sense told Eliza to continue up the stairs, to get away from this family and all their troubles, but she found herself instead pressing her eye to the peephole in the door.

It gave an imperfect view of the long drawing room, but good enough to see Mrs. Kittering's face and her daughter's back. The missus was clothed with her customary rigidity, but Louisa seemed to be wearing a dressing gown still, with a bright green scarf thrown over her shoulders. Whatever she said to her mother, it made Mrs. Kittering go even more rigid with fury. "I will not have such language in my house. Count your days of freedom, girl; I will have you gone from London this Sunday week. There is a sanatorium . . . in . . ."

Her voice trailed off into sudden listlessness, as if she had forgotten what she was saying. Then Eliza's breath did the same, as she saw Louisa's left hand float up to grip her mother's jaw.

No sound issued from the room. But Mrs. Kittering nodded three times, as if the hand on her chin were moving her without visible effort. When the third movement ended, Louisa murmured, "Now, let's have no more of this," and let her go.

Whereupon Mrs. Kittering turned and left the room, without another word.

Eliza still wasn't breathing. She tried to draw air, but fear stopped the motion, as if the creature in the drawing room might hear her. Her fingers ached, pressed hard against the plain-painted surface of the door.

Not until the quiet figure moved did her own paralysis break. And then it broke to flight, for the creature masquerading as Louisa Kittering turned toward the servants' door.

Eliza nearly tripped on the hem of her skirt, trying to take the stairs three at a time. She'd gone up another two flights before she realised the idiocy of her choice—*should have gone down!*—but by then she was nearly at the top of the house, with the changeling—*Holy Mary, Mother of God, it really is a changeling*—somewhere below. She wrenched the door handle around and stumbled through, expecting to see the servants' garret.

She was one floor short. She'd exited into Louisa Kittering's bedroom.

Her heart pounded, rattling her entire body, the sound pulsing in her ears. Despite the exertion of flinging herself up the stairs, she felt nothing but cold—shaking cold, that made her hands tremble like leaves. But what had been fear was turning instead to rage.

That beast. That bloody monster. It stole Louisa—like he stole Owen—

All this time, it's been toying *with me—*

She never heard the footsteps on the other stair. Or perhaps there were none to hear: another faerie trick. The bedroom door opened, and the creature wearing Louisa's face stepped through.

"Where is he? Damn you, what have you done with Owen?"

The changeling opened its mouth to speak, but never got the chance. Eliza's fist smashed into its cheek, stopping whatever charm it might have cast. The creature staggered into the wall; then Eliza's hands seized that green scarf and some of the dressing gown, hauling the creature up and throwing it farther into the room. She kicked the door shut with one heel and advanced on the fallen changeling, still screaming. "Bloody faerie, you've stolen the girl, I know you have—coming into this house, pretending to be her—you'll tell me where she is, damn your eyes, and Owen, too, if I have to roast you over the kitchen fire—"

By now the creature was shrieking, throwing its arms up to protect its face, leaving its ribs vulnerable. Eliza kicked once, caught her shoe in her skirts, and fell to her knees. "Tell me where they are! Tell me! By all that's holy—"

Someone caught her arm. Twisting, Eliza found that Mary Banning was trying to drag her off the changeling. It was no difficulty at all to shove her back, sending the maid onto her rump in an undignified sprawl, but the changeling crawled away while Eliza was so occupied. She flung herself after it, sending them both flat to the floor. It curled in on itself while Eliza bit and scratched; she pulled hair; she got the flailing arms pinned back, grinding Louisa's stolen face into the floor.

Then an arm wrapped around her throat, tight enough

to cut off the blood, and by that hold she was dragged back. Eliza clawed at the arm, reached back to try and catch eyes or ears, threw her elbow back into her captor's groin; Ned Sayers cursed, and his grip wavered. Then a fist slammed into her head, and Eliza went limp.

Sayers wrestled her to the floor, holding her down with one knee in her back. Feet appeared in the doorway, maids and footmen and everyone else crowding into the room; distantly she heard Mrs. Fowler demanding to be let through. Eliza no longer fought. There was no point.

She'd lost.

She'd failed Owen.

God had given her a chance to save him, and she'd thrown it away, in a moment of blind, drunken fury.

Sobbing into the carpet, Eliza waited for the constables to come.

THE GALENIC ACADEMY, ONYX HALL

1 June 1884

Dead Rick skulked along, belly close to the ground, only half-believing he was actually making this journey. Nadrett had sent him above again; it amused the master to use a skriker, a death omen, as a courier for the dynamite he sold to dissidents above. If Dead Rick were smart, he would have stayed up there, using that safe time to replace the bread he'd lost in the collapse.

He directed his paws instead toward the Galenic Academy.

He wouldn't have risked it, except that Cyma had vanished, and with her his one reliable connection to this place. Dead Rick hadn't seen the faerie woman since before the earthquake. In her absence, his only way to get information from the scholars was to defy Nadrett's orders and go to them himself.

He smelled the Academy before he got anywhere near it. A welter of chemicals and strange substances, hot metal and steam, burning in his nose. Odd sounds echoed through the corridors: buzzing and humming, clicking and clanging, like some kind of mad factory lay ahead. And voices, too, arguing in a variety of languages, most of them incomprehensible to him.

An arch of moon-silver and sun-gold marked the boundary, tossed only a little askew by the Hall's tremors. Letters wrought into its length spelled out THE GALENIC ACADEMY OF FAERIE SCIENCES, and beneath that, *SOLVE ET COAGULA*. Dead Rick knew enough to recognise that as Latin, but he had no idea what it said. Something alchemical, probably; most of what they did down here was alchemy of some kind, so far as he understood it. He paused beneath the arch, searching the area around him with every sense, and only when he was as sure as he could be that nobody was watching did he shift into man form and proceed.

He didn't get very far before running into someone. Quite literally: a mortal man came unexpectedly out of a side passage, nose buried in a book, and bounced off

Dead Rick's shoulder. "Terribly sorry," he mumbled, and wandered onward without ever looking up.

Dead Rick paused, staring after him, then down the corridor he'd come from. *Which way?* He had no idea; Nadrett had never brought him here. Tossing a mental coin, he followed the mortal.

It proved to be the right choice, at least if he was looking for people. The passage opened into an enormous chamber, blazingly well lit; startled, Dead Rick realised that some of the illumination came from electric lights. Also gas lamps, faerie lights, and even some candles scattered here and there, as if someone had decided to try everything at once. After the dimness of the Goblin Market and the crumbling Onyx Hall, it made his eyes water.

When they cleared, he found himself confronted with . . . he didn't even know what to call some of it. Machines of various sorts; a few were recognizable as clocks or engines, but others were completely unidentifiable. Chemicals in glass containers, doing things incomprehensible to him. And people of both faerie and mortal kinds, some of them English, some very obviously not; fae came from as far away as China to join the scholars here. They were hard at work all over the hall, tinkering and arguing and ignoring his presence completely.

Dead Rick hadn't cloaked himself with any charms of silence or invisibility. They wouldn't do much good, with so many fae around to pierce them, and he had no particular desire to surprise anyone; that led to violence, and he still ached from the beating Greymalkin had given him. But nobody seemed to care that he was standing in plain sight, watching them go about their work. All the bustle and clamour of the Goblin Market, and none of the suspicion.

Not immediately, at least. But if he went on standing there like an idiot, somebody would start to wonder. Dead Rick risked waving down a monkeylike faerie whose clothing marked him as being from India, like the naga he'd seen caged in the Market. *Wonder where that poor beast went?* Died in the earthquake, maybe. Or got sold to some collector of exotics. Or escaped, though he doubted it. Speaking loudly and slowly, with gestures to help, he said, "Irrith? Where? I'm looking for 'er—"

With a cool look and a flawless accent, the monkey said, "Dame Irrith? I believe she is over by the calculating engine. And if you need an interpreter from cockney to English, I can ask on your behalf."

"Cheeky bugger," Dead Rick muttered, embarrassed, and went in the direction the monkey pointed.

Of course Irrith couldn't be in some quiet part of the Academy, where fewer people would see Dead Rick. He found her in the shadow of an enormous machine, a mass of gears and levers twice the height of a man. She was arguing with a red-bearded dwarf about defenses for something, until Dead Rick drew close; then the dwarf cut her off with a raised hand, scowling suspiciously at the skriker. His distrust was weirdly comforting; at least it was familiar.

That distrust was echoed in Irrith's eyes when she

turned and saw him. Unsurprising; their last meeting hadn't exactly ended well. "What do you want?"

Uncomfortable, Dead Rick muttered, "Can we talk private somewhere?"

Her mouth pinched a little, but she said, "I suppose so. Niklas, can I have my gun back?"

"Not unless you vant it to blow up in your hand," the red-bearded faerie said.

The name triggered Dead Rick's memory—the part of it that hadn't been stolen. This must be Niklas von das Ticken, one of the pair of German dwarves who served as Academy Masters. The less friendly of the two. No surprise the web-gun was his doing; he could only rarely be talked into making weapons, but those he produced were remarkable.

Irrith stuck her tongue out at Niklas, then sighed. "Fine, I suppose I'd rather keep my hand. Come on, Dead Rick; I think Feidelm's out of the library. We should be private there."

Feeling a bit like a puppy who didn't know if he was going to be whipped or not, Dead Rick followed her. They wove a path down the chamber, dodging various people bent on unknown tasks, past a tall faerie in a turban watching two humans work on some kind of strange loom, and through an oaken doorway into a room filled with more books than Dead Rick had ever seen in a single place. He stopped, gaping at the shelves—and then whirled, but not fast enough, as Irrith kicked the door shut and aimed a pistol at his throat.

"Picked Rumdoring's pocket as we went by," she said, in response to his obvious surprise. "Did you think you could just stroll into the Academy, and we wouldn't care? You work for *Nadrett*. What in Mab's name are you doing here?"

She didn't look like she would shoot him, but the skriker put his hands up anyway. "Are we safe?"

Irrith's brow furrowed in confusion. "You aren't, not with me pointing a gun at you. I certainly hope I am."

"I mean, could anybody be listening to us?"

"Oh." She paused, considering. "Back up."

Finding his way with his bare toes, Dead Rick retreated the length of the library, toward the statues at the far end. As they passed each set of shelves, Irrith's gaze flicked sideways, checking the aisles. He made no attempt to jump her in those moments of distraction, and when they reached the end of the room, she shrugged. "Nobody in here, I don't think, and the whole Academy is charmed against eavesdropping. Why do you care?"

"Because I ain't 'ere on Nadrett's business."

Her mouth tightened. "Whether that's true or not, you still work for a slave-trader and thief. What happened to you, Dead Rick?"

He'd been an idiot, thinking she would want to help him. "It don't matter," he growled, toes digging into the carpet as if he had any chance to run. "I just came 'ere to ask a question, that's all. Ain't no danger to you; it might even be 'elpful. Will you put the bloody pistol down?"

The sprite bit her lower lip, teeth digging a sharp line,

then spoke abruptly. "Answer this first. Do you know anything about Nadrett having the ghost of Galen St. Clair?"

His hands dropped like stones. "Blood and Bone—'ow the 'ell do you know about that?"

Irrith sighed, and finally relaxed her arm, pointing the barrel at the ceiling. "Valentin Aspell. He wants to sell the Prince some information about it, but Hodge doesn't like his price."

"Blood and Bone," Dead Rick repeated, this time more quietly, but no less heartfelt. Had his ally sold that news to Aspell, or did it leak out by some other path? Old Gadling, maybe. Or it could be Nadrett, working through the other faerie to demand a ransom.

He hated this feeling, like he was playing some game, with rules he didn't know and players he couldn't see. Nadrett and the voice, Aspell and the Prince—even Irrith. Any chance he had of pretending not to be involved was long gone. She asked, "What do you know?"

Dead Rick opened his mouth to answer, then shook his head violently. "No. I can't. I'm probably dead already, but the more people I go telling, the more likely that is."

"You can trust me."

The laugh burst out of him, harsh and unamused.

Irrith paused, then laid the gun down on a table at her side. "But you've forgotten that, haven't you? You've forgotten *me*. Other people, too, I think; you didn't recognise Abd ar-Rashid out there, did you? Or Niklas—well, he didn't recognise you either, but that's Niklas for you. Now here you are, looking like you've been run over by a dustman's wagon, acting as if somebody might knife you in the back any second, and you're working for *Nadrett*. What *happened*?"

The sympathy, the warmth—the guilelessness of her face, as if she wouldn't know a lie if it bit her. Dead Rick shook his head, backing away again, but he'd run out of space; he ended up in a corner between the wall and a statue's pedestal. "It don't matter," he whispered.

"It matters to your friends. Which is what I used to be. Don't you remember *anything*?"

He stared at her: the large eyes, the stubbornly pointed chin, the auburn hair left to fall free of any arrangement. Desperately, he raked through his mind, grasping for anything—even a wisp, the slightest *hint* of a memory. Anything to tell him that he'd once known this sprite, that he could trust her. That maybe he wasn't alone.

Nothing.

He didn't realise he'd said it until her eyes filled with tears. Then she took his head in her hands, and for an instant he tottered on the knife edge of breaking, like a memory dropped onto stone.

With an anguished snarl, he tore himself free, escaping the corner. And found himself staring up at the statue into whose shadow he'd retreated a moment before.

The old-fashioned wig, its curls carefully rendered in marble, made the face beneath look different. Older. But he recognised it, from the sewers beneath London.

The Galenic Academy. Galen St. Clair. The ghost Nadrett had trapped.

"What I came to ask," Dead Rick said, eyes fixed on that stone face. It was young, and the sculptor had put eternal optimism into the young man's faint smile. "When I 'elped you out of the Market, I mentioned Nadrett doing something with photography. I saw 'is photographer—a French sprite, Chrennois. Used to be in the Academy, a while back. 'E's the one as trapped the ghost. Burn my body if I know 'ow it works, but I've got to find Chrennois."

Irrith wiped her eyes with the back of her hand and swallowed, visibly pushing her concern for him to the side. *But she* is *concerned. Ash and Thorn. So that's what it's like, to 'ave a friend.* "Will you punch me again if I ask whether this has to do with passages to Faerie?"

Dead Rick gave a helpless shrug. "I don't know. Maybe, though damned if I can see 'ow."

She nodded, as if that somehow made sense. "All right. Chrennois . . . I remember. Yvoir *hated* him. I'm not surprised he went to work for Nadrett; that bastard's collected more than a few people from the Academy. The nasty ones. I'd assume he's somewhere in the Goblin Market."

"I'm looking, but my guess is 'e ain't there. Nadrett's keeping 'im somewhere else."

"Well, he isn't here, or in Hodge's court. The night garden?" She frowned. "Or some back corner where no one would think to look. I can—"

She stopped, because the door to the library had opened.

Dead Rick whirled again, sinking to a half crouch; his heart instantly began to beat three times as fast. But it was only a mortal, shuffling in with a lost look on his face. From behind him, Irrith spoke, her voice gentled by compassion. "I'm sorry—Feidelm isn't here. I think she went to talk to Ch'ien Mu."

The mortal was scarcely more than a boy, only hints of stubble upon his cheeks. The vacancy in his eyes made him look even younger, as if he were an imbecile. And his scent had changed, too; it was contaminated by a thorough faerie stain, losing the markers of his mortal home. But for all of that, Dead Rick recognised him, just as he had the statue.

That boy was the second thing he remembered, in all the world. Right after Nadrett's face and voice, ordering Dead Rick to go into Whitechapel and steal him away.

The skriker was halfway across the room before he knew he'd moved. The boy cried out wordlessly and fled, running to cower between two of the tall bookcases that stood out from the walls. "Don't scare him!" Irrith cried, and ran after them both. When she caught up, her steps slowed. "Dead Rick . . . what is it?"

He was still staring at the boy, who had collapsed into a ball in the deepest shadow he could find. "Where did you get 'im?"

"From the Goblin Market. Amadea bought him off someone there, a year or so ago, out of pity. Do you know him?"

I'm the one as stole 'im. He couldn't tell Irrith that; bad enough she knew he'd fallen into Nadrett's grasp, without admitting what the master had forced him to do. "Saw 'im there," Dead Rick said, which was true enough. "What 'appened to 'im?"

Irrith shook her head, pityingly. "We don't know. Some kind of botched attempt at a changeling swap, Feidelm thinks. He's lost more than just his name. Poor lad can't speak anymore, though he understands us a bit. Latched on to Feidelm like a lost puppy."

Another Academy Master, a sidhe from Connacht. Dead Rick swallowed. "He's Irish. From Whitechapel. Probably likes the sound of 'er voice." He bit his lip, then said, "Is there any way to set 'im right again?"

He didn't know why he bothered asking. The optimism in the eyes of the statue that watched over them, maybe. But this wasn't the Goblin Market; if there were such a way, someone would have done it already, out of kindness. He wasn't surprised when Irrith shook her head again. "Not without knowing what exactly went wrong, and maybe not even then. I don't suppose you know anything about that?"

Whatever had happened, it was probably Nadrett's doing. There were more than a few broken mortals wandering around his chambers. But that didn't tell Dead Rick much. "Sorry," he muttered, and meant it. *They were both friends of yours,* the voice had told him. It would have been nice to do something for the boy, healing Nadrett's damage.

"Come on," Irrith said, drawing him away. "Let's not

scare him any more than we already have." Any more than Dead Rick already had, though she didn't say it. Maybe the boy always stared out with such fear; maybe he didn't remember the skriker after all.

Once they were on the other side of the library, Irrith said, "Chrennois. You said he trapped Galen in a photograph?" He nodded. "Where's the picture now?"

"With Chrennois, probably."

"Not with Nadrett?"

"I doubt it," Dead Rick said slowly, thinking. Nadrett had some photos around his chambers, mostly death portraits of mortals. He doubted his master would keep anything as valuable as the Prince's ghost where it might so easily be stolen.

Irrith muttered a curse. "Well, more reason to find Chrennois. I'll ask Yvoir if he has any ideas, but he's out right now, and I don't know when he'll be back. How long can you stay?"

His expression answered that question. Irrith's face settled into grim lines, that even he could tell were unusual for her. "I see. Let me ask a more useful question, then: What can I do to help you? Other than finding Chrennois."

"I'm fine," he said. It sounded thin even to his own ears.

"Of course you are. I could shoot Nadrett, if you like; I've been wanting to for years."

"Ash and Thorn, no!" He might never get his memories back. Those, too, were well hidden. "I've got to get back, is all."

Irrith frowned, but nodded with reluctance. "And secretly, I assume. There's a side way out of the Academy; ever since last year, one of the passages leads over to near the Hall of Figures. A small gift, from all the changes in this place. It's useful for sneaking out."

Outside the library, she led him left, avoiding most of the crowded hall. Dead Rick was both disappointed and grateful. He couldn't afford to stay, to speak to the fae who had known him before—but he wanted to. *It was easier when I didn't 'ave nothing to remind me,* he thought. But he wouldn't have traded his current pain for that numb despair, not for any price.

At a bronze-bound door, Irrith stopped, and faced him with a most peculiar expression. It looked like sorrow, turned into a smile. "The first time we met," she said, "was two hundred years ago, I think. Something like that, anyway. You were part of the Onyx Court before I was, and fought in a war, on the Queen's side. You mostly spent your time in the Crow's Head, drinking and playing dice, but I paid you once to help me steal something from the mortals, and after that we were friends. Once I decided to stay in London, you showed me all your favourite bits, and taught me to like coffee." Her smile brightened into real amusement, for an instant. "Tried to teach me to like gin, too, but nobody can do the impossible.

"I know that's not very much. If you could stay longer, I'd tell you more, but really—how do you boil two hundred years down into something you can say? So instead I'll say this: If there's anything I can do to help you remember, all you have to do is ask."

Ask. Not bribe, or pay, or bargain. She might as well have been speaking a foreign language, the words sounded so alien to his ears.

Dead Rick didn't know how to answer it. He clung instead to the familiar. "If you 'ear anything about Chrennois—" How could she get word to him, without Nadrett finding out?

Irrith clapped him on the shoulder, with something more like a natural grin. "I'll figure something out. Or somebody here will; we have a few sneaky sorts. If you get a message with the words 'British Museum' in it, that's from me."

He nodded. And then he turned his back on the Academy and left, before yearning could persuade him to stay.

ROSE HOUSE, ISLINGTON

6 June 1884

Any young lady who had recently suffered an outrage at the hands of a lunatic Irish maid might have been forgiven the desire to stay in bed. Indeed, that impulse was not so much forgivable as required; surely her nerves would demand the chance to recuperate, and in the meantime such bruising as she had suffered would have an opportunity to heal, before anyone saw her disfigured.

Louisa did not care a fig for her bruises, and the longer she stayed in bed, the more she would have to enchant Mrs. Kittering, who showed a most regrettable persistence in shaking off the persuasions laid upon her. Hearn, the Kitterings' coachman, was more easily managed; as for the drunken maid Mary Banning, she did not even need enchantment. Sherry sufficed for her silence. With conveyance and escort thus arranged, Louisa set out for a spa west of the city, and went instead to Islington.

It was better for her health than any spa could have been. While the mead from which the Goodemeade sisters took their name might not be able to cure everything—a pistol ball to the head, for example, was beyond its powers—Louisa felt worlds better after downing a mug with unladylike enthusiasm. Mortals could keep their foul-smelling and fouler-tasting patent medicines; she would take faerie mead any day, and twice on Fridays.

Some of the effect, she admitted privately, might be credited to her surroundings. Brownies were very, very good at creating comfort, and the sisters had spent several hundred years perfecting it in their hidden home. Louisa was convinced the sisters had invented the notion of stuffing chairs hugely full of padding long before mortals ever thought of it. Rose House always smelled of good, clean things, herbs and flowers and fresh-baked bread, with never a hint of the coal-smoke stink of the world outside their door. And the hospitality, of course, was unmatched. But even had Rose House been a dirty hole furnished only with benches and rushlights, Louisa would have basked in its shelter. Some deep-seated part of her soul still could not quite believe that she was safe in the mortal world; spending so many days there without pause had set her skin to crawling with nervousness.

All of which the Goodemeades, with their splendid care for others' well-being, seemed to sense. They held their questions back until Louisa had finished the mead and gave a satisfied sigh.

Then Rosamund pounced.

With the flat, disbelieving tone of one who knows the answer and does not expect to be surprised, she said, "What have you *done*?"

She had the decency to refrain from using a name. The sisters were far from stupid; undoubtedly they remembered a certain human girl who came to a few meetings of the London Fairy Society, and spoke to a certain faerie after the first one. They probably even knew that faerie had come to the meetings in hope of something particular, and it wasn't just bread. Rosamund might not be able to see the face that lay behind the changeling's mask, but that wasn't necessary for her to guess what name that face had formerly borne.

But the woman who was now Louisa Kittering would not have been able to answer to that name, not without losing what she'd gone to such great lengths to gain. So, in gratitude for Rosamund's discretion, she answered as meekly as she could. Not the question itself; that too was dangerous. Instead she addressed Rosamund's actual concern. "It's the only way I could see to stay. It isn't enough to have a mortal who regularly tithes bread; that person could die, or go away, and besides, eating too much of their food is dangerous, even when it has been tithed. What kind of life would it be anyway, with no more shelter than what you can put in your mouth?"

Gertrude spoke with obvious sympathy. "You didn't want to leave London."

"That doesn't justify—"

Rosamund snapped her mouth shut on the words that almost came out. Louisa hastened to add, "She begged me for it! The girl had a wild spirit; she felt trapped in her life, doomed to a future she didn't want, but she couldn't quite bring herself to go through all that running away would require. They would have tried to hunt her down—likely succeeded—and in a way, I suspect she was too soft-hearted to inflict that wound herself."

"So instead you'll do it for her."

Louisa shrugged, seeing no point in denying it. "If I choose to vanish—" She said *if*, but meant *when*. The notion of protecting Myers from Nadrett, once in her mind, had not left; she might not even wait for her face to heal before seeking him out. Who knew but that Nadrett might snatch him, while she waited around for the bruises to fade? "I'm far better able to escape their hunt than she was. And I do not care if I cause someone heartache."

"That's the problem," Rosamund said. "This is how it always goes with this kind of thing; the ones who suffer are the family. They don't understand what's happened, and you can't explain it to them."

Gertrude laid a hand on her arm. "Rose, two souls have been made happy by this—yes, perhaps other souls have been made *un*happy, but from the sound of it, that would have happened even if everyone stayed where they were. The girl is free, and—"

She paused, looking at their guest, who gave the name by which they must call her now. "Louisa."

"Louisa is safe." Gertrude fixed her with a sharp look. "The girl is safe, too, I hope. Does she have money?"

"Yes. It's real, too." Taken from the sale of her better jewels. The absence of which was covered for now, but eventually the deception would be found out. Louisa had half-considered blaming it on the mad Irish maid, but the notion pricked her conscience—and reminded her of why she'd come. It wasn't to hear a lecture from the Goodemeades.

The brownie sisters had dwelt in London since time out of mind; indeed, since before Islington had been a true part of the city. Their distance from the Onyx Hall meant fae did not visit them as often as they used to—the journey to Islington was fraught with peril, for an unprotected faerie—but they still kept abreast of rumours and gossip, by what means Louisa could only guess. If they could not answer her question, they would find someone who could.

Rosamund was muttering darkly about the odds of a sheltered girl from the better classes surviving on her own in London. When she paused to draw breath, Louisa broke in. "She went freely, but I've come across a rumour of another who didn't. Have you ever seen a boy who looks like this?" From her pocket she produced a battered, ill-quality photograph, showing a woman seated with three children. "Or heard of anyone called Owen?"

Both brownies frowned over the photograph, identical furrows appearing in their brows. "Welsh?" Rosamund asked.

"Irish, I think. At least, the maid who assaulted me was."

Gertrude's honey-brown eyes widened. "A *maid* did that to you? I assumed it was L—the girl's father!"

"She was a strong maid," Louisa said sourly, putting the photo away. *More like a woman boxer.* "She, er . . ."

While she paused to frame her next words, Rosamund came to her chair, and beckoned with one peremptory hand. Louisa bent obediently and let the brownie's gentle fingers probe her bruises. When Rosamund let go, she said, "She suspected me for what I am, and tried to trick me into saying things I shouldn't. When that failed . . . I'm not even certain she was trying to drive me out; she may not have had any particular purpose in mind, except to vent her spleen upon me. But she shouted a great deal about someone she called Owen, and how she wanted him back."

Looking to her sister, Rosamund said, "The bombings?"

"Oh!" Louisa said, startled. "I hadn't thought of that. It would make a good deal of sense. Do you know who's helping them?"

Gertrude tapped one plump finger against her lip.

"Eidhnin and Scéineach . . . Bonecruncher, though you didn't hear that from us; Peregrin would kill him if it came out he's been working with folk in the Goblin Market, even for a good cause . . . Nadrett supplies the dynamite, but only because he can profit from it. We suspect Valentin Aspell is behind it all, though there's no proof."

"Which almost *is* proof," Rosamund said, returning to her chair. "No one else is half so sneaky."

Louisa frowned. "Why should Aspell be so helpful? You can't tell me he cares about the Fenian cause."

Rosamund was shaking her head before Louisa even finished. "The Fenians are just a useful cover, a way to act in public without drawing attention. For Bonecruncher, anyway—the Irish fae see it differently, of course. Remember, some of those bombs have been on the underground railway. They can't destroy the tunnels themselves, not with how alert the police are—but the hope is that it would stop, or at least slow down, the plans to finish the Inner Circle."

The ring of iron that would destroy the Onyx Hall. Aspell had gone to prison for being a traitor, but he at least claimed he'd been trying to save the palace. Maybe there was some truth to it. "Did they carry off any of the Irish mortals? Bonecruncher wouldn't, I suppose, but Aspell might."

Rosamund spread her hands helplessly. "I'm sorry. It's terrible to say this, but there are so many mortals caught in the Market nowadays, we don't know who they all are."

Which meant that if Louisa wanted to know, she'd have to go below once more. With a guilty start, she remembered that she'd promised Dead Rick she would come back, even try to help him get away from Nadrett. There was a dearth of young men in her new life that might be persuaded to change places with a faerie, though. Perhaps she could convince the Goodemeades to divert a few pieces of the London Fairy Society bread from Hodge to Dead Rick; that would be better than nothing.

Well, it wouldn't kill her to walk into the Onyx Hall; it wouldn't even endanger her safety as a changeling. She just couldn't answer to anyone who guessed her old name. Dead Rick might not be the cleverest faerie there, but he would sort that out soon enough.

As for what she would do when—if—she found this Irish Owen . . . *Time enough to decide that once I've located him. The maid might just have been deranged, after all.*

But Louisa didn't think so. Not with those screams still ringing in her ears.

"Is there anything I can do for you two?" she asked the brownies, gathering the will to leave their comfortable home.

Rosamund laughed, and it was surprisingly bitter for someone ordinarily so cheerful. "Marry that Watkin fellow, who's in charge of finishing the Inner Circle, and convince him to stop. Oh, and you only have a few months in which to do it."

"If I could, I most certainly would," Louisa said, the warmth draining out of her. It was all well and good to escape to safety, but the Goodemeades had a way of making her feel guilty for those left behind.

"Is there an address where we can write to you?" Gertrude asked. "It may be we'll have something else you can do—and it would be nice to stay in touch, regardless."

Louisa wrote the direction on a scrap of paper Rosamund furnished, hugged both brownies, and went back out into the streets of Islington. "Now," she said to the passing traffic, not caring who stared at her, "I must decide: What do I owe to an Irishwoman who hit me in the face?"

Nothing. But her curiosity had been roused, and would not subside. Sighing, Louisa went to find the coachman.

THE GOBLIN MARKET, ONYX HALL
6 June 1884

Nadrett's boot came down on the back of Dead Rick's neck, forcing his face sideways, so that his throat was half-crushed against the cold stone. The skriker's entire body trembled, torn between the need to breathe and the knowledge that fighting would only make his master press harder.

"I sends you out," Nadrett said in a dangerously soft voice, "for my own purposes. Not yours. When you don't return on time, you know what that says to me? It says you've taken the good bread I've given you, and decided to use it for your *own* purposes. Which sounds an awful lot like stealing from me, don't it?"

Shallow breaths rasped into Dead Rick's throat. Nadrett had been busy when he returned from the Academy—off fucking some former court lady, according to Gresh, which always put the master in a better mood—so he'd dared to think he might get away with his disobedience.

He didn't have that kind of luck. He never had.

"What, *dog,* was so very important that you decided it was worth stealing from me?"

Dead Rick couldn't answer. The best he could manage was a hoarse noise, some movement of his lips. Nadrett let him suffer like that for a moment longer, then lifted the boot. "Yes?"

The skriker coughed, then hurried to speak before his master lost patience. "Bread."

"I know what you stole from me, dog."

"No. Bread. Debts. Tried to get more, to pay a few coves off."

Nadrett made a disgusted sound. "'Ow'd you end up with debts? You don't need no bleeding bread; you never go outside. And don't I give you everything else you need? Anybody comes to break my dog's fingers, they've got to ask me for permission first, don't they?" The toe of his boot thudded into Dead Rick's ribs, and the skriker curled up in pain.

By the time it faded, Nadrett had stepped away, going to an old cabinet in the corner of the room. Dead Rick looked up, cautiously, afraid he would be punished for doing so. But his master's attention was elsewhere; he unlocked the doors with a small key from around his neck, then opened them to reveal an assortment of shelves and tiny drawers.

This was where he kept minor valuables: bread for his underlings, mortal trinkets, other items for his business.

A flat piece of glass, rippling with indistinct shapes.

Black horror rose like bile in his throat. *No.* He tried to swallow his instinctive whimper—it would buy him no pity—but the sound escaped him nonetheless, thin and weak. Nadrett heard and smiled.

"Been a while, 'asn't it? Ain't brought out one of these in ages. This seemed like a good time; after all, I don't want you forgetting about them, do I?"

Dead Rick licked his lips. There was no dignity, no pride; any self-respect he might have gained by talking to Irrith was gone as if it had never been. He cowered on the floor, showing throat to his master, and said the words he knew Nadrett wanted to hear. "Please. Don't."

"You stole from me. You 'as to pay for that."

"I won't do it again, I swear."

"But you've already *done* it, dog. That's all fine and well for the future, but what about what I already lost?"

He was whimpering again, desperately keening, knowing it would do no good. "Please . . ."

Nadrett laughed, a soft, cruel sound. "You're pathetic."

A pause. Just long enough for him to start hoping—

The glass shattered.

Razor shards rebounded off the stone, scoring Dead Rick's skin. Physical pain was lost in the anguish that wrenched his heart. Light shone across his eyes for just an instant, like a will-o'-the-wisp; his hand shot out to try and grab it, but the glow slipped through his fingers and was gone, leaving only blood where the glass had cut him.

Another piece of his past, destroyed. Another piece of himself.

Gone forever.

He couldn't even take strength in rage, for fear Nadrett had more in the cabinet, just waiting to be broken. He just curled around himself, around the pain in his gut, until his master spat, "Get out."

Dead Rick went. He crawled, belly low, sick and on the verge of tears. Out the door, then into enough of a crouch to flee the bastards in the outer room, hearing their laughter and mockery fading behind him. Into the warren of the Goblin Market, not caring where he went, so long as it was away; surely there must be *some* place here that would hide him from everyone's eyes.

Rushing headlong as he was, Dead Rick didn't notice the woman until he slammed into her. He staggered sideways into the wall, regained his balance, lurched onward—and was pulled up short by her words. "Dead Rick!"

The skriker spun, lips peeling back in a snarl. *What in Mab's name*—It was some mortal woman. Obscenely out of place in the Goblin Market, with her silk gown and jewel-pinned hat and unstained gloves; he was surprised she'd made it this far, though if the bruises on her face were any sign, it hadn't been without trouble. How did she know him? He'd never seen her before.

No, that wasn't true. His memory was raw, an open

wound, left bleeding by the shattered glass; he remembered her face. Laughing, slack in the grip of opium. She'd been there with Cyma.

Then he took a better look, and his jaw fell open.

Her gloved hand came up in a rush, before he could say a word. "Don't! Think, Dead Rick. You know there are things I can't say, and it will become very awkward if I have to ignore you saying them for me. But yes—you know me."

Cyma. Wearing the face and name of her mortal toy. A changeling.

With a furious growl, he whirled and began to run again. But she ran after him, calling his name. "Please! I promised I would come back—Dead Rick, wait—what happened? Let me help you!"

Help him. So bloody generous of her, after running off like that. *I'm going away,* she'd said. He remembered her coy smile, her refusal to say where she was going. *Iron rot your soul, Cyma.* But she wasn't Cyma any longer, was she?

He wasn't looking where he was going; Dead Rick found himself facing a rockfall, the corridor ahead completely blocked. And that woman was behind him, gasping for breath, one hand pressed to her tightly laced side. *That's what you get for living as a human.* Dead Rick spat a curse at her. "Out of my way, bitch."

"My name," the changeling said, in between gasps, "is Louisa. Now. And I promised I would try to help you, Dead Rick."

"You can't fucking 'elp me."

He flung the words at her like knives, and she flinched. "I can find a man—"

"Why—so I can be a changeling? Like that would do me any bloody good!"

"Bread, then."

Another curse. "You've got no idea what I need."

"Then tell me!" The changeling—Louisa—finally managed to straighten up. "I can't be much use to you if you don't tell me anything, Dead Rick."

The pain still pulsed inside him, the gaping awareness of void where his self used to be. Before Nadrett stole it and started breaking it, piece by piece. He didn't care if she was any use to him or not; he didn't care about anything at all. *Nadrett's blood. Give me that, and I'll rest easy.* But she couldn't, and so he just wanted her gone.

Dead Rick spat that last part out, half-incoherent, but she understood. She held out her hands, though, stopping him when he moved to leave. "Please, one thing. It's small, I promise. Have you seen a mortal who looks like the boy in this photo?"

He'd been stuck in the dogfighting pit on more than one occasion, not just that fight with Rewdan. Simple boxing matches. One time a yarthkin had caught him a solid blow, right where a drunken goblin had knifed him a few days before.

This felt much the same.

The face stared out at him from the tattered paper, stiffly solemn, but alert, self-aware, *complete* in a way the half-daft boy in the library had lost. That was the face Dead Rick remembered, from those moments before the poor bastard vanished into Nadrett's control.

"You do know," the changeling said, staring into his eyes. "Can you tell me where he is? There's a maid in my household—well, not anymore; she's been arrested and sent to prison—she's searching for him. An Irish girl, Hannah someone."

So that was her name. Two syllables, empty sounds: they meant nothing to him. It might have been anyone's name.

She had once been his friend.

Both of them had. If the voice told the truth.

"The Academy," Dead Rick said. It wasn't Nadrett's blood on his jaws, but it was a tiny piece of revenge, putting right what his master had sent wrong. "Feidelm's got 'im. But 'e's broken."

"Broken how?"

The skriker shivered. "Like 'e lost half of 'imself. They think somebody tried to do 'im as a changeling, but it went wrong. 'E don't speak no more, and 'e's gone soft in the 'ead."

Cyma—Louisa—frowned. "I've never heard of that happening to anyone before. Normally they just lose their names, their identities. Could it be someone tried to force him into it unwilling? I don't know how they *could,* but—"

He cut her off with a swipe of his hand. "I told you all I know. We're done."

Her animated expression faltered, fell into sad acceptance. "I see. Thank you, Dead Rick. If there's anything I can do for you—"

"Don't bother making promises," Dead Rick snarled, shoving past her. "They ain't worth the air they're spoken on."

THE PRINCE'S COURT, ONYX HALL
9 June 1884

"Now you just drink that down," Rosamund Goodemeade said, "and you'll feel good as new."

She said it every time she gave Hodge a cup of mead to drink, and every time it was a little less true. He didn't begrudge her the words, though. In his private thoughts, he'd long since decided the mead was the only thing keeping him alive. It gave a man strength, and he needed as much as he could possibly get.

Today more than most. Hodge gulped the sweet liquid down without pausing for breath, then handed her the empty cup. "Thank you," he said; once, early in his reign, he'd forgotten to be courteous, and Gertrude had smacked him, Prince or no. "Now if you'll pardon me—it's probably better if you ain't 'ere for this."

The brownie's expression soured. She didn't like his plan; even her usually invincible talent for seeing the good in people faltered at times. But he *was* the Prince, and so long as he remembered to say please and thank you, she wouldn't defy him once his decision was made. "We'll be nearby if you need us," Rosamund said, and hastened out of the room.

Leaving him with his guard of two elf-knights. Peregrin had tried to convince Hodge to put on fine clothes; he insisted the Prince's dignity demanded it, especially when holding something like a formal audience. Hodge—who hadn't held anything one could plausibly call a formal audience in his entire reign—flatly refused. He was the son of a bricklayer; he'd never once worn a top hat, and he had no intention of starting now. *I'd look a proper fool, I would. And if I can't take me seriously, who will?*

Even Peregrin and Cerenel were there less for dignity and more for protection. None of them expected physical danger—but given that Hodge's death might very well mean the end of the Onyx Hall, nobody wanted to take any chances.

He took a deep breath, then nodded at Cerenel. The knight murmured to the moth perching on his finger, which fluttered out through a crack in the door.

A moment later, the door opened, and Dame Segraine escorted Valentin Aspell into the room.

Hodge's fingers curled tight around the arms of his chair. He loathed the fae of the Goblin Market; they indulged in all the worst vices of their kind, at the expense of humans, and flaunted it in his face. Their influence had grown through Lune's long decline, as she became less and less capable of calling them to heel, but since her seclusion they'd flourished like rats. Hodge's best attempts to check them on his own were laughably inadequate.

On the surface of it, Aspell wasn't the worst of the lot: that honour belonged to Nadrett. But he had a distinction the other Market boss didn't, which was that he was a confirmed traitor, sentenced and punished by the Queen herself. Hodge didn't trust the bastard an inch.

A spark of anger—the first of many, he was sure—lit in his stomach when Aspell made him an old-fashioned bow. Polite though it looked, he was sure the faerie meant it as mockery. His suspicion strengthened when Aspell said, "Thank you for seeing me, Lord Benjamin."

The formal courtesy twisted Hodge's mouth. He said roughly, "Don't waste my time on fancy talk. Why do you want to see Lune?"

Aspell's thin eyebrows rose, an elegant display of surprise. *But 'e ain't surprised at all.* "That," the faerie said, "is between me and the Queen."

"What's between you and the Queen is *me*. You don't answer my question, this meeting's done."

By the way things should have worked, Hodge had no right to say that; his authority had to do with the dealings between mortals and fae. Not two faeries. He half-expected Apsell to point that out. But the other merely drew in a vexed breath and said, "If you throw me out, you'll never hear what I have to say about Galen St. Clair."

"What's to 'ear?" Hodge grinned. "We already know Nadrett stuck 'im in a photograph. Oh, I'm sorry—was that what you was going to sell us?"

He could almost hear Aspell's teeth grinding. *You came in 'ere with your notions of 'ow this would go—but I ain't playing your game. I may be the last Prince this place ever sees; well, I'm going to be the best fucking Prince I can. And that means not letting you dance me like a puppet.*

When Aspell recovered his composure, the faerie said, "Do you know where the photograph is?"

"Do you?"

That was the one piece of information Hodge was willing to bargain for. But Aspell's fleeting hesitation told him he was out of luck. "I can find out," the faerie said.

Hodge snorted. "So can we. Try again some other time, guv. When you've got something of value to sell."

What looked like real frustration twisted Aspell's face. The Goodemeades had given Hodge a thorough warning about him; they said he was very good at hiding what he thought. Either this was a pose, or he wasn't bothering to conceal his feelings. Whichever it was, it boiled down to manipulation. "I am not a fool, *my lord*. I know the Queen has not been seen in years. Unlike many of her ignorant subjects, I know better than to think her dead—we would have felt it; likely we would not be here—but she cannot be far from her end. Is she even conscious? Is that why you refuse to let me see her, because she has fallen into a coma and can no longer speak?"

It came near enough the truth to make Hodge furious. "No, I won't let you see 'er because you're a fucking traitor. Or did you think I'd forgotten that? Even if you told me why you wanted in, I probably wouldn't believe you; there's no reason I should. But you stands there with your bloody 'that's between me and the Queen' rot, and you expects me to say yes? 'Ow stupid do you think I am?"

The heat in the faerie's eyes said, *Very*. Hodge heard Cerenel shift, as if ready to throw himself in front of the Prince—but without warning, the fire faded, and Aspell relaxed. Too abruptly; Hodge didn't trust it. Aspell said, "You know of the harm I did this court, of course. But I have also done good on its behalf."

"I know; you was Lune's Lord Keeper. That was 'undreds of years ago, mate."

"Not that," Aspell said. "Much more recently. Do you think I want to see the Onyx Hall fall into ruin? When the purpose of my treason was to prevent that very thing? I have tried to halt the progress of the Inner Circle, more than once. I arranged the bombs last fall, at Charing Cross and Praed Street." He grimaced. "There should have been more, a few days ago—enough to break the line completely, and force repairs—but I'm afraid those who took them were not so tractable as I had thought; they chose to direct their efforts elsewhere."

The Goodemeades had told him their suspicions about Aspell and the bombs. His surprise at hearing the faerie confess it so openly, though, was shouted down by his anger. "Oh, and you expects me to thank you for it? Man, if I wanted the line blown up, Bonecruncher would do it tomorrow. But people got *'urt* by that. And I didn't become

Prince so I could 'elp fae murder my own kind."

"Not even to save faerie lives?"

"You won't die," Hodge said grimly. "You'll just go away."

He hid the pain the words brought. Even his fellow mortals knew the Fair Folk were leaving; it was a common story in rural parts of the British Isles, as common as the flower fairies supposedly haunting the gardens of middle-class girls. Unlike the flower fairies, the stories of flitting were true. He wondered how many people telling the stories, though, knew their immortal neighbours personally. It wasn't so easy to accept when the faeries were friends.

Or even enemies, like Aspell. Nothing was showing through that bastard's mask, not anymore; Hodge might have been some exotic bird, stuffed and put on display for a ha'penny a look. "Your predecessors would have considered that a great tragedy."

"It don't matter 'ow great a tragedy it is; I ain't going to blow up London to stop it."

Aspell's gaze flickered, ever so briefly, to either side of Hodge. The Prince couldn't tell what he was thinking: wondering whether Peregrin and Cerenel would attack? Gauging whether he could fight them himself? Looking to them for support? Whatever Aspell saw, it didn't seem to please him. The frustration his face didn't show came through in his oily voice as he said, "I do not want the Onyx Hall to be lost. I have been fighting to preserve it for well over a hundred years. Yes, that has of necessity involved some violent acts—my treason of before, the bombs, the River Fleet—"

The lurch in Hodge's mind felt like another earthquake, this one internal. "What?"

"Twenty years ago, or thereabouts," Aspell said. "When they were building the first stretch of the Underground. I feared even then what damage it might do, and loosed the hag of the Fleet from her bonds, so that she broke through into the railway works."

Peregrin and Cerenel moved forward in one swift, coordinated movement, keeping themselves ahead of Hodge as the Prince catapulted to his feet. "*You're* the reason that 'appened?" He didn't wait for an answer. "My father bloody well *drowned* that day, you bastard. And you sits there telling about it like you're *proud*?"

The former lord's composure faltered; his jaw hung briefly slack. "I—did not realise."

Hodge spat a curse. "You didn't care. Just a fucking mortal life, eh? And those ain't worth a farthing. You *still* don't care, except that you picked the wrong bleeding man to brag to."

Aspell stepped back, hands out as if they could somehow calm the Prince's rage. "Please—you do not approve of my methods; so be it—but I can be of better use to you, if you'll only let me speak with her Majesty—"

A blow to the jaw stopped his words. The elf-knights didn't try to stop Hodge; they only caught Aspell by the arms and dragged him clear as he stumbled, so he could not strike back. "You ain't getting within ten yards of Lune. You ain't going to see so much as the tip of 'er shoe. Only reason I ain't telling my boys to blow your fucking 'ead off is that ain't the Prince's job. Now get out of 'ere before I change my mind."

He never had a chance to obey or refuse. Peregrin and Cerenel wrenched Aspell's arms up behind his back and shoved the faerie out the door, leaving Hodge alone with his fury.

Memory: 30 March 1859

Lune could have tried to conceal the truth. There were any number of rooms in which the Queen of the Onyx Court might choose to grant audience to a prisoner; some of them were quite impressive. But this prisoner would learn the truth soon enough. To delay that would only make her look weak.

She instructed the guards to bring Valentin Aspell to the greater presence chamber.

With so many refugees crowding the Hall, fae were living almost everywhere they could pack in—but not there. The chamber was haunted, Lune thought, by the ghost of the Onyx Hall itself, the glory that had once been her court. No one could live in the shadow of her silver throne, still placed like a sentinel against the far wall, guarding an empty hollow where the London Stone used to be. When the guards brought Aspell in, the only people waiting for him were Lune and Alexander Messina, her Prince.

Despite Aspell's near-flawless control, she saw him check at the threshold. He must have seen signs on his way from the cells beneath the Tower; at the very least, they would have taken a different path than he expected, avoiding rooms and passages that were no longer there. But it clearly had not prepared him for the crack that ran like a scar through the black and white *pietra dura* marble of the floor, the warped and missing columns where the greater presence chamber had *bent* during the shift of the London Stone. It violated all the laws of mortal geometry, and carried a chilling message in the language of faerie science.

While he slept for one hundred years, sentenced for his treachery, the world had changed around him—and not for the better.

If the sight of the presence chamber struck him a blow, the sight of him did the same to Lune. Aspell still dressed as he had a hundred years before, in the long coat and knee breeches of the Georgian kings. For nearly a century she'd put him from her mind, but now he came before her, unchanged, a traitor out of the past, who had tried to murder her for the sake of her realm. The unhealed wound in her shoulder, where an iron knife had stabbed her long ages before, throbbed with brief pain.

With four knights flanking him and rowan chains binding his hands and feet, he reached the edge of the dais and bowed.

"Madam," he said, "my one hundred years are complete."

He did not, she noticed, claim his punishment was done. Whatever sentence she had passed before, she was the Queen of the Onyx Court, and he, one of her faerie subjects; if she changed her mind, not even the Prince of the Stone could gainsay her. Aspell had never been one to choose his words carelessly.

But she'd been wrong to think him unchanged. Lune saw it in his eyes, when Aspell straightened: no one, not even a faerie, woke from a century-long sleep without consequence. A remoteness clung to him still, as if he gripped wakefulness in his hands, but had not yet claimed it for his own. "They are complete," Lune agreed.

She let the silence between them grow taut, then said the words she and Alex had argued over for days. Her Prince had never known Aspell, but he knew what common sense looked like, and this, he said, was not it. Lune granted him that point. The time for common sense, though, had passed.

"One hundred years ago," Lune said, "when I sentenced you to your sleep, I made a prediction. I said that by the time you woke, either the Onyx Hall would be whole once more, or I would no longer be its mistress."

Perhaps it was the lingering effects of sleep that made Aspell interrupt her, as he would never have done before. "Yet here you stand, with your realm cracking beneath your feet."

He would have learned it soon enough. Lune hoped that admitting it now, while he stood before her, would prevent the trouble that might otherwise follow. "Can you guess why?"

Shackled hand and foot, with two elf-knights more than ready to stab him should he blink wrong, Aspell tilted his head and studied her. The distant look in his eyes gave her a chill, as if he looked *through* her. "You have your share of pride," Aspell said, with uncharacteristic bluntness, "but that, I think, is not it. If you remain, it is because you honestly believe that is best for the Onyx Hall."

Left unspoken was the qualifier: *You may be wrong*.

Lune said, very simply, "I remain because I cannot leave."

His indrawn breath was audible.

With her crippled left hand, she gestured at the warped space of the greater presence chamber, the crack that split its floor. "The destruction begun in the eighteenth century continues today, and the Onyx Hall continues to break. An unwounded Queen would not be able to stop it. She might be able to slow it, better than I have done . . . but by the time I conceded that possibility, it was too late.

"If I withdraw myself from my bond with the Onyx Hall, the palace will not survive."

Alex watched silently from her side. There had been a time when she could rule for weeks, even months, without a Prince; it made her bond incomplete, but not fatally so. That time was past. He had been created Prince of the Stone when his predecessor Henry Brandon was not even one day gone, because Lune needed her consort; she could not hold the entire weight of her broken realm alone. If she let go her share of the burden, his mortal frame would not last one hour.

Aspell's thin mouth did not press into the sharp line she expected. He simply stood, eyes still remote, and then he said, "You have woven yourself too thoroughly into the fabric of your realm."

The accuracy of his description startled her. He saw it, and his mouth curved into a strange half smile. "Do you know how I passed my one hundred years of sleep, madam?"

Wordlessly, she shook her head.

Aspell said, "In dreams."

Fae did not dream. Were it not for that look in his eyes, Lune would have tried to correct his words, suggesting that he had experienced hallucinations, or some other kind of vision. But Aspell never chose his words carelessly, and his not quite wakeful state would accept no other term: he had dreamt, and some portion of those dreams held him still.

"I dreamt of many things, as the years slipped by," he said. "I felt the Hall continue to crumble, though I did not understand what it was I felt until I entered this room. I sensed your presence, madam, working itself into the cracks and gaps of this realm, holding together what would otherwise break apart. I sensed . . ." He trailed off, then shook his head, as if trying to escape the seductive clutches of something faerie-kind was never meant to experience. "Even now, much of what I dreamt is unclear to me. But I believe that you are right. Having given so much of yourself to preserve your realm, you cannot leave it now."

But she could have done it before. Lune trusted everyone else in the chamber, her knights and her Prince of the Stone; in front of them, she could admit her mistakes. Her gamble was to do so in front of Aspell. "I wish I had done it sooner. Whether that would have been better or worse, I cannot say—there is more at stake than merely the palace—but I wish I had not left the choice until it was too late."

Aspell's eyes widened in unguarded surprise. Then, with careful consideration, he bowed.

Lune did not let herself breathe out in relief. Not yet. "Valentin Aspell. You have been condemned and punished for your treason. If we should grant your freedom, how would you use it?"

As always, he chose his words with care. After a long pause, he said, "I do not know. But I would not seek to unseat or replace you. It would serve no purpose now."

Hardly a ringing declaration of fealty. But it was what she had hoped for. "Swear to it," Lune said, "and liberty will be yours."

He did not hesitate. Valentin Aspell went down on one knee, and swore the oath, and Lune let the traitor go.

ST. MARY ABBOTS WORKHOUSE

Kensington: 18 July 1884

Nothing would stop the shivering. It wasn't the cold, not anymore; the icy water into which they'd forced her head and most of her upper body had long since dried. The drafts blowing through her cropped hair still made Eliza feel peculiarly naked, but only when she let herself think about it.

She shivered because she was not alone.

Or because she was going mad. She couldn't be sure of the difference between the two. The gusts of misery and dread that kept surging through her—were those her own? Or did they belong to the woman who had died in this cell? She felt the ghost hovering about her, some poor soul who'd made the same mistake she had—trying to run, trying to flee, as if the workhouse were something that could be escaped. All it did was make things worse. Convinced the workhouse master that Mrs. Kitteirng was right, that Elizabeth White, called Hannah, was a dangerous lunatic in need of the strictest restraint.

How long had she been in the cell? A day, at first; then they'd taken her before a justice and gotten permission to keep her there longer. She'd laughed when they shoved her through the door, calling it a holiday; so long as they kept her in here, she didn't have to pick oakum or sew shirts or do any of the other tedious labour that was supposed to teach workhouse inmates virtue. But she'd never been forced to sit, for hours and days on end, in a pitch-black cell too small to pace, her only contact with the world coming when they opened the door to deliver food or empty her chamber pot. The single candle they carried hurt her eyes, and if she spoke, they struck her without answering back.

Lights burst across Eliza's vision, and she realised she was pressing her fingers against her eyeballs, just to have something to see.

Something other than the ghost.

"Leave me alone," she whispered, forgetting her resolve not to talk to the dead woman. Or to the figment of her imagination, whichever it was. "You want me to kill myself, as you did, and I won't. I *won't.*" A laugh caught in her throat—a laugh or a sob, she couldn't tell which.

Maybe it would be better to feign madness. Then she might be sent to Bedlam. She'd seen an article in the newspaper once, praising Bedlam for being a model of civilised, enlightened treatment for the mad—far better than a workhouse, anyway. But no, that would never happen; Mrs. Kittering would put a stop to it. Just as she'd prevented Eliza from being sent to the new women's prison in Brixton, where she might have been able to keep an ounce of dignity. Instead it was hard labour in the Kensington workhouse, and confinement as mentally unsound.

"Please." It was her own voice, whispering again, and then repeating itself more loudly. "Please. I won't try to escape again. Just take me away from her—" Then she remembered that she must keep silent, that every word she spoke might keep her in here longer.

When she heard the footsteps outside, she cringed, thinking they had come to punish her for talking. When the door opened, the flood of light made her whimper in pain; it was far more than a single candle. And then she heard a voice, actually *speaking* to her, for the first time since they shoved her back into the cell. A voice that didn't belong to the dead.

"Come on, then. Somebody wants to see you."

A rough hand grabbed the sleeve of her smock. Eliza did not resist. The woman was taking her out of the cell; that was all that mattered. Bringing her back to the world of light and sound—bringing her back to the *world*.

By the time she felt fresh air on her face, her eyes had recovered enough for her to see. She was being marched across to the main building, past workhouse men who could be trusted with the labour of keeping the grounds tidy. What could they want her for? *Please, Mary Mother of God, don't let them be taking me back to the justice, to ask for more time. If they've only brought me out to throw me back in again . . .*

The main building was not a place where she spent much time; only the best of the workhouse inmates were given duties here, where visitors might see them. The matron hustled her through quickly, into a nearly empty room, containing only two things: an ordinary chair, and a much heavier one with shackles on its arms. Eliza swallowed a whimper as they were closed around her wrists. *It's better than the cell. Anything's better than the cell.* Then the matron left, and Eliza had just enough time to wonder what was going on before a man walked in.

He was a round-faced fellow, not much older than she, with alert eyes beneath heavy dark brows. Both whiskers and hair were closely trimmed, and he wore a stern-looking suit, everything buttoned into place. In one hand he carried a leather case, which he set down at his side when he took the chair across from Eliza, and opened to reveal a sheaf of papers. These he took out, but did not look at; they sat forgotten in his hand as he studied her.

Eliza stared back mutely, wondering who he was. Then he spoke, and a shock of familiarity washed over her. The accents of western Ireland, which she had heard before.

"Elizabeth White," he said. "Formerly a housemaid to the Kittering family of Cromwell Road, in South Kensington. *Alias* Elizabeth Marsh, formerly a costerwoman. *Alias* Elizabeth Darragh, a drunkard seen in Newgate. *Alias* Elizabeth O'Malley, aged twenty-one years, of Whitechapel."

God help me—it's the Special Branch man.

She barely kept that behind her teeth. He knew who she was; the last thing she needed was to give away that she'd spied on him when he came to Cromwell Road. Eliza licked her lips and said, "Who are you?"

"Police Sergeant Patrick Quinn." He folded his hands over the papers he held, continuing to study her. "You've been a hard woman to track down, Miss O'Malley."

Not half hard enough. "Why did you bother?"

He gave her a pitying look. "I work for the Special Irish Branch, Miss O'Malley. As you've likely guessed. So let's pass over the bit where you pretend you don't know why I'm here." Now he did look down at the papers, thumbing through them briefly. "In October of last year, you were seen running out of Westminster Bridge Station, after a bomb went off on the train from Charing Cross."

"I had nothing to do with that."

"So you told Constable McCawley, when he questioned yourself a few days later. You claimed to be chasing somebody. The real culprits."

Eliza closed her eyes. She still didn't know whether it had been a mistake, telling the peeler even that much of the truth. At the time, it seemed like the right idea; after all, she needed to give some reason for why she'd been running that didn't make it look like she'd been fleeing after dropping the bomb. Not until she had repeated her story several times did she find out that nobody else at Charing Cross had seen the people she was chasing.

Not people: faeries. And that's why nobody saw them.

She should have said that to McCawley, let him write her off as a lunatic. It would have been harmless enough then. Saying it to Quinn now, though, would only trap her more thoroughly in the workhouse. Opening her eyes, Eliza said, "I don't know any more now than I did then. If you've come to ask those questions over again, you might as well just read your papers there, because they'll say everything I know."

To her surprise, Quinn nodded. "No doubt. It's new questions I've come with, about the new bombings."

"I wasn't at Victoria Station," Eliza said immediately, remembering Tom Granger's news, months before.

Those thick brows drew a little together. "Not Victoria Station. More recent than that. I mean the four on the thirtieth of May."

Four? She couldn't hide her startlement. Then she tried to remember when she'd attacked the changeling. Her thoughts were sluggish with cold and isolation; she couldn't recall.

Until Quinn refreshed her memory. "You were arrested the next day."

"Not for that!" Eliza protested. "I hit the Kitterings' daughter."

"Yes, I know." Of course he knew; that would have been the easiest thing to learn about her. Far more disturbing was his ability to put that together with her other deeds—especially the ones in Newgate. As if to remind her of that, Quinn said, "One of the bombs was found before it could do harm; the other three went off a little after nine in the evening on the thirtieth. Around two the following morning, Constable Mason found you drunk and disorderly in Newgate. Do you deny that was yourself?"

Not much point in trying, not when she'd foolishly given her name as Darragh. The police kept damnably good notes on everything; they would have a record of Owen's disappearance, even if they never did anything about it. And therefore a record of her complaints. "That was me," Eliza admitted. "But I had nothing to do with those bombs. I didn't even know about them until you told me."

More glancing through the papers in his hand.

"According to the housekeeper, Mrs. Fowler, your evening off was supposed to be June second, the following Monday. But on the morning of the thirtieth, you demanded to be given that night off instead."

How much did he *have* on those sheets? None of that had been part of her trial for assault; he must have questioned Mrs. Fowler himself. And probably the Kitterings, too. "I'd heard some bad news," Eliza said, giving the first explanation that came to mind. "I wasn't much minded to spend the whole day doing chores for nobs."

"What sort of bad news?"

Her wrists pulled against the shackles of her chair, involuntarily. She felt as if she'd been staked out for his target practice. If she tried to lie, he'd catch her out; good as she'd become, she doubted she was any match for this man with his friendly face and too-sharp eyes.

But she could hide behind something like the truth. "You know about Owen Darragh."

"Your childhood love. Disappeared seven years ago."

Hearing the word "love" from his mouth made her want to snarl, but she confined herself to a nod. "I'd heard a rumour. Thought I might be able to find out what happened to him. But it didn't come to anything."

From a pocket inside his coat, Quinn drew out a pencil and a small notebook. Bracing the latter against his knee, he scribbled a few words, while Eliza watched in dread. "What was this rumour?"

Would he never stop asking questions? *Of course not.*

"What do you care?" she asked, her tone deliberately nasty, to distract him. "I went to the police when he was taken, and do you know what they told me? That the Irish are an unreliable race, we are, and I shouldn't be surprised if he abandoned his mother and sister and me. That he'd probably gone to America, or fallen drunk into the river and drowned. And nobody bothered to search."

Quinn's pencil stopped. After a pause, he tucked it back inside his notebook, set the notebook and papers on the floor. Then he leaned forward, putting his elbows on his knees and looking her straight in the eye. "They may have said that, but do you think I would? About my own people? I was born in Castlecarra, Ballyglass, and lived there 'til I was near twenty, I did. We've drunkards aplenty, and unreliable sorts, but sure your lad wasn't one of them. And they did search, you know. Gave up because there was nothing to find. But if you've new evidence, I'll pass it to the fellows in the C.I.D., and see what they can do with it."

The distraction wasn't working as she'd hoped it would. Eliza wished he *could* help—but what could she do? Tell him to arrest Louisa Kittering for impersonating a human? "Ballyglass," she said, and laughed bitterly. "You're Irish-born, and yet yourself and your mates in the Special Branch spend yer time hunting Irish for the English."

Quinn's expression darkened. "You think I should let them go? Twelve people were hurt in the explosion at the Junior Carlton Club. Several servants at Sir Watkin Williams's house, one of them badly. Two coachmen and a police constable at Scotland Yard. If a boy hadn't spotted the parcel at the foot of Nelson's Column, the fourth bomb would have caught even more people in Trafalgar Square. And that's just one night's work; Praed Street hurt more than seventy last autumn. I should turn a blind eye, just because 'tis Irish lads who do the deed?"

"You know what they're fighting for."

"And I know this is a devil of a bad way to do it. Parnell's working for home rule in the Parliament now, and that might do some good—but not if there's another Clerkenwell outrage, or more murders in Phoenix Park. Your lads poison half the world against them, when they go killing people like that."

Eliza shifted uncomfortably in her chair. "They aren't my lads."

"Aye, you were a babe in your mother's arms when they blew up Clerkenwell. But now—"

"No, I mean—" She caught herself. What was she doing? All but spitting in Fergus Boyle's face when he accused her of allying herself with the Irish Republican Brotherhood, then turning around and defending them to Quinn. It made a bad preface for what she said next. "I'm no Fenian."

As she feared, he didn't believe her. "We know you've been helping them."

"I have not!"

"I understand being loyal to family, Miss O'Malley. But you have to see that there are things more important than kin."

He said it so seriously, and yet she had no idea what he meant. "They're Americans, aren't they? No kin of mine."

"But your father is."

It felt like the chair dropped two inches without warning; her hands clutched the arms for balance. "My father's in Newgate."

Quinn didn't bother to glance at his notes. "Not since the twenty-ninth of May."

She couldn't let go of the chair. James O'Malley, out of prison at last. If she'd been in Whitechapel, she would have known. But she'd done her best to hide from her own world, and so it fell to a police constable to tell her about the only family she had left.

Out on the twenty-ninth. On the thirtieth, Eliza asked for the night off, and then four bombs appeared around London.

She'd been visiting him in Newgate, the night she chased the faeries to Charing Cross.

"I haven't seen him," she whispered. "You must believe me." Surely her shock was proof enough. But Quinn just sat there, looking at her, until she asked the question eating away at her heart like acid. "Was he there? Did my da help them?"

"We have a man who says ye both did."

It wasn't true. At least for herself, it wasn't; she knew *that* beyond a sliver of doubt. In which case, who would—

Boyle. Like a slap to the face, she remembered Father Tooley warning her at Easter. *Fergus Boyle's been spreading trouble.* Did he hate her that much, to point a finger at her when the Special Branch boys came calling?

For Maggie's sake, he might. And that thought was bitter as poison, that *Maggie* might hate her so much, when they'd been sister-close in the years before Owen was stolen. But now she and her mother were tottering on the brink of starvation, and that made a woman harsh. Maggie could have told them, or told Boyle to do it. Or he'd done it of his own will, to make sure Eliza would never come to trouble the Darraghs again.

"Tell me what you know," Quinn said, very softly, "and I'll do what I can for you. No lass should be caught in a place like this."

The gentleness of his voice startled her. Why such sympathy, such kindness? Then Eliza sniffled, reflexively, and realised she was crying. And Quinn, not knowing her thoughts about Maggie, thought it was guilt that sent the tears down her face.

With the remnants of anger in her belly, she considered—ever so briefly—telling him to look into Fergus Boyle. That was a man she wouldn't mind seeing locked away; whatever Maggie's state, she could do better than him. But no: that would make her as bad as him, turning Irish over to the English for no better reason than hate. Quinn at least had a purpose for what he did that went beyond his own feelings.

Sniffing away the tears, wishing she had a handkerchief, or at least could lift a hand to wipe her face, Eliza met Quinn's eyes. "What my father's done, I don't know—but I'm no Fenian, and I've never done a thing to hurt the innocent, or to help anyone else do it, either. Do I want Ireland free? You may be sure of it. Christ knows the English haven't been any good for us. But I was born here; London is my home. I'd never do anything to change that."

Quinn held her gaze, eyes still creased with that unexpected line of sympathy. "Then why all the lies? What have you been doing, these nine months past?"

She knew it was weak of her, to give in to that sympathy—knew he was probably doing it on purpose, to soften her resolve. Still, she couldn't stop herself from answering him more honestly than she had any man in seven years. "You'd never believe me. You'd think me mad."

He didn't offer her any easy reassurance, even though she might have taken it. Instead he considered the words, then gave a faint, rueful smile. "And then you'd lose what? You're already locked up as mad, Miss O'Malley. If I don't believe you, then all it means is staying where you are. But if you know something true, and can prove it to me—"

"I *cannot* prove it." Her frustration felt like it would burst out of her skin. "Not from in here, and maybe not out there; but that's what I've been trying to do."

"Perhaps I could help."

If he believed her. *He never will,* she thought, with the wounded instinct of constant failure.

But as he said—what would she lose by trying?

In the end, it was his voice that did it, the familiar Irish cast to his vowels. Castlecarra, Ballyglass. She didn't know the place, but he was a country boy, and might have heard country stories.

Eliza took a deep breath, and told the truth.

Faeries at Charing Cross. Faeries in Newgate. Faeries that stole Owen Darragh away. Even the stories the traitor had told, about the fading Queen of a dying realm, though Eliza admitted they were probably empty. She held back nothing except Louisa Kittering, and that only because it would do her more harm than good; Quinn would never go after the daughter of such a rich family, and the accusation would make Eliza look mad after all. But the rest of it, she told, and Quinn listened to it all without speaking, almost without blinking.

He didn't take notes. When Eliza was done, he sat very still, then glanced down at the notebook as if he'd forgotten it was there. After a moment of consideration, he closed it. "Sure that's a fine queer story."

"And you don't believe a word of it."

"I didn't say that." He tucked the notebook away. "I've learned something, Miss O'Malley, working for Scotland Yard; I've learned not to make up my mind without evidence. And that means not disbelieving you, either. As you say, you've no proof—but at least it makes sense of what you've done, which is more than I've had until now."

"Let me out of here," Eliza said, "and I'll get you proof." In the form of an unconscious Louisa Kittering, if she had to.

He put up a cautioning hand. "I cannot promise you that. But I'll look into it, and see what I turn up. If there are faeries in London, I should be able to find them."

Eliza wished his confidence went deeper. *I should,* he said, not *we should;* he wasn't about to set his fellows in Scotland Yard to hunting. Well, she couldn't blame him. He hadn't laughed in her face, though, and that was something.

Quinn stood. "In the meantime, you behave yourself in here, Miss O'Malley," he said, replacing his papers in the case. "Mind what they tell you, and you'll have less trouble."

Spoken like a man always on the strong side of the law, who'd never been subjected to the abuses of a place like this. Eliza gritted her teeth and looked away, rather than speak the words that might have undone all the good of a moment before. Quinn waited for her to say something, then sighed and went out, closing the door softly behind him.

A few minutes passed. Then the workhouse matron came back and unlocked her from the chair. Eliza cringed, thinking of the black cell and its ghost, but the woman took her back to where the rest of the inmates were rubbing their fingers raw, picking oakum. She fell to work gratefully, drinking in every bit of light as if it were water. If Quinn had arranged this, then she blessed him with her whole heart.

RIVERSIDE, ONYX HALL
24 July 1884

Dead Rick's hackles rose uneasily when he returned to the chamber where he spoke to the voice. It looked worse than ever, cracks mazing the stone until he feared it would fall to gravel at a touch. He stretched one hand out, then stopped, fingers a breath away from touching. *It's the Queen, Irrith said. Trying to keep this place together. Blood and Bone—'ow long 'as she been doing this?* Fourteen years since she vanished; he'd asked. But the struggle must have begun long before that.

Back when he was a Queen's man. "Don't give up," he whispered, as if she could hear him through the black stone. "Not yet."

"Did you say something?"

The skriker jerked his hand back. It was his ally, of course, not Lune; but it made his skin jump all the same. "No, nothing."

"What a pity," the voice said, in cold tones. "I was hoping you might finally have word for me of where Chrennois is."

Dead Rick sat down on the last intact bench, hoping it wouldn't break beneath him. " 'E ain't 'ere, I'm telling you. Not in any bit of the palace. I've searched."

In the course of their conversations, there had been moments of something like rapport: not friendship—nothing so warm as that—but accord, a feeling that they were working toward the same end, and could lay aside the wary suspicion of the Goblin Market. All that vanished as if it had never been, obliterated by the sudden malice of the voice's response. "You could not possibly have searched the entire palace yourself. You must have had help from others."

He had. Irrith's first report had come while he lay

at Nadrett's feet, watching his master examine a string of mortal slaves; a beetle had crawled into his ear and whispered the sprite's short message. The sheer audacity of it startled him almost as badly as the bug had. It brought no useful news, though; just the assurance that they were searching. Every message since then had been the same. And Dead Rick scoured every surviving inch of the Market, without luck. Either Chrennois had been taken by one of the smaller earthquakes that continued to rock the palace, or he was somewhere else entirely.

Dead Rick thought of the grief in Irrith's eyes, and Nadrett's boot on his neck. The sprite knew his memories were gone; she'd offered to do something about that. And she was brave enough—mad enough—to charge into the Goblin Market to save a flock of mortal children, and to tweak Valentin Aspell's nose. If he told her about the glass, would she help him steal his memories back?

Maybe. The possibility was enough to make him brave. "I didn't 'ave much choice," Dead Rick told the voice, setting his shoulders as if for a fight. "This place may be 'alf gone, but I can't search it all, not with Nadrett watching me so often. So sure, I got 'elp. If you don't like it, then you can shove off."

"Do not tempt me," the voice said, each word cold and sharp as winter ice. "You are not indispensable, skriker, and if you ruin what I have spent all this time preparing, I will not hesitate to walk away from our arrangement. You may think you no longer need me, but believe me, you are wrong."

His newfound courage faltered. Differences of accent aside, the voice momentarily sounded so much like Nadrett . . . seven years of brutal control made Dead Rick want to crawl, show throat, beg for mercy. Swallowing hard, he said, "You said you thought I could be subtle; well, this is the best I could do. Anything else would 'ave gotten me killed, or taken so long we'd all be out on the streets anyway. Besides, all they know is where 'e *ain't*—and that's no use to anybody."

The voice made an impatient, irritated noise. "They must be wrong. The compounds would not survive long above. The mortal world behaves according to a set of strict natural laws; Faerie follows no laws at all, at least not consistently. Only in the spaces in between can something like this photography be carried out, where the laws are different, but discoverable and amenable to our use."

It sounded like something an Academy scholar would say. Could Dead Rick have been wrong when he assumed his ally was a Goblin Market faerie? If so, he would stand no chance of guessing the voice's identity—not when he didn't even remember the Academy fae he *had* once known.

He wished he dared ask Irrith—it would simplify things so much, if he uncovered his ally's secret—but the risk was too great, at least for now. "Someplace else, then," Dead Rick said. "A faerie realm, but not this one."

"Close enough by to be of use to Nadrett? The Goodemeades would never let him into Rose House, and there are no others within London."

There had never needed to be, not when the palace was a city unto itself. Even in its fractured state—

Dead Rick's eyes widened. *'E'd 'ave to be a bloody madman.* That didn't mean it was impossible, though. Fae dared the bad patches of the Onyx Hall when they wanted to escape the notice of others; that was why he and the voice met here, where no one else was likely to go. A daring enough faerie could take it one step further. "Maybe 'e's in another part of the palace."

"Another—" The question cut off short, as his ally realised what he meant. Dead Rick caught the soft exhalation of breath, understanding and incredulity. When the voice resumed, it raced quickly through thoughts much like those in the skriker's own mind. "One of the bad patches, perhaps, that no longer leads where it used to; except that those are known, and in the public view. There might be an exception, but the more likely answer is some isolated fragment still attached to an entrance."

The places where the Onyx Hall connected to the City of London above. A great many of them had been lost, in the course of the palace's decay. Dead Rick curled his lip in a bitter snarl. "I'm no bleeding use to you, then; I don't remember where they was."

"I do," the voice murmured, lost in thought. "Both above and below, but I think it will be necessary to search from the City. If such a thing exists, it would be perfect for Nadrett's purposes: he and Chrennois enter only from the mortal world, without anyone to see, but the enchantments on the faerie side give them a protected space in which to work. The question is where, and that, you will have to answer for me."

Dead Rick startled. "Me? Why?"

"Because I have no means of tracking them. The only way for me to determine if their laboratory lies on the other side of an entrance would be to try walking through it, and I don't fancy playing that particular game of chance. It would be a terrible disappointment if I buried myself in airless dirt or scattered my soul to the four winds, when I am so close to achieving my objectives."

It almost sounded like humour. Dead Rick was glad the voice had regained a measure of good feeling, but not so glad he lost sight of his own difficulties. "I can't go up there."

"I'll supply you with bread."

"To 'ell with the bread! Well, I need that, too, I suppose, but Nadrett's the real problem. I go missing again, 'e'll 'ave my fucking 'ead off. And then 'e'll make my 'ead tell 'im where I've been, and what I've been doing. You don't want me spreading your secrets around, then send some other dog."

The silence lasted so long, he wondered if the voice had gone to do just that. Dead Rick wasn't being a coward; in this case, preserving his own hide went hand in hand with preserving his ally's. But it seemed the other had simply been thinking the matter through, for when the reply came at last, it didn't sound angry at all. "I will take care of Nadrett."

Dead Rick frowned. "Take care of 'im? How?"

"I won't kill him, if that's what you're hoping for,"

the voice said dryly. "Not yet. But I think I can arrange a distraction, so that he'll not realise you've gone missing. You will have to be quick—the quicker the better—but a couple of hours should be sufficient for you to visit all the lost entrances, and look for signs that anyone has been through them recently."

He thought about asking what this distraction might be, then thought the better of it. *What I don't know I can't give away. Or be scared of.* "If they 'ave?"

"Do *not* go through." Dead Rick heaved a sigh of relief. "Return to the palace, notify me—by a different signal; we've used the night garden too often—and I will tell you what to do next."

If he moved fast enough, he could possibly even risk going back to the Academy, and telling Irrith what he had learned. But even as that thought took shape in Dead Rick's head, the voice spoke again. "Before you go, I will have your oath that you will not tell anyone else the location of Chrennois's laboratory."

Dead Rick's mouth fell open. "My *oath*?"

"Yes." The word was cold once more. "Since it seems you cannot be trusted to hold your tongue otherwise."

"Even Nadrett don't make us swear oaths!"

A contemptuous sound answered him. "For very practical reasons, I assure you; he would make his minions swear six times a day if he could. Fortunately for me, I enjoy more freedom in the matter. You will swear, or we are done."

Dead Rick could ask Irrith for bread, or go into the

City without it. Surely other people remembered where the entrances had been. But did he dare throw this ally away?

He ground his teeth together, remembering the original form of their deal. "Tell me something first. More about myself."

"After turning to outside help the way you have, you expect me to reward you?"

The coldness was back, and stronger. Dead Rick already crawled for Nadrett; he was damned if he'd do it for this bastard, too. Any more than he had to. "No, I expects you to *pay* me. Like we agreed."

Silence made him wonder if the voice had gone away, if that demand was one push too many. But the words came at last, clipped and hard. "You came to the Onyx Hall not long after Lune became Queen. Ostensibly because cities breed disease, and therefore death, which is in your nature; but the truth is that you were lonely in Yorkshire, and liked the notion of companionship. To put it in crude terms, you wanted a pack."

How in Mab's name could he know that? Even if the voice had been here centuries ago, he couldn't be sure what had been in Dead Rick's head. Unless they'd been friends—no, not a chance. And Yorkshire . . . that was just unexpected enough to be true. There were Yorkshire fae among the refugees, and their accents sounded nothing like Dead Rick's. But some fae changed their way of speaking, and others did not. *For all I know, eight years ago I didn't sound like a cockney.*

It was the payment he'd asked for, even if it came without proof. He didn't dare fight for more. Hanging his head, Dead Rick asked, "'Ow do I swear?"

As far back as he could remember, he'd never given his binding word, nor heard anyone else do the same. The voice instructed him, and Dead Rick spoke the oath. "In Mab's name, I swear not to tell nobody where Chrennois's laboratory is, except you, or if you says I can."

It was more than mere words. He felt the promise wrap around him like an unbreakable chain. Shivering, Dead Rick hoped his ally could be trusted. It had just become that much harder to look to anyone else for help.

HYDE PARK, KENSINGTON
25 July 1884

Despite the fine summer's day, Hyde Park was not well populated for one o'clock in the afternoon. The London Season was nearly done; soon the quality would be departing for their country estates, the men to hunt grouse, the women to visit with one another and either celebrate their escape from the city or bemoan the tedium of rural life, as their dispositions inclined them.

"When will your family be leaving?" Myers asked Miss Kittering, as they strolled down one of the park's graveled paths.

He was vaguely aware that they seemed to have

misplaced the maid who was supposed to be chaperoning the girl. Myers hardly regretted her absence—unpleasant woman—but it was not really appropriate for him and Miss Kittering to be walking alone, even in a public place such as this. Indeed, it might do damage to her reputation.

Miss Kittering did not seem to care. "Not until the fourteenth, I think. Mama is convinced she can arrange a match for me before then, and all my efforts to convince her that I *will not do it* fall on deaf ears." She sounded both disgruntled and impressed.

Startled, Myers said, "Do you not care to be matched?"

The young woman hesitated, concealing her uncertainty behind her fan. "I . . . perhaps I am a foolish girl, too easily swayed by sentiment, but I *cannot* marry where I have not given my heart."

Myers's own heart contracted with an unaccustomed pang. It was foolish, and he knew it; he hardly knew this girl more than twenty years his junior. They'd met only a handful of times, and during the first two of those—meetings of the London Fairy Society—he had scarcely registered her, noting only that she seemed more rebellious against her respectable class than was likely to end well for her. But then they had encountered one another by chance, outside the meetings, and something about her was so oddly familiar . . .

She reminded him of Annie, no matter how hard he tried to ignore it. The way she held her head, and her manner of speaking; had she not been born years before Annie drowned herself, Myers might have thought her his lost love reborn, like some Hindu tale.

It was foolish, and it was disloyal to Eveleen, his wife. He pushed the unquiet feelings of his heart aside, and answered her as innocuously as he could. "At least being married, or going into the countryside, will save you from your mother's unwise taste in servants."

His hand, damn it for a traitor, tried to rise and brush her cheek, from which the bruises had faded. Miss Kittering coloured as if he'd done it anyway. "Yes, well—the servant had her reasons. Which is not to say I *forgive* her, but . . ."

He thought at first that she she paused so the bored young gentleman passing in an open carriage would not hear her words. But when the gentleman was gone, Miss Kittering was still silent. "But?" Myers prompted her.

The annoyed crease between her brows was mercifully not much like Annie at all. "Oh, I—I can't get the blessed woman out of my *head*."

Myers had the distinct impression that she had almost used a different word than *blessed*. "Is it guilt, do you think?"

Miss Kittering's golden head whipped around to regard him indignantly. "Guilt? Certainly not! I had nothing to do with—" She stopped again and gritted her teeth. Then, taking a deep breath, she said, "I trust your good judgment, Mr. Myers. Perhaps you can guide me in a matter which has been troubling me for some time now."

"I certainly will do my best."

She looked away from him, fingers playing with her fan. "The maid, as I said, had her reasons for attacking me. She . . . lost someone dear to her, I suspect; a brother, perhaps. I fear it drove her mad. She somehow got it into her head that I knew something of this—which I most certainly did not—and was attempting to beat that information out of me. For the sake of the one she lost."

Myers, studying the tense line of her neck, the movement of the fan, considered her phrasing. *Most certainly* did *not*. "Have you learned something since then?"

Again that look, both disgruntled and impressed. "How do you know these things?"

I have spent a great deal of time watching women lie, usually about their ability to raise ghosts. Though he was nothing on Sidgwick, for such observations. Myers knew his own desire for success sometimes blinded him. "What you've learned—is that what troubles you?"

"No. Well, yes—" Miss Kittering sighed. "The question that plagues me is, what do I owe to a crazed Irish maid who tried to strangle me?"

"You mean, do you owe her your assistance."

She looked away again, then nodded.

Myers wanted to ask for more details, but her obvious reticence told him not to push. Considered in its most general terms, however, the crux of the matter was clear. "Would it do anyone any good for her to know? Either the maid, or this fellow she lost?"

A long silence answered that, until they had nearly reached the bank of the Serpentine. Finally—grudgingly—Miss Kittering said, "It might."

"Would it cost you much to help?"

Even more grudgingly, she said, "No."

"Then, from what you have told me, the only reason to refuse is spite toward this maid, for what she did to you. But your wounds healed, and hers, it seems, cannot. Unless someone helps her."

Staring out over the placid waters of the artificial lake, Miss Kittering spoke again, sounding oddly lost and confused. "I'm not accustomed to feeling this way. There was a time I would have forgotten her without hesitation."

Quietly, Myers said, "I must confess, I would think less of you if you did."

She turned to face him, skirts brushing pebbles into rattling motion. "That, too, is unaccustomed. I never thought I would care so much what you think. But I do; I find I cannot bear the thought of you condemning me." Miss Kittering sighed. "So be it, then. I know what I must do."

ST. MARY ABBOTS WORKHOUSE, KENSINGTON
27 July 1884

Following her release from the black punishment cell, Eliza heeded Quinn's advice and behaved herself, swallowing every bit of rebellion and reluctance. They churned uneasily in her gut—along with a case of the gripes she got from bad food—but she held her peace. To really get the sergeant's help, she would need proof, and she couldn't get it from inside here. Eliza doubted she could win free by model behaviour, but it was at least worth a try; and in the meanwhile, she would look for other options. She'd made a mistake, trying to run so early, before she knew enough.

So when the matron came to find her a little over a week later, Eliza was not locked away, pressing on her own eyeballs out of desperation; she was up to her elbows in scalding hot water and soap, scrubbing the battered tiles of the workhouse floor. "Another visitor," the woman said. "You're a popular one, aren't you?"

Her tone made it clear what she thought of that, but Eliza showed no offense. She dried her hands, curtsied, and followed the matron, wondering. Hoping. *Quinn back again? Has he found proof of the faeries?*

Not Quinn. The matron led her to a different room, which proved to be a small parlour, of the sort where ladies from the Workhouse Visiting Society would take their tea, while being told grand lies about the public good such places did. One such silk-clad lady was waiting in the corner, studying a bad landscape painting on the wall, when Eliza entered, with the matron close behind.

Then the lady turned around, and Eliza stopped dead. It was Louisa Kittering.

Who swept past her as if she weren't there and took the matron's hands in her own, nonsense courtesies spilling from her mouth— "*So* grateful to you, just rest yourself in this chair, please, there's nothing here you need worry yourself about in the slightest"—whereupon the woman nodded, smiling vacantly, and sat herself down as if she'd forgotten her own name.

"Don't say anything," the changeling told Eliza. She said it almost in the same breath, but her tone and entire posture changed, the bright silliness falling away like a costume. "And please, for the love of Mab, don't hit me again. If I scream, we'll have half the staff on us in an instant, and I can't charm them all."

The creature was between her and the door. Eliza backed away, wishing she had a crucifix. "Jesus, Mary, and Joseph—"

Louisa Kittering's face showed exasperation. "That won't do any good against me, you know—it doesn't even scare me anymore. Will you hush? I'm here to help you."

Eliza stopped. No, she really had just said that. "You're a liar."

"What I *am* is the one who can help you get him back." She held up the lost photo of Owen.

For all her apparent calm, the changeling squeaked in alarm when Eliza snatched the picture from her gloved hand. *I thought it gone forever.* Her heart thudded hard against her ribs. "Why—why would you do that?"

Composure regained, the changeling lifted her eyebrows as if she were wondering that herself. "Before we say anything more, a few basic rules. We aren't going to talk about who, and what, I am—"

"The devil we aren't," Eliza said violently.

A raised hand stopped her. "I'll have you know the girl you're so concerned about *chose* this. She had to; I couldn't have done . . . what I did unless she was willing. She's off to enjoy the life she wants, without fear her parents will chase her down. Isn't that a gift?"

"And I'm to be believing you did that out of the goodness of your heart?" Eliza snorted to show what she thought of that. "What do you get out of it?"

The changeling smiled. "The ability to stand here in front of you while you fling words of your God at me, without fear they'll harm me. The safety of knowing my protection won't wear off, the way other kinds do. The freedom to stay in London, so long as I keep to this life. She and I both got what we wanted."

For all the tales she'd heard of changelings, Eliza had never thought of the faerie side. She'd assumed the point was to steal mortals away—and maybe for some of them, it was. When it came to the faerie left in the mortal's place, though, she hadn't given it much thought, other than to call it mischief on their parts. *This one* wants *to live as a mortal . . . ?*

Not fully mortal—not given what she'd just done to the matron, who was still smiling at the far wall, not heeding a word they said. But partially so, enough to protect.

Eliza wouldn't believe it until she laid eyes on the real Louisa Kittering. But in the end, one spoiled, rebellious young woman mattered far less to her than Owen. For him, there was no aid she would not accept. And this seemed more promising than trying to arrange for the changeling to be delivered to Sergeant Quinn as proof. *That,* Eliza thought, *can come later.* "How do you mean to help me?"

The creature who was now Louisa Kittering looked around the workhouse parlour, her mouth forming a pretty expression of distaste. "First, by getting you out of here. Ash and Thorn, what a dreadful place. I confess I felt none too kindly toward you after you beat me black and blue—but I expect you've had three blows by now for every one I took. Wouldn't you agree? Of course you would, if it means seeing this end. It will take a while longer, I fear; it's a bit of a tricky thing, convincing these people to let you go, and I can't be quite as direct as once I would have been. You can wait a few more days, can't you?"

Eliza only stared, listening to the new Miss Kittering talk about workhouse overseers and justices of the peace—not to mention Mrs. Kittering—as if they were only tiny challenges, easily overcome. She collected herself with a snap and said, "What then?"

"Then," Louisa said, "you go back to Islington. I trust you recall the house where the London Fairy Society gathers? There's another meeting next Friday week; you should be free by then. Speak to the Goodemeade sisters privately, and tell them . . ." The young woman paused, and chose her next words with care. "Tell them you come in Cyma's name, and are searching for the boy in that photo. They will help you get him back."

"Why should they help me?" Eliza ran one hand over her ragged hair, and felt tears unexpectedly burning behind her eyes. "You still haven't even said why *you're* doing it."

Louisa became very occupied with her gloves, tugging

their delicate seams straight along her fingers. "Someone I . . . that is, someone convinced me it was the right thing to do. Someone whose good opinion I value, and do not want to lose." Her mouth quirked, as if at an unfamiliar taste.

Eliza was not about to question it. She was not certain about the changeling's advice, though. "A few months gone, I heard a lady from the Society tell Louisa Kittering that the others there were not ready for . . . certain truths." A lady who, she strongly suspected, had subsequently taken the girl's place.

"True enough, of some," Louisa admitted. "But not of others. You needn't fear saying anything to the sisters; they know more than you could imagine."

Even if the changeling was wrong—even if the Miss Goodemeades were not so eager to help as Louisa assumed—Eliza would find a way to convince them. "You haven't said where Owen is."

Again, Louisa would not meet her gaze. This time, though, she seemed less uncomfortable for herself than for Eliza. "You understand that he's been among the fae for a long time. And I'm afraid the ones who had him first were . . . not kind at all."

Anger and grief alike rose in her throat. "What did they do to him?"

"I don't know. But he's being cared for, now—by an Irish lady, in fact; her name is Feidelm—and if there's a way to mend him, the Goodemeades will find it."

If. Eliza squeezed her eyes shut, unwilling to let a tear slip free. But what had she expected? For Owen to emerge after seven years lost, smiling as he always had? All this time, the promise she'd repeated to herself over and over again had been, *I will get you back*. Now it seemed that would not be the end. Clenching her fist until it hurt, Eliza added another promise to it. *I'll find a way to make you well.*

And then make the ones who hurt you pay for it.

She opened her eyes to find Louisa giving the seated matron a considering look. "She'll be coming to before long. When she does, I will go."

A month ago, the sight of the new Miss Kittering had filled Eliza with fury; now the changeling felt more like the rope that was offering to draw her up from the abyss. Desperate, Eliza stuffed the photo inside her ragged dress, then closed the distance between them and grasped the young woman by her silk-covered shoulders. "Swear to me that all of this has been true. You'll free me from this place."

"I will," Louisa said, her body stiff with surprise.

"If you do not, then my oath to God, I'll win myself free, and then I'll hunt you down."

She meant it, and she saw that the changeling believed her. "I'll do everything I can. You have my word."

It would have to be enough.

THE CITY OF LONDON

30 July 1884

The hour was not quite midday, and London's beating heart was full of life. Men thronged the narrow, old-fashioned streets of the City, the business men nearly as uniform as soldiers in their suits and top hats, the street-sellers and beggars and musicians a less orderly lot. They carried with them a welter of scents, from food to horseshit to the macassar oil on the gentlemen's hair. Somehow, Dead Rick was supposed to pick his way through that knot to find the few thin strands that might tell him where Nadrett had been—and quickly, before his master noticed he was gone.

Dead Rick's faceless ally had, as promised, slipped a piece of bread to him. The skriker had found it in his waistcoat pocket earlier today—a trick that unnerved him even more than Irrith's beetle had, because he didn't know how it had gotten there. But that was the signal for him to go into the City, so he swallowed it and went. Hoping, with a devoutness few Londoners showed for their divine Master nowadays, that the voice was upholding his other promise, to distract Nadrett from Dead Rick's absence.

Just don't ask 'ow 'e's doing it.

Aldersgate, Crutched Friars, Threadneedle Street, and Ketton Street. Four places for Dead Rick to search. He knew where Aldersgate was—or rather, where it had been, before the gate itself was torn down—and Threadneedle was important enough of a street to be familiar, but for the other two, he would need help. The voice had tried to tell him where to look, but directions meant little when most of Dead Rick's memories of the City were gone.

He went to Threadneedle Street first. There had once been a well here, the voice said, that gave access to the

Onyx Hall, but it was long gone, replaced by pumps. Weakened by the loss of the wall, the palace below had fractured, taking the Queen's old lesser presence chamber with it. But some piece might remain, cut off from the rest.

Dead Rick circled the area in human form, wondering where the entrance had been, and how anyone would pass through it without the well. He sniffed the air, and got a nose full of smells, but nothing that hinted at Nadrett, Chrennois, or their photographic experiments. *'E should be up 'ere, not me. 'E knows right where they used to be. I ain't going to find nothing, searching like this.*

Scowling, he looked around for a private corner, and found none. In the end he slid under a cab that stood at the corner by the Royal Exchange, and changed in the shadow while the driver and passenger argued. But even in dog form, his nose turned up nothing. Did that mean there was nothing to find—or just that his quarries had left no trace of their passage?

On four paws, he trotted down Cheapside until he reached St. Martins le Grand, then went north more slowly, examining the ground once it became Aldersgate Street. The entrance here had been a tree, long ago, but everything around him was stone and brick, without so much as a shrub or a potted plant to soften the harshness. Dead Rick had to dodge aside when a man tried to kick him out of the way, but went back once the bastard was gone, to make certain he didn't miss so much as an inch. In fact, so absorbed was he in searching, he made it as far as Barbican before realising he'd gone beyond the reach of the Onyx Hall.

Back in man form, he retraced his steps to the City and began to ask directions. He ignored the gentlemen; they would look askance at his rough attire and bare feet, and probably only know the principal streets anyway. On Cheapside a seller of newspapers scratched through his whiskers and shook his head. "Crutched Friars, sure—over by the Tower. Go down King William Street, then Lombard, which'll turn into Fenchurch; then right on Mark Lane, and left at the church—that's St. Olave 'Art Street—and pretty soon the street will be Crutched Friars. But Ketton? I've been selling papers 'ere since I were nine years old, and I ain't never 'eard of Ketton."

"The cove told me it were a big street," Dead Rick said, hoping he could remember the first set of directions. "North of Cheapside, going from west to east."

The newspaper seller shrugged. "Gresham Street, then, or London Wall. All the rest is little poky lanes, unless you goes more north."

North would be outside the wall. It had to be one of those two. Even in the City, where streets mostly stayed the same as centuries before, sometimes things changed; what the fae still called the Fish Street entrance now gave onto Queen Victoria Street.

Dead Rick searched Gresham Street and London Wall both, from one end to the other, and the curved length of Crutched Friars, until it became Jewry Street around Aldgate. Every yard of roadway was paved and curbed, lined with buildings and trampled by people, without the faintest hint of any scent he recognised.

It had been a good notion—until it fell apart.

His steps dragged as he turned back toward the Goblin Market. They dragged even more as he went down the rest of Mark Lane, on his way to Billingsgate and the door there; hoardings blocked one side of the roadway, and a piece of paper glued to them promised in bold letters that it wouldn't be long at all before the new Mark Lane Underground station opened for business. "Bugger you all," he snarled under his breath, then hunched his shoulders and hurried by. The visible work here was already done, the roadway dug up and tunneled and covered once more, but the navvies were probably right beneath his feet, toiling away at destroying his home.

He wasn't even certain how safe it was to use the Billingsgate door. It had clung to existence after the rails were laid from Mark Lane to Eastcheap—*no,* he thought, *the* Queen *'eld onto it.* But if her grip slipped, any faerie in the middle of passing through might go along with the door.

His choice was that or crawling through the sewers, or else going into some other part of the Hall, and hoping nobody noticed him on his way back to the Market. Sighing, Dead Rick went into the pub that now covered the door, and put up a charm to hide himself briefly as he passed the owner on his way to the cellar stairs. Not that he needed it; the man's wits had been half-scrambled by all the charms used to make him forget the temporary invasion after the earthquake in May.

Down in the cellar, with one hand outstretched to open the door, he stopped.

The entrance was enchanted, just like the rest of the Hall. Enchantment was a faerie thing, and faerie things involved faerie elements. That was very nearly as far as Dead Rick's knowledge of science went, but he knew two things more. First, that one of those elements was aether.

And second, that the Academy had invented devices for detecting it.

He'd seen one in the Goblin Market, after someone brought in a load of things supposedly from the faerie courts of India and China. Jade figurines, strange weapons, things like that. A Greek trader named Arkheton had been interested in buying them, but only if they were genuine, and so he'd tested them with one of those devices. An aetheric versorium, that was the term.

All but two pieces proved to be false, and Arkheton kept the versorium in case anyone tried to swindle him again.

'E won't mind if I borrow it, right?

Dead Rick almost didn't make it out of the Goblin Market with his head attached, but not because Arkheton objected to him stealing the object. The skriker doubted his victim even knew the thing was gone. *Right now, you could steal a man's left nutmeg and 'e might not notice.*

His ally, it seemed, had decided to cover his absence

by laying an enormous charm over what remained of the warren, confusing both sight and sound. Smell was more or less untouched, and that was the only reason Dead Rick had been able to carry out his purpose; he'd closed his eyes, ignored what he heard, and followed his nose to the incense of Arkheton's stall. Then nearly lost his ears when Charcoal Eddie, convinced this was prelude to some kind of attack, began waving a rusted sword at anything resembling movement nearby.

"Blood and Bone," he muttered, climbing with relief back into the cellar. "I thought I was working with somebody *subtle*."

But it was effective. Nobody would be able to tell Dead Rick was gone. He didn't know how much longer the effect would last, though; best to hurry.

Nothing at Crutched Friars. Nothing at Threadneedle. At Aldersgate . . .

The device looked something like a compass, with a barrier to prevent the needle from swinging about to point at the faerie holding it. On the way up Aldersgate Street, the needle began to twitch, and a thin line of something shimmering copper began to show along its length; the line grew, and the needle moved more strongly as he neared a particular building. When Dead Rick held the versorium out, it pointed steadily toward the building's corner, and the line steadied to about a quarter the needle's length.

Not much, for what ought to be the most powerful enchantments in London. But enough to tell him that *something* faerie still existed there.

Dead Rick had no desire to find out what, not on his own. Chrennois could be inside; so could half a dozen Market bullies, all prepared to kill anyone who walked in without permission. He would leave that to his ally.

And why didn't that blighter get 'is own versorium and do this 'imself? It don't need a good nose—so why send me?

Stupid question. Standing out here was dangerous; it might attract attention. Much better, from the voice's perspective, to send an expendable skriker.

Dead Rick quickly put the versorium behind his back—as if that would save him, had anyone been watching. Then, with a shiver, he went back to the chaos his ally had made of the Goblin Market.

WHITE LION STREET, ISLINGTON
6 August 1884

There would be no waiting for Friday. Eliza walked through the gates of the Kensington workhouse late in the afternoon, and immediately turned her steps toward Islington.

She'd seen nothing more of Louisa, but the changeling must have kept her word; *someone* had persuaded the authorities to release a woman that only a little while ago had been declared a violent lunatic, a menace to those around her. Eliza kept to her best behaviour while waiting for freedom, but couldn't resist making a rude gesture once she was clear of the gates. They could go to the devil, the lot of them, from the workhouse matrons to the justice who put her there.

Put her there, and then put her back out, with nothing more than the dress and shoes she wore. All her other possessions had vanished somewhere between assault and freedom, save the photograph of Owen, rescued from Cromwell Road. How they expected her to feed herself, she didn't know. Begging, she supposed. And it would come to that soon enough, when she dared not return to Whitechapel. But before she did that—before she decided what, if anything, to tell Quinn about the changeling—she would do what she'd been trying to do for seven long years.

She would get Owen back.

This time, there was no spying from a neighbour's front steps, no disguising herself as more than she was. Eliza walked straight up to No. 9 and knocked on the door. When the maid opened it, Eliza said, "I'm here to see Mrs. Chase. Don't bother trying to keep me out; it's urgent business I've come on, concerning the London Fairy Society and the Goodemeade sisters. If she isn't at home, I'll wait until she is."

Intimidating people wasn't so very difficult; mostly what it required was an absolute refusal to back down. Eliza was prepared to shove the maid out of the way, if it proved necessary. It didn't: a door not far down the hall opened, and Mrs. Chase herself looked out. "What on earth . . . Miss Baker, wasn't it? Whatever are you doing here?"

The maid stepped clear. Eliza came into the hall—it

would be a good deal harder to force her from the house, now—and said, "I need your help."

Mrs. Chase's white eyebrows rose. "Oh dear. Do come in—shut the door, Mary; we don't need the whole of Islington knowing our affairs—and I will see what I can do."

The parlour had a much more lived-in look than the drawing room upstairs, with faded upholstery and a pattern of roses climbing the wallpaper. Mrs. Chase gestured Eliza toward a seat, but she didn't take it. "I need to see the Goodemeade sisters," she said.

The old woman's brow knitted in confusion. "I'm afraid they aren't here, Miss Baker."

"I know that," Eliza said. Belatedly, she realised she sounded like an Irishwoman. She hadn't attempted to pass for English since she attacked the changeling; after that, there hadn't been much point. Now she was out of the habit. *It doesn't matter—I hope.* "But you seemed friendly with them; you can tell me where they live."

Maybe the accent did matter; Mrs. Chase seemed deeply reluctant. "They are . . . rather *private* individuals, Miss Baker. It wouldn't be right of me to direct you to their house, out of the blue, without even asking them first. But if you would like to write a letter—"

"I do not have time for that!" Eliza grimaced, regretting the sharpness of her tone. "Forgive me, Mrs. Chase. This is very important. I come in Cyma's name; I'm searching for someone, a friend who's been missing for a very long time, and I was told the Goodemeades could help. Please, I *must* find him."

She didn't miss the way Mrs. Chase's face stilled at the name "Cyma." When Eliza finished speaking, the old woman sat in thought, one finger tapping on her lower lip. Then she nodded decisively. "I cannot send you to their house, but I can ask them to meet with you here. Go to the Angel on the corner—" Rising, she pressed a sixpence into Eliza's palm. "Have something to drink, and settle your nerves. Come back in half an hour, and we will see what we can do."

What pride Eliza had once possessed was long since gone. She took the sixpence without hesitation; it was all the money she had in the world. But when Mrs. Chase showed her to the door, Eliza did not go to the coaching inn on the corner of High Street. She started in that direction, but stopped as soon as she could watch the door of No. 9 discreetly, and there she waited.

It wasn't so much that she intended to follow Mrs. Chase—or Mary, if she sent the maid—to the sisters' house. Simply that there was something *decidedly* odd about this entire affair. Clearly there was more going on here than Eliza could see, and she'd had enough of that in her life; right now, information and that sixpence were the only things of value she had.

But the door to No. 9 did not open again. Eliza fretted, rolling the coin between finger and thumb. There might be a back way, some garden gate through which the maid could go, though it did not look like that kind of house.

She cursed her failure to look out the window during the meeting a few months ago. Or perhaps the explanation was simpler; Mrs. Chase had only intended to get rid of her, and was not contacting the Goodemeades at all. But in that case, wouldn't she send her maid to fetch a constable? She couldn't possibly believe Eliza would fail to return.

Twice she had to move to avoid suspicion, but she came back almost immediately, fast enough that she doubted anyone had slipped away in her absence. Which surely they would have done, if they knew she was spying, and wanted to go to the sisters unseen.

Eliza knew her thoughts were running like panicked dogs, inventing one wild theory after another, all of them probably wrong. She couldn't help it. To be so close, after all these years—her fingers ached, the coin's edge digging into them. She loosened her grip, and waited for half an hour to pass.

As soon as she thought it had, she marched back down the street and rapped on the door again.

This time the maid was expecting her. "They're waiting for you in the parlour," she said.

They? Eliza opened the door and found three women inside: Mrs. Chase, and the mirror images of the Goodemeade sisters. *Where the devil did they come from?* She was certain they hadn't slipped past her on White Lion Street.

Upstairs, perhaps. Mrs. Chase wouldn't be first widow to seek out female companionship in her old age; maybe the Goodemeades lived here, too, and didn't want that known.

It hardly mattered, though. They were here.

Now she just had to convince them to help her find Owen.

"Miss Baker," the rose Goodemeade said, "we're so terribly sorry about what you've been through. Please, do sit down—Gertrude, the tea, if you would—and we will do everything we can to help you."

The changeling had told the truth. Dumbfounded, all the arguments she'd prepared dying on her lips, Eliza took a seat. *That easily. They scarcely know me, let alone Owen—and yet, without so much as a single question, they offer to help*. She accepted the teacup from the daisy Goodemeade, Gertrude, and almost laughed. Sitting in a parlour, drinking tea out of a porcelain cup, as if she were a respectable woman. And preparing to talk about faeries.

Once she'd taken a sip of the tea, the other Goodemeade—Rosamund, that was her name; it should have been easy to remember—smoothed her hands over her skirt in a businesslike fashion. "Now. Where did you hear that name? Cyma, I mean."

"From Miss Kittering," Eliza said.

The sisters exchanged glances. "How *exactly* did she put it?" Gertrude asked.

Eliza thought back. "She said I should tell ye I came in Cyma's name."

They both seemed to breathe a sigh of relief. "And she sent you here for help, I imagine," Rosamund said. Eliza nodded. The tiny woman shook her head in fond exasperation. "Wouldn't bring you herself, I see. I wish I could say I'm surprised, but—well. Never mind. Tell us what happened, from the beginning."

A simple request. Yet when Eliza opened her mouth, nothing came out. She had told Quinn the truth, and that was far more dangerous . . . but what if they doubted her? The others had spoken so much at the Society meeting; she had no idea what these women knew or believed about faeries. *Because you left,* she remembered suddenly. It had been lost in the panic of chasing Louisa Kittering. *They were trying to invite you to something further. If you had stayed to listen . . .*

Rosamund seemed to guess her thoughts. Smiling encouragment, she said, "Tell us *everything*. Faeries and all. You won't surprise us, I assure you."

Hearing the word out of the other woman's mouth both unsettled Eliza and steadied her. Licking her lips, she began.

"When I was a girl, my friend Owen and I came across a group of boys tormenting a dog. They'd looped an iron chain around his neck, and they were dragging him about, throwing stones to make him yelp . . . boys do things like that all the time, and most people hardly take notice, but this dog saw me." Even now, years later, she remembered those eyes. However much she tried not to. "One look at him, and I—I made the boys stop."

Ran at them shrieking, actually, and knocked the biggest lad down before he could throw the broken bottle in his hand. Its jagged edge gouged her arm as they fell, but Eliza didn't feel that until later. She'd slammed his head against the ground, and one of the others got her around the neck, but by then Owen had come to her aid. Six boys, and only two of them; but they were fourteen, and the others a good deal younger. Besides, there'd been a fury in Eliza that none of them were eager to face.

Her hands clenched again, in the stained fabric of her skirt. Eliza stared at them as she said, "The dog let me take the chain from its neck. I knew even then it was in an odd way; sure any dog hurt like that would have tried to bite, but it just stood there and let me help. Once the chain was gone, it licked my hand and limped off, and I thought that was the end."

She brushed her fingertips across the spot, remembering the brief touch of a warm, soft tongue. Owen hadn't let her go after the dog, even though Eliza wanted to take it in and feed it. *You can't afford it,* a stór; *just let it go. You've done your good for the day.*

All three women were listening patiently. Eliza took a deep breath and went on. "A few days later, when I was returning from church, I met a man." Even then, before she knew anything about him, his eyes had seemed familiar. "He walked up to me in the street and said, 'Thank you.' Then he tried to vanish into the crowd, but I chased him; I wanted to know who he was, and why he'd thanked me. He said his name was Dead Rick, and that I'd saved him."

For the first time since she began, one of the women made a noise. Eliza paused, looking at Gertrude, but the woman waved her on. She obeyed; if she stopped for long, she might not have the courage to go on. "I kept asking questions—what did he mean, that I'd saved him; I'd never seen him before in my life—until finally he turned into the dog."

No one looked surprised. Rosamund actually nodded, as if Eliza had confirmed what she already suspected. Eliza could scarcely believe their lack of disbelief; she'd scarcely believed the sight when she saw it with her own eyes. The wiry, hard-faced man had thrown his hands up in disgust—*if you're going to keep pushing like that*—and then dropped, curling inward, clothes somehow becoming fur, until he stood on four legs before her. Then he'd licked her hand, in the same spot as before.

"How long ago was this?" Gertrude asked.

"A little more than seven years ago."

More nodding. Only the sisters; Mrs. Chase listened silently, but it was clear the Goodemeades were the true audience for her tale. "Go on," Rosamund said.

It was almost easier to tell the next part. Painful as the memory was, it hurt less than remembering how things had begun, the friendship they'd enjoyed once both she and Owen knew the faerie's nature. Running wild through Whitechapel. Tithing bread to him when they could afford it—sometimes when they couldn't—so he could be among them safely. Telling him of her mother's ghost, and him teaching her to make use of that gift, so that it might earn her money someday. "A few months later, I went to Mass, and Owen wasn't there. Mrs. Darragh was in a fine fury, saying Dead Rick had caught them as they were about to go into the church, and convinced Owen to go with him instead. I slipped out before the priest came in and went looking for them, and—"

The words lodged in her throat like a piece of chicken bone. Try as she might, Eliza couldn't get them out. If she spoke, she would burst into tears, and she refused to do that in front of these women, when she scarcely knew them. Gertrude patted her on the hand, and that nearly broke her. The woman said softly, "For now, just give us the shape of it. If the details matter, we can worry about them later."

It helped, a little. "The faeries took him," she said. There, it was out; now she could go on. "Dead Rick betrayed us. All those months we spent together, the friendship—it was a lie; it meant nothing to him. I was a fool to think it did. Faeries can't be *friends* with human mortals. The look he gave me, when I asked him how he could turn against us like that—" He might as well have been looking at a wall that suddenly began to scream at him. Mild curiosity, but nothing more. Cold. Empty.

Gertrude reached out again, but Eliza pulled away before the woman could touch her. "I chased them," she said, hearing her own voice high and tight, "but they got away. And I never saw Dead Rick again, until last year, when he helped the ones who bombed the railways. Since then I've been trying to find people who know something of faeries. I've told ye my tale; now ye tell me—who is this Cyma, and can ye help me find Owen?"

Rosamund nodded. "Cyma's name was . . . merely a

sign to us, to make certain we'd listen to you when you came. We already know where your lad is."

Her calm, casual words struck like a bolt of lightning. *"Where?"*

The woman hesitated before answering. Eliza nearly leapt from her seat and shook her. "With the fae, still. But not the ones who took him before. Kinder folk, who are doing for him what they can."

Eliza's heart pounded in her ears, making her whole body tremble. "Miss Kittering said he was with an Irish lady."

"An Irish lady *faerie,*" Gertrude said. "It's almost the same thing."

Rosamund spoke before Eliza could find the words to express how far from the same thing it was. "Please believe us, Miss Baker. There are cruel faeries in this world, certainly—far too many of them, and even more who are only good when someone gives them a reason. But there *are* those for whom it's in their nature to be kind. You've been badly hurt, you and those close to you, and no kindness after the fact will heal that hurt entirely; but please, believe that not all fae are like that."

The passion in her voice was startling. Mrs. Chase gave Rosamund a peculiar smile, then said to Eliza, "They're telling the truth. Remember that, Miss Baker—that I, too, believe there are kind faeries in the world. I've lived many long years, and seen more than you can imagine; I hope my word will count for something."

She said it as if her word should somehow carry a

different weight than that of the Goodemeades. Eliza didn't understand, and honestly didn't care. Kind faeries, cruel ones; there was only one thing she wanted. "Make them give Owen back to me."

Another hesitation. This time Eliza did leap to her feet, but Mrs. Chase's outstretched hand stopped whatever she might have done. "He's eaten faerie food," Rosamund said. "Lived among the fae for seven years. We'd have brought him out already, but for fear it would hurt him."

"Then take me to him." She said it without thinking. Damn the danger; she could be the heroine in this tale, going underhill to rescue her true love.

Even if it's been seven long years? Even if you need a photograph to remind yourself of his face?

Even then. If her love wasn't strong enough to win him free, then she would find something else. The faeries would regret the day they took Owen from her.

The sisters exchanged another one of their glances, as if they were carrying on a conversation no one else could hear. Then Rosamund shrugged, and Gertrude smiled up at Eliza. "Very well. We'll take you to your friend."

THE GOBLIN MARKET, ONYX HALL:
6 August 1884

The usual noise of the Goblin Market had taken on a harder edge of late. Voices were grimmer, laughter more shrill; and everyone kept their weapons close to hand.

Hardface's latest lover, a Greek maenad named Hippagre, told stories about Roman despots who, knowing that soldiers were coming to kill them, spent their final night hosting a grand party, squandering all their wealth and riches at one go. With tremors repeatedly shaking the Hall, the Market felt a good deal like that—though Dead Rick doubted many fae would take poison at the end. It explained the wild celebrations he witnessed: drinking, rutting, the torment of mortals.

But not the violence. That, he feared, was the fault of his ally—at least in part.

The versorium wasn't the only thing to go missing during the chaos laid over the Market. A great many things of value had vanished, from bread to weapons to enchanted mirrors. Every major power in the Market had been robbed: Nadrett, Aspell, Hardface, even Lacca, who lost most of what little she had scraped together in the last few months.

Dead Rick's absence had not been marked, but the outrage meant Nadrett kept Dead Rick near constantly on four feet and running at his heels, whether he needed to be there or not. Currently the master was pacing while Old Gadling took a horsewhip to the back of the clurican who had been the guardian of the bread lockbox. It was the third time he'd had the Irish faerie beaten, and Dead Rick was serving absolutely no purpose there, but Nadrett insisted on it anyway.

Slipping away to report to his ally had almost cost him another memory. After he came back, he'd been saved only by a fight outside the room; Lacca's few remaining allies tried to steal the string of new mortals Nadrett was going to force into tithing bread. Then there had been another earthquake—not as bad as the one that broke the Market, but more than a tremor—and by the time that was done, Nadrett had been distracted from his punishment. The voice insisted Dead Rick go with him to investigate the Aldersgate door, but how he could do that without getting killed on his return, the skriker didn't know.

Nadrett gestured to Gadling, who lowered the bloody whip and rubbed his right arm as if it were tired. The clurican sagged in his chains, weeping. While the thrumpin unlocked him, Dead Rick learned why Nadrett insisted he be there. "Run 'im out," the master said, turning away in disgust. "Into the sewers. Let 'im bloody well drown in shit."

With Nadrett's temper so uncertain, he didn't dare hesitate. Dead Rick snarled and advanced on the fallen Irish faerie. The clurican was so exhausted, he didn't move at first; Dead Rick had to bite his arm before he'd start running.

Then it was out the door, through the desperate merriment and half-veiled hostility of the Market, all the while wondering if any of it mattered one fucking bit anymore. Dead Rick ran heavily, his heart far less into the chase than usual, and he didn't pay the blindest bit of attention to anything around him until a net dropped onto his head.

It was made of bronze chains, and their weight bore him instantly to the floor. Dead Rick's snarls changed from menace to fear. *Stupid whelp—stupid and blind, and now you're going to die—* He twisted, trying to see who had trapped him, but someone was there, bundling the net around him and then flipping him upside down to be carried out of the room. Dead Rick saw legs, hands, the back of someone's head—*Blood and Bone. Mortals. But who are they working for?*

The answer waited not far away. The men carrying him dropped him to the floor again, chains and all, and Dead Rick looked up to see the rich green of Valentin Aspell's old-fashioned coat.

"My apologies," the faerie said, sounding not at all contrite. "As you told me before—so *very* insistently—it is necessary to give Nadrett some explanation for why you ended up in my presence. He will soon be receiving a message that his skriker has become my prisoner, along with various others of his minions; and while he and I negotiate what should happen next, the one who paid me to kidnap you has a job for you to perform." Long fingers laid a piece of bread on the stone near Dead Rick's face; then he heard a pocket-watch click open. "His instructions are that you are to meet him on the north side of St. Paul's Cathedral in half an hour."

Dead Rick's jaws had slipped through a hole in the net, which bound him almost as effectively as a muzzle. Aspell said, "My men are going to unbind you now. I do ask that you not attempt to attack me, as I only did this to get you away from your master without suspicion."

So this was how his ally intended to arrange the investigation of the laboratory. As soon as Dead Rick was halfway free, he shifted to man form and said, "Nadrett ain't going to *bargain*. 'E'll tell you to kill us all."

"I think not," Aspell said dryly. "Once again, you have no faith in my abilities. Perhaps I will take that dispute up with you on some future day. In the meanwhile, you have an engagement to keep."

One that would, at last, answer the question he'd been chasing since spring. *And then I'll make sure that faceless bastard makes good on* 'is *end of the promise.*

Scooping up the bread, Dead Rick flung a glamour over himself and ran for the Billingsgate door.

CITY OF LONDON

6 August 1884

Dusk was falling over the world above, turning the light murky and gray. Some of the gas lamps had been lit, but not yet all; in the shadows north of St. Paul's, Dead Rick needed no charms to hide.

He slowed as he reached the spot, ears and nose sharp for any movement. There were mortals about, of course, but that was it; no fae, no one under any glamour.

Because you're early, fool. Unlike Aspell, he didn't have

a pocket-watch, but it couldn't have been more than fifteen minutes since he'd left. Dead Rick settled behind a pillar on the curving stairs of the northern portico, where the shadows were deepest, and crossed his arms over his chest to wait.

Before the half hour was up, he saw someone approaching.

It looked like a mortal man, indistinguishable from any of the hundreds of clerks employed by the shops and financial establishments around them. As soon as the fellow drew near, though, Dead Rick sensed the presence of a glamour. The face was of course none he recognised, but—

He found himself staring down the barrel of a pistol. "If you attempt to see my face, I will shoot you on the spot."

The voice was the one that had spoken to him from the air. His ally had come in person.

Dead Rick licked his lips. Curiosity clawed at him; after so many months, he finally had a chance to see who he'd been working with—which he would need, if his ally backed out on the promise to retrieve his memories. But it wasn't worth risking right now. *Later. When 'e's not paying attention.*

"Sure," he said easily, not wanting his ally to think about demanding another oath. "If I needs to get your attention, though, what should I call you? Fred? Joe?"

The other faerie uncocked the pistol, looking unamused. " 'My lord' will do. Come along."

'E really must be a gentleman. Rolling his eyes, Dead Rick followed him up St. Martins le Grand to Aldersgate Street.

His lordship had to be shown which building to look for. He shook his head slightly when Dead Rick pointed it out, as if surprised by what it had become.

"Is anybody else down there?" Dead Rick asked, looking down as if he could see through the pavement to the faerie palace below.

"I doubt it." Milord paced around the building's corner, one hand on his chin in thought.

He *doubted* it? Dead Rick wished he'd stolen someone else's gun on the way out of the Market. "What if you're wrong?"

"Then we will take care of them." His ally paused and smiled at him, condescendingly. "It is likely to be only Chrennois. Nadrett knows how many can keep a secret."

Two—if one of 'em is dead. But Nadrett needed the French sprite's knowledge, so two alive it was. Dead Rick drew his knife and tested its edge. *Good enough.*

Milord stretched one hand out, just shy of touching the stone. "Take hold of my sleeve," he said absently, considering the structure in front of him. Dead Rick obeyed. "The alder tree used to envelop those who passed through; this, I think, should—"

The stone flexed outward, and swallowed them whole.

Eager as Eliza was to see Owen, the departure from White Lion Street was delayed when she staggered and nearly fell going down the house's front steps. Somehow the Goodemeades drew out of her the admission that she hadn't eaten since her workhouse supper the night before, and then the next thing she knew she was bundled into the Angel coaching inn for a good solid meal. Eliza was on her second meat pie before she realised she'd admitted to being in the workhouse—and that no one had so much blinked at the admission.

As if they already knew. The Goodemeades, and Mrs. Chase; the new Louisa Kittering, and this unknown Cyma: How much information had they shared among them?

It didn't matter, so long as she got Owen back. Eliza ate as fast as she could, and then Mrs. Chase hired a carriage to take them into the City. Along the way, the sisters extracted a promise from Eliza: that she would offer no harm to anyone who didn't offer it first. "And that's harm of all kinds," Gertrude added. "Fists and feet, any iron or weapons you might have on you—"

"Am I at least allowed to talk?" Eliza asked, meaning it as a jest.

"So long as you don't speak of religious matters," the woman answered her seriously.

Of course: holy things had power against faeries. So long as she had her voice, she wasn't unarmed.

It gave her courage, but only a little. She was going among faeries. And the Goodemeades had made it clear that the experience would be even more strange than she could imagine.

But they've done it, and so has Mrs. Chase; gone in,

and come out again to tell the tale. You can do the same. You will.

The carriage took them to a narrower road south of Cannon Street. In the light of the gas lamps, Eliza spotted the plaque on the wall: Cloak Lane. Mrs. Chase paid the driver and waited until he was gone, though it didn't mean they were alone on the street. Giving no heed to the people around them, the old woman took Eliza by the hands. "Trust me," she said earnestly, for all the world as if the trust of an Irish workhouse convict was a valuable thing to have. "We—myself and the sisters *both*—will make certain you are safe."

Eliza pulled her hands free. "Just take me to him."

"Watch closely, then," Rosamund said, turning to face the buildings at their side. "If you don't, you'll never see it."

Before Eliza could ask her what she meant by that, the buildings began to shift.

They moved without moving: surely the brick walls stayed exactly where they were, but somehow there was a space between them. It was unmistakable—yet people walked on past, stepping off the pavement into the street to avoid the four women, without ever glancing at the impossibility happening just a few feet away. The gap widened until it was large enough to admit them, and then it stopped; and Rosamund glanced over her shoulder. "Come along, then. It won't stay open for long."

Eliza's heart was beating far too fast, but it was

excitement as much as fear. Clenching her hands into fists, she followed Rosamund through the faerie door.

ALDERSGATE, ONYX HALL

6 August 1884

"Qu'est-ce que vous faites ici?"

Rootlike stone tendrils were still crawling off Dead Rick's body when Chrennois spoke. The sprite stood at a table, surrounded by crystal bottles and shallow tubs, and he blinked as if utterly astonished to see visitors.

The other creature in the room didn't bother with questions. It dove at Dead Rick and his ally with all three heads.

Milord dropped to the floor, slipping out of the entrance's grasp just as two sets of the serpent's fangs gashed through the air where he had been. Stone broke in the creature's mouth. Dead Rick, still trapped, beat desperately at the third head with his free arm, knocking it aside. Then he was clear, and threw himself out of the entrance alcove as the heads came in for another strike.

Blood and Bone—"only Chrennois," like 'ell. Dead Rick slashed wildly with his knife, and winced when his ally's gun fired, deafening in the small room. *So that's where the fucking naga went.*

It was small comfort to know who'd bought the three-headed snake from the Market. That didn't tell him how to stop the thing from killing him. Which it was energetically trying to do; its orders from Nadrett clearly said to kill anyone who entered without permission. A second gunshot, and a third. Everything was chaos and noise and scaly coils of snake. Dead Rick's back slammed into the shelves along one wall, setting the crystal bottles to rocking; he heard Chrennois crying out in alarm. Grabbing the nearest bottle with his free hand, the skriker hurled it, and was rewarded with a hiss from the naga—from all three mouths, and from its skin. *Acid.* He threw more bottles.

Then they all crashed to the floor, as the naga's tail swept around to seize Dead Rick. The creature pinned his arms, and reared its heads back to attack. Two more shots: the naga's body jerked, and one of its heads sagged limply. Dead Rick took advantage of the pause to shift to dog form, gasping as the muscular coils pressed against his changing limbs, and then bit as hard as he could into the topmost coil, digging for the flesh underneath the scales.

The naga dropped him. Dead Rick landed with agility that would have done a cat proud. His knife lay on the floor nearby, but that would require changing again; instead he leapt for another head, seizing it just beneath the jaw, where it couldn't bite him. Half of him expected to feel fangs in his back at any instant, from the other surviving head, but instead he was dragged along as the naga lunged for Milord and his gun. Blood burst into his mouth; if a snake had a throat, he'd just torn that one out. Dead Rick turned without pausing and leapt upon the remaining head, biting and clawing into the eyes, and then Milord fired his last shot, and the naga finally went still.

Dead Rick spat out a mouthful of foul-tasting blood and flesh and whirled again, intending to deal with Chrennois—but the sprite lay motionless on the floor, in a growing pool of his own blood.

Milord shook his head when Dead Rick's gaze shifted to him. "An unfortunate accident. The naga moved as I fired."

Maybe it was true; maybe it wasn't. *Probably is; I think 'e wanted to question Chrennois.*

He didn't feel much pity for the frog, and only a little more for the dead snake; the creature had been trying to kill him, after all. Changing back to man form, and then spitting more to clear his mouth, Dead Rick took stock of the room.

It looked as if it had been enlarged at one point; the entrance had dropped them in a narrow alcove, which widened to perhaps ten feet for half the room's length, before opening up into something more like a proper chamber. Shelving blocked one archway at the far end, with rubble visible behind, but the other was open.

His ally asked, "Do you think you can recognise the plate in which they trapped the ghost?"

"Recognise it? No. Find it? Maybe." He didn't even know what a photographic plate looked like—but he had other things to look with than eyes. Dead Rick plucked a clean rag from the table by Chrennois's body and wiped the blood off himself as best as he could, then licked an unstained corner for good measure. With the reek of naga thus reduced, he put his head warily through the open archway.

The naga was the only defender here; nothing else could fit. A rockfall closed off the end of the second chamber, and what little space remained was filled with crates. Dead Rick sniffed experimentally. Naga, hawthorn wood, chemicals, and straw.

Behind him, Milord said, "I've found his cameras. They're all empty."

Dead Rick joined him at the table. There were three cameras, two like the one he'd seen in the sewers, with pairs of lenses rather than single ones set into the front boards. Putting his nose right up against the wood, he sniffed along them both. As he'd hoped, the second still carried a faint stink of the sewers. *Now, let's 'ope Chrennois ain't been crawling around there regular.*

There were a lot of crates in the side room, but one was much smaller, laid atop the others near the door, and it held an elusive trace of sewer reek. "That one?" Milord asked, watching from the door. When Dead Rick nodded, he took it down and pried the lid free. The skriker couldn't see what was inside, but a triumphant smile curved Milord's lips. "Excellent. And more quickly found than I expected. We cannot stay long, of course—but let us take a brief look at the materials Chrennois has been using; they may be enlightening, and useful in dealing with this." He clapped the lid back down and retreated to the larger room.

Dead Rick followed, suspicion coiling into a hard knot in his gut. It was smoothly done—all very natural, as if it were only haste that made the fellow take so quick a glance—but Dead Rick saw with more than just his eyes, and knew his ally had been very deliberate in not letting him see inside the box.

He obediently followed the other into the workroom, and glanced over the carefully labeled bottles as if the words he saw there meant anything to him. *Vitreous humour (hawk). Lunar caustic. Vitriol of alder*. Most of his attention was on the small box tucked under Milord's arm. *Just as soon as 'e's busy . . .*

Milord bent forward to examine a camera. In that moment of distraction, Dead Rick snatched the box from his grasp.

Before the other could do more than cry out in protest, he'd torn the top free, uncovering what lay inside. Nestled in a bed of straw was something Dead Rick recognised all too well.

A plate of glass, held in a thin wooden frame.

Dead Rick glared at his supposed ally, furious. "You knowed. This whole bloody time."

Milord straightened slowly, warily, hands stiff at his sides. "I suspected. I *still* suspect; I have no confirmation. But the pieces of glass that hold your memories do sound a good deal like photographic plates, yes."

Before Chrennois stole ghosts, he stole pieces of faeries' minds. The same technique, advanced over the last few years? Or different things entirely? It didn't matter. What mattered was that his ally had lied. Promising all this time to get his memories back, but now that they were here, the deceitful bugger would have rushed him right back out again, with never a mention of what he needed to know.

As much as Dead Rick wanted to knock the smug bastard onto his arse, there was one thing he wanted more. He slammed the box down onto the table and ran back into the side room.

"We don't have the time!" his ally called after him, real desperation in his voice. "I promise, I *will* help you, but not tonight—it would take too long to search—"

"Iron burn you," Dead Rick snarled back. "If you think I'm bloody well leaving 'ere without my bloody *mind* . . ." Words failed him. His hands did not; they tore the lid off one crate after another, digging through the straw and other contents. Some things were photographic plates; others were not; he didn't have to look to know none of those were his memories. He would know them when he found them.

"You can be *valuable,* Dead Rick, staying where you are—work from within Nadrett's defenses, and it will be far easier to destroy him when the time comes!"

The time to destroy him was after Dead Rick had his memories back. Growling, he burrowed deeper into the room, following instinct deeper than any physical sense, until his hands settled on a particular crate, and he *knew*.

"Blood and Bone," he whispered, the lid falling from his hands to thunk against the floor. *So many.* Instead of straw, this box was lined with notched strips of wood, holding the small plates in tidy rows. Dozens of them, stacked several rows deep—and yet, when he thought about it, that wasn't so many at all. Not for a faerie's eternal life. How much did each plate hold?

This had to be all of them. Nothing else in the room called to him.

Dead Rick jammed the lid back onto the crate. It was almost too large for one man to carry, but he would be damned before he asked Milord for any more help. He ended up lifting it atop another box, then turning around so he could tip the weight forward onto his back, with his hands on the bottom edge.

Milord had given up his protests; he was in the outer room, looking rapidly over the bottles and other containers, as if snatching everything he could into his mind. The plate holding Galen St. Clair was tucked securely under his arm. It wasn't worth trying to grab, not when Dead Rick had his memories at last. The skriker passed without a word, walking carefully to the alcove and positioning himself beneath the fanlike arrangement of stone tendrils. Hands full, he resorted to tapping one with his nose, hoping that would wake it up.

It did. The tendrils came down, wrapped around his body, and lifted him toward the street.

THE CITY OF LONDON

6 August 1884

He stumbled leaving the entrance, and nearly dropped the box. Panic beat in his throat—visions of it falling, the memories tumbling free, every last one of them *shattering*—

By the time he had it steadied, his heart was racing. Dead Rick squeezed his eyes shut and thanked all the powers of Faerie for his good fortune. *Now, to get them back safe in my 'ead.*

Which meant going to the Academy, and hoping he could buy help there. Dead Rick opened his eyes and turned his steps toward the Onyx Hall—but not, for once, the Goblin Market. The thought lit a spark of joy in his soul.

A flare that died when he saw three men coming up the pavement toward him. No, not men: fae, under glamour. And the leader was recognizable as Nadrett.

He could have run—if he abandoned the crate. Dead Rick could have more easily abandoned his legs. Then they were there, and it was too late to flee. "Well," Nadrett said, his voice soft and malevolent. He cocked a pistol, but didn't point it at Dead Rick. Not yet. "So my dog's got a backbone after all. You'll regret finding that, you will."

Dead Rick's hands clenched on the box's corners. "Iron burn you," he spat. "I ain't your fucking dog no more."

A grinding sound, a whiff of new scent: the entrance had done its work once more, and his ally had emerged—at the worst possible moment. Nadrett looked past Dead Rick, and his eyebrows went up. "So that's what you've been doing all this time, sneaking about. Thinking I wouldn't notice. I notice *everything*, dog. Who's your friend 'ere, then?" No answer from Milord, though Dead Rick heard the other faerie's feet shift, as if he were settling himself to fight. Nadrett said, "I wonder what's under that glamour, boys?"

Quick as a snake, he raised his pistol and fired.

It brought the entire street to a halt. The enchantments over the door protected against mortals noticing people coming and going from the Onyx Hall, but nothing more; seeing the gun, passersby began to flee. Dead Rick staggered, flinching instinctively away from the shot, and then one of Nadrett's underlings seized him, unbalancing him still further. For one horrific moment, he was again on the verge of dropping his memories.

Iron. Not elfshot, or lead—the bastard's shooting iron*!*

Bread protected against it, but not perfectly. Milord screamed and collapsed to the pavement, and the glamour covering him shattered.

Revealing Valentin Aspell.

The faerie was bleeding from the shoulder; Nadrett hadn't aimed to kill. Aspell spat curses worthy of the lowest Goblin Market trash, and he sounded neither like his disguised voice nor his usual oily self; and Dead Rick kept staring. *Aspell. All this time.*

Nadrett was spitting curses of his own. "I thought you was up to something, sending your lackeys like that, not talking to me yourself. I'm going to enjoy—"

He never finished the sentence. Aspell had one more twisty trick prepared. What he pulled from his pocket, Dead Rick never saw; but it exploded into light and smoke. He staggered again, this time into his captor, and on instinct he sank his teeth into whatever part of the fellow was closest to his mouth. He was rewarded with a howl of pain and freedom from the other's grip.

For half an instant, his mind tossed out images. Putting down the box. Leaping on Nadrett. Helping the wounded Aspell escape.

Instead he ran. Away from the chaos, toward the Onyx Hall, nothing in the world but feet and lungs, his hands and his back holding his memories secure, and a devout hope that he could find safety in the Academy.

THE GALENIC ACADEMY, ONYX HALL
6 August 1884

The strangest thing was the familiarity.

Eliza knew well the look of a formerly decent neighbourhood fallen to decay; that described many portions of the East End. She hadn't expected to find it echoed in a faerie realm—even one that seemed to lie *below* London.

This is where they've been, all this time. Beneath my feet. And I never knew it.

Now they were all around her. She saw one, two, a cluster of four, all before she and her guides reached the arch of silver and gold that shone in the otherwise gloomy air. Even the most human-looking creature was nothing of the sort, and could never be mistaken for it. Yet she knew from experience how well they could change to look like humans. Here, in their home, they had no need to hide.

Their home: some kind of grand, crumbling palace, both timeless and very old. Eliza hunched her shoulders inward and wrapped her hands around her elbows, afraid to touch the stone. Mrs. Chase stayed by her side, but the Goodemeades walked as if they knew the way blindfolded.

Past the arch, familiarity vanished, and strangeness multipled a hundredfold. She'd been prepared for green fields, or hollow hills, or castles of crystal—not *machines*. They weren't even human things, dragged down here like a crow would drag a shiny bit of metal; they had to be faerie inventions. Even the notion of faeries bombing railways paled into sensibility, next to that.

Owen, Eliza told herself, trying not to stare at everything around her. *Owen is the only thing that matters.* If she held on to that, she might keep her sanity.

Her escorts hurried her onward, past the knot of folk clustered around something like an enormous loom. One of them greeted her companions, and Gertrude stayed back, asking after someone named Feidelm. "They'll fetch your friend," Rosamund said, leading her through into a library. "If you'd like to sit down . . . ?"

She couldn't. Eliza paced the room, up and down the length of the polished table, past shelves of books containing unknown wonders. Oddly, the two statues dominating the far end of the room seemed to be of a mortal man and woman, in old-fashioned clothing. The plaques at the base named them as Galen and Delphia St. Clair. She wondered who they'd been, and what importance they could possibly hold for faeries, that they would be memorialised here.

The *click* of a door's latch drove all such thoughts from her head. Eliza turned, and saw Owen.

The sight of him drove all the breath from her body. Owen, *exactly* as she remembered him—Owen from seven years ago, as if not a day had passed since they parted.

He'd been among the faeries. For him, time *had* stopped.

The fourteen-year-old boy shuffled forward, guided by the gentle hands of Gertrude and a tall, elegant faerie with ginger hair. He seemed nervous, uncertain, and he didn't look at her. Eliza had to force the syllables past her lips, a desperate whisper. "Owen."

He didn't react. She might have spoken another name entirely. And that was when Eliza knew the appearance was a lie; his face might be unchanged, but inside, he was not at all the boy she remembered.

They had warned her. But warnings didn't come close to preparing her for the horror of seeing him like this, fourteen years old and shattered.

By this place.

She made herself walk forward, slowly, hands outstretched. The others hung back, giving her the space she needed. *For more reasons than one.* The boy looked up at her, confused, wary, but he let her take his hand—

"Ave Maria, gratia plena, Dominus tecum. Benedicta tu in mulieribus, et benedictus fructus ventris tui, Iesus. Sancta Maria, Mater Dei, ora pro nobis peccatoribus, nunc et in hora mortis nostrae!"

The prayer spilled from her lips, as fast as she'd ever recited it. Only years of repetition, though, kept Eliza from faltering as it took effect.

She'd thought the faeries would flinch back, as the changeling had, but stronger. And so they did—but everything else flinched, too.

The walls, the shelves, the *floor*. The entire world shuddered, like a candle flame in the wind. Cries of utter horror came from within the room and without; machinery ground to a shrieking halt; an ominous rumble filled the air.

And Owen, with whom Eliza had intended to run for freedom—through the door, past the distracted faeries, out into the world above—howled and tore himself away.

The shock of it paralyzed her. Eliza was still standing there, gaping, when the door slammed open so hard it bounced off the wall, and a short, stocky figure charged through, swearing in German. His gaze swept the room, then fixed on Eliza with murderous rage. The ginger-haired faerie caught him as he tried to rush at Eliza, and she began speaking in a rapid Irish voice. "She didn't know, Niklas; she was trying to help her friend—"

"She is going to kill the Queen and bring this *verdammte* place down upon our heads!"

Rosamund was at Eliza's side, clutching her sleeve, babbling away beneath the dwarf's furious tirade. "You mustn't do that, oh please, you *mustn't*—I know you want to help him, and so do we, but if you pray again you'll only hurt us all . . ."

Eliza staggered. It was too much, all of it: the shouting, that disorienting lurch, the peculiar and unsettling feeling that the stone itself had been *screaming*.

And Owen, huddled in a corner. Terrified of her. Of the words she had spoken, that did not belong to this world.

Vision blurred, slid, vanished into a cascade of tears. Eliza cried, the sobs wracking her body, bending her over until she fell to her knees on the carpet. *Oh Jesus, Owen. I'm too late. Seven years too late. God help me—Owen, I'm sorry, I'm so sorry . . .*

Gentle hands stroked her hair, the Irish voice spoke to her soothingly with words she couldn't understand, and none of it did any good. All of it had been in vain. She had lost Owen forever.

PART THREE

August–October 1884

They say that "coming events cast their shadows before." *May they not sometimes cast their lights before?*

ADA LOVELACE,
LETTER TO HER MOTHER, LADY BYRON,
SUNDAY, 10 AUGUST 1851

Do not let us talk then of restoration. The thing is a Lie from beginning to end. You may make a model of a building as you may of a corpse, and your model may have the shell of the old walls within it as your cast might have the skeleton, with what advantage I neither see nor care [. . .] But, it is said, there may come a necessity for restoration! Granted. Look the necessity full in the face, and understand it on its own terms. It is a necessity for destruction.

JOHN RUSKIN,
THE LAMP OF MEMORY

Ah, Love! could thou and I with Fate conspire
To grasp this sorry Scheme of Things entire,
Would not we shatter it to bits—and then
Re-mould it nearer to the Heart's Desire!

EDWARD FITZGERALD,
THE RUBAIYAT OF OMAR KHAYYAM LXXIII

Even the tiniest shock threatens her grip, now. The substance of her spirit has been stretched as far as it will go; there is not much of the Hall to protect any longer, but not much of herself to cover it, either. Despite her resolution to protect her mortal consort, she finds herself drawing on his strength more and more, to hold on through these final days.

The worst of it is not the physical pain, not now. It is the knowledge that everything she has fought for all these centuries must end. Some few fae may find a way to stay in London; they will become changelings, or subsist on mortal bread until their spirits are altered beyond recognition. The era of the Onyx Court, though, is over. No more will faeries be a hidden part of the city's life. Magic will pass a little further out of this world, to fade and be forgotten.

She no longer even has the strength to rage against that loss.

All she can do now is postpone it for as long as possible. Hold on, and give her people as much time as she can.

They are fae. Miracles are not something they pray for.

THE GALENIC ACADEMY, ONYX HALL

6 August 1884

By the time he reached the gold and silver arch of the Academy boundary, Dead Rick was completely blown. His lungs burned and his fingers ached with the weight of the box, but he didn't dare pause or set it down. He'd run all the way from Aldersgate to Cloak Lane, all the way from the entrance to here, until at the end he was staggering like a drunk, for fear Nadrett's men might be following him. And they might still—but if they burst into the Academy, somebody would stop them.

He hoped.

Certainly the fae and mortals there looked as if they might stop *him*, when he lurched into the main hall. Dead Rick kept moving, both to avoid any questions, and because once he stopped he doubted he could start again. The library was a quiet place, the safest he could think of; if he collapsed there, surely Irrith would find him.

With his hands full, he resorted to using his foot to open the door. The room beyond was dismayingly full of people, but at that exact moment the only thing he cared about was the table, on which he could lay his burden at last.

He drew in one shuddering, relieved breath, hearing it loud in the silence around him. Then the silence was broken by a single, murderous word. "*You.*"

It was all the warning he got. Dead Rick's reflexes were shredded by exhaustion; he hadn't even turned his head before a body slammed into him from the side and carried him to the floor.

He howled, reaching out instinctively to protect his memories. Hands slapped his aside, then reformed into fists, striking his face two swift blows. The habits of seven years in the Goblin Market took over: he got one arm between them, grabbed the side of his attacker's head, threw her hard to the floor. He rolled with her, his free hand moving to crush her throat—

The strong arms that wrapped about his shoulders and arms to drag him back weren't necessary. He'd already stopped, frozen by the sight of the face beneath him. Seven years older, but he recognised that thick dark hair, the upturned nose, the furious hazel eyes. And the voice, shrieking curses at him, in which he recognised the name *Owen*.

He couldn't even answer. All he could do was sprawl on the floor, Feidelm pinning his arms like a wrestler, and stare at her. Of course she was here. The boy was, after all, and Dead Rick remembered her screams when he'd stolen the boy away. Of course she would come after him, no matter how long it took.

They'd gathered quite an audience. An old mortal woman and two fae under glamour; they'd been there when he came in. More crowded the doorway, crouching or stretching or in one case hovering on dragonfly wings to see past their fellows, until a voice said, "Let me through."

It wasn't a loud voice; it didn't have to be. The authority in it parted the crowd like a knife through soft flesh, making a gap for a tall, dark-skinned figure to pass.

Irrith had been right when she said Dead Rick didn't recognise the faerie. He didn't have to, though, to know this was Abd ar-Rashid, the genie who was Scholarch of the Galenic Academy. He murmured a quiet request to the ink-stained sprite at his side, and soon the door was closed once more, with Abd ar-Rashid and Niklas von das Ticken inside.

The genie's dark eyes glinted like two chips of the Onyx Hall's stone as he took in Dead Rick's presence and appearance. Still in that quiet, authoritative tone, he asked, "What is happening here?"

Feidelm had finally released Dead Rick. He remained slumped at her feet as she stood and answered. "The Goodemeades brought Miss Baker here to see the boy in my care. Then *this* one came in, and she attacked him."

The mortal girl scrambled upright and pointed at Dead Rick, her hand shaking. "He's the one who stole Owen, he is."

Abd ar-Rashid turned his gaze back to Dead Rick. "Is this true?"

The skriker was too exhausted to lie, even if he thought it would have fooled anyone. "Yes. It's true."

The genie gestured to the box on the table. "And what is this?"

That gave Dead Rick the energy he needed. He was up before he knew it, bracing himself between the genie and the box as if he would last two seconds in another fight. "It's my fucking property, is what it is, and anybody so much as tries to touch it, they'll bleed."

Niklas made a low, amused noise, and cocked a pistol that seemed to have come from nowhere.

Where was Irrith? Dead Rick wasn't doing a very good job of winning friends here. But he had a card to play, one he thought they'd like. "Before your dwarf there goes shooting me, you should know—I can tell you where the ghost of Galen St. Clair is."

"Nadrett has him," one of the glamoured fae said.

"Not no more, 'e don't." Presuming Aspell had gotten away with the plate. He was a tricky snake, maybe tricky enough to escape Nadrett. "Keep that girl from tearing my throat out—give me some 'elp on a little matter of my own—and I'll tell you 'ow to find your dead Prince."

"Dead Rick." It was the other glamoured faerie. She spoke his name gently, and came forward with slow, careful steps; then the glamour fell from her, revealing the same kind face on a brownie half the height. The mortal girl made a stifled noise and retreated sharply. The faerie said, "You don't remember any of us, do you?"

He knew enough to guess who she was. Within two tries, anyway. Even in the Goblin Market, he'd heard of the Goodemeades, the brownie sisters that had dwelt in Islington since the earliest days of the Onyx Hall. Whether she was

Rosamund or Gertrude, she would try to help him—if he let her. The pity and sorrow in her eyes threatened to choke him. They had him pinned with his back to the table, surrounding him in an arc with no way to escape, and if it weren't for the crate behind him he would have tried to bolt for safety . . . but that would mean leaving his memories behind.

Then the door opened, and Irrith stood framed in the gap. "He doesn't remember anything," she said softly, with a grimace of apology to the skriker. "Niklas, don't shoot him; I don't want to see what he'd do to you if you tried."

Dead Rick's shoulders knotted until they ached. That easily, his secret was betrayed. *I never should 'ave come here. It's that bloody sprite's fault.* Now his vulnerability was in the open, for all to see. If anybody took so much as one step toward the box he guarded, Dead Rick would rip their throat out.

But Abd ar-Rashid asked him again, "Is this true?" And there was no way out but to answer.

"Yes," he snarled, hands cramping with the need to use them. To fight his way free. "Is that what you wants to 'ear? I don't know none of you. I been Nadrett's dog for seven fucking years because of that, and the only reason I came 'ere is because I 'oped somebody could put my memories back where they belong. You do that, I tells you where your dead Prince went."

Everybody's eyes went past him, to the box. Dead Rick's lips skinned back in a snarl, and Abd ar-Rashid held up his hands in a calming gesture. "Peace, my friend. No one will harm you. What you've said explains a great deal, and we will do what we can to help."

A furious noise burst from the mortal girl. "After what he did to us?"

"He didn't have a choice—" Irrith began.

"Peace," Abd ar-Rashid repeated, quieting them both. "Miss Baker. There is a man in this place—a mortal man, like you—whose duty is to oversee such matters, the affairs between humans and fae. It will be for him to decide what the answer for that crime should be. Until then, we will do what we can to address the matter of memories."

They were going to give him over to Hodge? Well, he could bargain with the Prince, and run if bargaining failed. *After* he got his self out of the glass and back into his head.

Sounds behind Dead Rick made him whirl, nerves coming alive once more. The crouched figure that had begun to emerge from behind a bookcase flinched back again, but not before Dead Rick saw him. The half-witted mortal. With the box of his memories so close, it gave him an inspiration.

"Your boy there," he said to the mortal girl. Miss Baker; Hannah, Cyma had said. Still just empty syllables, without meaning. "I might know what 'appened to 'im."

"*You* happened to him," she said bitterly.

He shook his head. "After me. My mas—the bastard who *was* my master. 'E's got some trick with cameras. Used it to steal my memories, and a ghost; might be 'e used it on your boy, too. Took away some part of 'im, and stuck it in glass."

"Cameras!" She laughed in disbelief, but Feidelm and Abd ar-Rashid came alive with curiosity. "What—are you saying a photograph took Owen's soul?"

And there it was, laid out in a few simple words. Dead Rick's mouth sagged open. "That's exactly what 'e's doing."

His memories: he'd thought of them more than once as his *self*, torn away, so he no longer had any notion of himself. This boy's mind, mangled as if half gone. The ghost of Galen St. Clair. That was the technique Chrennois had been developing for Nadrett, refining it over the last seven years.

Abd ar-Rashid said, "There have been inquiries of late—"

Cyma, and probably Aspell, too. "Satyr's bile," Dead Rick said. The genie nodded. "I've been trying to find out what 'e's up to for a while now. You 'elp me, I tells you what I know."

Irrith let out her breath in a frustrated sigh. "Dead Rick, *stop bargaining*. We're already going to help you."

Her protestation made him twitch. He couldn't stop the words bursting out: "Why should you?"

The Goodemeades made identical noises of affront, but Irrith just grinned. "Why? Because I know something you don't: who you used to be. And I'll bet you every piece of bread I've got that as soon as you get your memories back, you'll help us in return. Not as trade, but because you *want* to. Because that's the kind of fellow you are. Or were, and will be again."

He couldn't help looking around to see what the others thought of her declaration. The Goodemeades were nodding, but the one that hit him like a blow to the gut was the mortal girl. She was biting her lip as if fighting something inside. As if she didn't want to agree with Irrith, but a part of her did anyway.

If he wanted to be any use, he couldn't wait until his memories were restored. He might have wasted too much time already.

He opened his mouth, and felt the oath he'd sworn to Aspell binding his tongue tight. Dead Rick growled in frustration, then stopped when he realised how carelessly that oath had been worded. "I can't tell you where to go," he said, enunciating clearly, so they would understand what he meant. "But if some of you was to follow me . . . you might see something interesting." If they were fast enough, they might even get Nadrett himself.

Abd ar-Rashid clapped his hands once, a sharp sound, calling everyone to attention. "Go, and we will follow."

They left in a rush, shuffling the box somewhere safe, gathering a small war party to accompany the skriker. When they were gone, Eliza fumbled a chair out blindly and sank into it, knees limp as rags.

Dead Rick. There and gone. She'd spent seven years dreaming of the revenge she'd have when she got her hands on him, and now she'd let him go.

"Would you like a cup of tea, dear?"

Eliza abandoned her chair and skittered backward when she realised the question came from Gertrude Goodemeade. Who was now a good two feet shorter than she'd been before, and so was Rosamund. "Ye're faeries, ye are!"

They had the grace to look apologetic. "With the story you told," Rosamund said, "we didn't think you'd take kindly to finding out halfway through that we were brownies."

Outraged, she turned to Mrs. Chase. "And you—"

"I'm as human as you are," the old woman said serenely. "And a friend to these sisters since I was a child. My house is built atop theirs, you see."

None of it was what she'd expected. Eliza couldn't muster the will to fight when Gertrude took her by the arm and led her back to the chair. "Just rest awhile, my dear; you've had a great many shocks today."

They were the only ones left in the library—the four of them and Owen, who had crept into a corner once more. "I was going to kill him," Eliza said numbly, staring at the carpeted floor. "Seven years, I planned it. And now—"

Gertrude reached out as if to clasp her hands, but stopped before Eliza could pull back. "I can imagine," she murmured. "To keep searching for your boy, after all that time—you must have been very angry, and very determined, too. But if you want a target . . ."

"Then you should look to Nadrett," her sister finished, in a colder tone than Eliza had yet heard from either of them.

The name had gone by, briefly, in Dead Rick's rage.

Eliza hadn't been able to follow any of it, dead princes and photography and all the rest. But she was willing to consider including someone else in her anger. "Who is he?"

For all the delicacy with which the Goodemeades phrased their answer, Eliza could read between the lines. Whitechapel had men like that, leaders of gangs who profited off the suffering of others. And they had ways of keeping their followers in line—if nothing so exotic as this.

Stolen memories. It was as if she'd been fumbling around a darkened room, and then someone lit a lamp, showing her in full what she'd only felt the outlines of before now. The blank unfamiliarity in Dead Rick's eyes, when they took Owen away—if the Goodemeades were right, if they were telling the truth, then nothing that day had been his choice.

Mrs. Chase had fetched tea, and now was coaxing Owen from his corner. Eliza could barely look at him; the sight bid fair to break her heart. More things she didn't understand. "How could a camera do that to a person?"

Rosamund gestured around. "This place we're in is the library of the Galenic Academy. It's a school of sorts—"

"More like the Royal Society," Gertrude broke in, naming Britain's foremost scientific institution.

Her sister gave her a mild glare for the interruption, then went on. "We have our own sorts of scholars and scientists, just as you do. One of the things they've been working on is photography. Light doesn't behave the same down here, you see, and neither do some other things, so the cameras used in your world don't work. Nadrett, it seems, has managed to bend it to another use."

"But why do ye need cameras in the first place?"

"Why do *you* need them?" Rosamund asked. "Capturing an image like that, all at once, exactly as it looks in life, and then being able to share it with others . . . we can do a great many things with glamours and illusions, and our memories don't fade the same way yours do, but why shouldn't we want photographs as well?"

"Because ye're *faeries,*" Eliza said stupidly. Her anger couldn't stay hot, not forever; it was fading down to a sullen glow once more, and leaving her exhausted in its wake. Her thoughts kept chasing around in a little circle, everything coming back to the same inescapable point. Dozens of faeries, living beneath London. "And what the devil do ye need with bombs?"

"Bombs?" They both looked entirely innocent, but Eliza no longer trusted it. Mrs. Chase looked confused; that part, she *did* trust.

"The Fenians. Dynamiting the railway, and other things in London. Don't pretend ye had nothing to do with it; I *saw* Dead Rick, and other faeries, too. Why do ye care so much about Ireland?" A sudden, wild thought struck her. "Is that why ye were trying to recruit me, at the meeting? To help them?"

"Gracious, no!" They seemed utterly dumbfounded that she might suggest it. Rosamund said, "We would never get involved with a thing like that. Some fae want

Ireland free, and some want to stop the railway, and a few—like Nadrett—just want to profit, but *we* are trying to prepare for the future."

In something of a confused muddle, Gertrude correcting Rosamund, Rosamund correcting Gertrude, and Mrs. Chase guiding Eliza past their arguments when she could, they told her why the Underground was a threat to this place, the Onyx Hall. It echoed the stories Dead Rick had told, years ago, about a faerie Queen ruling over a dying realm; but he had never told her that realm was *here*. "We've tried all manner of things to stop it," Gertrude said. "When the overland railways came in, we encouraged the City men who wanted to keep them out; that's why they all stopped at Paddington, King's Cross, places a bit farther out. We were afraid so much iron, moving in and out like that, would be a problem even if it was aboveground. Then we tried to prevent plans for an underground railway, and when that failed, we tried to stop the Inner Circle."

Mrs. Chase added, "Do you recall all those delays on finishing it? Sir Edward Watkin of the Metropolitan Railway and Mr. Forbes of the Metropolitan District Railway, all the arguments between them—that was also faerie interference. Though admittedly, those two loathed each other from the start."

Eliza had no idea what the woman was talking about; the affairs of railway directors were hardly the kind of thing she concerned herself with. All she knew was what she'd seen, when they crossed Cannon Street on their way to Cloak Lane. They didn't have much time left at all. "So what are *ye* about, then? If not trying to save this place?"

"We'd do that if we could," Gertrude said. "But our thought is, maybe your people need to *know* faeries are here. That's what we've been doing with the London Fairy Society."

"Originally it started as a way to get more bread," Rosamund added. "You know about bread? There isn't enough anymore, with so few people believing in faeries. So we set out to make new friends, like Lady Wilde. But then we began to think—"

"*Have* thought, for a long time," Gertrude interjected.

"—that perhaps we'd be better off coming out of hiding."

Eliza blinked. Gertrude's words a moment ago had taken a little while to seep through to her understanding, and she still wasn't sure she had them right. "Ye . . . ye'll *announce* yerselves?" She just barely held back the *Jesus, Mary, and Joseph* that wanted to follow. "And ye think that will make anything *better*? For the love of—just ask the Irish how it is, living among people who don't want ye here!"

Quietly, Rosamund said, "And how is it, living among people who don't even *know* you're here? We're already being killed and driven from our homes. At least if we announce ourselves, *some* people can be convinced to help."

And some would be convinced to try harder to eradicate them. Still, Eliza couldn't help but feel a touch of sympathy. There had been folk in Ireland who felt the same way, during the Hunger; they refused to leave their homes, too, no matter how bad times became. Many of them had died of it. But she understood the impulse.

Her thoughts were no longer running in a tight circle; they were rambling, drifting from one thing to another, exhaustion slowing their pace. Owen had drawn near when she wasn't looking, crouching on the floor with his hands wrapped around his knees. Did he remember something of her? Or was it just that she was human, in this faerie place? She had to find a way to help him.

Hesitantly, she slipped from her chair and reached out one hand. Owen did not look up from the floor, but he let her brush the hair gently from his eyes. It had grown shaggy; that much change, at least, seemed capable of happening down here. But his face—so *young* . . .

She'd seen her own face enough times in the Kitterings' mirrors. Hardened by work and grief, it belonged to a woman older than twenty-one. What would Owen think, when he had his wits back? What would they be to each other now, after everything that had passed while they were apart?

Eliza had no answers. But she didn't need them, not yet. First, help Owen; everything else could follow after.

ALDERSGATE, ONYX HALL

6 August 1884

Fast as the Academy fae were, Nadrett was faster.

By the time Dead Rick led them to the Aldersgate fragment, the chambers had been emptied out. Not completely; the corpses of Chrennois and the naga still lay sprawled across the floor. The shelving and tables remained, too. But the cameras, the bottles of chemicals, and all the photographic plates: those were gone.

Niklas von das Ticken cursed in German and kicked a shard of bottle across the room. It nearly hit a faerie kneeling beside the naga's body. It was the same monkeylike fellow Dead Rick had seen when he came to the Academy before; Irrith had introduced him as Kutuhal. His expression as he looked down at his dead kinsman was bleak. *If 'e asks, I'm telling 'im Aspell did it.*

His former ally was long gone, too, though he'd left behind a bloodstain in the street above. Stains were about all they had to study: Yvoir, the Academy's expert on photography, had come down once they knew it was safe, and was investigating the shattered fragments of the bottles Dead Rick had thrown. The sour smell of satyr's bile mixed with other unpleasant odours, under the stench of blood. The French faerie kept murmuring to himself, too quietly for even Dead Rick's ears to make out, and pointing a finger back and forth as if putting pieces together in his mind. The skriker hoped he was getting something useful out of this that he could apply to undoing whatever Chrennois's process was.

"Can you follow them?" Irrith asked. She kept bouncing on the balls of her feet, as if chafing to do something. Probably to hunt Aspell, given her long-standing hatred—though she presumably wouldn't say no to Nadrett, should he present himself.

Dead Rick shrugged. "Maybe—but they both know I've got a sharp nose. They'll 'ave done something to cover their tracks. Don't need no scent to tell me where Nadrett's probably gone, though; 'e's back in the Market by now." Unless he had another bit of palace to hide in, but the skriker doubted it.

Irrith grimaced. Going after Nadrett there would mean war; it was why Hodge never did more than send his knights on occasional raids. Nadrett, like the other bosses, kept his fellows well armed. And even if the Prince's men could beat them in a straight up and down fight, nothing in the Goblin Market ever went straight; within ten seconds it would be every faerie for himself, with bloodshed the Prince was too soft-hearted to risk. He certainly wouldn't do it for something like this.

Aspell was a more interesting question. Would he go back to the Market, as well? There might be war there already, now that Nadrett had uncovered his treachery. If Dead Rick were Aspell, he wouldn't risk it; he'd go to ground somewhere else, away from underlings that might take the chance to seize advantage for themselves.

He needed to find Aspell; he needed that photograph to help him bargain with Hodge. Irrith might help him out of the goodness of her heart, but he couldn't count on any such sympathy from the Prince. Especially not if the Prince recognised Dead Rick as the dog who had attacked him in Blackfriars a few months ago.

Yvoir sighed and stood up from the pitted floor stone

he'd been examining. "There is not much here I did not already know. I will look at the plates you brought; perhaps they will tell more."

Perhaps was a thin word for Dead Rick to hang his hopes on—but it was better than he'd had yesterday, because at least he had the plates. "I'll try to follow Aspell," Dead Rick said, even though weariness dragged at him like lead.

Irrith immediately drew her gun, as if she expected him to find the sod as soon as they went outside. "I'll come with you."

Uncomfortable, he said, "You don't 'ave to."

"What are you going to do, yawn at him? He may be bleeding, but that doesn't mean he isn't a threat." The sprite's lip drew up in a delicate snarl. "I didn't trust him not to be a threat even when he was in prison for a hundred years. And it looks like I was right."

Aspell wasn't half the threat Nadrett was. But Dead Rick could tell there wasn't much point in trying to convince Irrith of that. So long as she didn't shoot their quarry on sight, he supposed it couldn't hurt to let her come along. She was better company than Old Gadling or Gresh, at least.

In the end, though, it didn't matter whether she came or not. There were no trails he could follow in the street above. The snaky bastard was gone, along with the ghost of Galen St. Clair.

* * *

LECKHAMPTON HOUSE, CAMBRIDGE
12 August 1884

"If you need me," Eveleen Myers said in coolly polite tones, "I will be in my workshop."

Contradictory impulses twisted Frederic Myers's heart as his wife turned and swept down the corridor. He should stop her going; they should not leave matters as they were, angry and distant. But what could he say to mend that rift, when his mind kept drifting to another woman? Perhaps a few hours of work over her beloved photographs would calm her, and then they could talk. And in the meanwhile, he was guiltily glad of her absence, which would give him time to work on matters he could not share with her.

Had Louisa Kittering not come to possess his thoughts, he would not have hesitated to ask the Goodemeades and Mrs. Chase whether he could share the London Fairy Society—the true one—with his wife. Eveleen was not a psychical researcher herself, but the secret of the faeries' presence would surely fascinate her. Yet now, with the two of them more estranged every passing day, he worried what she might do with that secret. Would she use it against him? Even betray the faeries' trust?

Six months ago, he would have said no. But now his thoughts were so tangled, he could no longer tell what was sound judgment, and what merely the fearful whispers of his poor, overtaxed brain.

Work might settle Eveleen; it might settle him, too.

Sighing, Myers went to his study.

He had promised the rest of the Society that he would draw up a plan for how they might introduce themselves to the larger world, if they chose to begin with the Society for Psychical Research. It was difficult, when he himself was so new to their world; he could scarcely be sure anything he might say to Sidgwick and the others would even be accurate. Where did faeries *come* from? How did the realm of Faerie itself relate to this world, and to Heaven and Hell? Was there any truth in Miss Harris's theosophical speculation at the séance a few months ago, that a connection existed between the fae and the spirits of the dead? Fjothar, one of the faerie members of the Society, had given him three books written by their own scholars, describing the elements that made up their reality, but after reading through them all Myers still hardly understood it.

But he had promised, and he would try. The Goodemeades expected the fae had at most a few months before they must abandon London. Those who remained—in Rose House, or sheltering by other means—would wait until the exodus was complete, and then begin their emergence. It was the agreement they had formed with Hodge, the one they called Prince of the Stone. "By then, I won't be in no condition to stop you anyway," he'd said, with a gallows grin. Myers shuddered to think of what the fellow meant.

Safely closed away in his study, Myers searched for an empty notebook he could use to write up his plans. One he could hide from Eveleen. *I never used to hide things from her . . .* The thought slipped away, to be replaced by another. *Louisa came to a few Society meetings. I should ask if she might be permitted to join us for the private ones. I should very much like to share them with her.*

There ought to be plenty of empty notebooks, but he could not find them. *I haven't filled them already, have I?* Eveleen would know, but he did not want to ask her. Frowning, Myers rummaged around in drawers, on the shelves, wondering where they might have gone. Finally he came across one he might use; there was writing inside, but it could not have been anything important, for its cover was unlabeled, and the notebook lay at the bottom of a towering stack that must have lain untouched for years.

Paging through, looking for empty pages he might use, Myers caught a word slipping past. *Ectoplasm.* Now, where had he heard that before?

From Sidgwick, at that séance—the one with the physical manifestation, where Miss Harris had proposed her theosophical theory. Curious, Myers turned back until he found the word again. The page was filled with bits of Greek and Latin, combined into different possibilities; not just *ectoplasm* but also *teleplasm* and various other alternatives, all under a header reading *An Emanation of the Spirit,* which was underlined twice.

All of it in his own handwriting—but he had no recollection of writing it.

Curiosity deepened. Myers went back to the beginning

of the notebook. The pages were undated, but a reference to a row he had with Edmund Gurney told him it must have been started in early 1879. Strangely, it began with speculations not far afield from those of Miss Harris: links between ghosts and faeries, jotted notes about legends from different parts of the country, and then other things written down as if they were the true story, though he'd marked no references for them. *Three kinds of apparitions,* he'd noted; *recent; recurrent; recalled.* The recent, this notebook claimed, were swept away by the faeries every All Hallows' Eve, sent on to their eventual rest. Different kinds of fae could see them: fetches, skrikers, church grims, and more. Then musings on where exactly these spirits resided—the astral plane of the theosophists?—and how someone might not only call a ghost from that realm, but enter it physically. But he had abandoned that line of inquiry at the page headed *An Emanation of the Spirit,* and pursued instead the question of the gauzy substance that accompanied true physical manifestations.

Here he found the word *aether,* both underlined and circled.

Aether. Myers straightened up, staggering as his legs protested; he did not know how long he'd been crouched by that pile, but it hardly mattered. He unlocked a drawer in his desk and pulled out the books Fjothar had given him. Aether, according to *An Explanation of Alchemical Principles,* was the defining characteristic of faerie spaces; it was the fifth of their elements, after the classical four.

Fascinating material—and he did not remember writing a single word of it.

Nebulous dread tightened his throat. This was no mere absentmindedness; it was an entire branch of research he had undertaken—on the topic of faeries!—and yet he'd forgotten it completely. Were it not for Sidgwick's comments at that séance, he might even believe these notes had come from someone else's pen, and dismissed the similarity of handwriting as mere coincidence.

Eveleen would not like him going back to London so soon, but he had to ask the Goodemeades what this meant. Myers was accustomed to wondering if he was going mad—he feared he had for a short time, after Annie died—but this was unlike anything he'd felt before, a growing, clawing fear, as if someone had stolen part of his mind while he wasn't looking. Eveleen could not help him with that. Everything he needed lay in London, and he could not endure the thought of delay.

CROMWELL ROAD, SOUTH KENSINGTON: *13 August 1884*

Louisa began to suspect she had been rather too liberal in her use of charms upon Frederic Myers when he showed up at Cromwell Road, the day before the Kittering family was due to leave.

Or rather, two members of the Kittering family, and a

selection of their servants. She had not the faintest intention of going with them. There had been entertainment in spurning every potential suitor Mrs. Kittering brought forward, but now those revels had ended; it would be the countryside after this, tedium without end, and that held no interest for Louisa. Her plan was to part company with them at the train station tomorrow, in such fashion as to ensure they didn't notice her absence until they arrived in Bath. That would give her plenty of time in which to vanish for good.

What she would do after that, she had not decided; and then Frederic Myers showed up at her door.

Mr. Warren did not want to let him in; the argument echoed down the corridor and into the morning room where Louisa sat with her toast. She went out, saw Myers, and swept forward to intervene. Distracting the butler, she dragged Myers into the unoccupied dining room, where the chairs and table had already been covered with sheets against dust. "What are you doing?" she whispered, a seed of alarm taking shape beneath her delighted surprise at seeing him. "A married man cannot call upon an unmarried lady, Mr. Myers, not in such a manner—"

"Louisa," he said, and she nearly jumped from her skin. A married man should *certainly* not call an unmarried lady by her given name—not in that tone of voice. "I have discovered the strangest thing—"

What had been a mere seed of alarm grew, within seconds, to become a strangling vine, cutting off her air. The problem of his affection for her paled into insignificance next to this: that Myers had discovered the gap in his memories, the ideas Nadrett had stolen from him.

How could she have forgotten it herself? She had known, ever since that séance back in April; and she had known then that she ought to stay away from Frederic Myers. But then she'd taken on this name, this life, and then . . .

Horror had drowned out the words coming from his mouth, until she heard him say "Goodemeades." Louisa came back to herself with a jolt. "They have another society, you see," he was telling her, the words tumbling over one another. "I should not tell you too much of it—I should ask their permission before I do—but I suspect they may know something of these ideas, and be able to help me—"

"You aren't going to tell them!" she said, panic clutching her tight.

He blinked at her in confusion. "I am on my way there right now, only I had to stop and see you."

Out in the entrance hall, she could hear Mrs. Kittering's strident voice. Moving swiftly, Louisa wedged a chair under the dining room door so it would not open. Then she turned back to Myers, and took him by the arms.

She was no prophet, but she could see this future clearly enough. If he went to the Goodemeades and told them of the notebook, they would investigate, and that would draw Nadrett's attention. He would not like anyone looking into his secrets. What he would do to the brownies, she couldn't say—they had survived plenty of danger in the past—but the mortal man standing before her was all too fragile. Nadrett would either claim him once more . . . or dispose of him entirely.

And she could not let that happen.

The doorknob rattled, and Mrs. Kittering, thinking it locked, demanded the key from Mr. Warren. There was no time for subtlety, such as she had employed in the past—or thought she had; Louisa rose onto her toes and kissed Frederic Myers hard on the lips, willing him to *love her*.

As she loved him back.

Pulling back just far enough to look him in the eyes, she said, "Frederic, you must listen to me. What you have there is dangerous; you must not tell *anyone* of it. Do you understand? Your only safety lies in fleeing. We will go together, my love; I cannot be parted from you. Do not go to Islington, and do not go back to Cambridge; they will find you there. I will meet you in Hyde Park tonight, by the Serpentine, where we walked before. At midnight. We will hide until we can go away together, and find some place we can be happy. Please, my love, promise me—"

My love. Words she had spoken many times, as Annie Marshall, as the countless other women she pretended to be, through the long ages of toying with humans. She had never meant them before. Fae did not love, not unless they chose to—not as humans did. Passion could not sweep them away; devotion could not creep into their hearts unnoticed. And so the new Louisa Kittering had told herself that what she felt for Frederic Myers was only a rebirth of her early fascination.

She had not realised that a changeling's heart did not lie wholly under her control.

Now he loved her back, as fully as she did him. Frederic wrapped his arms about her and crushed her mouth to his own, kissing her with all the blind passion faerie enchantment could create, until Mr. Warren managed to force the door open, and they were dragged apart. Then there was shouting and crying, accusations and threats of arrest, and too many people for Louisa to charm into cooperative indifference—but they could not hold her, not if she was determined to get away. Tonight she would go to Frederic, and together they would find a way to escape Nadrett forever.

EAST END, LONDON

14 August 1884

Eliza soon discovered the Goodemeade sisters were the sort of well-meaning meddlers who couldn't see two people in conflict without wanting to heal the breach. That was made quite clear by their all-too-innocent suggestion that she take Dead Rick with her to find Dónall Whelan.

She refused, of course. The man who was supposed to pass judgment on him, this Prince of theirs, hadn't yet gotten around to doing so; he was busy with other matters, they said. Trying to save their Onyx Hall. Until he decided on a punishment, she was forbidden to take her own vengeance—she still didn't know how they'd wheedled such a promise out of her. Given that, the last thing she wanted was to spend time in the skriker's company.

But that was before she wasted a week in the East End, trying and failing to locate Whelan. He wasn't among the crowds of men seeking work at the docks. He wasn't in a pub, pickling himself with whiskey. He wasn't in the tiny room he rented above a butcher's shop in Limehouse, either, and his rent was due to run out today. The landlord didn't know and didn't care where his tenant had gone; nobody did.

If there was a photograph with part of Owen in it, nobody knew where it was, and she couldn't assume it would ever be found. Which meant she needed the fairy doctor's help. Which meant she needed help finding him.

The skriker walked beside her in human form, not saying a word. That was how Eliza wanted it. There was nothing he could say to her that she wanted to hear, except for directions to where Whelan might be—and nothing he wanted to say, it seemed. But she couldn't help sneaking glances at him as they made their way through the dockside streets. The hard face that had once been so familiar had hardly changed; it was perhaps a shade harder now, marked with cynical distrust, but he hadn't aged, any more than Owen had. It felt unfair, that everyone else should have stood still, while years of her life ground away.

At the butcher's shop, she led him up to Whelan's room. A simple thrust of his shoulder did for the latch; then he paced around like the dog he sometimes was, bending to sniff the bedclothes, an empty bottle, a lewd photograph tacked to the wall. "You have his scent?" Eliza asked, and when he nodded, she said, "Find him, then."

The faerie exhaled sharply, not quite a snort. "All of London to search in, and you think I can find one bloody man. My nose ain't *that* sharp."

He'd always sounded like a cockney, but these days his speech had a rougher edge: less colourful slang, more bitter swearing. "I know where he spends his time," Eliza said. "You can track him—"

"If we're lucky." He stiffened, and she knew he'd noticed the same thing she had, that casual use of *we*. "Come on," he growled, and shoved past her to the stairs.

A little way into the slow process of quartering the riverside districts, Eliza remembered there *was* something she wanted to hear from Dead Rick. "Last year, in October—when the railway was bombed. I saw you, didn't I?"

She was trailing behind him, letting his nose do the work; she saw his shoulders tighten, and that was answer enough. "The Goodemeades told me about the Underground. I'm surprised ye fellows stopped at a few bombs. Why not go further? Why not kill everyone working on them, until nobody will do it anymore?"

He whirled suddenly enough that she almost ran into him. "Because there's two kinds of people in the Onyx Hall," he snarled, inches from her face. "The ones as are too soft-hearted to kill mortals, and the ones as don't care a twopenny damn what 'appens to anybody else. The first keep thinking there's got to be some other way, and the second are too busy getting their own to do anything useful."

Eliza set her jaw. "And which kind are you?"

His mouth twisted with self-loathing humour. "The third kind. What gets buggered up the arse by the second."

He started off again. After a moment, she followed. He didn't remember anything, the little green-eyed faerie had said. In the library, Eliza had been too angry to think much about what he said and did, but observing him now, the difference was painfully obvious. His face might be the same, but the man beneath it had changed profoundly.

Or had he? They could make illusions to cover their real bodies; maybe they did the same with their behaviour. It could have been an act, before, and only now was she seeing the real Dead Rick.

She didn't think so, though. He'd always been such a bad liar. And the man he'd become was too raw for him to mask, even when he tried.

That makes two of us, Eliza thought.

They tried docks and pubs, boardinghouses and brothels. In desperation, Eliza pointed Dead Rick north, into Whitechapel; Whelan was a Galway man, and might have looked to others from that county for help.

They asked in all the quarters Eliza could think of, but with no luck. Not until they left one of the narrow back courts into which the poor Irish crowded, and Dead Rick stopped, then knelt without warning to sniff the base of a brick wall.

He gathered odd stares from those passing by. "What is it?" Eliza whispered, crouching over him.

The faerie grimaced. "Piss and puke. Might 'ave been 'im. Three days ago, would be my guess." He straightened and scratched at the back of his neck with dirty fingernails. " 'E don't smell too good. Sick, I mean."

Sick. Eliza grabbed Dead Rick's arm, dragging him up Turner Street, following a hunch.

The Royal London Hospital lay a stone's throw away on Whitechapel Road, across from the Jews' cemetery. Its beds were filled with the sick poor, and more waited for the next that might open up; sometimes the nurses didn't even have time to change the sheets before a patient took the place of a corpse. Fortunately, when Eliza gave her name as Whelan and claimed Dónall as her father, she discovered he wasn't in the infectious ward. When she asked what ailed him, the nurse snorted. "Too much drink, not enough food, old age . . . he'll recover or he won't; there isn't much we can do for him. But Father Tooley asked that we give him a bed, so."

Father Tooley? Whelan hadn't set foot in a church since coming to England, but as the priest had once said, it didn't matter how far a sheep had strayed from the flock; it still needed a shepherd's care.

They were directed to a third-floor ward, thick with the smells of chemicals and sickness. Eliza spotted Whelan along the left wall, but when she tried to hurry to his side, Dead Rick's hand clamped around her arm like a vise. "Careful. 'E's dying."

She froze. "What? How can you tell?"

His hard mouth twisted in something that wasn't a smile. "Skriker, ain't I? Death omen. I know when a man's about to snuff it."

They'd said he wasn't infectious—but doctors had been wrong before. "What's killing him?"

"Who knows? I don't see the way, only the when. Don't touch 'im, is all."

He released her arm, and Eliza went forward more carefully. Not that she'd been intending to throw her arms around Whelan in the first place, but now she kept a wary distance. "Mr. Whelan . . . Dónall Whelan, can you hear me?"

He didn't look like a dying man, any more than usual. But he didn't rouse at her voice, until she wrapped her shawl over her hand—she hadn't had gloves since the workhouse—and touched his shoulder. A firmer shake brought his head rolling across his pillow, and he opened his rheumy eyes. At first she wasn't sure he recognised her, but then he said, "You're no nurse."

"I'm not." Eliza wet her lips. *Damn that faerie.* The questions she wanted to ask had all but flown her mind; all she could think was that the man in front of her was dying. "Has it come to such a bad pass, Dónall Whelan, that you'd be looking to the priests for help?"

He mumbled something indistinct, and probably sacrilegious. Then, more clearly, he said, "I'll be up and about soon enough—if these doctors don't kill me. Never trust a doctor. Did you find the girls? The ones from West Ham?"

She swallowed. Those disappearances that Whelan had told her about in May. She'd clean forgotten about them, with everything that happened in between.

Instinct made her look up at Dead Rick, but he just shrugged. Whelan followed her gaze. "Who's that?" He blinked, as if he could not quite focus on the skriker. For once, he didn't reek of spirits; it must be illness that blurred his eyes.

Eliza bit her lip, wondering how to answer. *With the truth; he deserves it.* "It's a faerie, Mr. Whelan," she said, addressing him with far more courtesy than she'd used in the past. "I found them, just like I said I would. And I found Owen. That's why I've come, because Owen needs your help."

"A fairy?" He reached out blindly. Dead Rick hesitated, until Eliza gestured impatiently; then he took Whelan's hand, his thin lips pressed together until they nearly disappeared.

Eliza said, "Yes, Mr. Whelan, a fairy. Just like you used to see, back in Ireland."

His laugh was a dry, hacking thing, indistinguishable from a cough. "Never saw one," he whispered, when he could speak. "Only ever knew what my father said. The rest, I made up."

Her heart sank into her gut. She'd always thought the fairy doctor half a fraud; but it was another thing entirely to hear him confess himself one complete. "All the changelings you said you'd driven out—"

"Stories, lass. Stories." He turned to look at her, still gripping Dead Rick's hand. "Did they work?"

"I never tried them," she lied. What was she supposed to do—tell this broken and dying old man he'd done her no good at all? But no, he'd done *some;* she was sure her farce with the furniture had confused the new Louisa Kittering. Just not enough to make the changeling admit what she was. "What Owen needs is something else. He's half gone, Mr. Whelan—like they tried to make him a changeling, but it went wrong. He doesn't speak, he doesn't seem to understand much; he doesn't even recognise his name. Sometimes I think I'm the only one who remembers it. Like it's been taken from him somehow."

Whelan's breath rasped in and out for a few moments, and his eyes drifted shut; she was afraid he'd fallen asleep, or worse. Then he spoke. "To prevent a child from being taken changeling, you baptise him."

"Owen *was* baptised. It didn't save him."

He mustered enough energy to be impatient with her. "If he's lost his name, you give him a new one. Baptism, lass. To wash their stain from him."

Dead Rick grimaced when she turned to him. "It turns a faerie human; it ought to do some good for 'im."

"But what about his memories? Will he get those back?"

The skriker shook his head, free hand twisting up to show he didn't know. Whelan mumbled, "At least he'll be human."

It wasn't everything, but it was more than nothing. Especially if it kept Owen from wasting away after he left the faeries' realm. "Thank you," Eliza said, and strengthened her voice. "You should get some rest, now."

Whelan nodded, already drifting off. His hand slipped from Dead Rick's and fell to the mattress. For a moment Eliza thought Whelan had died, but the skriker shook his head again. When they were a few steps from the bed, she asked him quietly, "How long?"

"Tomorrow," Dead Rick said. "At the latest."

She didn't dare wait that long; too many people had seen her, and might tell Special Branch where she'd gone. Eliza hadn't decided yet what to do about her impulsive confession to Quinn, back in the workhouse, and he wasn't the only man working for them. Still, Whelan had awoken pity in her heart. She hated to leave him here, forgotten and alone.

Dead Rick stepped into the path of a passing nurse. The woman opened her mouth to snap at him, but closed it when he lifted his hand, a silver crown winking between his fingers. "The Irishman there. This is for 'is care. You give 'im a good supper, and some whiskey if 'e wants it; you treat 'im well, understand?" His voice hardened. "If you don't, I'll know."

She bobbed a curtsy, and snatched the coin from his hand. "Treat 'im like a prince, I will, sir."

Eliza stood, openmouthed, as the nurse hurried on down the ward. When Dead Rick saw it, he shrugged uncomfortably. "Irrith says I used to be a decent cove. I figures, if that's true, maybe I should act like one."

A decent cove who didn't mind the occasional threat—but that was more like the faerie she'd known, seven years ago. "The money's faerie silver," he added roughly, before she could say anything. "It'll turn to a leaf tomorrow."

She closed her mouth and followed him to the stairs.

THE PRINCE'S COURT, ONYX HALL
15 August 1884

"Still no sign of him," Bonecruncher said, wiping blood from his face and dabbing his nose, which seeped red. A souvenir of his venture into the increasingly chaotic Goblin Market. "I can tell you one thing, though: it isn't some cunning plan of his. Unless Aspell really thinks he'll gain something by letting his entire gang fall apart for lack of leadership."

The barguest didn't sound like he believed it, and neither did Hodge. They knew Aspell had been shot, with iron. Had he crawled off somewhere to die? Dead Rick had said it didn't look like a lethal wound, but the death might have been too far off for him to sense.

Hodge didn't care much what happened to the old traitor, just the photograph he'd been carrying. Admittedly, the Prince had bigger problems than a cove who was already dead. The impending end of the Onyx Hall, for example. Common sense said he should let Galen St. Clair go.

But one thing stopped him: Lune. He knew the stories; she'd loved her first Prince, Sir Michael Deven, hundreds of years ago. His successors had been friends and partners, nothing more. Still, she cared about them, all those names carved into the memorial in the ruins of the night garden. Just as she cared for her subjects, and her realm—but if Hodge couldn't save those, he could at least save one bloody ghost.

And there was the faintest outside chance that it might do some larger good. Nadrett, after all, had taken that photograph for a reason. If only they could figure out what it was.

A question from Bonecruncher interrupted his thoughts. "Guess who else is missing from the Market?"

Quite a lot of fae; there wasn't much Market left to hold them, not with the Inner Circle so close to completion. But Bonecruncher wouldn't have said anything if he just meant the general exodus. Stomach sinking, Hodge asked, "Who?"

"Nadrett. And about half his lieutenants, too."

Hodge stared, not sure whether to be overjoyed or appalled. His heart settled on the latter; instinct—not to mention his entire reign as Prince—told him that anything Nadrett did couldn't be good. Including going away. "Where's 'e gone?"

Bonecruncher shook his head, then dabbed again at his face. "Got my nose broken for asking. But it isn't like Aspell, vanishing without a trace. Nadrett's people, the top ones, know what's going on. They just aren't telling."

His pulse quickened. *Maybe it ain't just humbug.* Hodge believed there was *something* going on, deep within Nadrett's lair—but surely if it were a passage to Faerie, they would know by now. People were fleeing, the palace emptying at a steady rate; if they could flee beyond this world, rumour would have spread like wildfire. Could be Nadrett just didn't have it finished, but something about that didn't fit together in Hodge's mind.

He would ask the Academy blokes, but first, he had someone better. A former minion of Nadrett's, who had no reason to love him now. And he'd been meaning to deal with the blighter anyway.

"Bring Dead Rick to me," he said.

I wonder if 'e realises I'm the one as knocked 'im down in Blackfriars.

Dead Rick had vaguely hoped Abd ar-Rashid's comment about turning him over to Hodge had been something to mollify the girl. But that would require his luck turning good, and aside from getting his memories back, he hadn't seen much sign of that happening. Yvoir was doing his best to sort out what exactly Chrennois's cameras had done, but so far he had nothing useful to say, and they were running out of time.

At least the Prince's court wasn't much to speak of. Dead Rick had nothing to go by save Cyma's occasional nostalgic recollections, but he had an imagination; what he'd imagined for the court had been a lot grander than this. There was little ceremony, and even he could recognise the spindly furniture as old-fashioned. The Prince himself dressed like a working man, even down here, in trousers and shirt probably bought ready-made, if not secondhand. It gave Dead Rick the thin consolation that his punishment might be something as ordinary as a beating. Hodge didn't look like the sort to get *creative*.

To be honest, he looked too tired for it. Maybe the darkness that night in Blackfriars had just hidden the sick exhaustion in the man's face, but Dead Rick would have bet anything other than his memories that the Prince had weakened more since then, as the rails raced to join up in Cannon Street. All those earthquakes, at best half suppressed. *The Queen's got it worse,* he thought, remembering what Irrith had said. He wondered if the rest of what she'd said was true, that Hodge heard the Queen screaming.

The Prince sat with his face in his hands, scrubbing wearily at his eyes; then he drew in a breath and straightened. It was just three of them in the room, Hodge and Dead Rick and one of the Prince's knights, Sir Cerenel. Dead Rick wasn't even chained. Without warning, Hodge said, "Passages to Faerie. What do you know about 'em?"

Dead Rick blinked in surprise. He'd expected the Prince to read him a lecture about that mortal boy, not question him. Stupid of him; of course Hodge would want to know about Nadrett. "Scarce more than I did when I saw Irrith in the Market. Got the notion from Aspell; 'e comes to me—in secret; I didn't know it was 'im—saying Nadrett's trying to find a way to make one. I been looking for months, though, and the only thing I found was this business with the photos."

"I know about those. But what's 'e *using* them for?"

The question had been plaguing Dead Rick since that moment in the sewers. He wasn't any closer to an answer now than before. "Blowed if I know. I can't even invent nothing. It don't make sense."

Hodge pinched the bridge of his nose. "But you know Nadrett. Better than any of us do. Even if you don't know 'ow the thing works, you can guess about *'im*."

Dead Rick would have preferred never to think about the bastard again, except to tear his throat out. He couldn't get there without doing this first, though. " 'E loves power; that's what I know. Loves being the biggest rat in the sewer, with everybody afraid of 'im or owing 'im debts. If this place weren't falling apart, 'e'd probably stay right where 'e is, fighting Hardface and all the rest until there ain't nobody to challenge 'im no more. I'll lay a clipped penny to a loaf of bread, 'e wants to make sure 'e don't lose that when this all falls down. And that means making sure 'e's got something everybody wants."

"Something everybody wants," Hodge muttered, "and people to sell it to. Did you know 'e's vanished from the Market?"

"What?"

"Some of 'is lieutenants, too. We're thinking they've shoved off to Faerie already. But I keep wondering: Why would 'e go, and leave everybody else behind? What use is it being a king in Faerie, if you've got nobody to rule over? Does 'e think 'e's going to conquer 'imself a kingdom there, using cameras?"

Dead Rick frowned. "Could be 'e's making ready for people to follow—"

"Then why ain't 'e saying nothing? Getting everybody outside the door, ready to leap through?" Hodge got up from his chair and paced, not like a man with too much energy, but like one who simply couldn't bear to remain still. "Something 'ere don't make sense."

Sourly, Dead Rick said, "I ain't the one to tell you. My 'ead's more 'ole than memory, you know."

Hodge stopped, muttered to himself, turned back to face him. "Why did 'e take your memories, anyway?"

With Dead Rick's mind buried in the other matter, it took him a moment to understand Hodge's. "What?"

"I 'eard what 'e did to you. What was the point? What was 'e going to use 'em for?"

"Nothing," Dead Rick said, frowning. Irrith had told him to trust Hodge; he made himself answer more fully. "That is—they was just for keeping me in line, is all. Whenever I disobeyed 'im, 'e broke one. 'E wouldn't do that, right, if 'e was going to use 'em for something else?"

"Probably not. But do you think you knowed something, and 'e wanted to steal it, or—"

The Prince stopped again, and they both stared at each other. "Or destroy it," Dead Rick said, with lips and tongue that had gone quite numb.

He'd never prodded too hard at that ragged, bleeding edge within his spirit, the place where everything had been torn away. It hurt too much, and Nadrett seemed to know when he was thinking about it; his master had kept him close in those early days, and broken more than a few memories to teach his dog his place. But now—

"What's the first thing you remember?" Hodge asked.

The boy, Dead Rick thought, but it wasn't true. That was just the farthest back he ever really let himself think about. Before that . . .

His breath came faster, his heart pounded harder, his knuckles ached from the tightness of his fists, but he made himself think back. Before the girl's screams, before the boy's trusting cooperation, even before Nadrett's orders.

The earliest thing was pain.

Being thrown down onto a stone floor, puking-sick with pain that didn't come from his body, and only white light when he blinked. "Somebody 'ad been flashing a light in my eyes," Dead Rick said, hearing his voice flatten out with tension. "And somebody—Nadrett, I think—'e said, is that the lot, and whoever 'e asked must 'ave nodded or such, because 'e said, good. And then they dragged me out of the room, and somebody else chained me up, a chain around my neck like I was a dog even though I was a man, and then—" He stopped, unable to go further, and shook his head. There was nothing worth telling, no hint of whether he'd once known something useful. Something Nadrett would shred his mind to get.

Cerenel stepped forward, and Dead Rick nearly jerked into violence; he'd forgotten the elf-knight was there. Cerenel's hand floated just above the butt of his pistol, though he didn't draw. Dead Rick realised his own body had drawn wire-tight; to anyone watching from the outside, it must look like he was on the verge of something dangerous. Like hurting the Prince. Drawing in a slow breath, trying to convince himself it was calming, Dead Rick unclenched his hands. His knuckles creaked at the release.

Hodge was chewing on one fingernail, half-turned away as if trying to give Dead Rick some privacy. "Yvoir's got to put you back together. If you knows something we can use, I want to know it, too."

Swallowing down the memory of sickness, Dead Rick shook his head. "If I ever did, it's gone now. That would've been the first bit Nadrett smashed."

"We won't know until you do, will we?" Hodge's breath caught, his scent giving off a wash of unexpected pain, and he slumped abruptly down into a different chair. When he'd let the air out again, he said, "I'll tell Yvoir to 'urry it up."

After a brief wait, Dead Rick figured out that had been a dismissal. Startled into lack of caution, he said, "That's it? Ain't you going to—" His common sense caught up, and he snapped his mouth shut.

But Hodge understood him anyway. "Ain't I going to punish you, for that business with the boy? Blood and Bone, Dead Rick—you just stood there and told me as 'ow Nadrett tortured you into being 'is dog. I suppose I could make you pay for what *'e* did—but ain't I got worse problems?"

Dumbfounded, all Dead Rick could think to say was, "The girl—"

"The girl's got 'er own problems," Hodge said with exhausted finality. " 'Ere's an idea—you two take care of yourselves, and save me the trouble."

WHITECHAPEL, LONDON
16 August 1884

The light showing through the canvas over the broken window was dim, no more than a single candle's worth. But it was enough to tell Eliza that someone was at home, and so she raised her hand to the weathered panels and knocked.

This time she heard footsteps: slow, dragging ones, the steps of a woman exhausted past the will to raise her feet. They might have belonged to an old woman, but when the door opened, Eliza saw it was Maggie Darragh. The narrow court in which they lived was dark as pitch, and with the candle behind Maggie her face was entirely in shadow, but she was too tall for Mrs. Darragh, and her shoulders slumped with weariness, not defeat. "What do you want?" she said dully.

Eliza drew a careful breath. She'd been given a mirror to look in, before leaving the Onyx Hall; she knew the face she currently wore was not her own. Seeing Maggie fail to recognise her, though, both reassured and unnerved her.

It made her task more difficult, too, which was regrettable, but necessary. She still hadn't decided what to do about Sergeant Quinn, and after her suspicious release from the workhouse—not to mention the way she'd vanished after—she doubted the man thought well of her. The Darraghs' room would be the first place he'd come, if he went looking. So if Eliza wanted to come here, she needed a disguise, and a better one than just a deep bonnet. She needed a faerie illusion—a glamour, as they called them.

Now she needed to convince Maggie to let strangers into her lodgings.

"Miss Darragh?" she said, and the shadow in the doorway nodded. "Father Tooley sent us. May we come in?"

At the word *us,* Maggie squinted past her into the darkness of the court, where Eliza's companions waited. "Sent ye? Why?"

"For your mother's sake," Eliza answered. "We belong to a charitable society, and would like to help you if we can. I promise we won't ask more than a few minutes of your time." It happened occasionally, that well-meaning women from the better classes decided to help out the less fortunate. They didn't come by at night, when few honest people were out and about, but she hoped Maggie wouldn't think of that, not before she let them in.

From behind Eliza, a friendly voice spoke up. "We've fresh biscuits to share."

Maggie hesitated as if fighting with her common sense,

but the delightful smell that suddenly filled the court decided her. “Ma’s asleep, so be quiet.” She stood aside to let them in.

With the weak light of the candle now falling on Maggie’s face, Eliza saw what shadows had previously hidden. The young woman’s eyes were red-rimmed as if she’d been straining them on too little sleep, and indeed, a half-finished pair of trousers were draped across a three-legged stool, next to the room’s one light. Other fabric scattered around showed that this was no bit of personal mending; Maggie had taken on piecework to earn a few more coins. Not enough coins, if her hollow cheeks were anything to go by. Heart cramping with sympathy, Eliza wondered if the biscuits would be the first thing Maggie had eaten that day.

The small room seemed even smaller once six people were crowded into it. Mrs. Darragh lay on the bed, crumpled even smaller in sleep, with a moth-eaten wool coverlet pulled tighter over her shoulder. Maggie stood over her protectively, facing Eliza and the other three. With the door closed, they were alone as anyone could get in the back alleys of Whitechapel, where eavesdroppers were only a thin wall or floor away.

The plump woman who looked exactly like Rosamund Goodemeade, only a little taller, unfolded the napkin in her basket, revealing the biscuits inside. Their smell was sweet heaven in the drab little room, and Maggie twitched as if she wanted desperately to seize them in both hands.

Rosamund gave them over freely, but Maggie just stood clutching the basket. "What is it ye want?"

Eliza wet her lips. After seven years, the moment had come; she was surprised to find it terrified her. Whatever speech she'd thought up, to explain everything in a quick and sensible way, had vanished from her mind, leaving a roaring blank. But she had to speak; Maggie's suspicion was growing with every silent moment. The words burst out of her. "Maggie, 'tis me. Eliza. I've found Owen."

Maggie's hands went white on the basket. She gripped it now as if she would swing it into someone's face, should they gave her half a reason. "What the devil kind of joke—"

"It isn't a joke! The faeries had him, Maggie, as I always said, but I've found him, and I brought him here, but we had to disguise ourselves in case—" Eliza stopped herself. That didn't matter; all that mattered was bringing Owen home. "Rosamund, show her—"

Like a breath of wind whispering over the fine hairs of her arms and legs, the glamour she wore fell away. And Maggie, eyes wide and unblinking, hands still white on the basket's handle, stood rigid for a full three seconds. Then her legs gave out, and she fell hard to her knees on the floor beside the bed.

It woke Mrs. Darragh, who made a plaintive noise and rolled over. Her eyes opened; for a moment they swept over the room in unfocused confusion. When her gaze sharpened, she gave a wordless cry and sat bolt upright, one hand pressed to her heart as if it would give out on the spot.

Her own heart pounding like a navvy's hammer, Eliza turned to see for herself. Owen stood swaying by Feidelm's side, his face wrinkled with apprehension and uncertainty. Eliza didn't know if her plea to Rosamund had been meant to include his glamour or not, but the brownie had taken it that way, dropping them both at once. The two faeries' glamours still stood, but they were hardly needed; they could have been a pair of fire-breathing dragons and neither of the Darraghs would have paid an ounce of attention. They had Owen back at last.

Mute, half-witted, snatched out of time. Mrs. Darragh did not seem to see; she stumbled free of the bedclothes, moving faster than she had in ages, to throw her arms around a boy who did not recognise her but had nowhere to retreat. The last seven years might never have happened; for her, it was still 1877, and Owen the age he should be.

But Maggie saw.

Some part of her understood, even if she couldn't yet put the knowledge into words. Eliza read it in the desperate look Maggie directed at her. "How—" the young woman began, shaking her head; and Eliza answered her.

She kept it to the simplest points. They had never told Maggie about their friend Dead Rick; that had been *their* secret, hers and Owen's, not for a little sister to share. And the part about Nadrett would only confuse her now. What mattered was Owen's condition—and the solution Dónall Whelan had given them.

"We tried to take him to St. Anne's first," Eliza

admitted. The boy had struggled free of Mrs. Darragh, not understanding why she was so desperately glad to see him; Rosamund diverted the woman from him, breaking the news of his situation as gently as she could. "I would have liked to bring him back more healed than this. But he panicked on the steps and wouldn't go in. Will you go fetch Father Tooley here instead?"

Maggie's senses were apparently still reeling; she didn't ask why Eliza's companions couldn't go. They *could* enter churches, so long as they had bread to protect them, but neither Rosamund nor Feidelm was eager to explain this matter to a priest. Maggie nodded, still sitting on the floor. And she stayed there until Eliza added, "Better if 'tis sooner." Then the girl blinked and scrambled to her feet.

Feidelm stepped over to murmur in her ear once Maggie was gone. "The mother . . . is she well?"

Tears burned in Eliza's eyes at the question. Mrs. Darragh was busily telling Rosamund about Owen's apprenticeship to a bicycle maker, while her strayed lamb of a son investigated the biscuits Maggie had left behind. "No," she whispered back. "Her wits left when Owen did. I pray having him back will do her some good, but . . ." But no priestly ritual could mend what had gone wrong with her.

Whether one could help Owen remained to be seen.

The church was only a few streets away, and Maggie had gone out the door like a woman determined to drag the priest back by his collar if necessary. She returned in almost no time at all with Father Tooley at her heels—looking,

Eliza was glad to see, more curious and concerned than upset at being rousted.

He stopped in the doorway as if he'd slammed into a pane of glass, staring at Owen.

Maggie nudged him in before the neighbours could grow too curious, and shut the door behind him. *"A mhic ó,"* Father Tooley breathed, crossing himself. " 'Tis true, then."

He listened as Eliza repeated her explanation, this time going into more detail on what Whelan and Dead Rick had said. She looked to the fae for confirmation, only to realise they'd slipped out while she was talking; how had they done that, without drawing attention? Faerie magic, perhaps. They'd done right, though. Rosamund and Feidelm had come with her because Owen needed looking after, and trusted them more than the family that were strangers to him now. The question of what to do with him, though, belonged to the mortals.

To Father Tooley most of all. He folded his big hands into a neat package while she spoke, a sure sign that he was thinking hard; when she finished, he stood silent for a long moment. Then he shook his head. " 'Tisn't that simple, Eliza. Or perhaps I should say, 'tis simpler. Once a child's been baptised, he cannot be baptised again. There's no *need* for it; God's grace is indelible. The Devil himself could not wipe it away."

For all her doubts about Whelan, it seemed some part of Eliza's mind had seized upon his suggestion as the answer to their problems. Her bitter disappointment at

Father Tooley's words surprised her. "Your baptism didn't do much to protect Owen, now did it? Could be you aren't priest enough to do it right."

It was unfair, and he frowned at her. "Anyone can baptise, Eliza—even a Jew, so long as his words and intent are right. But I don't know if 'tis true that baptism protects against such things. That . . . is not the sort of thing they teach in seminary."

"But *look* at him." Helplessness made Eliza's gesture violent, flinging her hand out to where Owen had curled up on the bed, with Mrs. Darragh stroking his hair. "They say the faerie tried to take his soul, Father. You'll be telling me next that no one can do that, and maybe 'tis true, but the bastard took *something*. And if we don't find some way to wash Owen clean, he can never come back to us, broken or whole. He's eaten too much of their food. It would kill him, and that's the truth of it."

"If you pray—"

"You think I *haven't*?"

Father Tooley conceded the point, but still he frowned. "Some other rite, perhaps—an exorcism—"

Maggie made a furious noise, like a dog defending her pup. A pup who had once been her older brother. Eliza said, "Can you tell me honestly that you think he's a demon in him?"

The priest looked at Owen for another long moment, then shook his head. "No."

While he grappled with that question, Eliza's own mind

had snatched up one of its own, from something Father Tooley said before. "You said anyone could baptise."

"Don't you think of it for one moment," he said, alarmed. "Ministering the sacrament to an infant who won't live long enough for the priest to come—to a Protestant converting on his deathbed—that's a worthy thing, Eliza. But to do it when a priest has refused, when you *know* the boy has already been baptised, would make a mockery of the sacrament. And sure that would be a grave sin."

"Then what should I do?" she demanded, forgetting to keep her voice low. "Let him waste away? Abandon him to the faeries? If you think—"

She wanted to keep talking when he raised his hand, but his suddenly thoughtful expression silenced her. "I could," he began, then stopped.

"Could?" Maggie prompted him, fierce with hope.

Father Tooley grimaced. "The bishop would have my ears for even considering it, he would," he muttered. "But better to be sure than sorry, and if there's a chance it might do him good . . . when I said anyone could baptise, it was true, but not the whole truth. If a heretic administers the sacrament, who's to say they had the form and meaning of it right?"

"So you baptise the person again," Eliza said.

He made a cautionary gesture. "Not *again*. A baptism done wrong doesn't count in the first place. But if you don't know for sure, there's conditional baptism." A hint of rueful humour crept into his voice. " 'Tisn't much different from the ordinary thing. *Si non es baptizatus,* that's all I add—*if you aren't already baptised.* If you are, then all you get is a bit of Latin and a bit of water on your head, and no harm to anyone."

Maggie turned swiftly, as if something could be hiding from her in the tiny room. "Water—I can go to the pump on Old Montague—"

"No," Eliza said. "Sure it would be better in the church. During Mass—"

Father Tooley barked a laugh. "Oh, no. Think ye two are going to march him up the aisle, and me explaining to everyone what on earth we're doing?"

Then Eliza remembered Owen's refusal to enter St. Anne's. She described it to Father Tooley, and he folded his hands again, tilting his head as if arguing with himself. The debate ended with a decisive nod of his head. "This is what ye'll do. Next Friday—"

"Next *Friday*!"

He gave Eliza a quelling look. "'Tis the feast day of St. Symphorian, and the octave of the Assumption of the Blessed Virgin Mary. He's a patron of children, and if Owen is too old to qualify for his help, we can still beseech the Virgin to intercede. Ye bring him to the church a few hours before dawn. The rite begins on the steps outside; if we can't get him through the door, then I'll do it all in the street. And pray God it does some good."

Owen shivered and curled tighter. He'd gone into that posture, Eliza thought, when they began speaking of God.

The faerie stain, no doubt. They couldn't keep him out here much longer; soon he would have to go back to the Onyx Hall.

Silently, she offered up her own prayer. *Blessed Virgin, Mother of God—for Mrs. Darragh's sake, if no one else's, help our Owen be well.*

Humming an old lullaby beneath her breath, Mrs. Darragh bent over her son and kissed his forehead. "Sleep, my boy," she whispered. "Sleep."

THE GALENIC ACADEMY, ONYX HALL
17 August 1884

Yvoir's workshop stank of chemicals. Dead Rick made the mistake of trying to smell them apart, and sneezed four times in quick succession. The French faerie smiled at him. "Be glad you aren't mortal. I'm fairly certain the compounds they use have killed a number of photographers."

"And yours are safer, are they?"

He shrugged. "To mortals, perhaps not. But we are not so easily killed, are we? A moment, please." Yvoir returned his attention to the bowl in front of him, and the strainer balanced on its rim. The latter held a stone-green blob that jiggled as the faerie lifted it and scraped viscous material away from its underside.

Fascinated despite himself, Dead Rick asked, "What is that?"

"Cockatrice egg." Yvoir carelessly dumped the yolk into a bucket on the floor. "Almost any sort of egg should work, but I find the albumen of a cockatrice egg is more stable, if slower to develop the image."

Dead Rick came closer, peering into the bowl, which proved to hold a large quantity of clear, viscous sludge. "This is for photographs, then."

Yvoir nodded and tossed the strainer into a basin of water, then wiped his hands clean on a towel. "Not like yours, though. Have a seat, and I'll tell you what I've learned."

The skriker's heart beat more quickly at the words. The message hadn't said anything about Yvoir's progress, just that the scholar wanted to talk to him. He hadn't quite dared let himself hope that the news would be good. Too excited to relax, he perched on the edge of the chair and said, "Can you put them back?"

"This is what I called you for, is it not? I have a sense now of what Chrennois did." Yvoir steepled his fingers and glanced around his workshop. The walls were covered in more photographs than Dead Rick could count, of all different kinds; some had the silver gloss of daguerreotypes, while others glowed a warm amber, or showed the delicate colours of hand-tinting. Mostly they showed people—fae were always fascinated by people—but a few depicted landscapes, sometimes from as far away as Egypt or China.

His accent thickened by distraction, Yvoir said, "They are not quite photographs, not in the way I have created. Not images. You could not put them up on the wall like these. Chrennois was finding a way to capture the . . . *essence* of things."

The essence of Dead Rick's memories. A growl rose in his throat at the thought, but he swallowed it down.

Yvoir searched through a pile on the table by his left arm and produced one of the thin glass plates. Dead Rick had spent untold hours staring at them, after the failed attempt on Aldersgate. The other faerie was right; they didn't show images like a photograph. Still, he thought he could see something swimming in their depths—as if, should he stare long enough, he could make out the secrets they held. He'd gone half blind trying.

"This," Yvoir said, tapping the glass—Dead Rick held his breath in apprehension—"is like a daguerreotype. It is on glass instead of copper, but I believe it was coated in moon-silver and then in some fashion sensitised before being exposed, though I do not know how. Willow smoke, perhaps. Are you familiar with the alchemical connections of willow and the moon?"

Dead Rick waved off what sounded like an impending lecture. "Just get to the bit that'll 'elp me."

The Frenchman blinked as if not at all clear why anyone would want to skip the details, but he obeyed. "The coating on the plate was made reactive to things less visible than light—thoughts, passions, memories. Which is very intriguing—and so is this." His stained fingernail traced a nearly imperceptible line down the center of the rectangular plate, which Dead Rick had noticed before. "It seems he took two photographs at once."

"Two?" Dead Rick frowned. "What in 'ell would 'e want with two?"

Yvoir smiled, like a conjurer about to reveal his completed trick. "Have you ever seen a stereograph?"

Dead Rick shook his head.

The other faerie bounded to his feet and went to the nearest wall, hand floating across the assortment of pictures. "It should be . . . ah, yes. Here." He lifted a frame down, then rummaged in a cabinet until he found a small wooden contraption with a clamp at one end. After a bit of fumbling, he got the picture out of its frame and put it in the clamp, then handed the whole to Dead Rick. "Look through the lenses."

He glanced at the picture before doing so, and saw it was a pair of identical images, showing some tremendous chasm in the wilderness, probably on the American frontier. When he put his eyes to the lenses, though, the two images blended into one—and came to life. He pulled back with a stifled yelp, and found Yvoir grinning at him; grinding his teeth, Dead Rick looked again.

Nothing moved; it wasn't "life" in that sense. But he felt as if he were standing where the photographer had been, seeing not a flat image, but depth. " 'Ow in Mab's name . . ."

"It mimics the way your eyes work," Yvoir said. "You see a slightly different image with each eye, so if the photographer takes two images the correct distance apart, and you view the prints the same way, it creates the effect of proper vision. Don't you see? It's like an illusion that mortals have learned to make for themselves!"

The excitement in his voice made Dead Rick sour. Putting down the stereograph, he said, "It weren't no illusion they did to me."

Yvoir sobered quickly. "No, of course not. But the point is that the stereoscopic image has *depth,* in a way that a flat photograph does not. I suspect this is the key to your memories being *taken* from you. If we were to use Chrennois's techniques, but with only one lens, we would make only a copy—of a memory, or a thought; perhaps even a soul." He looked thoughtful. "Or perhaps not. Souls are more complicated. The stereoscopic camera may be a necessity for that. But had Nadrett wished only to copy your memories, he could have done so, I think."

It lent credence to the idea that Nadrett had wanted to destroy them completely. Or at least a specific one. "You know about this passage to Faerie business?" Dead Rick asked. Yvoir nodded. "'Ow could that fit in with this?"

The thoughtful look deepened to a frown. "I do not know. Stereography creates depth; I could imagine that being useful if one wishes to make a path that leads somewhere else. But photographs to make a path?"

"Photographs of ghosts and souls," Dead Rick reminded him.

Yvoir nodded acknowledgment of his point. "If I were to do this, I would be photographing faerie minds, not mortals. Gather different notions of Faerie, perhaps—

copies only—from those with clear memories of it, and then set them side by side. It would create something that is a combination of the two, and more than a flat image. But I still do not see how that makes a path *through* to Faerie, even with depth."

Neither did Dead Rick. Maybe Hodge was right, and the answers lay in his own glass plates. "Well, put my memories back in my 'ead, and I'll tell you if the answer's in there somewhere."

The faerie put up an apologetic hand. "I cannot—not yet."

The skriker's mood was an unstable thing these days, swinging easily from hope to rage. He almost put his fist into Yvoir's face. "What do you mean, you can't? Why call me 'ere, then? All this bloody lecturing about things what don't matter, but when it comes to the only thing that does, you're bloody useless!"

He knew he was angry; he didn't realise how much until Yvoir flinched back. "*Soit patient s'il te plaît!* I mean, I know *how* to do it—I believe so, at least—but it cannot be done *yet*. You must be patient."

The fear in Yvoir's voice reminded Dead Rick, yet again, that he was no longer in the Goblin Market. The differences kept taking him by surprise. Hodge's mercy, Irrith's gentle teasing, and now Yvoir's fear, because to these people he was scary. They had not lived with the likes of Nadrett or Lacca.

Or am I that much scarier than I used to be?

There was no need to cringe or scrape here, to show throat and beg for mercy. For the first time in ages, Dead Rick felt strong. Only for a moment, though: then his eyes went to the fragile glass of his memory, and he remembered how easily strength could be taken from him.

He took a slow breath and made himself think about what Yvoir had just said. "What are you waiting for, then?"

"Are you familiar with absinthe?"

A surprised snort puffed out of him. "That green stuff the mortals drink?"

Yvoir looked contemptuous. "What they drink is a pale imitation of the real thing. In Faerie, wormwood is an herb of the moon; the mortals know this, for they call it *Artemisia absinthium,* after the Greek goddess. And it will assist in visions, which is what we need. I have written to France, to obtain some. As soon as it arrives, we will try."

Something in the way he said it made Dead Rick apprehensive. "And the bit you ain't telling me is . . ."

"I said what they drink is a pale imitation. True absinthe—the Green Faerie itself—is much more powerful. You may find its effects . . . distressing."

The anger was still there. It had always been there, every moment he lived under Nadrett's heel, only now he could admit it without fear of dying. Dead Rick stalked toward Yvoir, who abruptly went rigid and did not move, and growled very quietly into the other faerie's face, "More *distressing* than 'aving everything of who I was—every bit of me that ain't Nadrett's dog—stuck in glass?"

A tiny, tremulous shake of Yvoir's head was his only answer.

Dead Rick's lip curled in a mockery of a smile. "Let me know when you gets your wormwood. I'll be more than ready."

ST. ANNE'S CHURCH, WHITECHAPEL
22 August 1884

Eliza had grown accustomed to having her heart in her mouth every time she went to Whitechapel. Usually it was because of Special Branch, but this time, her fears were of another sort entirely.

What if it doesn't work?

The question had no answer. If it didn't work, then . . . no. It *had* to work. Had to, because Eliza lacked any alternative, and surely God owed her this much.

Blasphemous thoughts to have in her head as she slipped through the Whitechapel night to church.

With Owen following like a meek and frightened lamb, she avoided the pimps and the whores, the cutpurses and the drunkards staggering through the streets, making her way to a place such sinners rarely frequented. St. Anne's was a solid, comforting bulk in the darkness, silhouetted against a surprisingly clear sky. Eliza was grateful for the lack of a moon, which would help to conceal what they did here tonight.

Grateful, at least, until a shadow detaching itself from the outer wall of the church made her nearly jump from her skin. "We've a problem."

Eliza pressed one hand over her pounding heart and glared at the Maggie Darragh–shaped shadow. "Jesus, Mary, and Joseph, Maggie, you scared me half to— What do you mean, a problem?"

Owen had scurried to hide behind Eliza, keeping her between him and the sister he didn't recognise. Or perhaps it was the church he cowered away from, or his mother, who followed her daughter into the street. Maggie gestured at him. "He needs sponsors, doesn't he? A godmother and a godfather, to answer for him, since he's no voice. I didn't think of it until now. Ma can't, not for her own child. I suppose I might, but shouldn't there be two?"

Eliza's heart sank. She hadn't thought of it, either, but should have. Even when an adult converted, they had sponsors at their side during the baptism, and Owen's position was more like that of an infant. It might be possible to do it with only one—she could ask Father Tooley—but her instincts rebelled against doing anything that might undermine the sacrament.

But who would they find to be his godfather? Not liking it, but not seeing any other choice, Eliza said, "Fergus—"

Maggie was already shaking her head, as if she'd known Eliza would suggest him. "It would never work; he hasn't come to church in years. And he—he doesn't know about my brother, not yet."

Now wasn't the time to ask why. Eliza bit her lip. Dónall Whelan had been buried days before, with more faerie silver to pay his way; but he, like Fergus Boyle, had been an unrepentant sinner, not a man in good standing with the church.

Did the second sponsor have to be a man?

Owen was a silent, timid presence at her back. In the days since she'd found him, he'd come to trust her, a little, if not as much as Feidelm and the others he knew better. She'd dared the police and the world under London to find him, and a godmother was supposed to stand between her godson and sin . . .

If she sponsored him through this baptism, though, they would be family. And they could never marry.

She'd been avoiding the question ever since she went into the Onyx Hall and saw her lost love, caught seven years back in time. Even if Owen regained his wits, he was just a boy. Eliza had spent a third of her life apart from him, growing and changing, not always in good ways. Would he *remember* her? Would he still love who she'd become?

Did she still love who he was now?

Another question with no answer. It *couldn't* be answered, not until Father Tooley baptised Owen and they saw what good, if any, that did. But Eliza had to make her choice now.

The creak of a door made them all jump. It was just the priest, though, emerging from the church in his robes and violet stole. He cast a quick glance around, then hurried over to join them.

In the few seconds it took for him to reach them, Eliza made her decision.

All that matters is helping Owen. You can't let anything get in the way of that.

She just hoped the decision wasn't cowardice, a way of avoiding the questions she couldn't answer.

"Father Tooley," Maggie said, "we didn't arrange for sponsors. I'll be his godmother, but for the other—"

"I'll do it," Eliza said, cutting her off. The declaration came out too loud, and she lowered her voice. "If two godmothers isn't blasphemy, I'll be the other."

Maggie gave her a sharp look, and Father Tooley one so filled with pity and kindness that Eliza flinched away from meeting it. She expected the priest to remind her of what that meant, or say she couldn't do it, but to her surprise— "I thought of that already, and arranged a godfather for him."

"Who?" Maggie demanded, before Eliza could find her tongue. For one irrational, bewildered moment, she thought of Dead Rick. But the Goodemeades had already told her that baptism was too dangerous a thing for them to go near, bread or no.

Father Tooley said, "I think that's him at the corner, there."

She and Maggie both whirled. In the darkness, with a cap on, the man's face was too deeply shadowed to make out the slightest detail, but Eliza didn't need it. The left sleeve, knotted at the cuff where a hand should be, made him recognizable at any distance.

She didn't know she'd cursed until Maggie elbowed her, and for a moment they might have been sisters again. Eliza spun again and glared at Father Tooley. "You'd call my *father* a good Catholic? Good enough for Owen?"

The priest had the grace to look awkward. "In the general sense, no, but—he's made confession, and done his penance. And he wanted to see you, Eliza."

By then James O'Malley had drawn close enough to overhear. Eliza snapped her mouth shut, too many emotions warring inside for her to be sure what would pop out. Her father was much as he had been when she visited him in Newgate last year: still a big-boned man, though with less flesh on him than before, and his face scarred by a life harder than Eliza cared to think. She knew what trials he'd been through—and she knew they didn't excuse his flaws. Other men went through as much without becoming drunkards, or beating their wives and children, or falling into a life of petty crime.

That he should stand as Owen's godfather was unthinkable.

He said nothing, and the silence grew tighter and tighter, until Eliza finally snapped, "Where the devil have you been, then—other than with the Fenians?"

Maggie drew in her breath sharply. James O'Malley's jaw hardened. But he didn't growl back, as she expected; he just said, "That's something we'll be speaking of later. For now, I think we've other things to do." He paused, his gaze on Owen. "Christ. Something *has* gone wrong with the boy, hasn't it?"

"Yes," Father Tooley said hastily, "and we ought to take care of that before someone notices what we're about. Eliza, he needs a godfather, and James says he's willing to stand for it. Will that do?"

She wasn't at all sure that it would—but she could hardly ignore the priest when he said Owen needed this. Her answer came out unsteady, but it came out all the same. "It will—but pray God this works."

In all seriousness, Father Tooley said, "I have been. Come, let's get started."

It took all Eliza's coaxing to get Owen to even approach the steps of the church. The closer they got to the door, the more he fought her, face twisting in apprehension, just as it had before; and Mrs. Darragh was no use, making soothing noises that influenced her son not at all. But finally Eliza got him onto the steps, and Maggie said, "Father Tooley, we bring this boy to be baptised."

The priest waited, then prompted her with a gesture, but the girl only looked confused. *No one calls him by name,* Eliza thought. *Not anymore.* They hadn't for years—three or four, now that she thought of it. That must have been when Nadrett took it from him.

In a strong voice, she said, " 'Tis Owen Darragh they bring."

Father Tooley accepted that and began. "*Quid petis ab Ecclesia Dei?" What do you ask for from the Church of God?*

James answered the questioning on Owen's behalf, giving the short responses in badly pronounced Latin. Then the priest began to cross Owen, first with breath, then with his thumb. Maggie held her brother by the shoulders; he twitched and gasped at each sign of the cross, and let out a wordless, desperate cry when Father Tooley placed his hands upon the boy's head and began to pray. Eliza bit down on her lip. If prayer alone hurt him like that, what would the blessed salt do?

Owen fought to avoid it, clamping his mouth shut and twisting his head away; mouth set in a grim line, James pried his jaw open with his one hand, while Maggie held her brother and wept into his hair. When Father Tooley set the salt on his tongue, Owen went completely rigid, and Eliza tasted blood—but as James said the last "Amen," the boy relaxed, his eyes opening once more and his body going slack.

Eliza's breath was coming fast, but she met Father Tooley's questioning gaze and nodded. It seemed to have done some good; Owen was silent through the exorcism, through the repeated signs of the cross and the second imposition of hands, Father Tooley praying in a voice that went no farther than their little group, admitting him into the church building. When the paternoster was done, Eliza beckoned Owen from the door, and he obediently followed Maggie and the rest into the nave.

He shivered as he crossed the threshold, but made no other sound. The solemn exorcism, Father Tooley's spittle upon his ears and nostrils, the renunciation of Satan, the anointing with oil; the interior of the church was lit only by a few candles, and the entire moment had a dreamlike quality that made Eliza hold her breath. Her entire spirit was bent in wordless prayer, as if she could compel Owen into wholeness just by the force of her hope.

This had to heal him. It *had* to.

Father Tooley changed his violet stole for a white one, shimmering in the darkness, and led their little group to the font. A hand slipped into Eliza's, startling a little sound out of her, but it was only Mrs. Darragh. The old woman shivered, and Eliza gripped her fingers, taking comfort in the strength that answered hers. "Owen Darragh," Father Tooley asked, *"credis in Deum Patrem omnipotentem, creatorem cæli et terram?"*

James O'Malley might not be a religious man, but he never doubted the existence of God the Father Almighty. *"Credo,"* he answered for Owen, and Maggie with him.

Eliza's breath came faster and faster as they finished the profession of faith, as Father Tooley asked whether Owen wished to be baptised, and his godmother and godfather answered on his behalf that he did. And then the moment had come, and she stopped breathing entirely.

Taking water from the font, Father Tooley lifted it above Owen's head. *"Si non es baptizatus,"* he said, *"ego te baptizo in nomine Patris—"*

Every hair on Eliza's arms and neck stood straight up as the priest poured the holy water.

"—et Filii—"

A second dipper of water. Every candle in the church seemed to grow brighter.

"—et Spiritus Sancti."

Owen drew in a deep, shuddering gasp, the third cup of holy water running over his closed eyes, streaming through his hair and down his cheeks. He straightened beneath Maggie's and James's hands, shoulders going back, and Eliza's skin tried to shake itself right off her body as she felt *something* go by, banished from the church—and from Owen—by the ancient ritual, repeated in this precise form for hundreds of years.

Holy Mary, Mother of God—please—

Hand shaking, Father Tooley anointed Owen with chrism, reciting the prayer in a near whisper. When he finished, Maggie and James opened their mouths to answer, but another voice spoke before they could.

"*Amen,*" Owen said.

THE GALENIC ACADEMY, ONYX HALL

22 August 1884

When Dead Rick saw what Yvoir had set up, he almost turned around and left.

The French elf had mostly talked about how they were going to shine moonlight through the translucent plates of his memories, running them one by one past his eyes as if they were pattern cards in a Jacquard loom. He'd spent a great deal of time explaining the principles behind the creation of that moonlight—something about a particular balance of the four elements in what he called a selenic configuration; Dead Rick didn't understand a word of it—and made one brief mention that the absinthe might have some lingering effects that would take a while to disperse.

He hadn't said a word about the chair.

It was a thick, blocky thing—heavy, not like the modern, fashionable furniture that sometimes made its way into the Goblin Market, but rather like the oldest pieces, the ones that predated the Onyx Hall itself. No padding softened its seat or back, and along the edges . . .

"Ash and *Thorn,*" Irrith said from behind him. "Yvoir, what in Mab's name are you planning to *do* to him?"

Yvoir blinked owlishly at them through the lenses over his eyes, which allowed the Academy engineers to better study the alchemical balance of the machines they built. "What?"

Tension gripping his throat too tightly for him to speak, Dead Rick gestured at the chair—at the bands on its arms, its legs, even where his head would rest.

"Oh." Yvoir turned the lenses up, so that his eyes were no longer refracted into weird layers. "I mentioned there may be muscle spasms, yes? It is necessary to make certain you do not move from the path of the light; if we do not send the image directly into your eyes, you may lose a part of what we seek to return. Is it a problem?"

Dead Rick's jaw ached from being clenched so hard. The sight of the chair called up a nameless dread in him—no, not entirely nameless; he could identify a portion of it very well indeed. Once he was locked into position, he would be at the mercy of those around him, unable to move so much as a single hand to defend himself. Every Market-honed instinct he had screamed at him not to be an idiot, not to trust these people, no matter what they promised . . .

Irrith had learned something of him in these last few days. She stepped around in front of him, lifted her hand, and when he did not flinch away, rested it on his arm. "I'll be right here," she promised. "The instant you say the word, I'll let you out. Even if Yvoir isn't done. If you want it to end, all you have to do is say so."

She was still asking him to trust *her*, and he was still petrified to do it. *But you've done worse, 'aven't you? Trusted Valentin Aspell, without even knowing who 'e was. 'Cause you was too desperate to pass up the chance.*

He'd been under Nadrett's thumb at the time. Now he was free of his master. He could hold on to the memories, and wait until—

Until what? Until he found someone else he *did* trust? Dead Rick looked around the room, at the alchemical diagrams on the walls and strange equipment littering the shelves. All the foreigners were here for a reason: because there was no other place like this in the world, where fae had found a means of describing the half-rational, half-symbolic rules that governed the realms existing in the cracks of the mortal world, and then translating those rules into mechanical devices. Once this place was gone, he could wander a century without finding anyone else with the necessary skills to help him.

And then there was the possibility Hodge had raised. Maybe he'd known something that threatened Nadrett, and that was why the bastard had stolen his memories. If there was any fragment left that might hurt his former master . . .

With stiff legs, Dead Rick strode over to the chair and dropped into the seat. "I ain't going to back out. Do what you 'as to."

Irrith bit her lip, and gave him a startlingly grave nod. "Here," Yvoir said, handing her a crystal vial. "Prepare this, and have him drink it."

The Green Faerie: absinthe from beyond this world. The moment Irrith withdrew the emerald that capped the vial's slender neck, a powerful scent filled the air, like bitter anise carried on ephemeral wings. Irrith emptied it into a small cup; then she laid a slotted silver spoon across the top, with some kind of glittering crystal balanced in the center. Over this she poured a liquid that shone like moonlight. When it dripped into the absinthe below, the concoction swirled into a thousand different shades, dizzying to watch.

Dead Rick meant to toss it off in one gulp, the better to get this over with, but it turned out not to be that simple. The first taste of the bitter liquid, blooming warm on his tongue, seemed to lift him partially from his body, so that he wasn't sure if it was going down his throat or not. He was suddenly very aware of the motions involved in drinking: the angle of the arm, the tilting of the head, tongue and throat working in a specific fashion. Only his intellectual understanding of these things allowed him to continue; he had to trust that his body was responding as it should.

Distantly, he heard Yvoir speaking. "—partial separation of the aetheric component from the rest of the elements; it will aid the reintegration of the memories into the spirit. And, of course, the lunar sympathy of the absinthe will play a role as well. Ah, my lord, you're just in time. Irrith, if you would be so kind . . ."

A peculiar sort of clarity settled over Dead Rick's mind. Without looking, he knew that Hodge had entered the room, followed by Abd ar-Rashid and Wrain. He knew that Irrith was apprehensive as she reached for the manacles on the chair, and that he was mad beyond question to let these people chain him down.

He also knew he had no other hope of regaining his memories. So he swallowed the keening whine that wanted to escape his throat, dug his nails into the worn ends of the chair's arms, and let Irrith bind him into place.

Two leather cuffs around his ankles. A band across his knees. Another across his chest, and his wrists bound to the chair; then, her face tight with reluctance, Irrith strapped his head to the back of the chair, and moved into position the side braces that would prevent him from twisting in place.

Dead Rick's heart beat an accelerating tattoo against his ribs. It was more than just his appalling vulnerability, but he couldn't tell what the rest was—

"*Pardonnez-moi,*" Yvoir murmured, and his delicate

fingers slid thin wires under Dead Rick's eyelids, to brace them open.

Was it his fear or the absinthe that made everything so sharp, both close and yet impossibly far away? This must be what faerie wine tasted like to mortals, bitter and compelling, lifting him partway out of the world he knew, into sight of something *more,* whose existence he had never before suspected . . .

Yvoir's machine rolled into position in front of him, something like opera glasses lowering before his pinned eyes, the precious chain of his memories set to begin scrolling in front of the box that would create the necessary moonlight. Dead Rick felt Irrith's hand slip into his and grip his fingers tight; without thinking, he gripped hers back, hard enough that he could feel the delicate bones grind together. The sprite didn't make a sound.

"Are you ready?" Yvoir asked, and Dead Rick answered with a wordless grunt. It was supposed to be a yes, and it seemed the French faerie interpreted it as such, for he began to turn a crank on the side of the box, and pure silver light filled Dead Rick's vision.

As if from the other side of the moon, he heard scattered words. *"Un moment—"* "Should I—" *"Commençons—"*

And then the memories clacked into motion, the first plate of glass falling into the path of the light, and the shapes hidden therein shining straight into Dead Rick's eyes.

* * *

Memory: 14 September 1877

He fought against the straps even before he knew what Nadrett and Chrennois had planned, because it didn't take a bloody genius to guess it wouldn't be anything good. But they'd drugged him before they chained him to the chair, and then they forced his eyes open with wires and pushed some kind of two-lensed camera right up into his face, and he didn't even have time to snarl before white light flashed and a piece of himself was torn straight out of his head.

Dead Rick's scream echoed off the stone walls. The straps dug into his body, hard enough to bruise, and when the spasm faded he heard Nadrett say, "Did you get it?"

Clattering wooden sounds, the gentle splash of liquid, and then an apologetic sound from the French faerie. "No. It is not precise; I can only take what is foremost in his mind. You must persuade him to think of what you want removed."

"Iron rot you," Dead Rick snarled, through teeth that would not unclench. All he could see was the camera in front of his eyes, but he knew Nadrett was out there somewhere, and directed his curses at the bastard. "I ain't going to give you nothing—"

"That," Nadrett said coldly, "is where you're wrong."

Another flash, another scream, his muscles knotting into hard points of agony.

"Your arrival in London, I think, sir," Chrennois said. "Closer, but not quite."

He had to hold on to it. Whatever the cost, he couldn't

let Nadrett take what he knew—

Dead Rick twisted his mind frantically away from that thought. *'Ave to think of something, anything other than what 'e wants—*

Drinking in the Crow's Head. With a rending flash, that was gone. The first Prince of the Stone—gone. The Great Fire, which had burned London to the ground—gone. Desperate, Dead Rick threw everything he could think of between him and the camera, and piece by piece it dwindled, as his body thrashed and his throat went raw with screaming. The moors of Yorkshire, where he'd roamed for ages before coming to London. Centuries of All Hallows' Eve rides, sweeping ghosts from the city's streets. Irrith. Other Princes. Mortals he'd known—Owen and Eliza—he'd told her about—

"Ah," Chrennois said in satisfaction. "We have it at last."

"Let me see."

Dead Rick's breath sobbed in his chest. Despairing, he reached into the bloody, shredded depths of his mind, knowing there had once been something there, something *important*, something that explained why he was here . . .

Nothing but a gaping hole remained.

"Excellent," Nadrett hissed, and the sound of shattering glass filled Dead Rick's ears.

The skriker's hands had cramped into fisted masses, useless so long as he was tied down. But as soon as they let him out, drugged or not, he would get his revenge. It didn't fucking matter what he'd known about Nadrett and lost, if the bastard was dead.

The sprite asked, "Do you want him killed?"

The question chilled Dead Rick's blood; Nadrett's thoughtful laugh turned it to ice. "No. We know it works, now; let's try something more. Let's see what 'appens when 'e don't 'ave *any* memories left."

A mindless, panicked howl burst out of Dead Rick then, long before the camera clicked once more into action. He fought like a rabid dog, until the straps cut into his skin and he thought he might tear his own arms off; he would have done it if he could, and counted it a worthy trade.

But mere flesh and blood could not buy him escape. Nothing could. And soon the pain in his body faded into insignificance next to the agony in his mind. The light flashed again and again, each burst tearing him apart piece by piece until even the memory of the tearing was gone, leaving behind nothing but a gaping wound where someone used to be.

The howling went from memory to reality, a primal sound driving up from his gut to split the air. *"C'est terminé, c'est tout!"* Yvoir was shouting, and Irrith's nimble hands were tearing at the buckles that held Dead Rick in place; he tried to fling himself from the chair before he was entirely free, wrenched his legs, snapped the last ankle cuff without waiting for anyone to undo it. Dead Rick fell to the floor, gasping, crawling away from the all-too-similar chair, staggering to his feet and forward until a wall stopped him, where he clung to the black stone, relying on it to hold him up.

Too many thoughts flooded through his mind at once, a swirling, incoherent mass of memory that even the clarity granted by faerie absinthe couldn't settle immediately. Faces stared at him—familiar faces; *Blood and Bone, Irrith, I 'elped 'er rob the British Museum*—everything piled atop everything else, arranged more by connection than time, so that he looked at the Prince and remembered every man who had preceded him, Joseph Winslow, Geoffrey Franklin, Michael Deven, who was buried in the ruins of the night garden. Galen St. Clair, who haunted the Onyx Hall every year after his death, lending what help he could to his successors, until the breaking of the palace stranded him in the sewers.

Nadrett. The bastard who ripped apart Dead Rick's mind until he got what he wanted, then tore the rest out just to see if he could make a puppet from what remained.

"I did know something," Dead Rick ground out, fingers pressed against the wall, not sure whether he was about to fall down or launch himself off it. "Fucking *bastard*. You was right, milord. I'd found out something about Nadrett; that's why 'e took my memories."

Hodge's eyes went wide. "What was it?"

Dead Rick shook his head, ignoring the way the room and everything in it danced at the motion. "I don't know. Burn my body—burn my *mind;* that's damn near what 'e did—'e broke it as soon as 'e 'ad it, to make sure nobody could get it back."

Groaning, Irrith squeezed her eyes shut. They popped back open, though, when Dead Rick laughed—a laugh as ominous as the one Nadrett had uttered before.

"I don't remember no more," the skriker said, baring his teeth in a fierce snarl. "But I knows somebody who does."

ST. ANNE'S CHURCH, WHITECHAPEL

22 August 1884

It might have been better to leave the church and go somewhere with fewer eyes that could recognise Eliza and James O'Malley. But they had nowhere suitable to go, and Father Tooley was not eager to throw the recipient of tonight's miracle out onto the streets; instead he hurried the five of them into the sacristy, where they might be cramped, but at least there was a bit of privacy, and the priest himself went to make sure no one else was stirring.

Tears kept ambushing Eliza when she least expected them. Crying after Owen began to speak again, that was understandable; but every time she thought she was done, a fresh spate would begin. It was all she could do to stand back and let the Darraghs at their son, Owen's mother hugging him as if the meager strength of her arms could undo all the separation of before.

It couldn't. He was still fourteen but not; he still seemed to remember almost nothing. But he spoke again, and looked at the world around him like he *saw* it, which was more than they had before. Eliza sniffed back the latest round of tears and told herself that was enough.

For distraction, she had her father. The success of the baptism did wonders of its own for Eliza's feelings toward the man; he'd been a part of that miracle, and for that she was grateful to him. But not so grateful that she didn't think to say, "It's later, Da. And long past time to talk."

His face settled into a grimmer shape. Keeping her voice low, so as not to distract the Darraghs a few feet away, she growled, "Isn't it enough, all the trouble you were for us before? Drinking and gambling and falling in with the wrong sort—and now the sort you've fallen in with are the bloody Fenians. I've had Special Branch after me, because of you."

Because of her own actions, too; but the boiling resentment in Eliza's gut left no room for that kind of nuance. James O'Malley grabbed his daughter and pulled her farther from the Darraghs, as if another two feet would make any real difference. "Because of me? It's Fergus Boyle who's had the loose tongue—"

"Aye, I know that—"

"And telling lies to boot," he finished. "Christ, Eliza, I've been in prison; I don't have a bloody thing to do with those boys. Don't you see what Boyle's doing? He's trying to protect *her.*"

And he jerked his thumb at Maggie Darragh.

He hadn't bothered to keep as quiet as Eliza; he spoke loudly enough that Maggie's head came up suddenly, the girl staring in their direction. She hadn't caught his words,

Eliza didn't think—but Maggie's eyes held a hunted look, like a stray dog that thought she heard trouble coming.

Maggie Darragh? Working with the *Fenians*? But she'd always said—

No. *She* hadn't said; *Fergus* had. Maggie had never voiced a word on the subject, not that Eliza heard—not since that fellow came by a summer past, dropping hints in the pubs about the Irish Republican Brotherhood. Then the dynamite incidents started happening, and Eliza was so caught up in her own troubles that she'd hardly spared a thought for Maggie.

Their gazes locked, and the hunted look grew. Eliza said, "Maggie," and that was all she got out before the young woman grabbed her by the arm and dragged her out the sacristy door.

"Not a *word,* where Ma can hear," Maggie said in a harsh whisper, when they were out in the nave once more. "Say to me what you like, but I won't be having her troubled with this, not when she's just got Owen back."

Eliza had not been short of curses and anger before, but it all seemed to have temporarily drained from her. "I—I don't even know what to say."

Maggie pulled her bonnet off, forgetting they were in church, and scraped a hand through her tangled hair. "'Tis Fergus who sent Special Branch after you; I never asked him to do it."

"And did you ask him to stop?"

The silence answered her well enough.

Eliza sagged into a pew. "Christ, Maggie—why?"

"Why not?" the girl said bitterly. "I look at Ma and I see what this place did to her; I see what it has done to *me*. Twice the English bastards have pushed me into an alley and flipped my skirts up, because being Irish is the same as being a whore, is it not? And God help me, but I've thought of doing it, because at least that would keep us fed. With Owen gone . . ." She trailed off, looking hopeless in the light of the few candles still burning.

It made Eliza sick to her stomach. "But the ones who have died—they aren't the ones who hurt you."

"I don't care, and that's the truth of it," Maggie said flatly. "I want them to know what it is like, seeing innocents die for crimes they never did."

Hideous, blasphemous words—spoken in front of the altar, no less, with the Son of God watching from the crucifix above. In the workhouse, when Quinn accused her of helping the Fenians, Eliza had wondered if Maggie hated her enough to spread that lie. But Maggie's hate wasn't for Eliza: it was for the English, and all of London. Poison like that could not be drawn by her brother's return.

There was no sound, but the hairs on the back of Eliza's neck rose. Turning, she saw Owen standing in the shadows, watching them both.

Maggie drew in a sob-tangled breath at the sight of him. Her elder brother, now younger than she. "Oh, Owen," she whispered, and went to wrap her arms around him once more. He stiffened, but let her do it; and Eliza, rising to her feet, wondered if he would embrace her back. A moment later, she had no more attention to spare for such questions, because the church entrance banged open and Dead Rick came darting through.

The sight of him knocked the breath from her. Not just to see a faerie there—in *church*!—making no effort to pretend he was human, though that would have been enough. But his *eyes* . . .

The soft dog-brown was gone, drowned in an acid green that flooded iris and pupil alike. In those absinthine depths, time came off its hinge; past and present abandoned their God-given places and danced a mad waltz, whirling such vertigo into Eliza's mind that she abruptly found herself on the floor, staring at the skriker's knees. Those, at least, stayed put.

Until he dropped into a crouch and seized her shoulders. "Eliza. I need you to remember. The last time you saw me—before that bastard sent me to take Owen—what did I tell you?"

He called me Eliza.

Not Miss Baker, or Hannah, or any of the other false names she'd borne. He *remembered*. She saw it in his posture, heard it in his voice; everything about him, everything but those eyes, was an echo from seven years gone. Dead Rick was himself again.

The friend she'd lost had returned.

And then was torn away from her, as Owen charged at him with a howl. Dead Rick lurched under the boy's weight as if drunk, not defending himself with the brutal skill she knew he had; terrified for him—for them both—Eliza leapt up and tried to force them apart. Tangled together, the three of them swung around, back toward the sacristy, from which her da and Mrs. Darragh had emerged.

It was chaos. Three other people had followed Dead Rick in: two mortal men, and a young woman who took one look at the altar and suddenly showed herself to be the sprite Eliza had seen before. That one blanched dead white and fled the church as if she was about to throw up, leaving the other two behind. They caught Maggie and her mother, while James O'Malley backed off, staring, and in the meanwhile words were pouring out of Eliza's mouth. "He never meant to do it, Owen—the bastard who hurt you hurt him, too—"

He let go, and the sudden release sent Dead Rick and Eliza both staggering backward into the sacristy. Owen advanced and slammed the door behind himself. "Then why is he here?"

In the relative quiet, she realised Dead Rick was still talking, his voice managing to be hard and begging at the same time. He didn't even seem to realise Owen was there. "Ash and Thorn, Eliza—you 'ave to remember. If you don't remember, nobody does. Nadrett smashed it; I'll never get it back. But it were a danger to 'im, and 'e's the one what did this to your boy; if you tells me, maybe we can make 'im pay for that."

She made the mistake of looking into Dead Rick's eyes again; time swirled, and she almost lost her footing. *The last time I saw him.* Not the one burned into her memory by the pain of betrayal, or any of their encounters since then; the last time she saw *him,* the skriker she'd saved. For his sake, Eliza tried to remember. "You told me a story."

He straightened, then caught himself with one hand against the wall; with that insanity in his eyes, no wonder he was unsteady. "A story?"

Piece by piece, it came to her. "About the Faerie-land. You said that all the tales we have of lands being drowned by the sea—Lyonesse and, oh, others I don't remember—they're all echoes of some place in Faerie, that *did* sink beneath the waves."

Bewilderment showed on Dead Rick's face; she was learning to watch his mouth and forehead, not his impossible eyes. "No, there—there 'as to 'ave been something else. Something about Nadrett." A shiver rose from his toes to his head. He leaned harder against the wall.

She wanted to help him so badly, but— "You never mentioned Nadrett. Only Seithenyn."

His sagging head came up so fast, she flinched back. What Dead Rick might have said, though, she never found out. The skriker took one step toward her and pitched over sideways as if the floor had gone vertical beneath his feet. Eliza cried out and managed to slow his fall, but not to catch his full weight; he hit the tile floor in a boneless heap.

Bewildered, she looked up at Owen. But he looked no less confused than she. "Nadrett. I—I've heard that name? . . ."

Before she could answer him, the door swung open, and on the other side was one of the men she'd seen a moment before. A dark-skinned heathen fellow—probably that genie from the Galenic Academy. He shook his head over Dead Rick's limp body. "Were it not for the absinthe, I doubt he would have made it this far. Come, please—your friend, too, if you wish—we will take him to a safer place, and see if we have answers at last."

HARE STREET, BETHNAL GREEN

22 August 1884

How they made good their escape from the church with Dead Rick's twitching carcass in tow, Eliza couldn't say, except that it undoubtedly involved faerie magic. What they'd planned to be a surreptitious baptism under cover of night had become a good deal louder than that, and attracted attention to suit. But somehow Eliza found herself being led north by the other man who'd followed Dead Rick, a fellow who might have been anywhere between thirty and eighty years old. The heathen came with them, carrying the skriker, and Owen and that faerie woman followed, but the rest had been lost along the way.

She expected to go to the Onyx Hall, but instead they crossed under the railway arches to the north—half their party gasping in pain as they went—and halted outside a tobacconist's not far from St. Anne's, where the man unlocked a door leading to the flat above. Through her shivering, the faerie woman said, "We can't take him below." She indicated Owen with her pointed chin. Irrith, that was her name. "It wouldn't be safe. And we can't risk somebody selling word of this to the Goblin Market, anyway."

This morning, it hadn't been safe to keep Owen out of the Hall for long. Now . . . *can he ever go back?*

Better for him if he couldn't. Eliza had no intention of it herself, except as much as was necessary to get revenge on this bastard Nadrett. And that, she supposed, was why Owen had come.

The rooms on the first floor reeked of dust and stale air, as if almost no one ever came here. "Hodge's flat," Irrith said, as the man went around striking matches for the lamps, illuminating a mismatched assortment of shabby furniture. The other fellow laid Dead Rick on the couch, where he shuddered as if caught in a winter storm.

Hodge said, "Not that I'm 'ere too often. Miss—would you?"

Eliza found him holding out a stale biscuit. After one staring moment—she had gone stupid with exhaustion—she realised what he wanted.

The tithe.

"We've got to get something inside him," Irrith said. "And me, if you don't mind."

Saying the words would cost Eliza nothing; even the bread was being handed to her. Even so . . . "Can't you do it?" she asked Hodge.

He shook his head. "Drank faerie wine, as part of becoming Prince. Once you do that, you're no good for the tithe; I doubt your friend 'ere could do it, either."

So this was the Prince who was supposed to pass judgment on Dead Rick for what he'd done. She hadn't seen much judging happen—but she was no longer certain she wanted it to. Not against the skriker, anyway. But Nadrett, yes. And Dead Rick had come to ask about Nadrett.

Stiffly, she reached out and took the bread. "A gift for the *Daoine Sidhe,*" Eliza said, laying the stale biscuit at Dead Rick's side. "Take it and plague us no more."

Irrith snatched up the food and tore a piece off, shoving it into her mouth like a starving woman. Chewing frantically, she broke off a second bite and slipped it between the skriker's thin lips. "Go on, swallow it," she murmured, shaking his shoulder as if that would do any good. Eliza edged her out of the way and lifted his head. Hodge gave her a hip flask, and she poured a dribble of its sweet-smelling contents into Dead Rick's mouth, stroking his throat the way she'd done for her brothers and sisters when they were ill, until finally she thought the morsel had gone down.

He continued to twitch in her grasp. "Shouldn't that help?" she asked, worried despite herself.

"Against all of this, yes," Irrith said, gesturing around. Her own colour had already improved visibly. "But it won't do much against the absinthe he drank."

Her worry grew. "I've never seen absinthe do this to a

man. Not unless it was mixed with something bad."

Irrith's breath huffed out in a quiet laugh. "Our version is . . . special."

Hodge's own breath followed hard on her words, but his was a sudden hiss of pain. The man dropped into the nearest chair, his Arab companion moving swiftly to his side. Irrith said, "Are they—"

The panic in her voice was clear. Hodge waved it, and the Arab, away. "No new rails; I've done what I can to make sure those get put off as long as possible. But a bit of the woven stuff just went, near the Academy. We should do our business 'ere and get back; Lune can't 'old without me for long."

"This business ye have," Eliza echoed. "It would be what, exactly?"

Hodge said, "Nadrett. You know who that is?" He waited for her nod before going on. "Then you know 'e's a nasty piece of work. We're trying to find out what 'e's doing right now. Seemed a good bet that Dead Rick might 'ave learned something about 'im, seven years ago, and that's why Nadrett took 'is memories. Looks like that was true, but if so, it's gone. We gave 'im back everything in that box. 'E thought you might 'ave what 'e'd lost."

Eliza hugged her arms around her body, feeling cold inside, despite the oppressive summer heat. "He said . . . Nadrett 'smashed' it?"

"The memories were on glass plates," Irrith said quietly. "Photographs. Nadrett broke one whenever Dead Rick made him angry."

The cold deepened to a sick fury. But Eliza couldn't see how what she knew would help them. "He never told me anything about Nadrett. The last time I saw him, the only thing he said—the only thing that seemed important—was a story about a fellow named Seithenyn."

By the looks on the others' faces, it didn't mean anything to Hodge or the Arab; the former was mortal, of course, and perhaps young Arab faeries learned different stories at their grannies' knees. Irrith showed more confusion than anything else. "Seithenyn and Mererid . . . he told you about the *Drowned Land*? What has that got to do with anything?"

"It means Nadrett's a fucking dead man." It was a bone-dry whisper from the couch. Dead Rick's eyes were still closed; Eliza was grateful to be spared another glimpse of that swirling, otherworldly green. He spoke like a medium in a trance, channeling information from some source outside himself. "Irrith—what 'appened to Seithenyn, after 'e killed Mererid and flooded the land?"

The sprite said, "He was cursed. By the waters of Faerie, because he killed Mererid, who was their daughter. If he hadn't fled—" Her eyes, a shifting green almost as unnerving as the absinthe in Dead Rick's, widened. "They would have drowned him. Ash and Thorn—you think Nadrett *is* Seithenyn?"

"Came 'ere," Dead Rick said. "And made 'imself somebody else. No idea 'ow I found out . . . but there's one way to know if I'm right."

"Throw water on him?" Eliza asked.

She meant it to sound scornful; the idea was ridiculous. But the fierce, predatory smile on Dead Rick's face told her it was no joke. "Show the waters where 'e went," the skriker said. "Then let the curse do its work. Even if 'e runs, 'e won't live; they'll find 'im."

Hodge let out a soft whistle. "Bloody well easier than trying to get at 'im by force. But first we 'ave to find 'im, and from what Bonecruncher tells me, 'e's pushed off to Faerie already."

A brief silence—and then Dead Rick sat bolt upright, mad eyes flying open once more. "Off to Faerie? Not bleeding likely. 'E'd die the second 'e set foot over there. Aspell was wrong!"

It seemed to mean something to everyone else there, save Eliza. Even Owen was frowning, as if trying to stitch his shredded mind back together. With the tone of a man making an argument he did not believe, but felt should be given due consideration, the Arab said, "He could still sell the right to use it, and then take his profits elsewhere. There are other lands than this, and not all are threatened by iron. Not yet, at least. Nor can he be bothered by things of your Heaven where men are not Christian."

While Eliza frowned at his choice of words—*your Heaven,* as if there were others—Dead Rick spoke again, with cold certainty. The whirling in his eyes had slowed, but still lent his words a skin-crawling cast. "And start scratch, in a foreign land? Not a chance. 'E likes being master too much for that. I don't think 'e's making no passage to Faerie. I think 'e's trying to make a kingdom for 'imself, right 'ere."

Eliza's oath would not have bothered anyone in the Onyx Hall; it had nothing of God in it. She might not give a twopenny damn for the fae, but the thought of the bastard who did such terrible things to Owen and Dead Rick setting himself up as some kind of lord made her go white hot with rage.

The expressions around her, though, showed varying shades of hope. Irrith said, "If he can repair the Onyx Hall—"

"Not repair," Hodge said, with certainty. "'E ain't in the palace—we're sure of that. But 'e might be trying to make a *new* palace. Maybe 'e already *'as*."

"How?" The Arab's deep voice had the abstracted quality of a fellow whose thoughts are buried deep in a puzzle. "This must involve the photographs; if we can determine *how*, we may have some notion of what to search for."

Eliza knew precious little about this sort of thing; her instinct was to stay silent, and let more knowledgeable people talk. But a useless silence had fallen, while everyone scowled or bit their lips and tried to find the answer, and perhaps the notion that had come into her head would help one of them. Even though it had nothing to do with the question of *how*. "What he's photographing—'tis people, is it not?"

"It seems to be so," the genie answered. "What are you thinking?"

Now everyone's eyes were on her. She shrugged

uncomfortably. "Only that I've heard tell of a number of people going missing in the East End. Not just missing: the story is, they were taken by the faeries."

As she expected, Hodge shook his head, frowning. "That could be anybody in the Goblin Market. They steals people all the time, now."

But Dead Rick said, "Where was it?"

"I think . . . I might know."

The answer didn't come from Eliza. The others all stared past her, and then she turned, and saw Owen standing, face paper white, hands tangled in a hard knot near his mouth.

"Did you see something? What—"

Irrith's burst of questions cut off when she ran into Eliza's outflung arm. She hadn't stopped the sprite in time to prevent Owen from flinching back, but Eliza turned and put herself between them, hands on her hips, returning glare for green-eyed glare. "He's about had enough of ye," she said, addressing all the fae. Even Dead Rick. "What ye did to send his family away just now, I don't want to know—but ye won't be coming near him again. Do ye understand?"

"If you're right about these missing people," Hodge said quietly, not moving from his seat, "then more than just 'is safety depends on us knowing."

"I know. But *I* will do the asking." She turned her back on him, and looked to Owen.

He'd retreated into the corner, and stood with his hands flat against the walls. He shook his head, confusion scratching a faint line between his brows. "They say they're my family, but I don't—I remember you from the library. You took me to the church. And I think I remember you from before, too, but 'tis all in pieces. I thought I had a sister, but she was younger."

Eliza's heart ached. *Healed—but not fully. He may never be completely well again.* Wetting her lips, she said, "You've been gone seven years. Perhaps—perhaps it will come back to you. Were you in West Ham?" The name only deepened the crease between his brows. "In the East End," she added. "Did Nadrett take you there?"

Haltingly, fumbling it out word by word, Owen said, "There was . . . a building. A warehouse. Or something. He kept people there. Like me. In cages. And one by one, they went away, until it was my turn."

"How many people?" Eliza whispered. Whelan knew of three; she'd heard rumours of two more.

Owen shook his head again. "A dozen. Or more. I did not count."

From behind Eliza, Irrith said, "When he took you away—"

Eliza cut her off again with a furious glare. Any idiot could see that was when Owen had been broken; his hunched shoulders proclaimed it. She had to swallow down tears before she could ask, "This building. Would you know if it you saw it?"

As gently as she posed the question, it still sent him rigid with fear. "No, no, I can't—"

In a low voice, Hodge asked Dead Rick, "Could you sniff it out?"

"Maybe," the skriker said, but he didn't sound confident. "Depends on 'ow 'ard Nadrett's trying to 'ide."

If Eliza correctly understood what the fae had said, he would be trying very hard indeed. She risked going closer to Owen, and following him when he slid down the wall to crouch on the floor, arms around his knees. "You're afraid of him, aren't you," she murmured. He nodded convulsively. "You don't have to face him. We'll do that part, Dead Rick and I will. But we need your help to find him first. I swear—" She hesitated, wondering if it was safe to say this to him; then she remembered the holy splendour of the baptism washing over him. "As God is my witness, I will keep you safe."

The words produced no shiver of antipathy. *That much, we've done; he's ours once more.* But Owen still looked afraid. Impulsively, Eliza reached out and took his hand in her own, gripping his fingers tight. "We don't want anyone more to end up as you did. Help us, Owen, and we'll stop him. You'll not have to be afraid again."

He might have been as mute as before, cowering on the floor like that. But after a moment, his fingers tightened hard enough to make her own ache, and he nodded.

"That's my lad," Eliza whispered. "We'll bring the bastard down together."

* * *

WHITE LION STREET, ISLINGTON

24 August 1884

How the Goodemeades had ever persuaded Mrs. Chase's cat to play messenger for the woman, Hodge would never know. The tortoiseshell creature had shown up in his chambers, reeking of affronted dignity, with a note tied around its neck, and vanished as soon as he took the paper, with enough speed that he wondered if they'd put a faerie charm on the cat as well.

Dear Mr. Hodge, Your Highness, the note began—Mrs. Chase had never quite grasped the proper address for the Prince of the Stone.

> *I hope you will forgive me for making bold to write you directly, but the Goodemeades are not here and I suspect this matter is one of which you would wish to be informed immediately. There is a faerie gentleman in my house, in a very poor state, who says his name is Valentin Aspell; and I believe him to be the gentleman you have been seeking but could not find. If I am mistaken, then I apologise most sincerely, but ask you to tell either Gertrude or Rosamund of his presence, as I fear he needs someone to tend his wounds. Your obt. servt., Theresa Chase.*

He left for Islington three minutes later, with the Goodemeades, short as they were, almost outrunning him in their haste. It was a risk, leaving the Onyx Hall, when he'd been out just the previous night; now it was afternoon, with trains running to threaten the palace's stability. But he could not leave the matter of Aspell for others to handle. They took a cab, Hodge paying the driver handsomely while the Goodemeades whispered to the horses, and the resulting trip to Islington would not have shamed some competitors at Ascot. They burst through Mrs. Chase's front door, and found they were in time—if only barely.

"In a poor state" fell far short of describing Aspell's condition. The former lord had always been pale as the underbelly of a fish; now that pallor had a grayish-green cast. If faerie bodies persisted long enough past death to need graves, Hodge would have said the bastard had just crawled out of his own.

Mrs. Chase stood by, twisting her hands, staring at the unconscious faerie on her canvas-draped sofa. "He all but fainted onto Mary when she opened the door. But I didn't dare fetch an ordinary doctor—"

"It wouldn't have done any good," Rosamund said, as Gertrude knelt to peel aside Aspell's blood-soaked shirt and coat. "Dead Rick said he was shot with iron."

Gertrude's breath hissed between her teeth when she uncovered the wound. Ugly black lines radiated from the torn flesh of his shoulder, spiking across his arm and chest. Enemy though he was, even Hodge flinched at the sight. He'd seen blood poisoning before, though never on a faerie.

"It looks as if he dug the bullet out himself," Gertrude

said, her fingers gently probing. Even the most delicate touch made Aspell jerk, moaning indistinctly. "But nobody drew out the poison the iron left behind. This . . . may kill him."

Hodge clenched his jaw. "Don't let 'im die yet. We need 'im to say where 'e 'id the Prince's ghost."

"I have no intention of *letting* him die under any circumstances," Gertrude snapped. A glare from Rosamund echoed her sister's sharp words. Hodge flushed in shame. He hadn't meant it that way—not *really*—though it had crossed his mind that it wouldn't be any great shame if Aspell were to croak. Now he felt like a terrible person, and Mrs. Chase was staring at him as though he were a grandson of hers not yet too old for a good thrashing.

"Let's shift him downstairs," Gertrude said, with all the brisk, no-nonsense confidence of a nurse. Mrs. Chase hastened to apologise, explaining that she had not been sure whether the sisters would want Aspell in their home; Rosamund waved it away, and bid the parlour wall open.

To make up for his earlier mistake, Hodge stepped forward without prompting and lifted Aspell from the couch. The disgraced lord weighed very little, even for his slender build, and hung limply from the Prince's arms. The only difficulty was making sure not to crack his head against the wall as Hodge navigated the narrow staircase.

Once within the tiny faerie realm of Rose House, Aspell breathed more easily. While Hodge settled him onto another couch there, the sisters hurried off to gather supplies, and Mrs. Chase closed the entrance behind them.

Hodge stood aside, letting the women do their work—and grim, unpleasant work it was, leeching what poison they could from the faerie's body, while Aspell sweated and whimpered under their touch. *Good job they can't see inside my 'ead,* Hodge thought. Neither the brownies nor their mortal friend would approve of the satisfaction he got from seeing his father's murderer in pain.

But he didn't want the treacherous sod to kick the bucket. Not now, and not like this. Hodge waited, crossing his fingers, and was rewarded at last with a stirring that looked more like life. Aspell's eyes opened a slit, their usually green irises darkened almost to black.

"Where'd you put the photo?"

The faerie's mouth moved soundlessly, not quite forming words.

Another glare from Rosamund stopped Hodge before he took more than one stride forward. Gritting his teeth, the Prince said, "Galen St. Clair. You 'ad 'is ghost; Dead Rick told us so. Where'd you put 'im?"

Gertrude helped Aspell sit up a few inches, and poured a dribble of water between his pale lips. It seemed to give him energy: when he had swallowed it, the faerie sank back, glared black venom at Hodge, and said, "I *put* him nowhere. He was taken from me. By Nadrett." He coughed, and a spasm of pain twisted his face. Once that had passed, he added, "Who has been my captor, as well. Until I escaped."

Bloody convenient. There was just one flaw in the notion

that Aspell was lying: the iron poison pervading his body. The snake might have had a good reason for abandoning all his people in the disintegrating Goblin Market—though Hodge could not imagine what that might be—but not for letting himself come so close to the edge of death. Being Nadrett's prisoner, however, explained it neatly.

Hodge thought about asking how Aspell had gotten away, but realised he didn't care. Other things mattered far more. "Where?"

The shaking of Aspell's head was almost imperceptible. "Don't know."

"You say you bloody well *escaped* from there; 'ow can you not know?"

"I leapt aboard a train," the faerie growled. Both brownies hissed in sympathy. Even Hodge flinched; with no bread to protect him, and that poison in his veins, it must have been agony. "Somewhere east," he added, in a whisper, as if that growl had taken most of his remaining vigor.

Thinking of Eliza and Dead Rick, even now searching the area for sign of Nadrett and a new faerie realm, Hodge asked, "Could it 'ave been West Ham?"

Aspell nodded, exhausted.

Well, it lent weight to Eliza's notions, at least. If Owen failed to identify his former prison, might Aspell succeed? Before the Prince could even think about asking, Gertrude told him quietly, "You should let him rest."

But Aspell's eyes flew open again, life flooding once more into his face, and he stretched out one gray-tinged hand. "Wait. What I said before. I *must* speak to Lune."

"You aren't going anywhere," Rosamund said firmly. "Not for a good long while."

"And you ain't getting anywhere near Lune," Hodge added.

"Then carry a message for me!"

Panic tinged the words. He *must* be desperate, if he was willing to trust Hodge with a secret that not that long ago had been too valuable for anyone else's ears. And—"What's your price for it?"

Aspell spat out a curse entirely at odds with his usual elegance. "For you to pay me, or me to pay you? This is for the Onyx Court, you cretin. I bargained because it was the only way to gain access to Lune, and she is the only one who might listen to me."

"She's the one you betrayed!"

"And she knows why. *To save the Onyx Court*: not to destroy it." Aspell sagged deeper into the embrace of the couch, his burst of vitality flagging. "You must promise to carry the message."

All three women were looking at him, now, not Aspell. If Hodge refused—or agreed, and then didn't follow through—he suspected there would be a second round of those looks from before, that made him want to crawl in shame. Through his teeth, Hodge said, "I promise."

Gertrude had to give her patient more water before he could muster the strength to speak. When he did, his words were enigmatic. "Francis and Suspiria."

Enigmatic to Hodge; the brownies sat bolt upright at the names. "Who are they?" Hodge asked.

Rosamund answered, to spare Aspell the need. "They made the Onyx Hall."

"With help," Gertrude reminded her.

Hodge knew the story, in its broad outlines; he'd been told it when he asked why repairing the palace was so hard. Mostly it was the abundance of iron, but also what had been lost in the interim: of the various powers that helped create the Hall, nearly all were now dead.

Including the mortal man and faerie woman who shaped it in the first place.

When Hodge said as much, Aspell whispered, "Dead, yes—but not gone. It took me far too long to understand what it was I felt. We are not used to dreaming, we fae; I could not make sense of it, not for many years. But I am certain of it now. The spirits of Suspiria and Francis Merriman dwell within the London Stone."

The Prince stared. Then reached out, blindly, for a chair; finding one, he lowered himself carefully into it. "I would 'ave felt them there."

Would he? He hadn't known about Chrennois in Aldersgate; as Prince, he could send his mind throughout the Onyx Hall, but it hurt so much he almost never did. The London Stone, though . . . it was the very point of his connection. Surely he would have known if there was another spirit there. Something besides himself and Lune—

And the Onyx Hall itself.

He clamped one hand over his mouth, fingers digging into his cheeks, to keep the words from bursting out. *Bloody fucking 'ell.* The palace—which answered to the commands of Queen and Prince; sometimes, he'd heard, as if it had a mind of its own. Which protected the bones of the Princes laid to rest within its ground against all attempts to desecrate them. Which acknowledged Lune as Queen, and refused others, when they tried to usurp her crown; that was the foundation of faerie sovereignty, that one ruled by right of that bond, the realm accepting someone as master or mistress over it all.

Suspiria and Francis Merriman stood with their hands upon the London Stone, beneath the eclipsed light of the sun, and dreamed the Hall into being.

Three hundred years and more later, they were still there—because they *were* the Onyx Hall.

Hodge unclamped his fingers, knuckles aching as he moved them. He licked his lips, swallowed, and said, "You . . . might be right. And I don't think Lune knows it, neither. But—what good does that do us?"

Aspell's eyes glittered through the fringe of his lashes. "It means Lune isn't the only one holding the palace together. Without her, it would not last long—but it would not collapse instantly, either. She would have a moment's grace, in which to escape: from the Hall, from London entirely, and into Faerie."

He'd once tried to *murder* Lune. But not out of malice, Hodge was forced to admit; like the Fenians with their dynamite, he'd thought it would serve a greater purpose, which was the preservation of the Onyx Hall. With that cause now lost beyond recall, it seemed Aspell was not without a degree of mercy.

The bastard had it backward. He was giving up right when victory for that cause could be within their reach. It all depended on what they found in West Ham.

Smiling ruefully, Hodge said, "You've known 'er for 'ow many centuries, and you don't see the mistake there? Lune will never run." He stood and grinned down at the pale, exhausted Aspell. "But maybe she don't 'ave to. Not if we can make 'er a new 'ome."

PADDINGTON STATION, PADDINGTON

25 August 1884

For once, it was not the abundant menace of iron that made Louisa Kittering's breath come fast.

She'd flinched when she and Frederic first came beneath the vaulting girders that covered the vast interior of Paddington Station, with its rails and trains and gas lamps, but it was nothing more than instinctive sympathy for those she left behind: the fae of the Onyx Hall, who even now were entering the final days of their home. Then she'd been taken aback by the chaotic activity of the crowds within: men of the suburbs going to or from work, mothers shepherding noisy and disobedient children, porters pushing trolleys full of baggage, voices crying food or newspapers from stalls along the sides. But Frederic had found a porter to take their trunk, and he'd known how to find the right platform, so now all she had to do was wait.

Wait, and think of what she had done.

Leaving the Kitterings hardly mattered. But what would Frederic think, in the days and months and years to come, about leaving his wife? He did love the woman, Louisa knew; and while it was possible to make him forget that love, it wouldn't be easy. Not when he hadn't chosen this path freely. She even felt a twinge of guilt, because she actually *cared* what he thought of her . . . and in the privacy of her own mind, where she could be honest with herself, Louisa knew he would not approve of what she had done.

But the alternative was to leave him vulnerable to Nadrett. Or to send him away on his own, without her—

She could not do that, either.

No. They would go away together: to Dover, to Calais, and once they had booked passage, to America, where they would make a new life among the emigrants, faerie and mortal alike, and they would have nothing to fear at all.

She should have known better than to believe it.

Trouble came without any warning at all: one moment Louisa was awaiting her train, dreaming of the life it would carry her off to, and the next there was a gun barrel pressing intimately against her spine, just above her bustle.

The gun remained there when Nadrett stepped into view, flanked by two of his men. He looked enough like himself to be recognised, though of course it was a human version of himself. But Louisa thought, despairing, that she would have recognised that cruel smile no matter what face shaped it. "There you are, my love," Nadrett said, with false cheer. "Going somewhere?"

At her side, Frederic was gazing patiently into the distance, taking no notice of the fae a few feet away. The ticket was in his hand; he didn't even blink as Nadrett twitched it from between his fingers. "Dover, is it? Now, why would you be going to Dover . . . and 'ello, who's this? Blimey, if it ain't Mr. Myers!"

His theatrical surprise might as well have been a knife between her ribs. The words were very nearly the worst thing she could have said, but Louisa could not stop them from bursting out: "Don't hurt him!"

Nadrett's sharp eyebrows rose. "Don't 'urt 'im?" he repeated, mocking her. "Mab's tits—don't tell me you've bloody fallen in love with 'im."

She tried to salvage what she could. "Not *love,* no, of course not—what an idea!" Her laugh sounded brittle and too bright, even to her own ears. "Just a passing entertainment, sir; you know how such things are. I thought you were done with him."

The Goblin Market boss looked speculatively at Frederic, who sighed and referred to his pocket-watch. "'E were a useful sort, I'll grant 'im that. Kept 'im around in case I 'ad more questions. But you know, it's all going splendidly. I think I don't need 'im anymore." Nadrett drew his gun.

"No!" Louisa threw herself forward, seizing his arm. There was no risk she would make him fire; she knew Nadrett, knew he wanted her to beg. "Please. I'll do anything—"

"I knows you will." Nadrett's free hand wrapped around her slender throat. Hissing into her face, he said, "You still belong to me, slut. So does 'e. So does *everybody* I touch."

The train had pulled up to the platform, in a cloud of coal-scented steam. All around them, the crowds of Paddington Station passed by, oblivious. Had she vanished completely from their eyes? Or did they just see some man disciplining his wayward wife?

"That little shell ain't enough to protect you," Nadrett said. "It breaks too easy, you see. All I got to do is make you admit what you are." His grip tightened. " 'Ow 'ard do you think it would be for me to do that?"

She wasn't sure she could speak, and he probably didn't want her to. She just shook her head, a tiny, trembling motion.

Nadrett smiled and released her. "Right you are. But I'm not without mercy, am I, boys?" The other fae grinned and made noises of agreement. "I'll let your cove 'ere live. For a price."

Passengers were flooding off the train, parting around their little group as if it were nothing more than a rock in the stream, of no interest to the water flowing by. Porters farther down were unloading the trunks and smaller valises, making room for the new baggage. Her trunk would make it onto the train, and so might Frederic Myers—but she would not.

It had been foolish to think that she might escape.

Awkwardly, hampered by the fashionably narrow skirt of her dress, Louisa knelt on the filthy platform. Another eternity of servitude . . . but it was worth it, to see Frederic safe. "I will serve you faithfully. Master."

"Good—but not good enough," Nadrett said, and snapped his fingers, gesturing for the other fae to move along. Grabbing her by the arm and hauling her to her feet, he said, "You'll 'ave company before we're done today."

WEST HAM, LONDON
26 August 1884

Dead Rick could scarcely bring himself to look at either of his companions. He felt like he was seeing two of each, and not because of the absinthe; those effects had only lasted for a day or so. No, he saw Eliza and Owen with two sets of memories: his own, and those of Nadrett's dog.

It wasn't honest to divide himself like that, and he knew it. However much he wished to deny it, the last seven years were as much a part of him as the ages that went before—ages his mind was still sorting into order, below the level of his awareness. And losing his memories hadn't completely changed who he was; some things went beyond simple recollection, into his nature as a faerie. But he had no better way to describe the strange disconnection he felt when he looked around, seeing two meanings to a single thing. Owen was both the mute, broken shell he'd found cowering in the Academy library, and the good-natured boy who'd had such hopes for bettering his family's condition. Eliza was both the furious young woman who tried to beat him senseless, and the fierce girl who'd protected him against those tormenting lads.

Two of most things; three of *them*. Because what those two had become, in the aftermath of Owen's healing, were different yet again.

He wanted so badly to have back the warmth they'd shared—a warmth that, thanks to the absinthe, he remembered as if it were just a few days ago. Owen had forgotten it, though, and as far as Eliza was concerned, it had long since died and been left to rot. At this point they operated in a state of uneasy truce; Dead Rick didn't dare hope for more.

Fed on Eliza's bread, he took the surface path to West Ham, following the road as its name changed from Aldgate to Whitechapel to Mile End to Bow. "The place makes sense," he said to break the silence, as the buildings around them began to thin. "The big sewer runs right from the Goblin Market to the pumping station out 'ere, don't it? Easy road for Nadrett's men." He didn't like to think who he might have met, if he'd had to go by the road below.

"Yes," Eliza said, but the conversation died there.

The strange mixing of his memories disoriented him, with its insistence on remembering Londons that were centuries gone. Tower Hamlets, they called this area; once it *had* been an area of hamlets, little villages scattered like seeds among fields that fed the City. Now all the villages had run together like stains, and the weeds of industry had taken root, choking the green grass with brick and soot.

As if she, too, could not bear the silence between them, Eliza said abruptly, "When this is done, perhaps I'll get myself a factory job. It can be good work, it can—better than being in service."

Dead Rick blinked. With his mind so filled by the past, it was hard to see the present, much less the future; but to Eliza, this must look very different. She saw not destruction, but opportunity. Which of them was right? Were either of them? Mortals had been arguing this very point amongst themselves for years. But it made him remember something Irrith said once, about why Lune ruled with a Prince at her side. Because they helped her see what she otherwise could not.

None of it was important, not right now—and yet, he needed the distraction, because if he let himself think about Nadrett he wouldn't be here, walking calmly down the street with Eliza and Owen; he would have long since taken to his heels, intent on nothing more than finding his former master and tearing out the bastard's throat. Which would have gotten him killed, and he knew it—assuming he could even *find* Nadrett—but the feral rage pumping through his veins with every beat of his heart didn't care. It had waited too long already for its satisfaction.

The road sharpened its gentle bend northward. In the

distance to the right, Dead Rick could see the ornate exterior of the pumping station, which brought all the filth up to a level where it could be vented into the river, safely downstream of the city. "Recognise anything?" he asked Owen.

The boy shook his head. He still communicated more in gestures than in words when he could, but sometimes Dead Rick thought that born of a similar confusion to the one in his own mind: whatever had been taken from him by Chrennois's cameras, and given back by the baptism, Owen was still sorting it into order. And pieces of it were clearly missing.

Dead Rick frowned at the pumping station. "If they been coming up out of the sewers, I can try to find a scent. But it ain't going to be Nadrett crawling up out of the muck, and I don't know who it *will* be."

"Might there be guards?" Eliza asked. Dead Rick nodded. "Then we'll try the town first."

She guided her companions past the depot for the Great Eastern Railway and into West Ham itself, working her way along Stephens Road toward Plaistow, with Dead Rick in dog form sniffing everything they passed, and Owen shaking his head. As sites for faerie palaces went, this one was frankly terrible: a grim industrial suburb, with nothing much to recommend it. Would Nadrett really come here? Eliza held an aetheric versorium like the one Dead Rick had used to find the Aldersgate entrance, but its needle only pointed at the skriker, with never a twitch in another direction.

Owen said the area smelled right, though—coal and marsh air and the stench of a leatherworks—and so they went on, up and down each near-lifeless street, watching in all directions for danger. At the corner of Liddington Road, the boy stopped with a whimper.

The building his eyes had fixed upon was unremarkable, a squat, hulking mass of mud-yellow London brick. Its walls were as uninviting as the Bank of England's; only a thin line of windows ran along the upper reaches, leaving the rest of the surface featureless and blind. A warehouse, perhaps, or a factory, with nothing obviously faerie about it.

They pulled back swiftly, of course, out of sight of the building. Dead Rick held out a hand, and Eliza gave him the versorium; angle it how he might, the needle did not point at the building. Owen insisted this was the place, though.

"What in Mab's name is 'e *doing* in there?" Dead Rick muttered. Surely if it were a new faerie realm, the versorium would sense it.

Eliza risked another glance around the corner, though Owen twitched as if to pull her back. "I don't see anyone," she said. This was not a busy part of town; at the moment, they were the only ones on the street. "But there could be any number of people inside."

"In cages," Owen said, in a voice made tight with fear.

She stroked his shoulder, calming him. "We'll get them out. We just have to figure out how."

Not easily, that much was certain. Eliza was the safest of them for scouting; with her bonnet pulled forward, she made a circuit of the building's perimeter, up Liddington Road and down the nameless alley on the other side. What she reported back cemented Dead Rick's unease. There were only three entrances into the building, two of them narrow, the third a set of double doors that looked to be securely barred from within. If Hodge could bribe Charcoal Eddie or somebody else capable of flying to look through the windows beneath the roof's edge, they might be able to get some sense of what was inside, but Dead Rick wouldn't care to bet on it. Which meant whatever forces Hodge sent would be going in blind.

"Who the 'ell is 'e going to send, anyway?" Dead Rick muttered, after they'd retreated to a safe distance. The Onyx Guard, the closest thing Lune had ever had to an army, was down to three knights: Peregrin, Cerenel, and Segraine. Irrith could shoot, and so could Bonecruncher; Niklas von das Ticken could, too, if dragged out of the Academy. Dead Rick himself would fight. Perhaps a few others, especially if Hodge offered something valuable in return. But Nadrett had a great deal more than half a dozen bullies working for him, and the means to hire more, too.

"You have magic—" Eliza said.

Dead Rick snorted. "And so does 'e. It's Nadrett's territory, too, so 'e'll 'ave prepared it. If we 'ad enough bodies to throw at it, I'd say damn the charms, we can just storm the place. But we've got 'alf a dozen people and a Prince who would fall over if you blew on 'im too 'ard."

In her eyes, he saw the same frustrated desperation that burned in his own heart. They were this close; it simply wasn't conceivable that they could admit defeat now. "There has to be a way," Eliza said.

The skriker closed his eyes in thought. He'd never been a general, not even before his memories were taken—but he did know a thing or two about fighting dirty. The weak point was the windows: too high to be used for invasion, too small to let people through at speed. *Which do you want more? Answers, or revenge?* He knew which one Eliza would say. "Give up on finding out what 'e's doing in there, and chuck dynamite in through the top. Blow Nadrett straight to 'ell."

The resulting silence gave him time to regret his words. The salvation of the Onyx Hall might lie inside that building; could he really sacrifice it, just to make amends? *You don't know 'e really 'as anything,* Dead Rick thought, and knew it was a justification. And a thin one at that.

Eliza whispered, "Dynamite."

Owen yelped, and Dead Rick's eyes flew open. "There might be people in there—" the boy protested, far too loudly.

She threw her hands up, stopping his appalled protest. "No, not blowing it up! Jesus, Mary, and Joseph; I would never hurt innocents. And there might be something in it the fae need. But Dead Rick—you said that if you had enough people, you could storm it. Was that true?"

"Where the bleeding 'ell do you think you're going to get an army?" he asked in disbelief.

Eliza drew in a careful breath, looking as if she was questioning her own sanity. "From the Special Irish Branch."

* * *

SCOTLAND YARD, WESTMINSTER
27 August 1884

No one clapped Eliza in chains when she walked into the offices of Scotland Yard. She felt foolish for expecting it; she was, after all, just a poor woman from Whitechapel, not some famous murderer or highwayman. The number of constables who knew her name, let alone what she looked like, was probably rather small. But she was walking into the lion's den, and she could not help but be afraid.

The man at the front barely even looked up at her. "State your business."

Eliza licked her dry lips, and had to make a conscious effort not to hide behind an English accent. "I'd like to speak to Sergeant Quinn."

"Which one?"

They had more than one man of that name and rank? She tried to remember his Christian name. "Patrick Quinn, of the Special Irish Branch."

The man jerked his thumb at the door she had come through, back out into the road of Great Scotland Yard. "Small building across from the Rising Sun. First floor, off to your left; look for the name. He might not be in, though."

Eliza hadn't considered that possibility. What if they tried to make her talk to Chief Inspector Williamson, the man in charge of the branch? She could hardly ask *him* for help. And if she walked in, she might not walk out again, except in chains.

Dead Rick's sharp ears must have caught what the man said, or maybe he just smelled her fear, for he rose from his slouch by the door and came to her side. "You can do this," he murmured in her ear. "Come on."

He'd promised he would see her safely out, whatever happened. Taking a deep breath, Eliza went in search of Special Branch.

They weren't hard to find. Repairs still marked the northeastern corner of the building, where the bomb had exploded in May; inside, the words SPECIAL IRISH BRANCH were painted black and gold on the door. It hung slightly ajar. Eliza listened at the gap, but heard nothing, and at last forced herself to knock and put her head in. "Hello?"

The man inside didn't wear a uniform, any more than Quinn had; Special Branch constables rarely did. Their job wasn't to patrol the streets and frighten off criminals by their presence; they operated like spies, more effective when not noticed. Eliza wasn't surprised to hear the Irish tinge to his answer. "Can I help you?"

Edging into the room, with Dead Rick close behind, Eliza said, "We need to speak to Sergeant Quinn. He—he told me to come to him if I had information."

"And you would be?"

She'd gone back and forth on the question of what name to use. But it was likely all these men knew the aliases she'd gone by before; even calling herself some form of Elizabeth might get their attention. And a totally new name would mean nothing to Quinn. Still, her heart pounded louder as she said, "Eliza O'Malley."

The man straightened immediately. She spooked, one hand going to the door as if pulling it shut behind her when she fled would do any good, but his manner wasn't hostile; more like a dog that just heard an interesting sound. He beckoned her farther in. "No, it's all right—the sergeant will be glad to hear you've come. I'm P.C. Maguire. No need to be scared, Miss O'Malley. Quinn's just down this way; you and your friend just follow me."

Deeper into the lion's den. Maguire led them through a large room with several men at work in it, to a smaller office holding four desks. Two were in use, and Quinn almost knocked a stack of papers off his when he sprang to his feet. "Miss O'Malley!"

The head of the other man came up sharply. Was her name so notorious? "Sergeant Quinn. I—I have some information you might want to be hearing." She glanced at Maguire and the other man. "Can we speak to you alone?"

Quinn frowned slightly, at her and Dead Rick both. She'd gotten the skriker to put on shoes, at least, but he still wore no shirt beneath his stained waistcoat, and generally looked like a ruffian. "If 'tis police business, ye should know, I'll be sharing it with the others. We can't do our work, otherwise."

" 'Tis what I told you of before," Eliza said. Habits of reticence made it hard to say the rest, even though these men certainly knew. "In the workhouse."

He hadn't forgotten. Quinn's eyes widened fractionally,

but his tone was perfectly level as he said, "All right. Maguire, Sweeney—let us have the room. And no listening at keyholes, ye mind!"

Dead Rick clearly did not trust it; he listened at the door, then nodded that the men were walking away. Quinn, in the meanwhile, dragged two chairs from the neighbouring desks over to his own, and sat facing Eliza, bracing his elbows on his knees. "You gave me a fair surprise, you did, vanishing from the workhouse like that. How did you get *Miss Kittering* to arrange your release?"

"She took pity on me," Eliza said briefly, not wanting to have to invent an explanation for whatever the changeling had done. "Sergeant, have you found any proof of what I told you?" He shook his head, and opened his mouth to answer, but she stopped him with a raised hand. "I brought some for you."

She would have expected Dead Rick to hesitate. His hatred of Nadrett ran deep, though; if stopping that monster meant showing his faerie face to half of Scotland Yard, he might have done it. Quinn's chair scraped backward across the floor, and she knew the skriker had dropped his glamour.

"Jesus, Mary, and Joseph," Quinn whispered.

"Wrong on all counts," the skriker said with aplomb. "Though it's an 'onest mistake to make. You believe 'er yet? I don't want some cove walking in 'ere while I'm 'alf naked."

Eliza hadn't heard such lightheartedness from him since before Nadrett stole his memories. The warmth it produced gave her the confidence to say to Quinn, "I showed you because I need your help. Yours, and as many more as you can get."

Quinn was still staring at Dead Rick, but he answered her. "To find your boy?"

"No, that bit I've done. 'Tis the one responsible I'm going after now."

He sat quietly as she explained it to him, though once or twice his hand drifted for a notebook, out of habit, before being called back. Nothing of the Onyx Hall, Hodge had insisted when they asked him; if what they found in West Ham saved the palace, they didn't want to lose it promptly after to a throng of hostile neighbours or curious explorers. But that Nadrett was possibly trying to make a shelter for himself, yes, and that he was apparently using ordinary humans to build it.

That he would defend the place. And that there were things men could do—especially mortal men—to fight back.

By the time she was done, Quinn's eyes had taken on a glazed cast. None of it, she suspected, was much like the fairy tales he'd grown up with. But he shook it off, alert once more, after she'd been silent for a few seconds. Then he grimaced. "I'll help ye myself, just to see the truth of it with my own eyes. But it's a devil of a hard thing to arrange more. Even if ye knew for sure he's the one kidnapping these folk, that isn't Special Branch business."

"But dynamite is," Dead Rick said, drawing Quinn's attention once more. "Nadrett supplied the Fenians. For

Charing Cross, and Praed Street, and the four in May. I doubt 'e's the only one they gets it from, but cut 'im off, and you've at least done them a blow."

"How do you know?" Quinn asked. Not suspiciously, but dutifully; he would have asked Queen Victoria herself where she got her information, if she offered some to him.

Dead Rick's answering grin was fit for a death omen, even on his human-looking face. "I carried it to 'em myself."

Eliza hastened to assure Quinn that Dead Rick had not cooperated by choice, but the sergeant waved it away. " 'Tisn't the first time I've taken help from somebody inside," he said absently. "Christ, though—I can't just go up to Williamson and say, give me a dozen fellows to hunt the faeries."

What came next was properly Dead Rick's to offer, but they'd agreed it would be better coming from Eliza. "There are ways to . . . persuade them," she said. Nervousness made her fumble the words she'd chosen in advance. "And to make it so they aren't too clear afterwards on what they saw—"

"Stop," Quinn said. Not loudly, not angrily, but it cut her off like a knife. "I do not know what you might be thinking, but I won't have your faeries fiddling with the heads of my boys. They know what they're doing, or they don't come at all. Do you understand me?"

She did—but she also knew what the other side feared. "Sergeant, they're afraid, too. They might not be hiding much longer, the good ones won't; but they don't want the first news of them to be a fellow like Nadrett. They'd be hunted for sure, then. So unless you can persuade your boys to be keeping quiet . . ."

Quinn seemed to be chewing on the insides of his cheeks. He rose from his chair and paced the room, casting the occasional glance at the door, as if thinking about the men outside. Eliza and Dead Rick let him keep his peace. Finally he said, "How many would ye be needing? Not how many ye'd *like,* but what would be enough to try with."

Eliza turned to Dead Rick. He knew far better than she did what kind of defenses Nadrett might have, and what men could do against them. He said, "If they're brave, 'alf a dozen. Two for each door. Religious, if you can."

The sergeant breathed out a quiet laugh. "That will be the easy bit. Half a dozen, then? So five, aside from me." He shook his head, like a man about to take a wager he knew he should refuse. "They won't all be Special Branch, but this won't be an official operation, either. All right, Miss O'Malley—ye'll have yer men."

WEST HAM, LONDON

2 September 1884

Dead Rick watched Eliza pace up and down the edge of Stephens Road, hands knotted behind her back, a general waiting for her troops to arrive. The upcoming assault was as much hers as anybody else's: she didn't know as much about tactics or charms as Sergeant Quinn or Sir Peregrin, but she had the connection to both worlds, so everybody on both sides looked for answers to come through her. And it had been her idea to begin with.

An audacious idea, that might yet blow up in all their faces. But they had run out of time for caution, and every faerie with a sense of self-preservation had already left the Onyx Hall. What they had left were the desperate and the mad. A few more of those than expected, at that: in addition to the three knights of the Onyx Guard, Irrith, and Bonecruncher, they'd managed to rouse out Niklas von das Ticken, the puck Cuddy, and even Kutuhal, the monkey fellow that had come with them to Aldersgate. Dead Rick didn't know if he was coming out of curiosity, loyalty to his Academy fellows, or vengeance for the dead naga, but ultimately the reason didn't matter. The Indian cove had a strong arm, which was all they really needed.

So there were three fae for each door, and the rest of their forces should be here soon enough.

"Can you tell?" Eliza asked abruptly.

It made him jump a bit; he was as tense as she. When he cocked his head at her quizzically, she made a brief, abortive gesture at the rest of the fae, waiting in a clump some distance away. "Whether they're going to die."

Dead Rick's hackles rose at the question. He shook his head. "No. It don't work on fae." Their deaths were always too far off to sense, until the moment they happened.

"But you'll know about the mortals."

"Only if I look."

Eliza shivered, and looked down. "Don't look."

He wished, with sudden intensity, that he were in dog form; he would have gone and slipped his head under her hand. It was the sort of thing he would have done before, and he thought she might not refuse it now—but he wasn't sure.

Hoofbeats and the rattle of iron-rimmed wheels gave him no time in any case. A boxlike carriage with iron-barred windows approached along Stephens Road, and drew to a halt nearby. Sergeant Quinn jumped down from the front seat. With an effort at humour, Dead Rick said, "Planning on arresting 'em, are you?"

"There might be fellows that need arresting," Quinn said. "The iron bars could be useful around the others."

The carriage's back door opened, and men began climbing out. None were in uniform, but they all had the sturdy, hard-bitten look of police constables. Also the ill-disguised nerves of men who knew they had not signed up for an ordinary fight. How Quinn had recruited them, Dead Rick didn't know, and didn't care to ask. After what Eliza had said, he couldn't *not* look—and as he expected, the possibility of death hovered not far from each man. Not a certainty, and that was something; but this might yet go very badly indeed.

He wasn't about to tell them, though. Without preamble, Eliza said, "It's this way," and their pitiful army moved up toward Liddington Road.

Three doors to assault; three groups to assault them.

Dead Rick and Niklas were under Sir Peregrin's command. Quinn had mustered six additional constables instead of five, so the sergeant himself came with their group; they would be taking the large double doors on the southern end of the building. Eliza joined them as well. One hand gripped a knife; the other, a vial of water, ready to be thrown. Whether it would have any effect coming from a mortal's hand, nobody knew, but it might at least scare Nadrett—or rather, Seithenyn.

Dead Rick was looking forward to seeing the bastard drown.

Around the corner from the building, they paused to make their final preparations. The fae tied green bands around their left arms, to distinguish them from the others inside. Every mortal had come wearing a cross or crucifix, in addition to the weapons of revolver and water. Niklas daubed their eyes with some kind of ointment, mixed by someone in the Academy; it should help them see through charms of confusion. As a final touch, each constable turned his coat inside out—whereupon Dead Rick's gaze slid right past them, refusing to notice Quinn and the other two men standing just feet away.

It settled on Eliza instead. "You should 'ide yourself," he said.

She shook her head, surprising him not at all. "I want that bastard to see me. I want to look him in the eye."

No time to argue; the other groups would be moving into position already. Peregrin beckoned them forward, and together they ran to the double doors.

Which burst open, the bar holding them shut splintering into two broken ends. Dead Rick tried to watch the constables do it, but he only saw Eliza and the fae run through the gap. Inside lay a shallow room, filled with empty crates and some odd bits of machinery, with another set of doors and a staircase leading up. Peregrin ordered Niklas and P.C. Butler to check above, but the door at the top was locked, and they retreated rather than make noise by bashing through.

The one at the bottom was barred from their side; no need to break this one down. Someone Dead Rick couldn't see lifted the bar, and it swung open enough for a man to slip through.

But no one moved forward, and Dead Rick froze, every hair on his body standing on end. Something hung on the other side, fluttering in the shifting air: a length of cloth, shimmering all colours and none.

No. Not cloth. Looking at it, Dead Rick shivered down to the bone. The stuff twanged discordantly against his skriker instincts: something not quite of death, but not far distant, either.

At his side, Eliza let out a stifled moan. Her eyes were wide, when he turned to her, and she looked rather like he felt. Memory swam up from the absinthe-riddled depths of his mind: teaching her to call ghosts, because she was a born medium.

Mouthing the words more than speaking them, he

whispered, "What in Mab's name *is* that?" The only thing he could think was, it felt like ghosts, like the stuff the physical ones were made of—but not even quite like that.

Eliza shook her head, as baffled and unnerved as he. The fabric covered the entire doorway, in overlapping sheets; they would either have to go through, or try another door. And he wouldn't be surprised if the others were similarly draped.

A skriker couldn't see faerie deaths, and he certainly couldn't see his own. Gritting his teeth, Dead Rick muttered an oath, and flung himself through.

The caress of the fabric over his shoulders made his skin try to shudder right off his body, but what he found on the other side was a complete anticlimax:

An empty room.

It was a huge, echoing space, going up to the clerestory windows above, with a walkway overlooking from the second floor. Another set of stairs up to it lay by the wall at the far end. There were doors along the walkway, but everything he could see was silent and still.

"Blood and Bone," Dead Rick whispered to himself. "What is going *on*?"

Movement along the wall made him jump, but it was just Bonecruncher, coming through the near entrance, and Irrith through the far. A familiar scent told him Eliza had followed behind him, and one by one the others came through as well, to stare about in confusion.

The answers had to lie in the fabric. Dead Rick turned to examine it. Not death, and not ghosts, though something like each. That it was Nadrett's work, he had no doubt—but what *was* it, and why was it draping the entire inside surface of this building?

"Wait," Eliza said. Not to Dead Rick; she was staring toward someone his eye refused to see. Of course; the inside-out coats wouldn't confuse her mortal eyes at all. "They think they see something," she told the fae, "and I do, too—up ahead—*wait*!" she cried, and leapt forward as if to catch someone; whereupon she vanished.

Dead Rick flung himself after her.

Three steps in, the entire room changed. Rattling, clanking sound filled his ears; the smell of oil and grease and unwashed humans filled his nose; and in the center of the floor stood an enormous machine.

It transfixed his gaze, a hulking monstrosity unlike any he'd ever seen before. No, not true: it reminded him of the thing he'd seen in the Academy, that strange loom, except only part of this seemed to be weaving anything. People stood all around it: boys and girls, men and women, at least a dozen of them at a glance, all working away in the dim light as if they hadn't noticed anyone rushing in.

Dead Rick's skriker instinct crawled along his bones, confused and afraid. *Death—but not.*

Every last one of them was more empty than Owen had been.

And while one end of the machine was producing more of that strange, shimmering fabric, a man at the other end was setting into place something Dead Rick recognised all too well: a photographic plate.

"Mab's bleeding 'eart," Dead Rick whispered, almost voiceless with horror. "It's their bloody souls."

A bullet cracked into the floor not a foot away. Dead Rick spun, gun coming up instinctively, and he fired; he caught a brief glimpse of Gresh on the walkway above, before the goblin pulled back through a doorway. The skriker yelled, even as common sense told him Peregrin and the others wouldn't hear; the illusion concealing this place wouldn't let his voice past. *Better 'ope they follow,* he thought grimly, grabbing Eliza and dragging her toward cover beneath the walkway. *Else I* am *about to die.*

They did—or at least the fae did; Dead Rick's eye still refused to track the constables, though he could see their effects. One of the mortals around the machine staggered, blood bursting from his shoulder; he regained his footing and went about his work as if nothing had happened. "Don't shoot 'em!" Dead Rick bellowed, wondering who had done it. "Get the bastards up above!"

But by then it was chaos. Nadrett's men came out of concealment at various places around the floor, their protection broken by crucifixes and the devout faith of the mortals holding them. They wrestled with fellows they couldn't see, and then someone tore Quinn's coat off, exposing the sergeant to hostile eyes. Bullets rained down from above. "We've got to get up there," Dead Rick snarled.

"In the first room," Eliza said breathlessly, knife and water in white-knuckled grips. "The staircase—"

Had to lead up to the walkway. Dead Rick gauged the distance to that door, wondering what their chances were. Then his nose caught the acrid smoke of a fuse. He tackled Eliza to the ground an instant before the dynamite exploded.

Metal screamed in protest. It wasn't any bomb, thrown from above; someone had jammed a stick into the machine itself. *Bonecruncher,* Dead Rick thought, through the ringing in his ears. He couldn't hear the gears and rods grinding against one another, but through the haze he saw an entire section shudder to a halt.

It was as good a distraction as any. Dead Rick ran for the door, setting his teeth against the ghastly feel of the soul-fabric against his skin. Up the stairs—Blood and Bone; Eliza had followed him—where he shot the lock off the door at the top, and then he was back in the main room, this time at one end of the walkway.

Old Gadling stood nearest. Dead Rick transformed midleap, and the ease of it shocked him so much he bowled the thrumpin over and went sprawling himself. He'd eaten bread, of course—but even with that protection, he usually *felt* the iron, the mortal world frowning at his change.

Not here. Aside from the iron the constables had brought in, the prayers wielded as shields, he might have been on the most deserted moor in all of Yorkshire. As if nothing outside this building existed.

Nothing outside the *fabric*.

He rose to his paws in time to see Eliza wrestle Gadling over the walkway rail. The thrumpin fell with a surprised yell, and then Dead Rick moved on, past Gresh, past a faerie he didn't recognise, toward the far wall, where Cerenel had lost his gun and was using a knife to drive Nithen up the other staircase. None of them mattered, except that they'd helped defend this atrocity; the only one who mattered was Nadrett. Dead Rick couldn't carry water in this form, but his teeth would do well enough, if only he could find a target for them. *Where did that bastard go?*

Eliza went through one of the doorways; he followed close on her heels. The rooms on the far side were smaller, and they had Nadrett's scent on them, but the master was nowhere to be found. Just tools, and cameras, and bits of machine, and a scrawny faerie cowering under a table, pleading for mercy.

And a room full of cages, twins to the ones Nadrett kept in the Goblin Market. These, too, were filled with people, and Dead Rick recognised two of them.

They wore the same face, and the same expressions of terror. But only one of them might be able to tell Dead Rick what he wanted to know. He shifted to man form and snapped, "Cyma! Where the bleeding 'ell is Nadrett?"

"He went back to the—"

Her words dissolved in a wail of horrified dismay. Unthinking, he had called her by her faeric name, and unthinking, she had answered. Louisa—the real Louisa—clutched her double's shoulder, but it was too late; the symmetry of their appearances shattered, leaving behind one mortal girl and one former changeling.

Cyma gasped for air, clinging to Louisa and the side of the cage. Eliza pressed her hands to her mouth, staring at them both, and the expression on her face made Dead Rick feel a brief stab of guilt. *I didn't mean to do it.* But it was too late now.

"Find a key," he said to Eliza, and she began searching while he crouched down to grip the bars of the cage. "Cyma—Blood and Bone, I'm sorry, but you've *got* to tell me. I ain't letting Nadrett get away. *Where is 'e?*"

She swallowed back tears and turned her pale face up far enough for him to see. "He went back to the Onyx Hall. Dead Rick, *he's going after Lune.*"

The skriker's heart stopped. He couldn't even think of a curse vile enough to suffice. Lune—if Nadrett did *anything* to her—

Eliza threw a key to someone he could not see and dragged Dead Rick to his feet, breaking his paralysis. "I know where we can hire a cab. Come on."

THE PRINCE'S COURT, ONYX HALL
2 September 1884

I can't die. Not now. Sweet mother of—oh Christ *it 'urts—don't let me die—*

The earthquake went on and on, inside and out. Hodge wasn't even trying to stand; he'd flung himself flat when the first tremor hit, pressing his body against the black stone of the floor, throwing every atom of his strength into the Onyx Hall. He could hear Lune's scream in his head, a constant shriek of agony, never needing to pause for breath; his own throat was mute, paralyzed by pain.

He had just enough presence of mind to choke back the prayer that tried to form. Hodge wasn't a praying man, never had been, save in the most extreme desperation—which most certainly described this moment. But he'd felt the extra strain when Christ's name went through his mind, and he knew, with the part of him that was still capable of analysis, that his own battlefield piety might be the thing that broke them both, and destroyed the Onyx Hall for good.

Cracking splintering shattering collapse. *The Academy,* Hodge thought, and knew Lune was thinking of it, too; they must not lose the Academy, which held all the knowledge they might use to craft their salvation. They could surrender any part of the Hall but that one—the Academy, and the rooms that held Hodge and Lune. Like a man caught in a trap, Hodge amputated his own leg, knowing that if he didn't he would die where he lay. And the blood, the *life,* poured out of him so fast he feared he would die anyway.

Not him. The Hall. The two spirits within the London Stone, Francis and Suspiria. He could neither hear nor feel them, but if Aspell was right, they were still there. And if they died—if their spirits were torn completely apart—

This is the one fucking thing I can do for this place. I can 'old it together. And I will. *No matter 'ow much it 'urts.*

And so he held.

The pain ended at last—the worst of it—and tears streamed without shame down his face. *Still alive. I'm still alive, and so is the Hall—for now.*

It was the smallest, most pathetic shred of victory. The iron chain had been linked together at last, the final pieces of rail laid down below Cannon Street. The Inner Circle Railway was complete.

It hadn't destroyed them—not yet. But when the trains began to make their circuit, Hodge was a dead man. Him, and Lune, and the palace: they had not enough strength among them to survive it.

Those sons of bitches were early, too. The navvies weren't supposed to lay the last bits of track until tomorrow; he'd thought Dead Rick and the others had just enough time to see what Nadrett was doing in West Ham. If that bastard actually had some way to make his own shelter, then this suffering could end at last.

Now he wasn't even sure he would live to *see* tomorrow.

The stone beneath him had spiderwebbed into a thousand pieces. His hand trembled with palsy as he pressed it against the shattered fragments, trying to push himself up—not to his feet, that was out of the question, but at least as far as his knees. There was no strength in his arm. When he heard the door open, running footsteps approach him, Hodge almost wept with relief; then Dead Rick hauled him upright, and the panic in the skriker's eyes killed that relief entirely.

" 'E's after Lune," Dead Rick said, fingers gripping hard

enough to bruise. "But I don't know where she is. You 'as to tell us."

Lune. And Nadrett. How the hell had that bastard learned where she was? It didn't matter. Alone and vulnerable, maybe shaking with weakness like Hodge, she would be easy prey. *I 'ave to warn 'er.* He pressed his hand against the floor, tried to reach out, but all he got was silence.

"I'll bloody carry you if I 'ave to," Dead Rick said, desperate.

Hodge's voice came out a near-inaudible rasp. "You'll 'ave to. Swore an oath; I can't tell you where the Stone is. But lift me up, and I'll show you where to go."

THE LONDON STONE, ONYX HALL
2 September 1884

Eliza followed Dead Rick's lurching run, one hand pressed to her side as if she could push away the stitch of pain there. When they came into the Onyx Hall, there had been a terrifying moment of dislocation, as if something were trying to rip her insides clear out of her body; she and Dead Rick had fallen hard when they finally made it through, and the skriker had begun crawling before the floor settled, even though it seemed the ceiling could fall in on him at any moment.

The Goodemeades had spoken of destruction; so had Dead Rick. None of it had meant much to Eliza, until now.

Until she felt their world tearing apart around her.

And now they were braving it in search of the Queen, the faerie woman who ruled over this dying place. No—in search of Nadrett, and revenge.

Hodge gestured Dead Rick to the left, then through an arch. In the distance, Eliza could hear cries of fear, the sounds of other people running. She cast a nervous glance at the walls around them, which seemed on the verge of collapse. *We only need a few minutes more.*

A sudden tremor sent Dead Rick sprawling. Hodge grunted in pain as he hit the floor. Eliza caught herself against the wall, then went to help the Prince. His pointing hand stopped her. "Not far. She walled 'erself in. But if Nadrett's there—"

Eliza didn't wait for anything more. Gripping the knife and the water so tight her knuckles ached, she ran in the direction Hodge pointed.

The first room was hung with faded tapestries and cluttered with rubbish, echoes of a forgotten past. Eliza had no eyes for them: her gaze went straight to the right-hand wall, where broken black stone formed a jagged mouth. Weapons raised, Eliza hurled herself through to the room beyond.

The woman within sat in serene perfection, eyes closed, heedless of her surroundings. Her cloth-of-silver gown was old-fashioned, with the full crinoline and sloping shoulders of decades past; it shone in the dim light of the room. *She* shone, pale skinned and silver haired, like some poet's vision of the moon, and a sword was thrust into the black stone at her feet.

So arresting a sight was she, it took Eliza a full second to notice the other faerie in the room—the creature that had been the source of all her pain.

She'd expected something more. Some grand demon, maybe not horned and clawed and dripping venom, but showing outward sign of his evil. Instead she saw a faerie much like any other: dressed like a man, in the tattered elegance she associated with the leaders of gangs in the slums of London.

Holding a gun to the woman's head.

"Stop!" Dead Rick wrenched the vial from Eliza's grip, when she would have hurled her water at the other faerie. "Stop," he repeated in a whisper, and she felt the skriker tremble against her back.

Nadrett's laugh held all the malice she'd imagined in her nightmares. "That's right, dog. You know what this means, even if that mortal bitch don't. I pulls the trigger, and this all comes tumbling down."

Fear roughened Dead Rick's voice, alongside the anger. "You'll die with us."

"Maybe so," Nadrett said, seemingly unconcerned. "But you ready to kill everybody else, too? No, I don't think so. You've got your memories back, don't you? Which means you remember fighting for this place. Being a good little dog for the Queen. She wouldn't want you to throw that away, now would she?" He gestured at Eliza. "Are you ready to kill *'er,* your little mortal pet?"

Dead Rick slid in front of Eliza, pushing her back with gentle, shaking hands. She retreated, thinking of that terrible dislocation as they came into the Onyx Hall. It would be like that again, if the Queen died. Only worse.

The skriker said, "What do you want?"

Nadrett's lip curled. "Your guts on an iron platter would be a pleasant start. Or no, I've got a better idea—I want all of your memories gone again, all except this moment. So the only thing you remember is 'ow you failed, and fell back into being my crawling, whining *cur*."

Eliza dug her fingers into the black stone of the wall at her back, gripping it as if that were the one thing keeping her from leaping at Nadrett. The malevolence of him turned her stomach. This was what had broken Owen; this was what Dead Rick had lived under for years, until the kindness and trust in him had been beaten almost to death.

Dead Rick snarled low in his throat, but said, "I mean right now. You came for Lune. You planning to walk out with 'er? Take 'er away from that? Might as well shoot 'er, and you know it."

He'd jerked his chin upward on the word "that." Following his motion, Eliza saw a stone in the ceiling above Lune that did not belong with the rest of the palace. It was a simple, rounded block of limestone, pitted and chipped, scored with grooves along its tip, as if carriage wheels had ground across it for years—but it hung ten feet above their heads. Surely nothing could touch it up there, least of all carriages.

Then she realised she'd seen it before, during her costerwoman days. Or rather, a stone just like it, set into the outside wall of St. Swithin's Church. An old relic that they called the London Stone.

"I ain't got no interest in seeing everybody die," Nadrett said, in answer to Dead Rick. "You ought to know that, dog; if there ain't no fae in London, I ain't got nobody to make a profit from. So 'ere's what we're going to do.

"You're going to go out and tell everybody there's a new place for them to live. Out in West Ham. Anybody as wants to stay in London can, so long as they pays my price. You clear them out of this place; that Prince of theirs 'as enough bread piled up to give everybody a bite. Once that's done . . . You see that camera over there?"

Eliza couldn't risk taking her attention off Nadrett, but out of the corner of her eye she could just glimpse a box on a tripod stand. "I use that camera," Nadrett said. "I take the Queen's soul. I carry it off to West Ham, and use 'er and that dead Prince to pour what's left of this place into what I've got waiting there. New faerie realm, new 'ome for everybody. Ain't it grand?"

Eliza's heart lurched against her ribs. So that was how he would do it: with human souls and the captured spirit of the Queen. That was the secret they had risked themselves to capture.

Or rather, destroy.

"Sounds very grand—except for one thing." Her voice shook: with rage, with fear, with the fruitless need to *do* something. She couldn't possibly kill him before he shot the Queen. But if she made him angry enough . . . "We blew your machine to pieces."

It almost worked. Nadrett snarled in fury, and Dead Rick tensed, about to throw himself forward in that moment of distraction. But Nadrett saw it, and spat a curse. "One inch, dog, and I blows the Queen's brains out."

Let him.

It was a stupid, reckless, suicidal thought—so Eliza believed, at first. But the tone wasn't reckless in the least; it was perfectly calm.

And it wasn't her thought.

The whisper ghosted into her head, and no one else seemed to hear it. *Let him fire. If you can hear me . . . make Nadrett do it.*

Madness. They would all die; Dead Rick had said so. But Eliza would have put her hand on the Holy Bible and sworn her oath to God that the whisper came from the silver-haired woman in the chair: the Queen of the Onyx Court.

Whose mind she was somehow feeling, as if the woman were a ghost she had raised.

Trust me.

The tenuous sense of connection faded as Eliza shifted forward, releasing her grip on the wall. Nadrett redirected his snarl to her. "That goes for you, too, bitch."

In the end, Eliza was sure of one thing: that it would be better to kill every faerie in this place, even Dead Rick, and herself with them, than to let Nadrett tear people's souls out and feed them into his terrible machine.

"Devil take you," she said, and threw herself at Nadrett.

The sound of gunfire was deafening in the small space. Eliza never made it near her target; Dead Rick caught her, in a desperate, failed attempt to prevent disaster. But as her ears rang with the aftermath of the shot, as smoke wisped through the cool, dry air, the expected earthquake did not begin.

And Lune sat, untouched, in her chair.

Nadrett stared, disbelieving, at the Queen. So did Dead Rick; so did Eliza. The pistol was an inch from her head; he could not possibly have missed. The wall showed a fresh pockmark where the round had struck, and the line between the two went straight through her skull.

Trembling, Nadrett reached out with his free hand to touch Lune's hair.

His fingers went right through.

"What in Mab's name . . . ?" he whispered.

Clinging to Dead Rick, Eliza felt the growl in the skriker's chest, before it ever became audible. Then understanding caught up, and she released him, freeing his arm to throw.

A tiny arc of water leapt from the vial, cloudy and stinking of the Thames from which it had been drawn. In a fierce, triumphant growl, Dead Rick snarled, "Seithenyn, I name you, and mark you for death. Let the waters of Faerie carry out their curse!"

Only a few droplets of water caught Nadrett. Nowhere near enough to hurt anyone. The entire vial couldn't have hurt a man, even if poured into his lungs. Nadrett raised his gun again, and Eliza thought they were dead; Lune might survive that, but she and Dead Rick never would. Before Nadrett's arm made it all the way up, though, the water began to *move*.

Move, and grow. It twisted up from the floor, from his sleeve and collar where the droplets had landed, twining into ropes and waves. Nadrett screamed, trying to claw it away, but the water only clung to his hands, like animate tar; then, understanding, he tried to run.

He didn't get more than three steps. The waters raged higher around him, a whirlpool binding his body tight, and in their surface Eliza thought she saw faces: beautiful nymphs, twisted hags, and through them all, the solemn, bearded face of an old man. A voice spoke, resonant but clotted with mud and filth, the voice of the Thames itself. "For the destruction you wrought, and the death of Mererid our daughter, we bring this justice upon you."

Nadrett's scream died in a choking cough. Then there was only rushing water; then silence, as it drained away, leaving only a damp slick on the floor.

Dead Rick spat at it. "Wanted to tear your throat out, you bastard. But they 'ad first claim."

Sick to her stomach, Eliza turned away. To the broken edge of the wall that had closed Lune into this chamber—Lune, who was some kind of ghost. Beyond its edge she found Hodge, limp on the floor, having dragged himself almost to the Queen before his strength gave out. Eliza knelt and rolled him onto his back, fearing the worst, but

Hodge opened his eyes. "Is she . . ."

Eliza didn't know how to answer. Instead she slipped her arm around his chest and helped him upright, and together they staggered back into the chamber of the London Stone.

Dead Rick gestured helplessly toward the Queen. "Lune—"

Hodge stretched one hand out to the wall. Not for support; his fingers touched the stone, and he closed his eyes. After a moment, Eliza did the same.

She felt that presence again, tenuous and weak, but undeniably there. A sense of gratitude breathed over her, so painfully weary that it brought a gasp of tears into Eliza's own throat. *I began to suspect some time ago. I have poured so much of myself into the Hall, I am no longer in my body; the Hall* is *my body. The scholars would say my spirit has released its grip upon the aether that made it solid. I could not hold both that and the palace at once.*

It was more than just words. The Queen's whisper carried with it overtones of sensation and memory that gave Eliza vertigo: in that moment, she came untethered from human notions of time and existence, growing into something vaster and more elemental than her poor mortal mind could conceive. But then, as from a distance, she felt Hodge's arm tighten around her shoulders, and she knew she wasn't alone; he was mortal, too, if not entirely so, and he helped anchor her to the reality she understood, against the tide of the Queen's ancient soul.

Whether she heard Dead Rick's voice with her ears or

her mind, Eliza didn't know. "Your Grace. I should 'ave stopped 'im sooner—"

No need for apology. Another wash of weariness, so intense Eliza wondered how anyone, human or faerie, could bear it. *I know of your purpose in West Ham. Did he have an answer? Can his . . . machines be used?*

It must have been mental communication, for Eliza felt the surge of Dead Rick's repugnance alongside her own. "No," she said, and then words failed her; they did not suffice to describe the horror of what Nadrett had built.

But it seemed the Queen took the sense of it from her mind, for she felt Lune's grim resignation. *Then we do not have long. At most, until the first train passes by the London Stone above. Perhaps not even that long. Hodge . . . the time has come. The Onyx Court must flit; the Hall can shelter us no more.*

"No!" That *was* out loud, and it came from Dead Rick. Hand still on the wall, Eliza opened her eyes, and saw the skriker fall to his knees at the feet of his phantom Queen. "We can't just bloody well give up. There *'as* to be a way to save the palace."

Hodge slipped from Eliza's arm to lean against the stone, exhausted. His answer was flat and unyielding. "There ain't. We've tried. I wish it weren't true—but your time 'ere is done."

The naked despair on Dead Rick's face echoed through the stone, into Eliza's own heart. "But this is our *home.*"

His words tore her in half. One piece growled that

it would be good riddance; after all the evil the fae had done, London would be better off without them. No more Nadretts, stealing people and memories and souls, profiting from the misery and suffering of others. These were not godly creatures; they were alien, and unwanted. The occasional exception—Dead Rick, the Goodemeades—did not redeem the rest of their kind.

The other piece of Eliza had heard such words before—coming from men like Louisa Kittering's father.

Maggie Darragh, starving in Whitechapel, until her anger could only express itself in dynamite. James O'Malley, who'd stolen more than a few things in his time, and other crimes besides. All the drunkards and thieves and murderers, the unwashed pestilential masses of Irish hidden away in their rookeries, where the respectable folk of London didn't have to see them; some were bad at heart, and others were led into sin by those around them, and still others had it forced upon them by circumstance. And then there were the men like Patrick Quinn, that those respectable folk liked to forget: decent, hardworking Irish, not living in poverty, not committing crimes, but they couldn't redeem their race in the eyes of those who judged.

Eliza had told Quinn that London was her home. It was Dead Rick's home, too—and Lune's, and the Goodemeades', and all the other fae who sheltered in the dying ruins of the Onyx Hall, criminal and citizen alike. How could she look him in the eye and say he had to leave, that his kind were not wanted here?

This moment wasn't hers; she was all but a stranger here, ignorant of so much that she hardly dared open her mouth. But she had to do something to lift the blackness from Dead Rick's heart, and so she said, "How did this place get made? Can't you make another one?"

The fierce blaze in the skriker's eye repaid her courage tenfold. "You said it two 'undred years ago, your Grace—that if the palace burned down, we'd build another one! If we can't save the Hall, then let it go, and start over!"

But Hodge shook his head. "The giants of London are dead; Father Thames 'asn't spoken in more than a 'undred years; the city's shot through with iron. We know what they did the first time, but the world's changed too much for that to work."

"Then find a *new* way," Eliza said, with all the bold confidence of a woman who had no idea what such a way might be, but wasn't letting that stop her. "Pull Nadrett's machines to bits and figure out how to make them work with something other than souls."

For a moment, she thought Hodge would say no. The weariness was in him, too, going beyond what she thought any man could endure; it would have been easier for him to give up, to send the faeries away, and then to die alongside Lune, with the last of the Onyx Hall.

But he wasn't some overbred twig off the royal tree of Europe. This Prince was made of sterner stuff, and had the will to go down fighting. "It can't 'urt to try," Hodge said, and managed a smile. "Any more than not trying will. I can only die once."

Dead Rick stood, bowing to both the Queen and the Prince, and said, "I think I might know somebody who can 'elp you put that off a bit."

THE GALENIC ACADEMY, ONYX HALL
7 September 1884

The closing of the Inner Circle had, in one brutal move, severed the Onyx Hall into two pieces, along the line of Cannon Street. For days afterward, the southern half shuddered through its death throes, the last of the Goblin Market fracturing smaller and smaller, taking with it anyone, faerie or mortal, not smart enough to run for the door while they could.

For the northern half, survival took precedence over security: Dead Rick and Eliza helped the Academy's engineers dismantle the great loom and move it to the chamber outside where Lune sat in desperate trance, supported by the ghost of Galen St. Clair. The young man had not hesitated, once Yvoir freed his spirit from the plate found in the West Ham factory; he had only to hear that Lune needed his aid, and went immediately to her side. In the meanwhile, Bonecruncher and others had braved the dying southern half to gather as much material as they could, salvaging it to feed the loom, so they could weave protection for what had become the two most vital pieces of the Hall.

The London Stone and the Galenic Academy.

The former would hold their present for as long as it could. The latter, perhaps, held their future.

It was the irrational hope born in those moments after Nadrett's death: that they could, in these final days, discover some acceptable use for the horror he had invented. Some way to make a new home for themselves, on some foundation other than the destruction of mortal souls.

"I'm sorry to say that was, in part, my doing," said the bearded man who presented himself to the Academy, five days after the raid. The Goodemeades had brought him, introducing the fellow as Frederic Myers, of the London Fairy Society. "I do not remember the details—it seems that memory has somehow been taken from me—but according to what Fjothar and I have reconstructed, some years ago, Nadrett sought out my expertise on ghosts.

"His original interest was in the notion of the 'astral plane'—a place where spirits dwell. I believe he was interested in establishing some dominion there, if he could. A different portion of my research, however, proved more fruitful to him: the physical manifestation of spirits. I theorised that *ectoplasm,* as I called it—the ghost-substance—was an emanation created by the human soul itself."

Here Fjothar took up the thread. He was a svartálfar, with patches of wiry hair sticking out in all directions; he had a habit of pulling on these as he spoke. "We all know that mortal souls can shelter fae against iron and faith; it is that property which allows tithed bread to do its work, and also protects changelings who take a mortal's place. With Mr. Myers's help—and, I suspect, the assistance of Red Rotch, a former Academy scholar who was killed some time ago in the Goblin Market—Nadrett discovered that ectoplasm is in fact *solid aether*. And it retains its protective capability."

With her usual bluntness, Irrith said, "But if we have to grind people's souls down into thread to make use of it, then we might as well put our coats on now, because that isn't going to happen."

They had gathered in the Presentation Hall, all those who remained, to pool their knowledge and answer the final question: could they, with the Academy's wisdom and Nadrett's machines, with their memories of the past and their visions of the future, find a way to build a new palace? They made a strange assortment, ranged across the benches and chairs and boxes scavenged for seating; not just scholars, but courtiers and mortal allies and Goblin Market refugees. Everyone who cared enough to risk staying. *Damned if I know what I can add,* Dead Rick thought wryly, *but I ain't about to run now. Not after what I said to Lune.*

They'd salvaged what they could from West Ham. Whether anything could be done for the empty human shells that had operated the machines was doubtful; Mrs. Chase was attempting to find caretakers for them all. Those faeries not killed had fled, and nobody had the energy to chase them, nor to do more than beg the constables not to speak of what they'd seen. All their remaining will went into the scientific problem instead. Parts of the equipment were intact or repairable, and some fellow with a strong stomach had examined the fabric for its secrets—but could they turn any of it to good?

Bonecruncher helped Rosamund up onto a barrel so she could stand high enough to be seen by the others. "A human seer helped before," the brownie said, once she had everyone's attention. "Back when the Hall was created. He and a faerie woman worked together to do it, and his spirit is part of what has protected this place. One possibility—and it's only a possibility, mind you—is that somebody else could do the same."

Creaks and scuffing sounded around the room, as every mortal in the place shifted and tried to avoid meeting anyone's eye, lest they be asked to volunteer. Not just the men; Dead Rick saw Eliza bite her lip. If she tried to do it, he would stop her.

But her thoughts, it seemed, went in another direction. Hesitantly, as if not sure she had the right to speak up in this place, Eliza said, "Would ghosts do? Could ye . . . harvest this stuff from them somehow, without harming them?"

"I know a genuine medium," Cyma offered, from where she sat on the far side of the room, a wide-eyed Louisa Kittering at her side.

So do I, Dead Rick thought. Did Eliza mean to offer her services? Before she could, though, others in the room took the idea and began to elaborate upon it. Ch'ien Mu, the Chinese faerie in charge of the great loom, seemed very excited by the prospect; he began muttering, "Weft thread! I say before, if we have aether for weft, it is stable." Fjothar tried to explain something about the configuration created by Nadrett's machine, but it was lost in the hubbub, scholars and nonscholars alike flinging suggestions atop one another, making a confused jumble of it all.

Dead Rick couldn't understand more than one word in ten. Instead he watched Abd ar-Rashid. The Scholarch listened quietly for a time, hands folded behind his back, before bringing out something like a golden pen. Without speaking, the genie began to move the pen through the air, and lines of glowing gold appeared in its wake, as if he were writing on an invisible slate.

Most of what he wrote consisted of the alchemical and arcane symbols the scholars used in their science, and those, Dead Rick could not read. Two things, however, Abd ar-Rashid wrote in plain English, letters big enough to be seen from across the Presentation Hall: CONFORMATION? and FOUNDATION?

He tucked the pen away and clapped his hands sharply, halting a discussion that had begun to veer off in a dozen directions, each less comprehensible than the last. "If we are to make a new faerie realm," Abd ar-Rashid said, "then we must address these two questions, before we go any further. Supposing we overcome the obstacles to making the substance itself—which may be within our grasp—what will be its conformation, and to what will it be anchored?"

At Dead Rick's side, Eliza looked completely lost. Pretending for a moment he knew the first thing about these matters, he leaned toward her ear and muttered, "Like this place. It reflects the City of London—the way it was when the palace were first made—and it's anchored to certain bits up above."

She nodded, frowning. "The Goodemeades told me. The old wall, the Tower, and so on."

"Right. Too much of that's broke, though, so we needs to pick something new."

What the "something new" should be rapidly became the primary point of discussion. Someone rolled out a huge map of the city and stuck it to the wall; this had lines marked on it for both the Underground and overground railways, and everyone was arguing over which landmarks to choose for the new foundation. Geographical arrangement, symbolism, and distance from the tracks seemed the primary points of contention, as Wilhas von das Ticken and a Spanish-accented mortal began a vigorous debate over the relative merits of a pentagram versus a hexagram.

That Myers fellow leapt into it with a will, but others sat back, looking as useless as Dead Rick felt. Louisa Kittering, he saw, was murmuring to Cyma; Bonecruncher was spinning a gun around one finger; Sir Cerenel's violet eyes had fixed on the far wall as if determined not to show how lost he was. Eliza, to his surprise, was listening closely, though unless she'd spent the last seven years studying the

Pythagoras fellow that the Spaniard was going on about, she couldn't possibly understand it any better than Dead Rick did.

As if feeling the weight of his gaze, she glanced sideways at him, and her brow furrowed. "Are they stupid, or am I?"

"I'm pretty sure *I* am," he muttered. "You actually follow them?"

"No—but I think I see a problem, all the same." She shifted her stool closer, an intent look in her eyes. "Tell me if I'm wrong. Isn't yer problem right now that yer foundation is cracked, because the things ye used for it got moved or destroyed?"

Dead Rick frowned. "Yes, but they're choosing new things—"

"Which might be destroyed in a hundred years, or ten," Eliza said. "Oh, I suppose no one will be in a hurry to knock down Nelson's Column, but still—that doesn't mean the problem goes away. Does it?"

He cocked his head, listening as best as he could to the conversation. They were talking now about the significance of the original anchor points, their symbolic meaning and the effect that had on the Onyx Hall. Trying to find new anchors that would carry similar meaning, or better. But it all still sounded like physical things, and to his way of thinking, Eliza was right. The Great Fire had destroyed much of the City of London, and came terrifyingly close to destroying the Onyx Hall, too. Anything man-made could be unmade, too.

Natural features, then—but no, those didn't work either, did they? All those bridges spanning the Thames, some of them with iron, and the various embankments narrowing and shaping its course. The Walbrook, buried underground, and the Fleet, too; year by year, London buried more of its rivers. Hills were flattened, valleys filled in. Mortals might not see it, with their short and blinkered lives, and the timeless memories of fae might overlook it; but with his memories half in a tangle still, Dead Rick knew very well how much London had changed.

The more firmly they planted their feet on the ground, the more vulnerable they were to an earthquake.

What could they choose, that couldn't be destroyed?

Eliza didn't think Dead Rick's words were meant for her; he spoke them under his breath, his teeth clenched hard together. *"Fucking Nadrett. Useful after all, you bastard."*

Before she could ask what he meant by that, the skriker shot to his feet. He wasn't tall, nor large of build, but the sudden conviction in his posture made him seem twice his usual size. In a growl that cut straight through the clamour, he said, "You're wasting your bleeding time."

Few of the expressions he received were friendly. Dead Rick still looked and sounded exactly like what he was: a black dog, a goblin creature from the Goblin Market, uneducated and barely literate. Neither the scholars nor the swells here much liked being told they were wasting their time by someone who had, until recently, been Nadrett's dog. But even the glaring ones had given him their attention, and that was enough. Shaking his head, Dead Rick said, "Eliza 'ere already figured it out. You can't just pick new places; you'll end up 'aving to do this again in a few 'undred years. Or less."

Ch'ien Mu snapped, "Must have anchor! Describe in symbol, tell machine, so machine go—"

He waved his hands, clearly frustrated with the way his mind had outpaced his English. Wrain said, "We realise the problem, Dead Rick, but—" Ch'ien Mu spat something out in rapid Chinese, and Wrain translated. "With samples from the locations we choose, we can create instructions for the loom; without that, we don't have conformation *or* foundation. We must work with what we have, flawed though it may be."

"And 'a few 'undred years' is more time than we have now," someone else said in a nasty tone.

Dead Rick took no offense at the mockery. "Ain't it better to pick something that ain't flawed? Something that can't *be* destroyed, that'll go on forever—or as close to forever as any of us needs."

Several people seemed ready to shout him down, but Abd ar-Rashid spoke before they could. "What do you have in mind?"

Dead Rick grinned, in a way that made Eliza's stomach tense in both apprehension and excitement. "London."

A full three seconds of silence followed, before a

skinny mortal said, "What the blazes do you think we've been discussing?"

"Not the stuff *in* the city," Dead Rick said, still grinning. "The city *itself*. The *idea* of the place. So long as there's Londoners, there'll be a London, right? Ash and Thorn—I'm the last bleeding sod to tell you we should thank Nadrett for anything, but 'e got Chrennois to figure out a way for photographing things that can't be touched. So photograph the city, the *idea* of it. Use that for your foundation. It'll fall apart when the city gets abandoned, maybe—but by then, we won't need it no more. Because there won't be no London to live in."

More silence. Then Irrith said, "But how in Mab's name do we photograph *that*?"

"We don't have to," Wrain said, leaping up in excitement. He flung one arm out toward the large machine that sat at the other end of the room, across from where the loom had been. "We can calculate it instead. Once we know how to represent the nature of London in symbolic notation, we can use that to instruct the loom. A *conceptual* conformation and foundation, instead of a physical one!"

The genie was writing this in the air as he spoke, in glowing letters of gold. Like a teacher waiting to see what his pupils knew, he said, "What, then, is the nature of London?"

Not far from Eliza, the Goodemeades had been whispering to each other. Now Rosamund cleared her throat and scrambled back up onto the barrel. "Gertie and I have been here longer than just about anyone. Longer than the Onyx Hall, even. London is, and always has been, the heart of England."

"They say that one in ten Englishmen lives here," Gertrude added. "Maybe more. Nowadays it isn't the only city—there's Liverpool, Manchester, Birmingham, and so on—but they're not a tenth the size of London."

Sounds of startlement, from a few of the fae; none of the mortals looked surprised. *These creatures may know history,* Eliza thought, *but they don't know the world around them very well.* Even she knew about those cities—many of them swelled by the emigration of her own people.

"Size is not the only thing that makes London the heart of England," Sir Cerenel added. "The government is here, too. Or rather, in Westminster—but I suppose that is part of London now, isn't it? Queen Victoria and Parliament are also England's heart, and they are here."

Not as much since Her Nibs went into mourning and never came out. Eliza couldn't help but notice, too, the way they kept speaking of *England*. Not Britain, or the United Kingdom. Three hundred years and more, they'd been here. It showed.

Louisa Kittering spoke up boldly. "You mustn't forget money, either. All the trade that comes into London, and the banks, and the investors; I don't know what fraction of the nation's wealth is here, but it must be vast. Anyone who wishes to count for anything must come to London eventually, if only for the Season."

One of the mortal men gave a dry laugh. "You and

Sir Cerenel are talking about the same thing, really: power. That's what London is about. It is the heart of power. And the trappings of power follow with it, all the fashion and art and commerce and such."

Voices rose up in agreement, murmuring about the elegant terraces of houses, the museums, the grand monuments, all embroidering upon the theme of London's glorious power. Eliza sagged in her chair, excitement draining away. She'd felt, for a few moments, as if she belonged—but not in this conversation. This was for the Louisa Kitterings of the world, the educated folk and the wealthy, the privileged swells, whether they were faerie or mortal. At her side, Dead Rick was equally silent; their eyes met, and his lip curled upward cynically. She knew what he was thinking, as clearly as if he'd said it. *That ain't* my *London.*

Eliza sucked in a sudden breath. The half sneer on Dead Rick's face turned into wide-eyed thought, and then to a remarkably evil grin. As well it should; *he'd* stood up a moment ago and told everyone they were a pack of idiots. Of course it would please him to watch her do the same.

Months of hiding, of doing her best to make sure nobody took notice of her. Months of lying about who and what she was, the better to blend in. Hard habits to break, after all that time. But if she didn't do it now, she would regret it forever.

Nobody heard her clear her throat. Should she wave her hand, or wait for a lull? *The devil with being polite.* Planting her shoes—her battered, secondhand shoes—firmly on the floor, Eliza stood and declared in a clear, carrying voice, "That's the London ye see, is it? Well, 'tisn't mine."

The conversation staggered and trailed off. The genie turned an inquiring face upon her and said, "Please, Miss O'Malley, do share your thoughts."

He might be a heathen, but Eliza couldn't help but like him at that moment; she suspected he knew what she was about to say. There were enough of his kind—heathens, not genies—in the East End, especially around the docks. Where the city pushed much of its unwanted refuse.

"What is London?" she asked, and licked her lips, clenching her hands for strength. " 'Tis thousands of servants scrubbing the floors of yer rich and mighty, so the missus's skirt won't get dusty. 'Tis boys sweeping mud out of the street for pennies, and scooping up dog turds to sell to the tanners. 'Tis cholera and measles and scarlet fever, poverty, starvation, drinking yourself half dead with gin, and being thrown in prison for debt. 'Tis paying fourpence to sleep on a bench with a rope holding you up, then going out to sell buns from a barrow while your fingers freeze with the cold." She paused for breath, and found she was shaking so hard it came in a ragged gasp. "All yer power, all yer wealth, all those things that make this place important—they don't come from nowhere. They're just the top layer, the crust on the pie, and underneath is another city entirely. The Irish, and the Italians, and the lascars—even the Jews—all those people who are *not* English, and are not a part of the world ye see, but they are bloody well part of London, too."

Quietly, Gertrude Goodemeade said, "Just as we are part of London, the hidden faerie folk. We, too, have been a part of making this city what it is today."

Sir Cerenel offered Eliza what he probably thought was a sympathetic smile. With the anger trembling in her veins, she found it hard to accept as anything other than condescending. "Your point is well taken, Miss O'Malley. But we must ask ourselves: Are those layers what we want to choose? The new palace will reflect its foundation; surely we want to make that the best London has to offer."

Of course a knight would say that. She spat at his feet in fury. "And power makes things best, does it? Money and fine clothes? Never mind the hard work, the folk who come here because they hope for a better life; ye would never want to reflect *that,* now would ye—devil knows what it might do."

Behind Eliza's shoulder, Dead Rick rose to his feet. "You want a strong foundation? I ain't no architect, but I knows that a broad bottom works better than a narrow one. It don't tip over so easy. And there's a lot more poor than there is rich."

"Who says we cannot include both?" Abd ar-Rashid asked. "Include *all* the visions of the city, high and low alike?"

In a tone that suggested his head was on the verge of exploding, the man who'd spoken of power said, "But we can't include *everything*. It would be chaos!"

"Only if it is rendered in fragments," the genie said, and looked significantly at Wrain.

Who turned to look at the machine he'd mentioned before, the calculating engine.

Lady Feidelm murmured, "Is this not the purpose for which it was built? To take certain values and bring them to bear upon one another, conducting the operations which will tell you the difference between them, or the average, or any such relationship?"

Multiple ideas of London, calculated into a whole. Eliza knew nothing of mathematics beyond bare addition and subtraction, and what the sidhe spoke of sounded only half like mathematics to begin with—but if they had some way to do it . . .

But Wrain sank with sudden exhaustion back onto his chair. "We can't possibly calculate it all in time. Even rendering a single concept into symbolic notation would be a huge undertaking. A dozen or more? The Hall will be long gone before we can do it. If the Calendar Room had survived, then it would give us the time we need, but that last earthquake broke the chamber's clock, and we cannot restore it."

The only reason Eliza knew the French voice that answered was because she'd thanked him for returning Dead Rick's memories. Yvoir said, "Then work from photographs, as Dead Rick said! As Nadrett did. But not souls, only thoughts, and a single lens only—we do not wish to remove the thoughts from anyone's head, merely to copy them. Use the glass as a filter; what passes through, and what does not, can be translated for the calculating engine—"

"Which will carry out the necessary operations—"

"And print the result onto another photographic plate? Use that as the instruction, instead of the crystal cards, for the elemental threads—"

"Aetheric weft—"

"—the configuration Nadrett used—"

"There is one problem."

The grim declaration came from Yvoir, as dead as his previous words had been animated. Eliza had been caught up in the excitement, herself; seeing the French faerie's expression fall, she blurted out, "What?"

He directed his answer to Dead Rick instead of her, and shaped it as a question. "Did Nadrett send anyone far away, earlier this year? To Australia, perhaps, or the American frontier, or the far reaches of the Orient?"

The skriker stared at him. " 'Ow'd you know that? Sent a fellow to Japan, 'e did. Rewdan, the same one as brought 'im those compounds."

Yvoir nodded. "He must have done more than just acquire compounds. In studying the photographs from West Ham, I realised what Chrennois did to sensitise the plates. He exposed them during a lunar eclipse."

An impressive curse from Irrith told Eliza what the problem was, before the sprite put it into words. "And we broke most of his unused plates when we stormed the factory."

"When is the next eclipse?" Eliza asked.

In a place like this, no one had to reach for an almanac. Abd ar-Rashid said, "October fourth. And its totality will be over London."

Nearly a month away. No one asked the final question. *Will this place survive that long?*

Eliza startled again, as Dead Rick spun to face her, hands gripping her shoulders. "Eliza. You can give the Queen more time. Maybe enough."

"What? How?"

"Ghosts," he said, holding her gaze steadily. "Lord Galen ain't enough. But there's others, other Princes I mean, that don't 'aunt the palace, but they used to be bound to it. Call 'em back. As many as you can get. With their strength, Lune can 'old, I *know* she can. Long enough for the others to do their bit, to get the photos and set it all in motion. Then we can take what we've got and shape it into something new, something that don't care if there's iron in the ground, because it ain't *in* the ground no more. A new reflection of London. But we need time, and the ghosts can give us that."

Ghosts. Seven years ago, he'd discovered her untutored gift, and trained her to use it. *Started* to train her; Nadrett had put a stop to that before she mastered it, enough to make her living.

The changeling who had taken and then lost Louisa's place had said she knew a medium, a real one. Surely it would be better to seek that woman out—

And how long would it take to find her? To explain what this place was, and persuade her to help?

Eliza remembered the voice whispering through her head, from the black walls around the London Stone, and the phantom Queen who sat beneath it. Pouring every last drop of her strength into holding the palace together. How much longer could she endure?

"I don't know if I can do it," she whispered, for Dead Rick's ears only.

He gave her a fierce smile. "I know you can."

She heard what he really meant. *I know you have to.*

Memory: 29 May 1870

While men in top hats applauded and congratulated one another on a job well done, Alexander Messina died.

Lune had known the shock would come, and she had known it would be bad. They'd discussed it, long before the navvies broke ground for the extension of the Metropolitan Railway to Blackfriars Station. Iron pipes were dangerous enough; iron rails carrying iron trains, stabbing in and out of the Onyx Court's domain dozens of times a day would be a threat the likes of which they had not yet faced.

But they had survived the test train, run late at night to make certain the signals worked, and in the aftermath she allowed herself to believe they would have at least a brief period of grace. Time during which she and her Prince could find some way to adapt, as they had before.

When the inaugural train crossed the line of the wall, Alex's heart stopped.

For a few horrifying moments, she thought her own

would, too. The double shock of the train and the Prince's death crushed her to the floor, driving all the breath from her; she could barely hear the frantic cries from Amadea and Nemette, begging their Queen to answer them. By the time her vision returned, she knew what she needed to say; the instant she regained her voice, she said it. "Get Hodge. Now."

After centuries of joint rule, the death of Princes no longer caught her unprepared. She knew who would succeed each man when he passed on, and the men themselves knew it, too. Later they would mourn Alex as he deserved; later they would consider how long any mortal could survive the cataclysm that was the world's first underground railway.

In this instant, all that mattered was replacing the Prince. She could not bear the weight of the palace alone. Not anymore.

He came at a run. Little more than a boy; she couldn't remember how old he was, except to be shocked at the youth of his face. But Lune could not afford that reaction, and so she crushed it ruthlessly. Youth was necessary. Youth, and the strength it brought, and birth at the heart of London, which was why this cockney lad would be her next—perhaps final—Prince.

Benjamin Hodge knew perfectly well that the title carried a sentence of death. And still he came running, to lift her to her feet and help her stumble toward the London Stone, where she would bind him to what remained of the

Onyx Hall, a marriage until death did them part. His death, or the Hall's.

Not hers. She refused it. Lune would die when her realm did, but not before.

No ceremony, beyond the few steps that were absolutely necessary; the days of her court's glory were gone. It was only the two of them: she with the London Sword, chiefest of her crown jewels, Hodge swearing the oaths and drinking the faerie wine and laying his hand upon the London Stone, the heart of her—their—realm. Lune wept when she kissed him, and she could not have said the cause. The pain still reverberating through her body, perhaps. Or grief for Alex. Or for Hodge, and what she was doing to him, in the name of preserving her people's refuge for as long as she could.

He gripped her good hand hard enough to bruise, when they were done. "I'll find a way," he promised. He didn't need to say more. *I'll find a way to save the Hall.* They'd all promised it, and they'd all meant it.

"Go," Lune whispered softly, knowing her smile of thanks looked more like a rictus. "I . . . need a moment alone."

He did not question it. Later, he might—after he'd assimilated his new dignity as Prince—but for now, he obeyed her as any mortal in the Hall would. When he was gone, Lune drew in a long, shuddering breath, and looked at the London Stone.

It hung like a dagger from the ceiling of the chamber: the key to her entire realm. Though the Stone had moved from room to room, as the original was moved above, it remained at the center; wherever it lay *was* the center. Through the Stone, she had become Queen of the Onyx Court, and at times it felt like that block of battered limestone was her oldest and closest friend. It was eternal, after all, as her Princes were not.

She could not save Hodge—not without saving the Hall. If there was to be any chance of doing either, the Prince and those who supported him would need time.

Lune went into the outer room. After the Stone moved here, they had filled this chamber with rubbish, broken ends too useless for anyone to bother stealing. That, and the cathedral overhead, were the best defense they could muster for the Stone, short of a constant guard that would draw the very attention they sought to avoid. She rummaged through the debris, coating her cloth-of-silver skirts with dust, until she found a chair whose missing leg could be jammed back into place. This she carried into the inner room, and placed it beneath the Stone. When she settled herself carefully upon it, the chair held her weight.

With one swift move, she thrust the London Sword into the floor, to serve as her conduit and anchor point. Beneath her skirts, she kicked off her shoes, settling her bare feet against the black stone. Measuring out her breathing like the ticking of a slow clock, Lune closed her eyes, and sank her mind into the wounded body of the Hall.

Her realm. A part of her flesh, a part of her spirit, for nearly three hundred years. She had done all she could outside—in the chambers of the palace; in the world above—

but there remained one final thing she could do for Hodge.

She could *hold*.

Soundlessly, the black stone of the wall grew shut, sealing the way to the outer room. Darkness closed in about the London Stone, and the Queen of the Onyx Court.

THE LONDON STONE, ONYX HALL

16 September 1884

When Dead Rick took Eliza's hands in his own, he found her fingers ice cold. The smile she attempted showed equal parts embarrassment and tension. Quietly enough that only he could hear, she whispered, "What if I can't do it?"

An echo of her words in the Academy; she kept saying it, though fortunately never where anyone else could hear. Dead Rick squeezed her fingers. "You can. You ain't one of them fake ones; you've got the knack for it. And you're in the right place. They'll come, never fear."

If they could. Just because Galen St. Clair haunted the Hall after his death didn't mean the ghosts of the other Princes could be drawn back. But Eliza needed confidence as much as anything else, so he gave it to her, and was repaid in the strength of her grip. "You ready?" he asked, and biting her lip, she nodded.

They'd set a chair facing Lune's, a little distance from the London Stone. With the Queen insubstantial from the effort of holding her realm together, she had no hand for

Eliza to take; Hodge had offered, but in the end the mortal woman had refused. "I'd feel a fraud," she'd said, and Dead Rick understood why. His restored memories included a few recollections of spiritualist meetings; the theatrical ritual some mediums engaged in bordered on the ludicrous. Instead it was this: Lune in her trance, with Hodge at her left hand, and Eliza facing them in her chair.

She'd spent days preparing for this, listening to stories about the past Princes, those men who had ruled the Onyx Court alongside their immortal Queen. As many days as they dared: according to the railway newspapers, a test train would be travelling around the entirety of the Inner Circle tomorrow. The proper opening of the new stations was not planned until the beginning of October; Cyma was doing her best to persuade certain gentlemen the date should be *after* the eclipse. But if the Hall were to last until then, the Queen would need more strength.

The Irishwoman shifted on her seat, brushing sweat-lank strands of hair from her face. She took a breath, and then another, each one slower and deeper than the one before. Silence settled over the room like a blanket, her breathing the only sound.

Dead Rick clamped his arms across his ribs, and waited.

The moments passed, one by one. Hodge swayed, then steadied. *We should 'ave given 'im a chair, whether 'e wanted it or not.* Eliza's breathing had gone all but inaudible, though the scent of her sweat grew. The woman held her breath—then let it out explosively. "I can't do it."

He crossed to her before anyone else could move, kneeling and gripping her cold, shaking hands. "Yes, you can."

"I *can't*—"

"I'll 'elp you." Dead Rick tightened his grip. "Skriker, ain't I? I knows death. Look into my eyes, and I'll show you."

Just like they had done seven years before. They'd both traveled a long road to come back to where they started, and been changed by the journey. Not weakened—*no,* Dead Rick thought, *she's stronger than she ever was.* The Eliza of seven years ago could not have done this. But the one in front of him, he believed, could.

She sniffed back the wetness of tears and clutched his fingers painfully tight. Dead Rick stared up at her, not moving, not blinking, casting his thoughts upon death. Age, the rot of the body, impending calamity that cut the thread of life short. The final breath, rattling free of the chest. Eyes clouding over. Blood growing cold. And the soul, slipping free . . . had this been All Hallows' Eve, it would have been as easy as breathing, but they could not wait for that night to come. Instead he filled his mind with ages of such nights, reaching for the connection he felt then, the sense that one could pass across that boundary with only a blink.

Eliza's hands grew colder and colder, and her breathing stilled almost to nothing.

Barely moving his lips, Dead Rick whispered, "Call 'em."

In a voice so distant it might have arisen from some source less material than lungs and throat, Eliza began to recite the names of the Princes of the Stone.

"Michael Deven. Antony Ware. Jack Ellin. Joseph Winslow."

Through the stone beneath his knees, Dead Rick felt Lune reach out, echoing Eliza's call.

"Alan Fitzwarren. Hamilton Birch. Galen St. Clair. Matthew Abingdon."

Behind Eliza's left shoulder, a glimmer, taking familiar shape. Galen's ghost was certainly here.

"Robert Shaw. Geoffrey Franklin. Henry Brandon. Alexander Messina."

Names Dead Rick remembered. He'd been here almost since the beginning—not the earliest days of the Hall, but not long after Lune became Queen. Memories swirled through his head: faces, voices, the individual habits of each man who stood at Lune's side, for thirty years or three.

"Benjamin Hodge," Eliza whispered, and began the litany again.

A chill that had nothing to do with cold swept through the room. Dead Rick's vision blackened at the edges, as if he were holding his breath—but this was different; the blackness closing in was not any kind of blindness. He could still see through it, could see *more clearly,* the ghostly figure of Galen St. Clair whispering along with Eliza and Lune.

Hodge joined them; so did Dead Rick. The names echoed off the stone, again and again, a mesmerizing litany. The room grew colder still, and then the air began to thicken into shapes.

Alexander Messina came first, the most recently dead:

a dark man, showing his Italian ancestry, and dressed like a prosperous tradesman. Then the others, in irregular order: Colonel Robert Shaw, colour bleeding slowly into his red-coated uniform. Dr. Jack Ellin, mouth ready for its usual wry smile. Dr. Hamilton Birch, a man in his middle years, showing no sign of the unnatural age that had killed him. Sir Antony Ware, a solid and dependable presence. Matthew Abingdon and Joseph Winslow; Alan Fitzwarren and Henry Brandon and Geoffrey Franklin, bearded and clean-shaven, dressed in all the styles of centuries past.

Michael Deven came last of all, into the gap at Lune's right hand. A dark-haired Elizabethan gentleman, in doublet and hose, and Dead Rick felt the swell of unspeakable joy in Lune's heart, as the man she had loved three hundred years ago returned at last to her side.

Joy, and also the lifting of his hackles. Not at the ghosts, but at the *tension* shivering through the air. It was as if cords stretched from each dead man and the single living one to the London Stone, and those cords were drawn to their tightest. At the same time, the stone beneath his feet suddenly felt more *stonelike,* in a way he had forgotten—not the photographic loss of his memories, but simply the forgetfulness brought on by more recent experience. Not until now, when the solidity returned, did he realise how insubstantial the Onyx Hall had grown over the last century and more of decay.

The Princes had come to serve their realm one final time. With this strength behind her, Lune—and the palace—

would survive what was to come.

Dead Rick hoped.

"Eliza," he whispered, rising to a crouch. "It's done. Time to go."

She did not respond.

Alarmed, he repeated her name, more loudly, then reached out for her shoulder. But he paused before he could shake it, because fear gripped his heart: What if disturbing her caused the ghosts to vanish?

She spoke without warning, in a flat, distant voice, like a badly recorded phonograph cylinder. "I am the channel through which they pass. While I remain, so do they."

Meaning that if he woke her from this trance, they *would* vanish. *Blood and Bone.* He hadn't thought of that.

September sixteenth. Eighteen days until the eclipse. Could they risk letting the ghosts go after the test train was done? Dead Rick knew without asking anyone what the answer would be. Even if they knew for certain there would be only one test, and no other trains until the formal opening, the risk of collapse was too great.

In the world outside, such a duration would kill her. But this was a faerie realm, where time and the body did not behave as they otherwise might. With care, she might survive.

Might. Or might not.

Guilty horror ate away at Dead Rick's heart, like acid. *I should've warned 'er.* He should have *guessed*.

Then he wondered if Eliza had—and had chosen not to say anything.

She ought to bloody well hate us, he thought. She certainly had, when they came face-to-face in the library. She had hated *him*. But once she learned the truth—once she saw him restored—

Stupid whelp. You got what you wanted. Your friendship back, and now she might die 'elping you.

No. He wouldn't let that happen.

Gently, so as not to disturb her, the skriker bent his head until his brow touched hers, his hand upon the back of her neck. "I'll see you through this," he whispered.

Releasing her was one of the hardest things he'd ever done, but one thought made it possible. If she were to survive until the eclipse—her and Hodge both—they would need the Goodemeades' help.

THE LONDON STONE, ONYX HALL
4 October 1884

By they time the engineers were done, machinery filled the outer chamber almost to the ceiling. If they could have fit it into the room with Lune and the ghosts, they would have done; Niklas said it should be as close to the center point as possible. But the sprawling mass was far too large, and there was a risk of disrupting the ghosts besides.

Instead it trailed through the available space: calculating engine and loom, elemental generators filled with raw material and aetheric filters to process it, photographic machinery and all the secondary pieces that joined the whole together. A portion even extended into the chamber of the Stone, to draw on the link between Lune, the Princes, and the realm, and to capture the ideas of London in *their* heads. "After all," Lady Feidelm had said, "between themselves, they have three hundred years of the city's past; and that, too, is worth including."

It was the brainchild of Charles Babbage and Ada Lovelace, Joseph Marie Jacquard and the Galenic Academy of Faerie Sciences: the Ephemeral Engine. Nobody seemed to know who had coined the name, but they were all using it.

The last pieces were coming in now: photographic plates sensitised outside, where the Earth had cast the moon into shadow. Yvoir had babbled something about a morphetic configuration of the vitreous humour and lunar caustic coating the plates, and what followed that had been even less comprehensible, but Dead Rick understood the effect: they would not have to bear the plates around the city, or shove cameras into anyone's faces while asking them to reflect upon London. They had gathered tokens from select individuals, so that tonight the plates would receive impressions from their dreams, even at a distance; and once imprinted, would be added in to the calculations.

Wrain, standing by the calculating apparatus, said, "I am ready."

"As am I," said Ch'ien Mu, by the loom.

More confirmations, all around the chamber. Dead Rick took a deep breath, and went into the chamber of the Stone.

The ghosts still stood in a ring around the center chair, where Eliza sat unmoving. Despite being fed Rosamund and Gertrude's best fortifying mead, she was nearly as pale as a ghost herself; Dead Rick half feared his hand would go through her arm, that she, like Lune, had gone insubstantial. But she was a human, composed of matter as well as spirit, and her arm was solid—if ice cold.

Leaning to whisper in her ear, he said, "It's time."

There were mirrors around the room, to assist the Princes in focusing what they held upon Lune; from her it would transfer to the machinery, and so the process would begin. Wilhas von das Ticken waited by the first lever, ready to set everything in motion as soon as Dead Rick gave the signal.

He *felt* the pressure of it, the strain: twelve ghosts, one living man, and a faerie Queen struggling to shift the weight of the entire Onyx Hall. It wasn't a matter of the few chambers that remained; there was more to it than that, he sensed, though he did not understand how. Perhaps this was what the others meant, when they said it was impossible to make a new palace as the first one had been made; the burden was too great for ordinary souls to bear, be they mortal or fae, and the greater powers that had once helped were now gone.

What would they do, if the Queen and her Princes could not complete their task?

Dead Rick looked up to ask Wilhas that very question, and choked on it as he saw movement in the outer room. With a few swift strides, he moved to block the hole broken in the wall, so that no one could pass.

Only those needed to operate the machine were supposed to be present: Wrain, Ch'ien Mu, and the von das Tickens, and Dead Rick for Eliza's sake. But in came the Goodemeades—somewhat battered by their passage through the only remaining entrance—and between them, looking faintly ridiculous leaning on the two tiny brownies, Valentin Aspell.

With Irrith behind him, gun in hand as if she planned to shoot him should he so much as breathe wrong. "He insisted," the sprite said, in response to the stares.

Aspell's smile was twisted. He looked like death: gaunt and weak, and lucky to be alive. But alert enough to answer Dead Rick's question before the skriker could ask it. "After a hundred years of dreams in this place, I cannot let go of it easily. And when the Goodemeades told me what you intended, I knew you had overlooked something. I forgive the sisters forgetting, as they scarcely understand this contraption you have built; and Hodge, of course, has been dying for years. It does much to explain his intellectual deficiency. But tell your medium, she must call two more ghosts."

Dead Rick managed to tear his gaze away from Aspell long enough to glance at Hodge. The Prince showed no sign of hearing; the trance into which this communion had put him was too deep to be disturbed. The man who had barely risen from his bed to come here stood as steady as a rock—had stood thus for *days*. He might as well not have been flesh anymore. So it was the Goodemeades Dead Rick addressed when he asked, "What does 'e mean?"

"Suspiria and Francis Merriman," Rosamund said.

The names meant nothing to Dead Rick. Gertrude said, "They're the ones who made the palace. They had help, but they were the heart of it—Suspiria was the Hall's first Queen. Aspell said, and Hodge agreed, that they're still here. In the London Stone. Now Aspell insists you need them."

By the way she said it, she agreed with him, however reluctantly. But Eliza had already maintained the connection for days, holding twelve ghosts at once; it was a feat of endurance that made Dead Rick shudder to think of it, and now Aspell wanted her to call two more. If she tried, she might lose the lot.

If she didn't try, then the Ephemeral Engine was useless.

But at least that wouldn't put 'er in danger.

He wished now they *had* brought in the medium Cyma spoke of, or one of the ones Mr. Myers suggested. It might have been possible for them to share the burden, though he'd never seen it tried. But all they had was Eliza, and no second chance: if this failed, he doubted they would be able to try again.

"Iron burn your soul, Aspell," Dead Rick growled, and went to kneel once more in front of his friend.

In a voice meant only for her ears, he said, "Eliza. I've got one more thing to ask of you—but it's *your choice,* you 'ear me? If you don't think you can do it—if you think it's too dangerous—then don't try. We'll find another way. I don't want you getting killed for this."

No answer. Of course not; he hadn't yet told her what

they needed. He just hoped that was it, and not Eliza being unable to answer.

The words dragged out of him. "We needs two more spirits. They ain't far; they're in the Stone. Can—can you sense 'em? Do you think you could call 'em? Would that be something you could do?"

He waited, not breathing, for Eliza's response. Some kind of nod or shudder; something to say yes or no, that she could try it or could not. He couldn't bring himself to *look,* to see if her death hovered near. If it did . . . he could not guess what he would do.

Then Eliza spoke. Two names she could not have overheard, two names she could only have gotten through her gift: either from the ghosts around her, or from those she now called. "Suspiria. Francis Merriman."

The London Stone rang like a bell.

Two last figures flared into view, behind Eliza's chair. A slender man, black hair falling loose around his sapphire-blue eyes, and a faerie woman, tall and regal, Lune's dark shadow.

Two spirits, bound within the Stone for more than three hundred years.

A perfect ring, surrounding Dead Rick and Eliza. Fourteen men, and the two Queens they'd served. Among them, they held everything the Onyx Hall had ever been, from the moment when Suspiria and Francis Merriman called London's shadow forth from the sun's eclipse until these final, fragmented days.

Held it ready for the machine.

Dead Rick could scarcely breathe for the power choking the air. It poured out of them all: the ghosts, and the fae, and himself; and Eliza most of all, holding them by force of will, here in the living world where they did not belong, and *Blood and Bone she's going to fucking kill 'erself—*

He couldn't draw enough air to shout the cue. But through the pulse thundering in his ears, Dead Rick heard someone say, "Do it."

A flash of light, a rattle and a metallic *clank*—and the Ephemeral Engine shuddered into motion.

The world blinked. Not darkness, but a fleeting eclipse of reality: a shutter snapping open and closed. The first stage of the machine captured the Onyx Hall itself, held in the Princes' heads, in the memories of its Queens, and translated it into the language necessary for the calculating apparatus.

In another part of the Engine, other images of London took shape. Photographic plates, sensitive to the evanescent touch of dreams, caught images out of the minds of Londoners: high and low, young and old, English and immigrant alike. Light streamed through, here stopped by the shape of the image within, there permitted through, rendered from one kind of abstraction to another.

Then the calculation began, metal wheels and crystal gears and rods and levers clicking smoothly into action. Poor subtracted from rich, East End multiplied against West, all the interactions and operations that made up the intricate and ever-changing reality of London. New plates slotted into position, received the imprint of intermediate concepts, slid aside until they were needed once more. Again and again the machine elaborated upon its calculations, first-order answers becoming variables for the second round, second for the third, third for the fourth, until it seemed there would never be an end—

But in time the machine ground out a plate, larger than those used within its confines, and this slid along a chain until it clanked into place alongside the elemental generators.

There was not enough material within them to create an entire palace large enough to shelter the fae who called London home. But if the Engine worked—if it created a structure that could withstand the strains of the world in which it stood—in time, that could be the starting point for more.

Earth and air, fire and water. The arms of the loom began to move, first a rattle, then a thunder, heddles rising and falling to change the warp, a shuttle of ectoplasmic aether flying back and forth, and on the far side of the mechanism, an image began to grow.

Dead Rick *felt* it, like the touch of Faerie itself. A power beyond any he'd known in this world—but no, it wasn't that distant realm; it was something else, born of the union between mortal ingenuity and faerie enchantment. What they sent through the Engine was not a series of cold numbers, abstracted from their meaning, but rather thoughts, dreams, beliefs, everything that London meant to those who dwelt within its reach. And the Engine, animated by such power, became more than mere metal and glass.

Dreams flooded in, faster and faster. Like wildfire, the thought of London spread from those early dreamers to inflame the minds around them. First the sleepers where they lay in their beds; then those who kept wakeful watch in these late hours of the night. A maid in Camden Town, sitting red-eyed over her mistress's pelisse, mending it for the morrow. A Lambeth solicitor, reading through the documents of a case, in search of anything that might spare his client from prison. An omnibus conductor, trudging on aching feet home to his flat in Battersea, beneath the light of the eclipsed moon. One by one, then by the hundreds, they found their thoughts turning to the city in which they dwelt, and those thoughts, high and low alike, took shape on glass in what remained of the Onyx Hall.

Which began to unravel.

The generators had run dry, but the Engine did not stop; it drew in the substance of the palace around it. Rumbling filled the air, ominous and low beneath the noise of the machine. Dead Rick clutched at Eliza's chair, terrified of disturbing her—but all at once fear overwhelmed that consideration and he seized her hands. His vision blurred, swam, reality falling apart around him. The palace was going; they had to get out!

But there was no escaping this final collapse. What door would they pass through, what floor would they walk upon? They hung in a shuddering maelstrom, everything breaking apart, the only solid thing their hands joined together in a desperate clasp. Something was growing, in the distance, right next to them, a radiant weave too bright to look upon, and they teetered upon its brink, an instant from falling.

The weave exploded.

Images, sounds, scents, textures; all burst outward in an unstoppable flood as time opened up. Five different cathedrals to St. Paul, spired and domed, in wood and in stone. Three Royal Exchanges. Whitehall Palace, vanishing in fire; docks growing like man-made lakes in the Isle of Dogs. A wall along the river's north bank, open wharves, a walkway of stone. Buildings rose and fell and rose again, some too tall to believe, while sewers threaded through the ground below. The clop of horses' hooves, the rattle of carriage wheels, the thunder of trains—and even stranger sounds, that had not been heard in London yet: music from no visible source, and a low growling in the air, as shapes like coaches without horses flooded the streets.

Men in doublets, top hats, Roman armour; women in crinolines and farthingales and glittering dresses that scarcely covered anything at all. Indians. Germans. Chinese. Iceni. People who dwelt there thousands of years before the Onyx Hall ever was; people who would dwell there in centuries to come. The flood kept going, into the past, into the future, everything the city had been, everything it could be—for Francis Merriman had been a seer, and through him, they saw it all.

London.

* * *

The weave flung itself outward, sweeping through the City of London, Westminster, Southwark, Whitechapel, and beyond. Every hair on Dead Rick's body stood on end. He *had* a body; gravity had returned, and so had air, and the proper spaces between things. He wasn't in every London at once, all the centuries interlaced; he was in a room, clutching Eliza, and the simultaneous pressure and tension that had threatened to destroy him were gone.

Nearby, the Ephemeral Engine clattered away, tireless and steady.

Movement in his arms. Warmth, too, and when he drew back enough to see, Eliza's eyes were open and alert. She had survived.

And so, he realised, had he.

Dead Rick sagged to the floor, exhausted beyond the telling of it. The tiles were cool against his cheek, and he might have stayed there forever; but Eliza, damn her, had actual energy, though Mab knew where she'd gotten it. She tugged at his arm. "Dead Rick—come and see."

With great effort, he braced his other hand against the stone— *Stone? Weren't it tiles, a moment ago?*—and pushed himself to his feet.

The room kept shifting. It wasn't just his imagination; every time his attention drifted, something changed, and if he tried to follow it his brain might melt. Dead Rick kept his eyes on Eliza, on her hand in his, and followed her through the gap in the wall to where the bulk of the Ephemeral Engine stood.

The gears still turned, the rods still rose and fell; on the far side of the weaving apparatus, something still shimmered. People circled the Engine, whispering quietly; the Goodemeades were hugging one another and sniffling. Irrith stood a few steps away, staring unblinking at the machine. "Shouldn't—shouldn't it be stopping now?"

Wilhas laughed, a sound of mixed astonishment and glee. Wrain licked his lips and said, "It—may never stop."

"But if it keeps weaving—" Eliza said.

The palace was growing still. Dead Rick could feel it, if he concentrated. He imagined it expanding, farther and farther, until it covered not only London but England, Europe, the *world* . . .

Wrain said, "It has to keep going. I think. This place . . . doesn't *resist* the world outside. Not like the old one did. It will break down; rooms will fade and go away. But the Engine will gather their substance back in and weave them anew. It hasn't *made* a palace—well, it has—what I mean is, it *is making* a palace, and will go on doing so. For as long as it needs to. That's how it will last."

So it wouldn't cover the world. Dead Rick suspected its boundaries would be those of London: the farther one got from areas that could truly be considered part of the city, the weaker the Engine's power would be, and the faster it would fray. If the city grew more, though—

It *would* grow more. He'd seen it, through Francis Merriman's eyes.

The thought brought Dead Rick around in a sudden whirl, to stare into the room he and Eliza had left behind.

Benjamin Hodge lay on the floor, curled fetal on his side. Eliza cried out and ran toward him; Dead Rick opened his mouth, but she saw the truth for herself soon enough. Hodge stirred as she touched his shoulder, and opened weary eyes.

"She's gone," Hodge said.

The room around him was empty. The ghosts had dissipated, Galen St. Clair and all the rest, Francis, Suspiria.

Lune.

Her chair remained, a battered thing beneath the London Stone, and a crack piercing the floor where Sword had been, with a pair of embroidered silver shoes between. These alone marked the Queen's fourteen-year battle to preserve her realm, and the three hundred years of her reign.

Dead Rick knew a few things about death. The scholars of the Academy said faerie souls and faerie bodies were not separate things, that the latter was the former made solid. When most fae died, their souls were destroyed; there was no afterlife for them, whether Heaven or Hell, and their bodies soon crumbled to nothing.

Soon, but not immediately. Sometimes, though, when a faerie died, she vanished on the spot. And then, they said, it meant her spirit had moved on, going to somewhere beyond anyone's ken.

Suspiria had gone into the London Stone, following the bond placed there when the Onyx Hall was created. Where Lune had gone, now that she was free of both body and Hall, Dead Rick could only guess—Faerie, perhaps—but wherever it was, he suspected Michael Deven was there with her. Lune's love, and the first Prince of the Stone. They, and their predecessors, had moved on at last.

Dead Rick joined Eliza, and between them they got Hodge on his feet. The man was still old before his time, still exhausted; his years holding the palace together had taken things from him that could never be restored. But he was alive, and while the Onyx Hall was gone, something new had taken its place. Lune's last Prince had served her, and her realm, very well.

The von das Tickens stayed to watch over the Engine, already conducting an argument in German that sounded more excited than angry. The rest of them, those dedicated few who had witnessed the rebirth, went out through a portal that shifted from wooden beams to brass arch to cleanly carved stone, to explore the new faerie realm of London.

THE ANGEL, ISLINGTON

6 October 1884

Benjamin Hodge did not look like a man who should be out of his sickbed. "I would have been happy to come to you below," Frederic Myers said, as one of the coaching inn's young maidservants set hot meat pies on the table before them.

Hodge waited until she was gone, then shook his head with a weary grin. "I spent fourteen years 'ardly daring to come up 'ere, for fear the place would fall apart as soon as I turned my back. And believe me, it ain't good for one of us to stay down there so long. It's a breath of fresh air, being outside."

The way he attacked the meat pie said the journey had taken a good deal out of him, whatever he claimed. Myers said, "I will endeavour not to tax you too much. Indeed, I would not have written to you at all, except that I have a rather pressing matter which I believe must be laid before you, as Prince of the Stone."

"'Old on," Hodge said through a mouthful of crust and gravy. Myers paused while he washed it down with a swallow of stout. "I ain't Prince no more."

Given the man's exhaustion and ill health, it wasn't surprising. "Who is?"

Hodge sucked a bit of meat out of his teeth and said, "There ain't one." Another swig of beer, and a rueful smile. "What we did with the palace . . . I don't know if it's the machine, or all the people's ideas we poured into that thing, but it don't 'ave a Prince no more, nor a Queen neither. So ask what you want, and I'll tell you what I think—but it'll be just one man's notion."

The revelation unsettled Myers, less for the change in

faerie society than for the loss of an authoritative voice to tell him yea or nay. This was the sort of question that ought to be answered by someone official—but it was also a question that could not be left until later, after the fae had decided how they would proceed.

He might as well ask Hodge. "Very well. I believe you are aware of the London Fairy Society, and the Goodemeades' plan for it?" Hodge nodded. "They had, of course, assumed the city would be mostly deserted of fae, with the remaining few largely scattered, and that announcing their presence to the general populace would therefore create trouble only for themselves and their associates. Given your recent miracle, however . . ."

"It ain't so simple," Hodge finished. "More than you know, guv. You got any notion what's 'appened, with the new palace?" Myers shook his head. Apprehension meant he was making but slow progress on his own pie, though Hodge managed to gulp down healthy bites during pauses. "Anchored it to the *idea* of London, didn't they? Now it's everywhere. Next to London. All around it. Inside it. Step to the left, and you're there. So says Abd ar-Rashid, anyway, and 'e's the sort of cove to trust on this."

Myers's appetite vanished entirely, though whether it was from fear or excitement, he couldn't have said. "And with the dreams so many had that night . . ."

"Won't be long before they starts puzzling it out," Hodge said. "Ain't 'ad nobody wander in yet, but it's only a matter of time. Not to mention there's 'alf a dozen constables as saw some bloody peculiar things in West Ham not long ago, and no telling 'ow long they'll stay quiet."

"In that case," Myers said, "I hope it is not too presumptuous of me to suggest that the Goodemeades and the London Fairy Society should proceed with their plan? Suitably modified, of course, for the circumstances—but I had thought to present some introductory information to the Society for Psychical Research, who would take a very great interest in this matter. I—I cannot promise the results will be entirely positive—"

Hodge waved it away with gravy-stained fingers. "Ain't going to be, and we knows it. More like bleeding chaos. But it was that or leave, so . . ." He shrugged. "Them as doesn't like it can live quiet somewhere else, or push off to Faerie. Same as they would 'ave done anyway."

It wasn't quite that simple, of course; as soon as it became public knowledge there were faeries in London, curiosity seekers would be poking under every hedgerow and hill in England. Likely elsewhere, too. Myers imagined there would be no little resentment of London's fae for that. But for better or for worse, that was the consequence of their decision, and refusing to face it would not improve anything.

"I will consult with the rest of the Society, then—the London Fairy Society," he clarified. "And, of course, take suggestions as to how you, or rather they, wish to make their debut. But it should be done swiftly."

Hodge nodded and drank down the last of his beer. "I'll 'elp as much as I can."

Myers dropped a shilling onto the table and rose, intending to begin work immediately—he had taken a room in a hotel nearby—but hesitated. "If I may ask one other question?"

The former Prince gestured for him to go on.

"During the meeting where the notion for the Ephemeral Engine was drafted, I believe I saw a young lady of my . . . acquaintance." The word stuck in his throat. Myers had not gone home to Cambridge since that inexplicable day in Paddington Station, when Louisa Kittering vanished from not two feet away. Confused and shattered, he had clung to what sent him on that disastrous journey to London in the first place: the notebook, with its record of ideas he did not remember. That led him back to the Goodemeades, and to the meeting down below, and somewhere in between the two, his feelings for the young woman had vanished as completely as the young woman herself. And with as little explanation.

Into the pause, Hodge suggested, "Eliza O'Malley?"

"What?" Myers said, startled. *Ah, yes—the Irishwoman. Though I thought her English, when I saw her in Mrs. Chase's house.* "No, Miss Louisa Kittering. She was sitting with a faerie woman—"

"I know the one you mean. And I'd wager it's the faerie woman you actually need. I'm done 'ere," Hodge said, rising from his seat like a old gaffer with aching joints. "I'll show you where she is."

* * *

OAKLEY STREET, CHELSEA
6 October 1884

Had Cyma felt a whit less pity for Hodge, broken and scarred as he was by his long ordeal as Prince, she would have thrown her shoe at him for bringing Frederic Myers to see her.

She had successfully avoided him in the Academy, hurrying Louisa Kittering away before the man could escape his fellow scholars and come after the girl. But while Hodge had lost his authority, he hadn't lost the habit of paying attention to what went on around him; he knew about her brief tenure as a changeling, and would not let her escape its consequences so easily. He ran her to ground in Chelsea, where she and Louisa had taken refuge with Lady Wilde, and then he left her and Myers alone.

She felt awkward in ways she never would have believed possible. Though her changeling face had gone, the memories stayed, of caring so intensely what he thought of her. Of *loving* him.

Only the memory of that love, though. Not the passion itself. Cyma's heart was her own—and so was the choice to withhold it.

"I don't understand," Frederic Myers said, his sad eyes clouded with pain and confusion; and because she remembered caring for him, but did not crave his love anymore, Cyma told him the truth.

All of it, from Nadrett onward. Haunting him as Annie

Marshall, keeping his grief alive. Surrendering him to the Goblin Market master, to be used, broken, and discarded. Encountering him once more at the London Fairy Society, where she had gone to seek out someone who might be persuadable to a changeling trade; taking the place of Louisa Kittering, and only then finding that what had been mere faerie infatuation, a fascination with his imagination and his grief, bloomed without warning into an obsession.

Through it all, she could not help but absorb every detail of his reactions: the incredulity, surprise, anger, and hurt. It was a relief, to be able to enjoy that rise and fall, without having her own emotions shackled to his.

"You are a monster," Frederic Myers whispered, when she brought the story to its close.

Cyma shrugged gracefully. "Undoubtedly I seem so to you. I am a faerie, sir; I am not human." For all the sympathy she once thought she had for them—perhaps it would be better to say *interest in them*—in the wake of her changeling experiences, she was glad to be herself again.

"To the best of my knowledge," he said with biting precision, "a faerie nature does not require one to be heartless. You have my forgiveness for those actions you took while under the fist of your former master—but what, pray tell, justifies your deeds since then? Charming me into an affection I did not naturally feel, and estranging me from my wife? The most infamous trull, ma'am, would shame to use your methods."

She would not have them to use. But Cyma did not

want to deal with the fury that might result if she said it, so instead she told him, "I did not know how else to respond. The panic I felt at the thought of not having you made any method seem reasonable, so long as it produced results."

Myers stared at her, then released his held breath in a sound that was half sob, half laugh. "You are not a monster. You are a child, stubbing her toe for the first time, and weeping that she cannot walk for the pain. Heaven preserve us against your innocence; it runs a bare second to your malice for cruelty."

Something in his tone made uneasiness stir in the depths of Cyma's mind. Myers turned to go, and she would have been happy to let him; but concern made her say, "One moment. My understanding is that you were to help the Goodemeades with their plans. Will you now refuse? Because of what I did to you?"

He halted, and his stooped shoulders had a beaten angle to them she remembered from their earliest encounters, when the grief over Annie Marshall was fresh upon him. But then Frederic Myers straightened. Without turning to face her, he said, "No. Though your people are fortunate indeed that I made the acquaintance of those sisters, before I learned of your perfidy. They alone persuade me that it is possible for faeries to be kind."

Satisfied with that answer, Cyma let him go, and went back to the task of reestablishing her life.

* * *

THE UNDERGROUND, CITY OF LONDON
6 October 1884

Eliza insisted on riding the train. Never mind that the new stretch of track opened with hardly any fanfare, compared to years past; it was commonplace now, the extension of the Underground, though most of its growth was to the west. To most Londoners, this addition meant little, except that gentlemen in their top hats were saved a minute's walk from the slightly more distant Mansion House Station. Now they could alight at Cannon Street, or Eastcheap, or Mark Lane.

Dead Rick resisted coming with her—more, Eliza thought, out of superstitious dread than any real danger. Iron still had power to harm him, though the bread she tithed kept it at bay; he would never be happy in the cold body of a train carriage. In some ways, she couldn't blame him: the noise and clammy foulness of the air meant the journey would never be pleasant, not until the railway companies made good on their promises of smokeless, steam-free engines.

They would, someday. She had seen glimpses of it, in that moment when the enchantment burst outward. Gleaming trains capable of terrifying speed, clean as the promises made twenty years ago, when the Underground first opened.

Faerie gold bought them a place in a first-class compartment at Blackfriars, and Dead Rick glared away anyone who tried to join them. Alone on the padded seats, with the gaslight flickering overhead, they passed from

Blackfriars through the underbelly of London.

Hands cupped against the window, Eliza peered into the darkness. "So we aren't going through the palace anymore?"

"You never was," Dead Rick said. He didn't look out, but closed his eyes and drew in a slow breath, as if tasting the air for something. "I mean, you sort of was. Two things in the same space, mostly not touching."

"And now?"

He grimaced in a way she recognised; his mouth took on that twist every time he had to deal with the scholars' theories. His thin lips had softened, though, from their hard set of before. "Sort of yes, sort of no, but in a different way. The palace is all over London now, not just in the ground. But 'ere, too. Blood and Bone, don't ask me to explain it. You just 'step sideways,' is all."

It was as good a phrase as any for what had proved to be their first challenge: getting *out* of the palace. The old entrances were gone, lost alongside every other physical landmark except the London Stone, and after some amount of fruitless effort Dead Rick had finally turned to her and said, "You're the mortal; *you* puzzle it out." She'd almost called on God, just to see what would happen. But she was nervous of disrupting the Ephemeral Engine's work, and so in the end she took his hand and concentrated, thinking about the world she knew. They walked forward—but yes, sort of *sideways,* too—and then they were on Whitechapel Road, a stone's throw from where the Darraghs lived. There was a possibility that going from faerie to mortal

London would always require the assistance of a mortal, and a faerie for the reverse, but no one yet knew for sure.

Mansion House rattled off behind them; soon they were slowing into Cannon Street. Somewhere just above their heads, the London Stone sat in the wall of St. Swithin's. Its reflection was the one thing that persisted below—that, and the Engine itself—but it wasn't the heart of the palace anymore, not like it had been before. Dead Rick glared away another gentleman who otherwise could have joined them, and when he was gone, Eliza asked, "Who is staying?"

The skriker shrugged, putting his bare feet up on one of the leather-padded seats. "Not sure. A lot of them foreigners is still around, from the Academy and the Market; they ain't bothered by the same things as us, iron and such, so they just cleared out while everything was crashing around our ears, and will come back now it's safe." He snorted. "It'll be a cross between the East End and the Royal Society down there."

Eliza pressed her lips together. "Just so long there's order. Ye may not have a Queen anymore, but *somebody* needs to make sure ye don't get another like Nadrett." She gave Dead Rick a sidelong grin. "Or I'll sick the constables on ye again."

Eastcheap Station, close by the Monument to the Great Fire of London; once the fae had captured lost time and placed it in a room beneath that column, to help them combat the threats against their home. Such grand deeds they had done, and so few of them known to the people above. She still marveled at it.

"Want to 'ear something mad?" Dead Rick asked.

Eliza laughed. "Always."

"Niklas thinks 'e can figure out a way to make this"—the skriker rapped the side of the carriage with his knuckles—"drive the Engine."

She stared at him, thinking she must have heard wrong. "The *train*? But—what about the iron?"

"You asking *me* to explain it? 'E said it 'ad something to do with magnets. All this iron circling around generates power, or some such. Damned if I understand it. But then we wouldn't 'ave to worry about keeping the thing going."

They certainly needed *some* source of power. As Wrain had predicted, the Engine was still clanking away, weaving more and more of the faerie palace. The growth had slowed, and aside from the immediate vicinity of the Engine—where things still changed every time one blinked—the result appeared stable, but if it was to go on functioning, it would need fuel. And no one had any intention of letting it stop.

The train drew into Mark Lane. Eliza and Dead Rick alighted there, for the nearby Tower of London Station had been closed when the new track opened. "You going back to Whitechapel?" Dead Rick asked.

Habit made Eliza draw her shawl around herself, as if to hide again. "I . . . don't know." She hadn't yet. Whitechapel was complicated; Quinn might not be hunting her anymore, but there was still Maggie Darragh to consider, and Fergus Boyle, and Owen. None of those were matters that could be dealt with in the space of a few days.

Including her own self. The work of seven years had ended; now what would she do? Find factory work, as Tom Granger had suggested all those months ago? Go into service with some other rich family, and hope they were better than the Kitterings? Perhaps Mrs. Chase needed another maid. The expansion of the palace had swept the Goodemeades' home into itself without faltering, so Eliza would be able to step through into Rose House any time she liked.

A gust of wind gave her a better reason to wrap her shawl close. The day was a chill one, and gloomy enough that gaslights still burned in many places, although it was early afternoon. A reminder that, whatever she did, it had better pay well enough to buy a warmer shawl. Winter was coming on.

Dead Rick, bare-armed in the cold air, noticed her discomfort. "If you'd like—" he said, then stopped.

They'd never truly had the conversation, the one where they settled all the pain and questions between them. Looking at him, Eliza realised she no longer needed it. Somehow, in the course of healing Owen and hunting Nadrett, calling ghosts and creating the new palace, they'd found a new balance of friendship. And she was comfortable with that.

He caught her smile, grinned, and kicked a broken cobblestone with one dirty foot. "You *is* a real medium, after all. And there's that Myers fellow, as studies ghosts. You probably don't need *my* 'elp no more, but . . ."

"I'd be glad to have it, I would," Eliza said quietly. As they had planned, seven years ago. She might not make a fortune, might never tour Scotland and France and the United States—but she could make enough to live on, and even to help the Darraghs. For now, that would more than do.

"Right then," Dead Rick said, a bit too loudly; that last crossing of the breach had made him awkward. "And any time you want to come on below—inside, I mean—Ash and Thorn, 'owever I'm supposed to say it—you just let me know. We'll always 'ave a place for you."

THE NEW PALACE, LONDON
31 October 1884

They could not call it the Onyx Hall anymore. The name had suited the old palace, with its halls and chambers of gleaming black stone, but the new one showed too much variety to be captured with so simple a description. Some rooms were like rustic cottages, black-tarred timbers between whitewashed walls; others were bare stone, or papered with William Morris designs. As before, some of it echoed what lay above—or outside, or whatever the term should be—while some was pure faerie invention.

They gathered in a place clearly born from the memory of the Great Exhibition, thirty years before: a green, tree-studded space not unlike Hyde Park, dominated by an edifice of silver and glass, a recollection of the Crystal

Palace even more wondrous than the original. Sunlight shone down through the panes, warming and brightening the grass-carpeted area inside. The Galenic Academy was already making noises about claiming the place as their own, a Presentation Hall grander than the one they had lost.

Outside, it was nearly night. In a few hours London's remaining goblins would go outside, to see what ghosts needed sweeping away this All Hallows' Eve. Ch'ien Mu, after examining the Ephemeral Engine, had concluded that it was gathering stray wisps of aether from the mortals of London, probably through their dreams; what effect that would have on the population of ghosts, no one knew. It didn't really matter. Right now, all Dead Rick wanted was the tradition, the sense that he was upholding his duties as a skriker, after being misused by Nadrett for so long.

Before then, a gathering of faerie London. The Goodemeades had been emphatic that it wasn't a formal, organised event; there had been talk of organizing some sort of Parliament, or at least a council, to govern the fae now that no royal authority held sway, but no decision had been reached as yet. This was simply a gathering, and a chance for everyone to hear of the changes taking place outside.

As Dead Rick had predicted, many foreigners were there: Abd ar-Rashid, and Ch'ien Mu, and that monkey fellow Kutuhal; Feidelm and Yvoir and the von das Tickens; Po from the Goblin Market, with Lacca at his side, and a faun Dead Rick now remembered as Il Veloce. Others from his memories, and strangers he did not know. Mortals, too;

not just Eliza and Hodge and various Academy fellows, but that girl Louisa Kittering, dressed in a *japonnais* gown that suggested she had used her faerie-granted freedom to run off and join the aesthetic set. She had come in with Cyma and an elderly woman Mrs. Chase had introduced as Lady Jane Wilde, but now was deep in conversation with a fellow who looked like the lady's son.

Irrith appeared at his elbow. As Dead Rick lagged a sleeve for her to tug on, she pinched a bit of the hair on his forearm instead. "Ow!" he said, and glared at her. "I'm right 'ere, you know. You could just say 'ello."

"Actually, what I came to say is, Gertrude's gone mad."

He looked across the gleaming expanse of the room to where Gertrude stood, in animated argument with her own sister. "I think they was always a bit cracked."

"*Extra* mad, then," Irrith said. "Come on; you have to help me convince her—"

What precisely he was supposed to convince Gertrude of, Dead Rick didn't know, but he followed before Irrith could decide to drag him by some sensitive bit of anatomy. As he drew near, Gertrude caught sight of him and brightened. "You can tell her! Didn't you take Miss Eliza to a meeting of the Society for Psychical Research? And wasn't it perfectly unobjectionable?"

"He didn't 'take' me, and it wasn't a meeting." Eliza rejoined him, having freed herself from a pair of revolutionary-minded fae, Eidhnin and Scéinach, who wanted only to talk of Irish nationalism. "I sat down with Mr. Myers and the Sidgwicks and a few others, with Dead Rick there, and we talked about ghosts. It went well enough, I suppose."

"And did they know you were a faerie?" Rosamund asked Dead Rick, hands braced on her hips.

Suspecting where this was going, he said, "They did, but—"

"You see?" Gertrude demanded, before he could say anything more. "So it's perfectly safe for us to attend a meeting."

She was a damned sight braver than Dead Rick, if she was willing to stake herself—and apparently her sister—out as targets for those insatiably curious bastards. If anyone could talk the Goodemeades to death, it would be the Society for Psychical Research. Myers's presentation to them had ignited even more curiosity than the man predicted; their reports and editorials in various newspapers were currently doing battle with sensational stories from a few constables and a pub keeper in Billingsgate who swore his cellar had once been invaded by faeries. Before Dead Rick could think of what to tell Gertrude, though, his nose caught a new scent on the air.

A little girl, no more than ten years of age, with the lollipop in her hand hovering forgotten, tangled in the ribbons of her bonnet. A pretty little thing, her hair in careful ringlets; she was obviously born to a pampered life, and wandered the grass with her eyes so wide, it seemed only the upward tilt of her head kept them from falling out.

The reactions were comical. Everywhere people fell

silent, fae and mortal alike, drawing back warily if the girl wandered so much as a single step in their direction.

Irrith whispered, "Ash and Thorn. Where did *she* come from?"

It was clear that nobody there knew her. Which meant nobody there had brought her in. Dead Rick licked his lips and said in a whisper, "My guess would be Hyde Park, or else Sydenham." Where they'd moved the original Crystal Palace, after the Great Exhibition ended. Or it could be somewhere else entirely; they were still sorting out what rules governed entry into this place.

But now they had evidence that people—at least one small, beribboned, female person—could enter unannounced.

The girl's gaze swung toward where Dead Rick stood, with Irrith and Eliza and the Goodemeades. Before it reached them, instinct made him shift shape; however disreputable a dog he might make, it was better than his appearance as a man. Unfortunately, this proved to be a miscalculation.

"Doggie!"

He rolled his eyes upward, hoping for rescue, but found the Goodemeades urging him toward the girl, Eliza failing to smother a smile, and Irrith grinning ear to ear. Then the girl was upon him. Dead Rick bolted, for all the good it did him; that, of course, made this a chase, and chasing was even *more* exciting.

It was ridiculous, undignified . . . and *fun*. He could have escaped by fleeing into the rest of the palace—leaving behind the unrepentant laughter of his so-called friends—

but Dead Rick found he did not want to. So long as he stayed clear of sticky hands that would undoubtedly try to pull his tail, it was pleasant to run across the soft grass. Not to hunt—not out of fear—just to run, and to trip up his friends, Eliza cursing him cheerfully in Irish, and Dead Rick grinning a canine grin, his tongue lolling out as he went.

Let others plan for the future. At this moment, beneath the bright, glittering expanse of enchantment and glass, Dead Rick was content.

EPILOGUE

BURLINGTON HOUSE, PICCADILLY

2 September 1899

"... and to those who say, we have charted all the configurations there may be; there are no more to uncover, and it remains now only to refine the applications of those already known—to those people, I say, *nonsense*. We stand upon the brink of a new century, and I feel—I *know*—that it will not be the end of discovery, an age wherein the best to which we can aspire is to perfect the knowledge already within our grasp. There are new mountains we have not climbed, and the vistas that we shall see from their peaks can scarcely be imagined, even by those with the rare gift to part the veil of time and catch glimpses of what is to come. I exhort all curious minds, whatever their origin, not to rest complacently upon the laurels of those who have gone before, but to seek out those new discoveries, and to share them with others, that all may partake of the knowledge that is our most precious wealth."

Master Wrain had much improved as a speaker, Lord

Lister thought, as he rose with the others to applaud. The sprite had delivered the first Galenic Visiting Lecture on Faerie Science, more than a decade before, and only the novelty of the subject matter—not to mention the lecturer himself—had kept his audience's attention. No, he most certainly had improved; that, or someone else was writing his speeches nowadays.

Fifteen years had dulled that novelty somewhat. Back then, people had flocked to any event that offered them a chance to see a faerie, and protestors had thronged the streets outside. Lord Lister would not call the matter settled even now, but a scientific lecture no longer attracted disproportionate attention, and Inspector Quinn didn't have to send constables to keep the peace. He was glad for the return to ordinary business—relatively speaking.

The President of the Royal Society made his way to the front of the room, to shake Master Wrain's hand and pose for a picture. Eveleen Myers promised she had a better technique than before, something that would balance the demands of mortal and faerie photography. Her husband was there to test it; Lord Lister only hoped his skill with a camera had improved as much as Wrain's speeches.

It was still a bit questionable, he thought, having scholars from the Galenic Academy and the Society for Psychical Research both come speak before the Royal Society. What they did was not exactly *science,* not so far as Lister was concerned. It was neither physical nor biological in nature, and it had a sort of inconsistency—a *mysticism*—that did not fit in here. But the London Fairy Society urged the connection; and after all, the Academy had made something from that deranged engine Charles Babbage had bothered Lister's predecessors about, the one Babbage himself had never built. Some of the gentlemen here were quite excited about further developments in that vein. It did no harm to let the fae come speak.

And there were certain matters best addressed through cooperation. After Wrain had finished answering questions—a great many questions—and the last stragglers had gone on their way, Lister said, "If you can spare a moment before you leave, I should like to talk to you about medical matters. There is something of an epidemic building in London, if I may use that word for something that is not a disease; and I am quite concerned to address it before the matter grows any worse."

Wrain did not need explanations. "The current fashion for eating faerie food? Yes, of course. We have been working on more reliable ways of treating those affected by it, but I would be glad for any suggestions you might make . . ."

Lord Lister would not enter the faerie realm; it was, he often said, a trick for the young, and not one he was eager to try. But he and Wrain strolled about the grounds of Burlington House, nodding greetings to men from the other scientific societies that shared the premises, and discussed the matter, with fruitful results.

Outside the gates of that eminent estate, the two cities went about their business: mortal and faerie London, lying atop and between and alongside one another. Not merged into one, but not separate either; a mere step *sideways,* and daily bridged by men and women of both kinds, for good and for ill, for education and for mischief, and sometimes just for curiosity's sake. Their coexistence was not perfectly peaceable—not yet, and perhaps not ever—but then no great city ever lay fully at peace, and this one had survived the influx of strangers before. It was the dawning of a new age, and London would endure.

ACKNOWLEDGMENTS

Like its predecessors in the series, *With Fate Conspire* owes a great deal to the people who assisted me in my research. During my trip to London, this included: Josephine Oxley of Apsley House, Lin and Geoff Skippings of Carlyle's House, and Shirley Nicholson of the Linley Sambourne House, all for answering questions about the furnishings and daily life of the period; Helen Grove and Caroline Warhurst of the London Transport Museum Archives, for helping me research the progress of the Inner Circle Railway; Donald Rumbelow of London Walks, my guide on a Jack the Ripper tour (which may eventually result in a short story); and Paul Dew and Philip Barnes Morgan of the Metropolitan Police Service historical archives, for opening their filing cabinets and display cases to me so that I might research the Special Irish Branch, and also for showing me Inspector Abberline's personal scrapbook. (Irrelevant to this novel, but still very cool.) Regrettably, I do not have the names of the dedicated librarians at the Guildhall Library and London Metropolitan Archives who helped me unearth an 1893 map of London's sewers, but they have my thanks. And a very special thank-you to Sara O'Connor, who waded through one of those sewers on my behalf, and also to the folks at Thames Water who helped arrange that visit.

Then, of course, there are the e-mail queries. Jenny Hall of the London Museum answered questions about the destruction of London's city wall; Jess Nevins pointed me toward a variety of Victorian resources; Sydney Padua of the excellent webcomic *2D Goggles* gave me assistance on both Ada Lovelace and the Analytical Engine; John Pritchard was invaluable on the history and occupancy of various houses in London. Dr. William Jones of Cardiff University provided me with references on Irish nationalism, Sarah Rees Brennan advised me on Irish dialect, and Erin Smith answered questions about Irish Catholicism. Rashda Khan and Shveta Thakrar advised me on Indian folklore, and Aliette de Bodard did the same for Chinese. Christina Blake translated things into French on my behalf. Finally, I thank all the readers of my LiveJournal who answered questions along the way, and most *especially* everyone who suggested possible titles for The Novel More Commonly Known as "The Victorian Book," during the long and arduous quest to find one that would work.

This book was more complicated than most to write, so I owe a large debt of gratitude to those friends and family who let me talk their ears off about it: Kyle Niedzwiecki, Adrienne Lipoma, Kate Walton, Alyc Helms, and Kevin

Schmidt, the last of whom made the very excellent and timely suggestion of ectoplasm.

Finally, I must thank all the historians and scholars whose research I relied upon to keep my facts accurate. The terrifyingly long list of these may be found on my Web site, www.swantower.com.

ABOUT THE AUTHOR

American fantasy writer Marie Brennan habitually pillages her background in anthropology, archaeology and folklore for fictional purposes. In addition to the Onyx Court series, she is author of the Doppelganger duology of *Warrior* and *Witch*, the urban fantasy *Lies and Prophecy*, and the highly acclaimed *Natural History of Dragons* fantasy series, as well as more than forty short stories.

ALSO AVAILABLE FROM TITAN BOOKS

IN ASHES LIE

MARIE BRENNAN

The year is 1639, and King Charles I and Parliament vie for power, fighting one another with politics and armies alike. Below the streets of London, the faerie court has enemies of its own. The old ways are breaking down, and no one knows what will take their place. A greater threat is growing, and under a new king, mortal and fae will have to lay aside the differences that divide them, and fight together for the survival of London itself...

"You will swallow this book whole, wishing it would never end."

Sacramento Book Review

"Compelling and well-plotted... paint[s] a seventeenth-century London with vivid colours."

SF Crow's Nest